SHANGHAI YESTERDAY

A WWII DRAMA TRILOGY BOOK THREE

ALEXA KANG

D1528423

ACKNOWLEDGMENTS

Shanghai Dreams has been a monumental project, and I would like say a special thank you to those who had helped me along the way. This book wouldn't have been possible without them.

Thank you to my editor Kristen Tate, for making sure I stay grounded and keeping me in the right head space when, after working on my manuscript for months, I could no longer view my work in an objective light. Thank you, too, to my other editor (and U.S. veteran) Aaron Sikes, for his insights and advice on my action scenes.

Thank you also to Keri Knutson of Alchemy Book Covers and Design for creating such beautiful covers for this series. So often while I was writing, I would look at the covers to imagine what Clark and Eden were like in various scenes.

Thank you to my friend Mylius Fox, author of the thriller novel *Bandit*, who has been on my author journey with me since my first book, *Rose of Anzio - Moonlight*. His input and advice on writing and publishing, as well as moral support, have been wonderful and invaluable.

Lastly, thanks to my husband, Dan, for being the most

understanding, the most patient, and the most supportive person to me all summer as I buried myself in the bat cave writing this book.

Dedicated to the Memory
of
Ms. Elizabeth (Betty) Martin

December 21, 1920 - July 14, 2019

My acquaintance with Ms. Martin began several years ago when she read my *Rose of Anzio* WWII historical fiction series. Her late husband, Joey, served in Kunming, China during the war and was part of the U.S. Army 14th Airforce (a/k/a the Flying Tigers). After reading *Rose of Anzio*, Ms. Martin reached out to me, and has been a huge supporter of my works ever since. I was blessed to have a chance to get to know her through our correspondences. It touched me greatly that my stories resonated with a reader who had lived during the war era. She had also sent me wonderful gifts of the last newsletters of the 14th Airforce veteran group before it was disbanded. One of the newsletters included a reprint of a speech by Madame Chiang Kai-Shek.

Ms. Martin passed away this summer in July. She was 98 years old. I was heartbroken to hear the news. I know that she had been waiting to read the final volume of the *Shanghai Story* trilogy, and I am so sorry that she would not be able to find out what happened to Clark and Eden in the end.

I would like to dedicate this book, *Shanghai Yesterday*, to her, as a way to thank her for all her support, and as a tribute to her husband Joey for his service to China and the United States.

Ms. Martin, you will always be missed.

CONTENTS

PREFACE

AUTHOR'S NOTE ON LANGUAGE

The following information on Chinese language had already been given in Book One of the *Shanghai Story* trilogy. Minor details have been added in Book Two, *Shanghai Dreams*, and are indicated below. I hope these explanations will help readers who are not familiar with the Chinese language, and ensure they have a fully immersive read and a good reading experience.

(i) Dialogues between Chinese characters have been written as closely as possible to how Chinese people actually speak, with inclusions of Chinese colloquialism to add authenticity. In some parts, the dialogues of Chinese characters may defy an English reader's expectation of how something would be said. Some parts might also come across a little bit odd. However, I assure you these are not errors. I made a sincere effort to ensure that the dialogues would read smoothly and naturally to English readers, and also be true to how these dialogues would be spoken in Chinese.

In a few instances, dialogues between Chinese characters contained phrases that would be anachronism if spoken in English. But as spoken in Chinese, they are not. Whenever possible, I tried to avoid this confusion. If such apparent anachronism are written in dialogues that would've been spoken in Chinese, then they are there because that would be the only natural ways for a Chinese person to speak.

(ii) To adhere to authenticity, the use of honorifics was unavoidable. Chinese people often address others by honorifics instead of names. Simple salutation would not be enough, and depending on the person being addressed, salutation as used in English would also be wrong. My editorial team and I considered adding footnotes, but ultimately decided it would disrupt your reading experience. Therefore, I have decided instead to provide below a list of honorifics used in this book and their explanations.

(iii) [*Added*: There are some parts of the Chinese dialogues in this book that sound like contemporary colloquial English. These were not oversights nor anachronism. In these instances, the statement would actually be spoken in Chinese the same way as it would be spoken in English. I found this very interesting, and it shows that people have similar ways of expressing themselves, even if their languages are different and they live continents apart.]

(iv) Finally, except for references to certain locations in Shanghai, I have chosen to apply *pinyin* for Romanization of Chinese names and words used in this story. For those who are not familiar with the pronunciation of *pinyin*, I hope this will help:

"q" is pronounced "ch"
"g" is pronounced like "g" in "gas"
"x" is pronounced "sh"
"c" is pronounced "ts", as in "bit**s**"
"zh" is pronounced like the Polish "**cz**"

Honorifics:

- *Ge*: means older brother.
- *Jie*: means older sister.
- *xiao jie*: means Miss.
- *Da xiao jie*: means "first Miss." Before and up to the prewar era, servants addressed the daughters of the family they work for as "Miss." When the family has more than one daughters, the servants would address the daughters by their birth order. *"Da"* means "biggest." *Da xiao jie* means "first Miss."
- *Shifu*: means driver.
- *Amah*: means "a mother" and was used to address a female servant, often one whose work involved childcare.
- Uncle, Aunt, Auntie: the honorifics are often used to address someone who is a friend of one's parents, as well as siblings of parents.
- *Xiong*: also means older brother. But when used for addressing someone, it would only come up when the speaker is speaking to someone who is not a blood relative or in his own family. It is used more commonly between two men in a conversation, as a polite way to address each other.

Note also that *Ge* and *Jie* are often used to address someone who is not a blood relative, but who the speaker holds in higher regards. In such cases, *"Ge"* or *"Jie"* is always added to the first name (and occasionally the last name) of the person being addressed.

I hope the above guide will enhance your reading experience.

List of Main Asian Characters

Note: Surnames of Chinese and Japanese characters are placed first except when shown last and separated by comma.

The Yuan Family

Clark Yuan (Yuan Guo-Hui) - Son of a prominent Chinese family in Shanghai. He recently returned from America after studying abroad and graduating college. He is addressed as **Young Master Yuan** by Chinese servants and in public. He is also addressed in honorific as *Guo-Hui Ge* by his younger sisters, with *Ge* (pronounced "guh") meaning "older brother", and **Yuan Xiong** by non-blood relatives sometimes, with *xiong* also meaning "older brother".

Wen-Ying, Yuan - Younger sister of Clark. Her family servants address her in the honorific as **Daxiaojie**, meaning "Eldest Miss".

Mei Mei/Wen-Li, Yuan - Youngest sister of Clark. **Mei Mei** is her nickname. Her family servants address her in the honorific as **Erxiaojie**, meaning "Second Miss".

Master Yuan Ren-Qiu - Clark's father. He is addressed as Master Yuan by Chinese servants and in public.

Madam Yuan - Clark's Mother.

Other Main Characters in Alphabetical Order
(Minor characters excluded)

Chen Lu - Minister of Foreign Affairs of the interim puppet Reformed Government of Republic of China established in southern China from 1938 to 1940.

Chiang Kai-Shek, Generalissimo - President of the Republic of China and leader of *Kuomintang* (KMT), the Chinese Nationalist Party.

Dai Li - Head of *Juntong*, the Chinese Secret Police.

Director Dong - senior Chinese member of the Shanghai Municipal Council.

Gao Zhen, Director - Family friend of the Yuans. Director of the Shanghai Commercial and Savings Bank.

Hayashi Yukichi - senior Japanese member of the Shanghai Municipal Council.

Ho Feng-Shan, Consul-General - Chinese consulate official in Vienna, Austria.

Huang Shifu - Yuan family chauffeur. *Shifu* is not a name but a way of addressing drivers.

Konoe Kenji, Captain - Member of Japanese *Kizoku* (Japanese equivalent to nobility), of the family Konoe, who ares descendants of the Fujiwara clan. Military attaché to the Japanese consul.

Liu Zi-Hong - Boyfriend of Mei Mei (Yuan Wen-Li), Clark's youngest sister. Communist sympathizer.

Mao Ze Dong - Leader of the Chinese Communist Party.

Ming Zhu (Pearl) - Clark's point of contact for Juntong, the Chinese secret police; owner of the brothel Chamber of Golden Clouds.

Okamoto Izamu - younger Japanese member of the Shanghai Municipal Council.

Ren Tian-Ming - member of underground renegade resistance group Whangpoo Brigade and supporter of the Chinese Communist Party.

Shen Yi - Clark's ex-fiancée by arranged marriage.

Sun Xiu-Qing - Girlfriend of Xu Hong-Lie. Xu is Clark's right hand at the Yuan Enterprises.

Tan Shao-Yu - Japanese appointee to head the interim puppet Provisional Government of Republic of China established in northern China from 1938 to 1940.

Tang Wei - Clark's friend, former schoolmate, and former colleague who became a collaborator after the Japanese invasion.

Wang Jing-Wei - President of puppet Reorganized National Government of Republic of China established in March 1940 to replace the interim puppet governments in all regions of Occupied China.

Xiaochun, Liang - Maidservant of the Yuan Family.

Xu Hong-Lie - Clark's right hand at the Yuan Enterprises.

Ye Ting - Chinese starlet who became Eden's confidential source.

Zhou Ke-Hao - former police officer of Chinese Public Security Bureau before Japanese invasion. Member of underground renegade resistance group Whangpoo Brigade.

Cross-over Characters from the spinoff novella
The Moon Chaser

Fan Yong-Hao - Member of the underground resistance group Tian Di Hui (the Heaven and Earth Society).

SHANGHAI YESTERDAY

LOOSE SAND

SMOKE BILLOWED into the darkened sky. Still stunned, Clark ran to the platform where the local train had carried away Xu Hong-Lie only moments ago. The moon peered out from behind the gray clouds floating across the heavens above. Its faint rays could not defeat the arrival of night and he couldn't see what was happening from afar.

Clark swung around and grabbed the station agent's arm. "What happened?"

The man's mouth dropped open. He was still gawking at the sight.

"What happened?" Clark shouted.

The station agent shook his head. "I don't know."

Clark let go of the man. Pushing aside all the passengers and people roused by the explosions, he ran toward the station depot to the ticket window. Inside the depot, the station master cried out into the phone, "What? . . . What? The freight train to the Kailan Mines blew up? . . . Ay-yah! Disaster!"

Clark's eyes widened. A layer of sweat dripped down his back.

The dynamite. Their plan.

If the train exploded, how would the resistance fighters follow through with their plan to blow up the mines?

"How many injured?" the station master asked the person on the other end of the line. "Did anyone die?"

Clark moved closer and put his hand on the ticket counter. His heart hammered.

"You don't know yet?" The station master turned toward the wall.

Clark shook his head. No. No.

Xu Hong-Lie. His trusted, capable right hand. His most reliable friend. What happened to him?

The station manager's voice ebbed. Clark's trembling hand fell from the ticket counter to his side. He took a shaky step backward and might have fallen if it weren't for the stranger in a conductor's uniform who called his name. "Young Master Yuan."

The stranger's voice prompted him to focus. Instinctively, his fear for Hong Lie switched to fear for himself. Without answering the man, he stiffened his chest. How did the man know his name?

"Come with me." The stranger held out Clark's small suitcase and the Agatha Christie novel which Clark had dropped when the train exploded. Subtly, he glanced about them and whispered, "Dai Li sent me."

Clark exhaled and his body eased, but he remained silent and stood still. Why should he believe this man?

The man took a coin out of his pocket. He flashed it at Clark to show a split-second glimpse of a triangular symbol. Clark recognized the insignia. Wen-Ying wore the same one on her necklace. It was the secret sign of Tian Di Hui, the Heaven and Earth Society—the underground resistance group waging terroristic attacks against their enemy.

Clark took his book and suitcase.

"You have to leave now. Your train to Peking is arriving." The man tossed his head at the direction away from the crowd.

"Follow me." He started toward the platform where Clark had been waiting earlier.

Still not moving, Clark asked, "What about the explosion? What happened? What about . . . "

The man gave him a firm look to signal him to shush. "I don't know. Even Dai Li doesn't know yet. I received a call instructing me to make sure you get on your next train. You're to check into your hotel as planned. When you arrive, someone will be in touch."

The train to Peking chugged on its track. The rumble of the engine grew until it drowned out the buzz of human voices. Clark gazed out ahead. The shriek of the train's horn warned him to move. He took one more look at the scene behind him, then followed the man.

They reached the platform and Clark stepped up into the car. The man stopped and muttered, "See you again." He turned and hastened away.

Clark made his way onto the train. Alone, he sat gripping his novel. The train pulled away from the station and he looked out the window into the black void. The train's wheels clacking against the tracks thwacked his ears and he could not form a single coherent thought.

In his room at the Grand Hôtel des Wagons-Lits, Clark lay on the soft damask duvet covering the bed, trying to listen to music on the radio and calm himself. The sweet voice of singer Zhou Xuan crooned from the speaker across the room but it failed to soothe his mind. He reached out to the nightstand and turned the knob to change the station. It was no use. The bouncy notes of Mozart's "Little Night Music" ascending and soaring exasperated him even more. He felt like an ant in a burning wok, circling in search for an escape and unable to stay still. Why was there an explosion? Did the Japanese discover their plan? Where was Hong-Lie now? Was he dead or alive? What became of their plot to disable the Kailan Mines?

He switched off the radio. Above the dresser, the gilded French clock showed the time to be one in the morning. He watched the second-hand tick for a while, then shifted from his side onto his back. If the country weren't at war, he could easily fall into a deep, peaceful sleep on this opulent bed with these plush pillows under his head. The company that owned this hotel took pride in ensuring the same luxuries continued when their guests on the Orient Express arrived.

What was happening next? He stared at the ceiling and clasped his hands under his head.

The elegantly engraved golden telephone on the desk remained silent. The conductor at the Hai River station who urged him to get on the train—if he really were a conductor—told him someone would be in touch. He'd been lying here for over an hour. His shirt and pants were all wrinkled.

A light knock on the door nearly stopped his heart. He bolted up from the bed and went to open the door. Instantly, his hope of receiving news vanished. A woman in a silk *qipao* tilted her head and smiled at him. She placed her hand on her hip and gazed seductively at him with her half-closed eyes. A strong whiff of perfume forced its way into his room, but the scent was not unpleasant.

Annoyed, Clark scowled. What was this? A hotel of this class should be more vigilant in keeping prostitutes out. Had the Japanese occupation corrupted Peking so much that solicitation of hotel guests at night was now acceptable even here?

"Go away. Not interested." He started to close the door.

"Wait." She pushed the door and held it open. As she did, the KMT emblem of the blue sky and white sun with the twelve rays of white light flashed from her silver bracelet.

Clark looked at her, a bit stunned. "You're . . . ?"

"Juntong," the woman said. "Would you let me come in?"

Slowly, Clark opened the door again. The woman from the Chinese secret police sauntered in, swaying her hips as she walked. Clark was expecting a man, not a woman who, at first glance, looked like a harlot.

The woman dropped her large purse on the sofa. Her wayward air toned down as she turned around. "I'm Ming Zhu."

Ming Zhu—luminous pearl. A beautiful name. Clark doubted it was real. He closed the door and invited her to sit, then took a seat himself on the other side of the coffee table. "Did Dai Li send you?"

Pearl nodded. "I'll be your primary contact from now on for all your dealings with him."

"You're a Juntong agent?" Clark asked, still feeling a tinge of doubt.

"Yes, but that's not something you should ever mention again," Pearl said. She adjusted her bracelet and hid the secret sign. "I'm one of the girls at the Garden of Apricots." She smiled proudly with a lift of her head. "It's Peking's number one playground for wealthy and powerful men."

"Is it?" Clark watched her cross her legs, the deep slit on the side of her skirt revealing her smooth skin. This made sense. Pearl could probably coax more secrets and information from their enemies than Juntong's other regular operatives—provided she could be trusted. And she could slide in and out of places without raising attention, like she was doing now. Making her his main contact was a brilliant move.

"You should come for a drink." She lightly bit her lower lip.

Clark ignored her invitation. "Do you know what happened to the train going to Kailan? Were we found out?"

"No." Pearl stared back at him, her eyes now serious. "It was the Communists. We're not the only ones trying to sabotage the shorties' army. The Communists came up with a dumb scheme to blow up the local train to scare the Japanese demons. Their little game ruined our chance to shut down the mines. We had to abort everything. The Japanese army is now on high alert. We won't be able to try again." She took a pack of cigarettes out of her purse, lit one up, and blew out a frustrated puff.

Clark sagged in his seat. Chinese people. This was precisely their problem. They were like a basin of loose sand. Even now, with the Japanese trampling over their land, they could not unite. The left hand didn't know what the right hand was doing. They were wrecking their own resistance efforts.

"What about Xu Hong-Lie?" he asked. "Do you have any news about him?"

Pearl raised her brows. "The whole train blew up. Those Communist yokel bandits. Their grenades set off the loads of dynamite it was carrying. Dai Li's contacts with the emergency rescue operation didn't report finding any survivors. The passengers who died must have all turned into human slag. I think . . . he more likely had little luck and met a violent end."

Clark dropped his face into his hands. This was all his fault. If he hadn't convinced Xu Hong-Lie to come on this mission, Xu would still be alive. Now what was he to do? How could he break the news to Hong-Lie's parents? Or Uncle Six? Uncle Six dedicated his whole life to serving the Yuan family. His nephew's death was now his payback? Clark raked his fingers through his hair. He wished he himself had died in Hong-Lie's place.

"What will I say to his family?" Clark asked, a rhetorical question to no one in particular. What would he tell Hong-Lie's family indeed? They were supposed to be in Peking for a business trip. How would he explain to his friend's parents why their son had disappeared and would never come back?

"We can at least resolve that question," Pearl said. She put her cigarette on the ashtray and took an urn out of her purse. "You will delay your return to Shanghai for three days. When you go back, you'll tell everyone Xu Hong-Lie died in a car accident. You'll tell them the Japanese won't let you bring the body back.

Therefore, you had his body cremated. You had to stay longer in Peking to make the arrangements." She put the urn on the coffee table and pushed it toward Clark.

Warily, Clark reached out for the urn. When his fingertips touched its surface, he flinched. "Whose ashes are these?"

Pearl shrugged. "It came from the morgue. I didn't ask. Dai Li told me to bring it to you, so I did. Take it back. It'll do as an explanation. No one will know the difference."

No one would know the difference? Clark imagined himself delivering the urn to Hong-Lie's family. A pang of sadness came over him. The poor parents. They lost their son, and they couldn't even mourn his dead body. They'd be mourning a pile of ashes of a stranger.

Pearl softened her voice. "A person who dies can't come back to life. Don't be distressed anymore. The only thing you can do now is to continue our resistance against Japan. If we can revive our country, then Xu Hong-Lie's death won't be a waste."

Clark closed his hands around the urn. Yes. He had to give his all to help the resistance. Xu Hong-Lie gave his life. He himself could not give anything less until the day the Japanese were gone. And then, Hong-Lie's death would mean something.

"I have to leave." Pearl closed her purse. "Do as I tell you. In three days, go home and attend to your company's business as usual. In a few weeks, I'll come to Shanghai and find you. Now that the Japanese army has chased away Big Ear Du and his Green Gang, Shanghai's wide open for new business. I'm bringing a group of sisters down there to open a new place. It'll be even bigger and more beautiful than the Garden of Apricots. It'll be a paradise. There'll be a garden of exotic plants, a fish pond for guests to fish in, even an indoor hot spring. We'll serve the finest wines money can buy. Also, we'll have the most beautiful girls. More beautiful than girls in any other houses." Pearl's eyes lit up. The excitement on her face nearly had Clark convinced that her only aim was to open Shanghai's number one brothel.

But then, she stared at him and whispered, "We expect a lot of new Japanese clients and their Chinese friends to come. Military generals, officers, principals of the new puppet government."

Clark understood immediately. What better way to deceive and spy on the enemy than through a brothel?

"Setting up something new in Shanghai's current climate won't be easy," he said. "I guess you have support behind you?"

Pearl smiled but didn't answer. Her eyes gleamed with the confidence of someone with all the right cards up her sleeves.

"I really must get going." She rose from her seat and walked to the back of his sofa. "Even though I know how much you wish for my company to last till the morning." She ran her hands softly down his chest. He turned around and stood up. She crinkled her eyes and smiled, then let herself out.

After she left, Clark locked the door and returned to the coffee table. The urn sat there, holding the ashes of their failed plan.

Pearl's cigarette burned to the butt. Its ashes crumbled into the tray. Clark's mind returned once again to the Hai River station when Hong-Lie boarded the local train to the Kailan Mines. He still couldn't believe that would be the last time he saw his friend alive.

He wasn't a man of superstitions. He never took it seriously when his mother told him stories of ghosts and spirits. But now, he wondered. Was Xu Hong-Lie's soul wandering along the Hai River, lost and forever searching for his way home? Would his spirit drift along for eternity, seeking to know why he was left behind in a foreign town he never knew, only to be trapped in another dimension in which he would never find any answer or peace?

Clark closed his fists. This thought tore his own heart and soul to a thousand shards.

2

A WOMAN SCORNED

AT THE BEAUTY PARLOR, Yelena, the hairdresser, fluffed out Eden's hair and parted it to one side. "Are you sure you don't want to try something a little different? How about a finger wave?"

Eden glanced over at the woman seated next to her, who was having her hair done exactly that way. The process would take hours. "No, not today."

Yelena showed her a page in a fashion magazine. "How about we set your curls tighter and pin them up to one side? See? Myrna Loy does her hair this way. This look will suit you perfectly."

Eden considered the idea. No doubt the look was sensational, but again, how many hours would it take? "No. Just a trim and a simple wet set and curl will do."

"All right, I'll be right back." Yelena walked away. Another hairdresser turned on the radio to a station playing George Gershwin's "Summertime." Yelena returned with several magazines and gave them to Eden. "Would you like a manicure today too?"

Eden held up her chipped nails. "Yes."

"Wonderful. We'll do that after we finish with your hair." Yelena picked up the comb and scissors and began to work.

Eden picked up an old issue of *McCall's* with Amelia Earhart on the cover. The American aviator disappeared last year during her attempt to fly across the globe. What happened to her? Eden wondered. American women could be so adventurous.

Her American friend Ava was adventurous too. Ava always had something exciting or outrageous happening in her life. One could never get tired of hearing her tell her stories.

But Ava was gone. So were many of the women and children from the West. The men too, if they didn't have business ties or anything else at stake in Shanghai. Every day, ships departed, carrying away people who had once reaped fortunes from this place. But at the first sign of war, they took everything they gained and fled.

At least, Ava never exploited this city except for the myriad of entertainments it offered. She was a good friend too. She even cried at the port when Eden saw her off. Crying was something Ava never did.

Stalling till the last minute, Ava kept apologizing. "I wish I didn't have to abandon you here."

With a brave face, Eden told her, "You're not abandoning me. This is the only place I could be. There's nothing you can do about that."

Ava wiped her tears. "This damn world. Everything's gone crazy." She gave Eden a tight hug. "I'll come back as soon as this dreadful war is over. You hear me? I promise."

Not wanting to distress her friend more, Eden returned her hug with a reassuring smile.

"You know something? Here." Ava opened her purse and dug out a set of keys. "I don't know when I'll see you again, but these are the keys to my apartment. While I'm not here, you can use it anytime." She pushed the keys into Eden's hand. "Treat it like it's your own."

"Ava—"

The ship's horn blew from behind them. Ava's maid, who was standing nearby with the pet monkey Mr. Bernard, said to Ava, "Ma'am, the ship's about to depart."

Ava patted her face with her handkerchief. "Goodbye, love," she said to Eden. "Take good care of yourself." She hugged Eden again and turned to board the ship. Her maid followed, the monkey squeaking as she pulled him along.

"Goodbye!" Eden waved. "I'll miss you," she whispered, knowing they could not hear her anymore.

And she did miss them. When Ava left, she left behind a big void.

Nine months had passed since the Japanese took over the Chinese-controlled sectors of the city. The foreign concessions, surrounded by Japanese forces on all sides, felt like a lone, isolated island. One could feel the oppressive cloud of malevolence shrouding them even as the champagne continued to flow and the music continued to roll. If the terror of war encroached further, who could break through the cloud to rescue them?

Trying to turn her mind to something else, Eden opened the magazine. What use was it to think about it? She and her family didn't have the option to leave. They were stateless Jews.

At least, Clark was here. Her heart warmed thinking of him. He had no place else to go either, and she was glad she could be here for him. He looked so broken at his father's funeral. And when he returned from his trip to Peking, all he could do was to hold on to her hand all night and say sorry over and over again to his friend Xu Hong-Lie, who was no longer alive to hear his apology.

Poor Clark. She wished she could say something to make

things better for him. Xu died in a car accident. Yet, Clark took so much guilt upon himself. It was almost as if he felt guilty for not being able to save all of Shanghai or China himself.

He was all alone too. At least it seemed that way. His KMT colleagues had fled. His best friend betrayed him and joined the collaborators. His father died suddenly and left him with the responsibility of caring not only for his family, but an entire staff of workers who depended on him for their livelihood and safety in these dangerous times. And now, even his right-hand man was gone.

He didn't tell her this, but she knew it all the same. She was the one bright thing left in his life.

She smiled to herself and flipped the page of the magazine. She couldn't wait to see him later today at the Public Garden.

The music on the radio ended, followed by the jingle for the eleven o'clock news.

"Is that Alex Mitchell?" the woman in the next seat shouted out. "Can you girls turn up the radio please?"

Eden moved her head slightly. Yelena answered, "Yes, Thelma! I've been waiting for him to come on too." She went over to the radio and dialed up the volume. From the speaker came a friendly but authoritative voice.

Good morning, everyone, this is Alex Mitchell reporting from XMHA. Today's broadcast is brought to you by Maxwell House.

"Ooooh!" The lady named Thelma fanned herself with her hand. "My heart flutters just hearing him talk."

All the hairdressers giggled, as did the other salon guests. Eden recognized the name too. Alex Mitchell. What Shanghailander hadn't heard of him? Since his debut on XMHA three months ago, everyone in Shanghai had become a fan of this reporter from Missouri. The American network NBC struck gold when they stole him from the *Shanghai Evening Post and Mercury* and made him a radio news host for one of their affiliate stations.

What made him so popular? Right from the start, Alex Mitchell eviscerated the Japanese. He gave no quarter to their violence against the Chinese people or the deteriorating conditions of the city now under their occupation. While the Shanghai Municipal Council, which governed the International Settlement, and the French government, which controlled Frenchtown, floundered in confusion over how to respond to the Japanese, Alex Mitchell spoke for everyone who wanted to denounce Japan for what it had done. He gave everyone a voice.

In no time, the popularity of his broadcast soared. Twice a day, three times a week, he would go on the air. Plus a special weekend broadcast. When he talked, people in every home, hotel, bar, and consulate who could understand him would tune in. Even those whom he mocked. Especially those whom he mocked. What he said carried weight.

"What do you all think he looks like?" Thelma asked with dreamy eyes. "With a voice like that, I bet he looks like Errol Flynn."

"Not at all," said the blonde sitting next to Thelma. "I saw him in person once. At a party at Farren's. He looks nothing like Errol Flynn. Actually, he looks better. He's tall, with dark brown hair. He has these amazing, daredevil eyes."

"Really?" Thelma gasped. "Did you talk to him?"

"No. I didn't dare." The blonde turtled her head.

After the Maxwell House commercial, Alex Mitchell's voice returned.

Thank God for Maxwell House because, once again, the Mikado sent me another useless communiqué today. Reading their daily propaganda puts me to sleep. There's never anything newsworthy in them. But with Maxwell House's fine coffee, I can now stay awake for this morning's broadcast . . .

The women in the parlor laughed. Thelma turned to her hairdresser. "May I have a cup of Maxwell House too?"

"Certainly!" Her hairdresser went to fetch her a cup.

So let's see . . . I'm going through this communiqué here . . . battle victory, more battle victory—because we know the Japanese army never loses, right? I mean, according to their daily bullshi—excuse me, I mean, their daily bulletin. According to them, the Japanese army hasn't lost a single battle since this war began—a war which they started, might I remind you. Let us not forget that. Now, if you believe them, they've never lost a single battle in their entire history.

Thelma snickered and wiggled her brows at Eden. Eden politely smiled back.

Why do I even bother reporting this? The problem is, Mr. Yamato complains I don't give enough of their side of the story in my broadcast.

The thought of Alex wisecracking to a stern, irritated Mr. Yamato popped into Eden's mind and she smirked. On the radio, Alex Mitchell often derided Mr. Yamato's various requests and demands. Most listeners thought it was just his way of mocking the Japanese authorities, although she wondered sometimes if a Mr. Yamato in fact existed.

They keep asking me why I don't report good news about them. I'd like to. Every day, I look in vain for something positive I can say about them. I find nothing good to report and they accuse me of being biased. Well, what can I say? Mr. Yamato, when you stop killing women and babies, maybe I'll finally have something good to say about you.

Yelena and the other women groaned in agreement. Eden stared at the floor. Even at the *China Press* where she worked, no one was ever this blunt, and they prided themselves on exposing the Japanese too.

I will now throw their communiqué into the trash where it belongs. Wait a minute, here's something interesting. According to Mr. Yamato, Imperial Japan is now working hard with the new Chinese leaders in Shanghai to build the Greater East Asia Co-Prosperity Sphere. Who are these new Chinese leaders? Did Chiang Kai-shek appoint them? Did the people of Shanghai elect them?

Thelma sneered and nodded her head in agreement. "Oh no, don't move," her hairdresser told her.

And what do they mean when they say a 'prosperity sphere'? What have they ever done to bring prosperity to China? Or Shanghai? I'm talking facts here. A hundred years ago, this city was nothing but a swamp. The British and the Americans were the ones who put up all the skyscrapers and built the infrastructure and utilities. They brought in all the modern industries. I'm not saying this to give undue credit to the white men, and it's a fact that all of this couldn't have happened without the hard work and labor of the Chinese people. And I'll freely admit the white men have profited handsomely, even unjustly, from all of it. But we also gave back. The Americans invested a million dollars buying and developing Shanghai's power plant. They reinvested almost all of the profits back into improving the plant and paying dividends to their shareholders living in the city, not the stockholders back in the United States. They also built the city's telephone system, and the Britons built the public transportation infrastructure, the waterworks, and the gas company. What was Japan's part in all of this?

"That's right!" the blonde next to Thelma called out.

And I don't want to hear any lies about the Britons and the Americans playing monopoly or having special advantages. Look at all the buildings in this city. The Japs are entitled to build anything they want within the foreign concessions. They have the same privileges as any other foreign nationals to buy land, to build apartments and offices. Even the Chinese themselves have done that, and I'd argue they're the least privileged people here in their own city. Why didn't the Japs take part in modernizing and industrializing this city? All this time, they haven't built a single building. Not one. Why doesn't Mitsubishi invest in any development project? Why doesn't the Nippon Yufen Kaisha? Why didn't they open at least one school for the Chinese kids? What the Japs did do was bomb everything that was built.

"He sure does not mince words," Thelma said.

Eden agreed. This was what they all loved about Alex Mitchell.

And now they tell us they're going to bring prosperity? By doing what? Bombing to pieces all the buildings other people had built and razing every city to the ground?

The fervor in his voice. It did more to rouse people than anything Eden herself could've ever written.

I just thought of something else. The Chinese practice ancestral worship. When the Japs invaded the city last year, the Chinese funeral homes had a crisis when they ran out of paper tael and currency, and paper cars, mansions, and wardrobes for people to burn for their family members who were killed. It wasn't just Shanghai. Every city the Japs demolished had the same problem. Maybe that's what Mr. Yamato means by 'prosperity sphere.' With all that paper money, mansions, cars, and what-have-you, the dead can now build a great prosperity sphere in hell.

Everyone in the beauty parlor burst out laughing. Eden bit her lip and grinned.

All right, everyone. This concludes my broadcast for the morning. I'll be back this evening. Goodbye to all you listeners, and don't forget to tune in again at six.

Behind her, Yelena had finished setting her hair. "Okay, all done. Would you please come this way?" She invited Eden to sit under the hairdryer.

Eden got up and followed her. Sure. She would tune in at six to listen to Alex Mitchell's evening broadcast. Her parents would too even if she didn't. Alex Mitchell's news hour was now a regular family affair.

But before then, she planned to spend the afternoon with Clark, alone.

With Eden by his side, Clark strolled along the path in the Public Garden, searching for a place on the grass where they could spread out the blanket and lay down the picnic basket. Here, under the shade of the trees, among the bushes and the summer flowers, local Chinese families still brought their children out to play, and foreign men still came to read their newspapers on the benches. A semblance of normalcy had returned, thanks to the Shanghai Municipal Police patrolling the park and keeping everyone in order. In the summer air, butterflies still flew, and chickadees still chirped.

How odd, Clark thought as he walked. The collapse of the city and the dire situation of the people living outside of the foreign concessions had no impact on nature. When lives were lost and cities were ruined, the sun still rose.

The sun still rose. His heart stung at the bitterness of the thought.

"How about there?" Eden pointed at an open space near a bed of camellias.

"Okay." Clark exhaled and relaxed. The breath of fresh air revitalized his spirits a bit. He watched as Eden walked over to the spot, the skirt of her checkered dress swaying with her gait. Sometimes, it still felt like a dream. He still couldn't believe she had chosen to be with him.

And right now, she was the only bright spot in his life. If it weren't for her, he wouldn't be indulging himself coming out to a picnic. Not when so many people were homeless and sleeping on the streets, and the rising price of food was keeping so many people hungry. Day and night, he feared for his mother and sisters' safety. Not that Shanghai was ever a safe city. But since the occupation, Japanese ronin marauded the streets. They kidnapped wealthy Chinese and demanded ransom. He himself no longer left home without carrying a gun.

People said the Japanese military hired the ronin to collect ransom to fund their army. He wouldn't put it past those murderers to fund the war with the victims' own money.

For countless nights, these thoughts kept him awake.

But it wasn't wrong to do something to bring joy to the woman he loved, was it? Even if it meant a little frivolous leisure for himself too?

Truth be told, he could use a few hours of escape without worrying about anything else.

He set down the picnic basket and helped her spread the blanket.

"Look what I brought." She reached into the picnic basket.

"What?"

She took out a round cake wrapped in a cloth. "It's a *Gugelhupf*. Have you ever tried it?"

"No." He sat down. He had seen them before though. In America, they called it a Bundt cake.

"Well, now you will. I baked this myself." Her smile widened and she took out the sandwiches.

"Thank you." He looked into her eyes and took her hand.

"You don't have to thank me." She laughed. "You sound so formal."

"No. I mean, thank you for being here. Thank you for being a part of my life." He pulled her hand close to his chest.

She gazed at his troubled face. "You're still upset about your friend Hong-Lie?"

Clark sighed. "It's not only him. Without him, I don't know if I can keep up with running my companies and factory. I haven't been at the job very long. It would be hard enough even if the country wasn't at war. And now . . ." He frowned. "I can't fail. If I fail, what would happen to our workers?"

Eden moved closer. "You'll do fine. Have faith in yourself. If you don't, then you'll fail for sure." She peered at him, trying to catch his gaze. "I believe in you."

He relented and smiled back. "There's something else I need to tell you."

"What's that?"

"The people I'm collaborating with to organize resistance activities designated a new contact for me."

"Yes?"

"The new contact's a woman."

"Like Ekaterina? Do you have to pretend you're having an affair again?"

"No." He hesitated. How to explain this the right way? "This one's a . . . courtesan."

"A courtesan?" Eden squinted. Holding back a smile, she whispered, "You mean a prostitute? Who uses the word courtesan anymore?"

He gave a small, nervous laugh. "Her name is Pearl. I'll be publicly seen going in and out of her brothel. How long I'll be doing this, I don't know. It's an intentional setup."

"To make it look like you're one of her clients."

"Yes," he said. He couldn't tell her much about what the resistance was doing, but he had to tell her about this. He'd rather she didn't find out on her own. "I'm only associating with her to communicate with the people I'm helping. I need you to understand that."

Eden drew back. Clark watched her lower her eyes, afraid to breathe in case she became upset. She gazed back up. "I trust you."

Relief washed over him. He held up her hand. "I know this is a lot to ask of you. It would be hard for any woman. Pearl . . . I don't know much about her. She's a member of a highly organized underground resistance group. She came to Shanghai from Peking a few weeks ago. I assume she has some very powerful people behind her. She's setting up a new brothel to attract high-level Japanese officials and Chinese collaborators."

"She's a spy," Eden said.

"I'd say so." Clark nodded.

"Do you trust her?"

"I have no other choice."

Eden gripped his hand. "Will you be in danger?"

Clark didn't answer. He didn't want to worry her, but he didn't want to lie either. Of course there would be danger. By working with Pearl, he was putting his life in her hands, as she was putting her life in his.

"I understand." Eden turned and looked away.

"You're not happy about this." Clark pulled her back. "I wish I didn't have to put you through this."

"It's not that," she said. "It saddens me more to see all the new brothels cropping up. Have you noticed? All the new casinos, gambling dens, and brothels along the Western Road?"

Of course he noticed. That area lay just outside of the International Settlement, and many foreigners lived there. They built their mansions there. The Shanghai Municipal Council even collected taxes from them. Now, control of that whole area was in flux. The puppet Chinese government claimed it was Chinese territory, and a new wave of underground criminals was making it their home.

"I'm sure some of them are Japanese comfort houses," Eden said. "I see the lines of Japanese soldiers outside. I recognize the kanji letters on the banners beside their doors. My little attempt to shut down one comfort house last year feels so useless."

"You tried." Clark put his arm around her.

She smiled back at him. "Anyway, don't worry about me. What you're doing is bigger than both of us. Don't let me be a burden. I want to be here for you."

"You're not a burden." He pulled her closer. Her radiant eyes now shone only for him. He ran his fingers across her lips. In that moment, he only wanted to live. To be free and in love. Their faces only inches apart, he leaned in, wanting to feel the warmth of her breath on his own lips.

But suddenly, his senses jumped to high alert. Someone was watching him. He raised his head to see who. On the path, two women were walking toward them. The one holding a parasol was Shen Yi, his ex-fiancée. The other was her best friend, Su Kai-Lin. He'd met Su once when he and Shen Yi were still engaged.

Clark sat up. Of all the people who could run into them. How awkward.

He stared in Shen Yi's direction. She glared back, her face frozen like ice.

Did she still hold a grudge against him? Why? She was married now.

Eden, too, realized her presence. "What should we do?"

"Nothing," he said. "You don't need to do anything."

"But—"

"But I do." He braced himself. He wouldn't ignore Shen Yi. No matter what, he had wronged her when he broke off their engagement. Nothing he could do would ever make up for the humiliation she suffered because of him. He couldn't let her walk by without the courtesy of acknowledging her, even if she ignored him or lashed out at him in public. Even if she would humiliate him back ten times over, he had to go and greet her. He was a man. It was the honorable thing to do.

"I should go greet her. I'll be right back." He dropped Eden's hand and stood up. Gritting his teeth, he started toward the path.

Seeing him approach, Shen Yi turned her face away and continued walking.

Clark quickened his steps after her. "Shen Yi! Shen Yi!"

Shen Yi stopped. She shot him a cold stare.

"Young Master Yuan." Su Kai-Lin linked her arm protectively around Shen Yi's. "What a coincidence. How is it that you too would have the idle sentiment to come to the park to talk love with a girl?" She glanced over at Eden.

Clark ignored her. With all sincerity, he asked, "Shen Yi, how are you?"

Refusing to answer, Shen Yi jutted her chin and looked away.

"The other person's doing fine," Su Kai-Lin continued, unfazed. "How thoughtful of you to ask."

He held back his urge to respond. A man ought to be more gracious and defer a step when women were displeased. He tried to smile at Shen Yi. "You look well."

"Of course she looks well," Su Kai-Lin said. "She's Madam Liu Kun now. What? Did you think no one would want her just because the other person didn't please your eyes?"

"That's not what I meant," Clark said. He wanted to say something appeasing, but he didn't know what. The reminder that Shen Yi had married Liu Kun made him feel even worse. Liu Kun was a collaborator. He couldn't help feeling he had a hand in causing Shen Yi to marry a traitor.

Shen Yi finally spoke. "Kai-Lin, let's go." She started walking away. Su Kai-Lin smirked and left with her. Behind them, he could hear Shen Yi say, "Someone's been bewitched by a fox sorceress."

Clark sighed and shook his head. Slowly, he went back to Eden.

"That went well," she teased him as he sat down.

He shrugged. Eager to put the encounter behind them, he picked up a sandwich. "Come on, let's eat. I want to try your *Gugelhupf.*"

A bright smile returned to Eden's face, erasing the shadow of Shen Yi and bringing him back into the light.

3

LUMINOUS PEARL

IN HIS SEAT, Clark crossed his legs and clasped his hands as he watched Cornell Franklin, the chairman of the Shanghai Municipal Council, pull a large yellow envelope out of his drawer.

"Here are the registration papers of your new company, Merrick International," Franklin said. He handed the envelope across the desk to Clark. "It's registered under the name John Hastings. John's leaving Shanghai next month for good. Can't blame him. The market's unstable and the price of everything is skyrocketing. Your offer to buy out his company came just at the right time. He couldn't have gotten your offer price from anyone else in such a hurry."

"Thank you." Clark accepted the papers. He did pay a decent price. But on his end, the purchase was a bargain. More importantly, he needed a trading company registered under foreign ownership.

"I tried to tell everyone not to panic." Cornell Franklin picked up his cigar. "If you look outside the stock market, the economy's showing every sign of improvement. We got hundreds of new companies moving in from the Japanese occupied territories.

Some of the cotton mills and flour mills are doubling and tripling their profits. Germany, America, Free China. Demands for goods are coming in from everywhere." He waved his cigar at Clark. "Anyhow, I'm glad you feel confident enough to expand. Since it's registered as an American company, you should be able to run it without any trouble from the Japs."

"I hope so," Clark said, keeping an amicable face. He hadn't told Franklin the real reason he acquired Merrick was not to expand his company's businesses.

Sure, he would continue Merrick's regular operations. It was important for everyone to continue to believe Merrick was still a real going concern. No one could know his real purpose was to compile lists of Japanese stores in Shanghai. All Japanese stores in the city served and supplied the Japanese military. Some overtly, some covertly. As a trading company, Merrick could gain access to detailed information on the movements of goods in and out of Shanghai. Through Merrick, he could monitor and trace all the shipments for the Japanese into the city and their final destinations. With this information, Dai Li and Juntong could disrupt the enemy supply chain.

In other words, they could blow them up.

"Now that we've settled that," Franklin said, "can we talk about the next SMC election?"

"The next election?" Clark asked. "We just had one. The next election's not for another two years."

"Yes, but I don't think this is a problem we can hold off," Franklin said. "If we want to avoid serious problems in the future, now's the time to nip it in the bud." He tapped the ashes of his cigar into the ashtray. "Hayashi Yukichi came to me two days ago. He wants us to increase the number of Japanese representatives on the Council." Franklin raised his brows. A half-amused, half-worried smile crossed his face.

"Did he?" Clark asked. Hayashi was one of the two Japanese

members of the SMC. Currently, fourteen members comprised the SMC. Five British, five Chinese, two Americans, and two Japanese. The Council representatives were elected by vote of the ratepayers, who were people who owned and paid taxes on land within the International Settlement. The allotment of representation by nationalities originated from a gentleman's agreement. No one had ever proposed anything different. Until now.

Those cunning Japanese. Now they wanted to exert control over the foreign sectors. They were testing the Western nations' will.

Franklin waved his hand holding the cigar. "Hayashi said the United States and Japan are friends. He thought the United States ought to extend a gesture of friendship to show we would work together to rebuild Shanghai."

"Are you considering accepting his request?" Clark watched Franklin closely. With so much investment at stake in the city, the Americans had plenty of reasons to avoid a conflict with Hayashi. But what would that mean for the Chinese?

"Hell no." Franklin laughed. "More than ever now, we need to keep the Japs in check. What is it that you Chinese say? Give them an inch, they push further a foot? We can't let them think we're pushovers."

Clark kept his hand still on the armrest. For a moment, he was worried Franklin would consider giving in to appease the Japanese. "What do you plan to do? Will you tell him no?"

"I told him I'll think about it. Like you said, it's too soon to talk about the next election. But I have a feeling this won't be the last time I'll hear about it. If they press the issue, I'll need everyone else on the Council to stand firm. Can I count on you to rally the Chinese council members?"

So that was what Franklin wanted. If that was the case, Clark was more than happy to oblige. "I'll do everything I can."

Franklin smiled and took another drag of his cigar. His eyes, though, betrayed a glint of worry.

And Clark knew why. Franklin was talking tough. But if Japan insisted on their wish, would Franklin have the support to resist? Not the support of the SMC members, but the support of his country and its military. If the Japanese became openly hostile, would America come to the aid of their own people in China?

No one could be sure. The whole Settlement was now surrounded by the Japanese army. Japanese cruisers were coasting up and down the Whangpoo River stream. One would think the U.S. military would boost their forces here, even if only for appearance's sake. Yet they had made no change to the number of Marines stationed in the city.

Where did Shanghai stand in the view of the people in Washington, D.C.?

Clark did not ask. No point in getting false promises. "I'm with you as long as we can keep Chinese people safe here." He stood up. Franklin, too, got up from his seat.

"Thank you for your help." Clark held up the envelope with Merrick's registration papers. He shook hands with Franklin and left the room.

On his way out, he checked his watch. Time to go see Pearl. But before then, he needed to stop at the bank. Franklin's talk about the economy reminded him the market was not stable. Currency values could diminish overnight, especially with the Japanese trying to force the use of their own new version of Chinese yuan in the occupied territories. Just to be safe, he should exchange his own family's cash for gold and American dollars, and transfer everything to an American bank.

At the sidewalk, Huang Shifu exited the car when he saw Clark approach. In the past, Huang liked to stand outside and take smoke breaks while waiting for Clark. These days, he didn't dare to leave the vehicle. Too many Japanese soldiers and ronin roaming around. They showed little fear for the Shanghai

Municipal Police as long as the victims they harassed were Chinese.

"Young Master," Huang greeted Clark as he opened the car door.

Clark acknowledged him and climbed in. "Head to the National City Bank of New York," he said when Huang returned to the driver's seat.

The view of the SMC building diminished in the rearview mirror as the car rolled along. Clark gazed ahead to the road. How much longer could he rely on the West for the little they could still do to keep this place safe?

———

Six blocks away from the newly established Chamber of Golden Clouds, Clark told Huang Shifu to stop.

Huang Shifu pulled to the side of the road.

"Wait here till I get back." Clark grabbed the bag of gifts and climbed out of the car. He would walk the rest of the way. For one thing, he didn't want his driver to see him go to a brothel. Moreover, it would be madness to drive a Cadillac into the heart of Western Road. That area had taken on a new name, the Badlands.

He moved into the stream of pedestrians and tried to blend in, except . . . why did he have a feeling he was being followed?

He reached under his suit jacket for the gun he carried holstered to his waistband. As subtly as possible, he glanced to his left.

Was he being paranoid? He continued to walk. His breath quickened but he tried to maintain a normal pace. As he reached the brothel's front steps, a man in a gray *tangzhuan* with his face hidden under his fedora appeared out of the corner of his eye. From a distance, the man casually passed Clark, but Clark couldn't shake the feeling this man was following him. Quickly, he entered the building.

"Young Master Yuan!" The pretty young hostess greeted him.

Clark took off his hat. He still couldn't get used to being inside a place like this.

"I'll tell our Pearl you're here." The hostess gave him a knowing glance, then went to the back. Two girls passed by the greeting area and flashed him their seductive smiles. Clark forced himself to look their way with a lustful gaze. One of the girls wetted her lips. She tilted her head and signaled for him to follow.

Thankfully, Pearl came to his rescue. "Young Master Yuan. I've been waiting for you." She hooked her arm around his. "I've got the best *maotai* ready for you." She led him to a private room upstairs deep in the back of the building.

Once in the room, Pearl locked the door. "Have a seat." She walked to the table set with small plates of snacks and poured them each a cup of *maotai*. "Do you know the special treatment you're getting? Very few clients are personally greeted by me." She put down the wine bottle and laughed. "Look at you. Could you hold the handle of that bag any tighter?" She tossed her chin at the bag of gifts he'd brought. "I know you're a straight person, a *junzi*, but you don't need to get so tense around my girls. They won't devour you."

Clark dropped his eyes to his hand. He didn't know his nerves were so tight. He loosened his grip and put the bag on the table. "I'm sorry. I didn't mean to be rude. It's just . . . I thought a man was following me when I came in."

"Oh? Was the man wearing a gray *tangzhuan* shirt and a matching hat?" Pearl picked up one of the little cups of wine and offered it to him.

Clark sat down and accepted the wine. "How did you know?"

"Don't you know you're important to our cause? You don't really think Dai Li would let you go around on your own without protection, do you?" She raised the other cup, covered her mouth, and drank the wine.

"What?" Clark held his cup, stunned.

"The man you saw is with the Heaven and Earth Society. Their members have been shadowing you. Your sister arranged it."

"My sister? You mean Wen-Ying?"

"Who else? With your wealth, you're a prime target for the Japanese for kidnapping. You haven't hired bodyguards for yourself. She worries about you." Pearl pointed at the wine cup in his hand. "Do you not want to drink?"

Clark glanced at his wine. In one shot, he drank the entire cup.

He had no idea people were shadowing him. All this time, he thought he hadn't met any danger because he was alert and careful. "How do you know this?"

Pearl returned a mysterious smile. "I have my sources." She peered into the bag of gifts. "What have you got for me?"

Still stunned, Clark opened the bag and took out the boxes of Chanel perfumes, face creams, and silk scarves. From the bottom, he pulled out a set of papers. "This is a list of all the shipments of drugs I sent to Changde in the last two weeks, including their delivery locations. The drugs are concealed in containers marked herbal medicine."

Pearl ran her eyes down the list. "These won't be enough. The army of shorties will keep sending their planes to dump germ-carrying fleas down to infect people."

"These are all I could get for now," Clark said. "We'll have more coming. Joseph Whitman said his contacts at the hospitals are doing all they can to get us more."

Disappointed, Pearl folded the list. She was right though. The amount of drugs Clark sent would not stem the plague in Changde, where the Japanese were deploying biological weapons and poisonous gas. Joseph Whitman, the agent at the U.S. Consulate who Clark still trusted as a real friend, was privately procuring medicine and supplies for him. Joseph had alerted his superiors in Washington of this issue, but they didn't believe him. They didn't believe the Japanese—the yellow people—could be scientifically sophisticated enough to launch a full-fledged biological attack. Not without the white men's help.

Still, Joseph lent a hand. Like he'd told Clark before the war, they were diplomats. They didn't have the power to make sweeping changes, but they were each a link in a chain. At times, they could rescue those caught in the tide. Relying on his own connections, Joseph secured for Clark what they needed most now.

Pearl picked up one of the boxes of face cream. "Next time bring some lipsticks too." She put the face cream back down and pushed a plate of red dates soaked in white wine toward him. "Eat something. At least, look like you were entertained."

Clark picked up his chopsticks. With the thoughts of the people suffering in Changde, he wouldn't be able to savor the taste of the food even if he ate.

Watching him, Pearl propped her chin in her palm. "You don't look like someone who would work with Dai Li."

"No?" Clark threw her a glance and picked up a piece of drunken chicken with his chopsticks. "You don't either."

"Because I'm someone who sells her body?"

Out of courtesy, Clark didn't answer directly. "I thought celibacy was a Juntong requirement."

Pearl laughed. "Dai Li, basically he's no different from other men. He demands celibacy from the Juntong agents, but . . . as for himself, doesn't he seek out flowers and ask for willows everywhere too? Although, I don't have that kind of relationship with him."

That didn't surprise Clark. He could see her value to Dai Li and the secret police. But what about her? What could a woman of wind and dust like her get out of risking her life for Juntong? Were they paying her that much money?

Pearl gazed back at his doubtful eyes. "I didn't join Juntong for my own self-interest." She lifted her head from her palm. "When I was eight years old, I was sold to a brothel. Since then, my only path was to become a harlot. My existence served no other purpose." She blinked and lowered her eyes. "Four years ago, a man came to the Garden of Apricots with a group of Japanese. He was introduced to us as the shorties' Chinese interpreter. They came often to visit. After a while, he started coming alone, always only to see me. He never asked me to service him. He only ate and talked to me, like you and I are doing now." She chuckled.

Clark, too, lowered his chopsticks and chuckled.

"We talked about a lot of things," Pearl said. "I never had anyone listen to me the way he did, like my thoughts and my feelings really mattered. He would tell me things too, about the horrible things the Japanese were doing to our people. It made me so angry. I already didn't like servicing the Japanese. And then, the more I learned, the more I wanted to throw up each time a Japanese client asked for me. I told him that too. I couldn't understand how he could work for the Japanese either, but maybe he was like me, and didn't have a choice."

"What happened next?" Clark asked.

"One day, he took me out for a walk. He took me to his home, locked the door, and shut all the windows. He asked me if he could trust me. He told me about Juntong. He said he was an agent and he wanted me to work for them. He told me I could use my position to elicit secrets from the Japanese. It would help China defeat Japan. He said there would be no monetary rewards. In fact, there would be a lot of risks. But the choice was entirely mine. I was shocked. I couldn't believe he trusted me enough to tell me his real identity. I would have agreed on that alone, but there was more. For the first time in my life, I could do something more than being a whore. Even something big for the country is not beyond me. With what I'm doing now, I can play in my hand everyone who thinks they're better than me." She raised her head. Her eyes shone with the fire of a huntress.

"Of course you can do more." Clark softened his voice. He held her gaze. "And no one is better than you. I can see why he chose you. You're a very intelligent woman." It wasn't an empty compliment either.

Pearl twitched her lips. Her fingers shook as she brushed a lock of hair behind her ear.

Clark refilled his wine and raised his cup. "To China."

Pearl closed her fists. A smile came to her face and she raised her cup. "To China." When they finished their toast, Clark took her wrist. Surprised, she gazed at him.

"Do you know what a pearl is?" He ran his thumb over her pearl bracelet.

"A kind of jewelry."

Ignoring her answer, he held up her wrist. "It is a weapon. When parasites break through the shells of an oyster, the oyster releases a fluid around the parasites, destroying them. The fluid eventually hardens into a pearl." He turned her arm to show her the pearls on her bracelet under the light. "Without the pearl, we wouldn't be able to fend off the parasites."

He released her hand. Stunned, she drew in a quick breath. Under the light, she pulled her wrist back and took a closer look at the pearls of her bracelet.

While she pondered what he told her, Clark wiped his mouth. "I have some news for you to pass on to Dai Li."

"What?"

"The Japanese found their running dog for the northern region. They're negotiating with Tan Shao-Yu to be the head of their puppet provisional government."

"Tan Shao-Yu?"

"That man used to stand for something. When he was young, he was one of the leaders in Sun Yat-Sen's revolution. Many times, he refused Sun Yet-Sen's offers to appoint him as the national treasurer because Sun Yat-Sen decided to give himself the title of Extraordinary Top President. Tang thought that was an act against the spirit of democracy. And now?" Clark poured himself another cup of wine. "The Japanese Consulate informed the SMC yesterday he's ready to come out of retirement and accept their appointment."

Pearl lit a cigarette. "What made him change?"

"Antiques, apparently," Clark said. "He has a penchant for antiques, and the Japanese fronted a huge sum of money to purchase a large set of porcelain vases from the Sung Dynasty for him."

"A set of porcelain vases to exchange for a country?"

"Yes," Clark said. Even a once honorable man could be bought today by nothing more than porcelain.

His heart sank.

He thought of Tang Wei too, his former schoolmate, friend, and colleague, and shook his head.

"All right." Pearl blew out a ring of smoke. "I'll pass on the word."

"Also . . . " He pulled a piece of paper from his pocket. "Tan Shao-Yu's new address. It's in the French Concession. Number 42 Ferguson Road."

Pearl gave the address a cold glance. "Dai Li won't want someone like him to be used by the Japanese."

No, he wouldn't. As soon as Dai Li found out, Tan Shao-Yu would be marked as a dead man. That was the purpose of giving Pearl the address.

Clark held on to the paper, trying to steady his trembling hands. Enabling murder was not something he'd ever done, but Pearl waited for him to turn over the address with her open hand. Hardening himself, he gave her the paper.

"Very well." Pearl put the paper into the gift bag along with the list of locations of medicine delivery in Changde. She switched to a sweet, flirtatious voice. "You've been so generous,

Young Master Yuan. Please come see me again soon." She kissed the box of Chanel perfume and placed it back into the bag with the rest of the decoy gifts.

Slowly, Clark stood up. He followed Pearl to the brothel's door.

Soon, a man would be killed, and blood would be on his hand.

But it was too late to turn back.

4

FREEDOM OF THE PRESS

AT HER DESK, Eden gathered her purse and notebook, ready to go to her meeting with the SMC chairman Cornell Franklin. Clark had arranged the interview. She had so many questions to ask the man. What plans did the Council have to stabilize rising prices? The cost of rice had soared to more than three hundred percent of what it was before the Japanese attack. What would the SMC do about the telephone company's opportunistic gouging of their customers during this critical time when the city was trying to rebuild? Their fees had become astronomical! And what about safety? Bandits were attacking and robbing Chinese and foreigners alike even in full daylight. Were they really sent by the Japanese? What about the Japanese soldiers bombing Chinese schools and theaters? And the angry Chinese who were retaliating and bombing Japanese cars and shops? What, if anything, could the SMC do about all this?

She pushed her chair into her desk and turned around, nearly bumping into her colleague, Emmet Lai. "Sorry." She took a step back. He slumped and dismissed her with a wave.

"Emmet, are you all right?" she asked.

"Um hm," he mumbled, his eyes cast down to the floor. He

must've just come back from his rounds at the police stations. It had always been his job to visit the Shanghai Municipal Police and Le Guarde Municipale stations in the morning to get the latest updates on crimes reported the night before. Drunken brawls, armed robberies, even murder. Violent crimes were nothing new to the city. Nowadays though, a new kind of violence had emerged. Gun battles and terrorist attacks between bands of Chinese and Japanese. For Emmet, the war between China and Japan in Shanghai never stopped. Seeing his own people killed every day, and knowing no one else in the world was coming to their aid, took a toll on him.

She watched him walk away. But Dottie Lambert, the secretary, stopped him. "Come with me to the front," she told him, then signaled to Eden. "You too. Charlie has something to say to the staff."

"The whole staff?" Eden asked.

"Yes. The whole staff," Dottie answered. She left to round up everyone else on the floor.

Eden glanced at Emmet. He shrugged and followed Dottie, not looking particularly interested. Eden checked the clock. She was running out of time. She'd be late to her meeting with Cornell Franklin.

Up the aisle between the desks, Dottie motioned again for her to come forward.

Eden sighed. She dropped her purse back on her desk and went to hear what Charlie wanted to say.

When the whole staff had gathered, Charlie came and stood before the group. She'd never seen Charlie like this. His face showed something like raw anger, mixed with a dose of uncertainty.

"I got a call just now from the Le Guarde Municipale Police Commissioner. An hour ago, they found Tsai Tiao-Tu's head propped up on a telephone pole."

The staff let out a collective gasp. Eden raised her hand to her lips.

"As you all know, Tsai Tiao-Tu is the manager of *Shen Pao*. Many of you personally know him. He was also a good friend of mine."

Several of the female staff began to cry. *Shen Pao* was one of the few Chinese newspapers that had the audacity to openly criticize Japan.

"They haven't found the rest of his body. There was a note attached to the phone pole. It warned newsmen to cooperate with the New Order in East Asia."

His words knocked Eden over. She glanced over at Emmet. Next to her, Emmet clenched his fists so tight, his knuckles turned white.

Charlie swept his eyes over the room. "I'm going to say out loud what everyone already knows but no one wants to admit. The Japanese are moving in on us. Yes, even those of us from the West. We've seen them take over the entire strip along Western Road. Nearby, the puppet government is setting up their own police bureau on Jessfield Road, even though we have always controlled that part of town. We've also seen our own police quietly retreat. As a result, Japanese soldiers are flaunting our laws. They're harassing us, robbing us, and provoking fights. Their attitude and intent is clear. What is also clear is, neither the SMC nor the Consul General of France will do anything serious to try to stop them."

The floor fell dead silent. The staff lowered their heads and shifted their eyes. Dottie handed a handkerchief to one of the typists who was crying.

Charlie loosened the knot of his tie. "For some time now, the Japanese have been exerting pressure on the press. They've tried to intimidate us. There have been multiple incidents of bombings at the Chinese newspapers' headquarters. In the last five months alone, *Shen Pao*, *Hua Mei Wan Bao*, *Xinmin Wan Bao*, and *Wen Hui*

Bao had all been targets. I'm expecting things will get worse." The staff started muttering among themselves. Their voices and demeanors exhibited nervousness and doubts, but Charlie's face became more determined. "The one thing we from the occidental countries hold sacred is our freedom of speech. This is especially true for those of us who work for the press. I want you all to know, as long as the *China Press* is under my direction, we will continue to report the truth. We will not shy away from telling the world what's happening in China, and the violence and transgressions Japan is inflicting on its people. The *China Press* will not be threatened. Our paper will not be silenced."

The staff exchanged glances. Their uncertainty gave way. An air of strength and resolve returned, and one of the reporters called out, "That's right, Charlie."

Eden felt her heart roused. She loved her colleagues. What a brave group of people.

"Now, I warn you," Charlie said. "Given the inaction we've seen from our own governments, you're all exposing yourselves to risks as long as you're working here. Therefore, I will understand if any of you feel you cannot continue your employment with us." He looked at Emmet, their most senior Chinese reporter. "This is doubly true for those of you who are Chinese. If you wish to resign, I will understand, and you should not feel ashamed. I don't expect any of you to put your life on the line for our paper." He paused for the staff's reaction. No one showed any sign of wanting to retreat.

Charlie's eyes gleamed. "We will be implementing more safety measures from now on. I'll be in consultation with the Shanghai Municipal Police to see what steps we need to take to protect our office and to ensure the safety of each of you. If you feel frightened, if you're being threatened, I want you to tell me at once." He checked to see if everyone understood.

Watching him, Eden felt so proud. She raised her hands and clapped. Everyone followed and the room broke out in applause.

Charlie dipped his head and let slip a smile. Eden clapped even harder. How glad she was to be working for him.

"All right, all right." Charlie gave a wave of dismissal. "Now get back to work."

Slowly, everyone dispersed. Eden stole a glance at Emmet. How alone, how helpless he must feel right now, without a government that would protect him. How depressing it must be, to watch his own people being attacked, yet be unable to do anything to make it stop?

She knew those feelings well. Too well.

The bus finally came and Eden joined the rush of people jostling their way in. She'd waited in line for an hour, and she was not going to be left behind.

The public transportation system couldn't handle this many people. Chinese refugees, Jewish refugees, riders with cars who could no longer afford to pay the obscene prices of petrol, they were all jammed in the already overcrowded trams and buses.

She pushed through the thick of the crowd and squeezed into a tight spot next to an old woman lugging a large basket. The bus started to move, and she gripped the nearest pole to steady her feet. Outside, swarms of bicycles rolled past as the bus slowed to a crawl and stalled behind the traffic.

Maybe it was time she got a bike too.

The bus plodded on. When the traffic light turned red, the bus slowed to a halt. A donkey pulling a wheelbarrow walked alongside it until they all were forced to stop.

Yes. Some people had resorted to using donkeys.

The light turned green and the bus started again to move. Eden watched the donkey and the coolie leading it fall behind as the bus pulled ahead. All she wanted was to go home and shed the horrible news she'd carried with her all day. The photos of

Tsai Tao-Tu's decapitated head that came in from Le Guarde Municipale were not something she ever wanted to see again.

During her interview with Cornell Franklin, she tried to ask him about it. He skirted her questions. The French police were still investigating, he said, so at this time, he felt it inappropriate to comment.

The bus eventually reached her stop and she made her way back to her apartment. When she opened the door, she found her father on the sofa, looking depressed and drained. Her mother was patting his back, consoling him.

Eden exchanged a glance with Joshua. With a lost and worried look on his face, he silently pleaded for her help.

"What happened?" Eden closed the door.

"Your father's office was robbed," Mrs. Levine said.

"What?"

"Someone broke into his office during his lunch hour."

"My goodness." Eden rushed over. "Father, are you okay?"

"I'm fine. I'm fine." Dr. Levine held up his hand. "It's just the shock, that's all. The robbers were already gone when we returned. Good thing I got back before my nurse did. If she'd come back to the office before me and ran into them alone, I don't know what would've happened."

"Father . . . " Eden sat down. Rising crime was becoming a huge problem, but a medical clinic was now a target too? "Did you report it to the police?"

"We did," Mrs. Levine said. "We spent the whole afternoon at the police station. They came and took pictures, but I doubt it'll do any good. They wouldn't spend too much time on a case of robbery." She sighed. "The robbers ransacked the place. The cabinets were turned over. They opened all the drawers, and they threw all the papers on the floor. They stole all the cash too."

"How much money did you lose?" Eden asked her father.

"Not much," Dr. Levine said. "Around thirty dollars. I don't keep a lot of cash in my office. They took my stethoscope, my radio, and the medicine." He shrugged. "Oh, and the oddest thing. They took the notebook with the names and addresses of my Chinese patients."

Immediately, Eden thought back to how Neil employed Dr. Green at the Hospital St. Marie to discover embarrassing private illnesses of his business competitors. He would threaten to use the information against them. "Could it be an enemy of one of your patients? Maybe they were looking for secrets they can use to extort money?"

"What kind of secrets?"

"Secrets like syphilis?"

"Syphilis?" Dr. Levine laughed. "If that's their purpose, they're in for a disappointment. I've never treated anyone with illnesses of that sort. At worst, I've had a few cases of opium addiction, and that's not something people could hide well anyway. They wouldn't need to come to my office to find out." He clasped his hands. "I probably should still call and warn them, but how? I don't have their phone numbers and addresses anymore."

"Eden," Mrs. Levine said. "Could your newspaper print a notice?"

Before she could answer, the doorbell rang. Eden got up and opened the door. "Isaac?"

Isaac stumbled in, his face twisted in fear.

Mrs. Levine rose from the sofa, "Isaac, are you all right?"

"No." Isaac sat down. He pulled out a handkerchief and wiped the sweat off his forehead. "I just got a letter from my parents." He took a letter out of his pocket and showed it to her. "They didn't make it to Italy. They missed the ship."

"Why?" Eden asked. The Weissmans were supposed to leave for Trieste to board the *Conte Rosso* to come to Shanghai. Neil had arranged it despite her having broken off their engagement. It was the last favor he did for her before he sailed back to England with Collette and their son.

Whatever faults Neil had, he delivered on his promise to help the Weissmans find a way out of Germany. They thought the Weissmans were finally safe. And now, this happened.

How much more bad news did they need today?

"A group of Hitler Youths attacked my father," Isaac said. His face wrenched. "He and my mother were heading to the train station in the afternoon to go to Trieste. They passed by a Jewish elementary school. Those punks in brown shirts were waiting outside. When the Jewish students came out, they threw stones at the kids. One of the students got hit and his head started to bleed. He fell, and my father tried to help him. And then, the punks attacked my father."

"Oh, dear." Mrs. Levine gasped.

"My father got seriously hurt. They broke his ribs and gave him a concussion. My mother had to take him to the doctor and they missed their train."

"I'm so sorry." Dr. Levine took the Weissmans' letter from his wife. He scowled and read the letter, then lowered it to his lap.

"Can they take another train?" Joshua asked.

"It'll be no use," Isaac said. "The *Conte Rosso* already sailed. They won't be able to leave unless they can get on another ship."

"Isaac . . ." Eden didn't know what to say. How could this be? She'd thought the Weissmans could finally escape. She stared at the letter. She could try to write to Neil for help, but, how awkward. Besides, he'd already begun his new life with Collette. The last thing she wanted was to appear as if she was interfering with them. Collette would surely not welcome it.

Could she reach out to Victor Sassoon? She had only spoken to him once since she and Neil parted ways. Victor had personally called her to say how much he regretted that she'd chosen to leave Neil. In any event, he had now gone to Bombay for the summer, and she had no idea when he planned to return. And how would she ask? When she walked out of her wedding, she made him lose face in front of all of his friends in Shanghai.

"Isaac," Dr. Levine said. "Don't lose hope. We'll find a way to get them out."

Eden looked away. She couldn't bear to see Isaac in such despair.

How? How could they ever find another way to help them get out?

5

THE LOVER LEFT BEHIND

IN HIS OFFICE, Clark straightened the stack of contracts, letters, and financial reports piled on the desk waiting for his review, signature, and approval. One by one, he leafed through the documents, doing his best to make the right call. Here at the headquarters of Yuan Enterprises, everyone looked up to him as the master with all the right answers. Now he wished he had worked with his father and gained more experience. Running a business would be challenging anyhow. Managing one in China, where *guanxi* preceded written agreements, and tricks and breaches of faith for extra gain were the rules of the game, how could he be sure he wasn't making any mistakes?

Should he worry about inflation? Not yet, it seemed. Sales were growing more than enough to match. The global surge in demand for goods from countries at war or under the threat of war was creating an economic boom in Shanghai, so much so that he'd hired even more people since the war in China broke out.

But if things turned, what would he do? He couldn't lay people off. Tony Keswick, the British taipan of the Jardine Matheson conglomerate who served with him on the SMC, told him a man had to make sound business decisions.

Perhaps so, in the Western men's eyes. But he was Chinese. For all their unscrupulous ways in business, leaving a large number of workers unable to feed their families wasn't the Chinese way.

He couldn't fail his workers. If he failed, they, their families, and their children would all become destitute. And there were his own mother and sisters. He couldn't let his family lose everything from his hand.

If Xu Hong-Lie were still here, Clark thought. Then, he would have a voice he could trust to consult.

He stared at the empty chair across from his desk. Only a few months ago, Xu Hong-Lie was sitting there, debating whether to join the plot to blow up the Kailan Mines.

Guilt, shame, and sadness besieged him.

"Director Yuan?" His secretary knocked.

"Yes?" Clark answered and shook off his thoughts.

"A woman is here and she wants to see you. She said her name is Sun Xiu-Qing."

"Sun Xiu-Qing?" Clark drew a blank. "I don't know such a person. Is she from any company we work with?"

"No, and she won't leave. She said she has to see you. I told her you're very busy, but she said she'd wait out front until you agree to see her."

Clark put down the contract. Who was she? What did she want?

His secretary stole a glance at him and clasped her hands. "She looks painfully sad."

Painfully sad? Clark's frown deepened. About what? And how did it involve him?

His secretary rounded her shoulders and tucked in her chin. She darted her eyes away, then raised them again without raising her head. "Do you need me to call security?"

He watched his secretary talk and the way she averted her eyes. "No. Send her in."

"Yes," his secretary said and left.

He took a sip of tea. Whatever the problem was, he might as well put it to rest. If this woman sat here all day and refused to go, the entire staff would wonder what was going on. If he called security, it could cause a scene. His reputation outside was one thing. False rumors and gossip about him among his staff were another.

Minutes later, his secretary returned. A young woman in a simple gray Western suit dress followed behind her. The woman's face, though sad, exuded a gentle grace.

"This is Miss Sun Xiu-Qing," his secretary said.

"Miss Sun." Clark stood up and walked out from behind his desk.

Sun turned to face him. She looked vaguely familiar. Where had he seen her before?

"Please sit." He invited her to the couch in the sitting area, then asked his secretary, "Can you bring in some tea?"

Before his secretary could answer, Sun said, "No need." The curtness in her voice took Clark aback, and his secretary gave him an awkward glance.

"Then . . . please sit." He held his arm out toward the couch. Sun quietly sat down and he nodded at his secretary to signal her to leave.

After his secretary closed the door, he took a seat across from the stranger. "Miss Sun, how can I help you?"

"Young Master Yuan." Sun folded her hands on her lap. "I'm Xu Hong-Lie's lover."

"Xu's . . ." Of course! Clark sat up. He remembered now. On the train on their way north, Xu Hong-Lie had shown him a photo of Sun. He said he and Sun grew up together and they were planning to get married.

Sun looked even prettier in person.

Poor young woman. She must be heartbroken.

"Miss Sun. Hong-Lie talked about you. I . . ." Clark bowed his head. "Hong-Lie's passing . . . we at the Yuan Enterprises deeply regret this too. To go on a trip and run into an accident, leading to him perishing early in his strongest youthful years, it's a loss to everyone."

"Is it?" Sun looked him in the eye. "Young Master Yuan, you already said these pleasant words to Hong-Lie's family. I'm here to ask you, how did Hong-Lie really die?"

Surprised, Clark drew back. "I don't understand. What do you mean?"

"You don't need to lie to me. Hong-Lie told me. The reason he went to Peking with you was to carry out a plot to demolish the Kailan Mines."

"He told you that?"

"Hong-Lie would never lie to me." She squeezed her hands together. "Since he left, I've heard no news about the mines being destroyed. So, what happened? What happened to him?"

"He . . ." Clark looked away. Should he try to deny the truth? She didn't look like she'd be fooled, but their covert activity was a top secret.

She already knew about the resistance, his own mind talked back to him. If he lied, she wouldn't believe him. The cover-up could be exposed if she kept talking to people to try to find out what happened. Besides, Xu Hong-Lie trusted her.

Clark decided to take a chance. "It's true. Hong-Lie and I went up north to carry out a plot to blow up the Kailan Mines. We didn't succeed."

Xiu-Qing's stern demeanor broke and fear rose to her face.

"Hong-Lie boarded a local train transporting the dynamite from Hai River to Kailan. Halfway through, a band of Communists attacked the train to sabotage the Japanese. The train exploded. None of the passengers survived."

Tears swelled in Xiu-Qing's eyes. Clark dropped his head even lower.

"The ashes?" Sun asked. "What about the ashes you gave to his parents?"

Clark shifted in his seat. Heaven. How should he explain that?

He sucked in a deep breath. "They aren't his."

Xiu-Qing stared at him in disbelief. "You gave them fake ashes?"

"I'm sorry," Clark said. He'd never felt more ashamed.

"Very well. Very well." Xiu-Qing nodded, tears now raining down her face. "Hong-Lie said to me, you wanted to resist Japan. You wanted him to join you. He said Japan attacked China, murdered our people, and we need to fight back. He told me he wanted to support you. I'm only a woman without any abilities. I don't know anything about resistance, country, or politics. He believed this was the right thing to do, so I followed him. However, I know if you hadn't asked him, he would never have joined in any resistance activities. Yes, Japan is ruling over us, but Hong-Lie would still be alive."

"I'm sorry," Clark said. She was right. And if there was anything he could do to change what had happened, he would.

"Why weren't you on the exploded train instead of him?" Sun asked. "Everything happened because of you. Why did he have to die instead of you?"

Clark grimaced and looked up. He'd asked himself the same question too so many times.

"I don't have anything anymore," Xiu-Qing said with a hopeless gaze. "Without Hong-Lie, I don't want to live either. Young Master Yuan," she said and clenched her fist, "from now on, I hope you'll remember forever Hong-Lie died because of you."

He tried to think of the right words to say. Suddenly, she bent forward and grabbed the scissors next to the pens and ruler on the coffee table. With a hard, determined glare, she raised the scissors and pointed the sharp end at herself.

"Miss Sun!" Clark jumped out of his seat. "Miss Sun! What are you doing?" He lunged forward and grabbed her wrist. "Miss Sun, stop! Stop!"

"Don't get in my way!" she cried back, pulling her arm to free herself from his grip. "Go away!"

"Stop! Please!" Clark held on and wrestled the scissors out of her hand.

"Let me die!" She tried to grab the scissors back from him.

"Calm down." He pulled his hand away and begged her. "Calm down. Whatever the problem is, we can slowly talk about it."

Still crying, she fell back down onto the couch.

Clark dumped the scissors into a drawer of his desk and returned to his seat.

Sun narrowed her hardened eyes. "Even if you stop me now, you can't stop me after I leave."

"What good would it do for you to die? I know Hong-Lie's death is hard for you, but I believe he wouldn't want you to kill yourself." Gently, he handed her a handkerchief from his pocket. She ignored him. Undeterred, Clark remained by her side. "Hong-Lie would want you to continue to live, and live well. He would want you to have a happy future."

"Live well?" Xiu-Qing sneered. "A happy future? You don't understand. It's all too late. I won't have any future anymore."

"Why would you think that? Because Xu Hong-Lie is dead?"

"Hong-Lie and I were planning to get married when he came back to Shanghai."

"Yes, he told me."

"Before he left, we . . ." She blinked down a tear and stared at the floor. "I'm with child."

"You . . ." Clark fell speechless. "It's Xu's?"

Xiu-Qing nodded.

Clark's chest and face eased. "Little Xu will have a child?" He sat down beside her. Joy rose from his heart, and a smile broke out on his face. "That's great. That's really great."

"Great?" Xiu-Qing glared at him. "I'm a single woman. This matter that can't be known by people . . . how will I face anyone now?"

"That . . ." Clark scratched his head. "But—"

"How will I explain this to my father and mother? Hong-Lie's no longer here. What will I do?" She wiped her eyes with the back of her hand. "The best thing for me is to die. In the underworld, my child and I can reunite with Hong-Lie."

"No," Clark said. "In that case, it's all the more important that you can't die. You're carrying Hong-Lie's child. Would you want him to have no descendant?"

Xiu-Qing sat still. "What would you have me do? No one will forgive an unmarried woman giving birth to a child. If anyone knows about this, my father and mother will lose face. They'll kick me out of my home. I will have no way to take care of a baby. The whole world will laugh at us, push us around. In the end, my child and I will both have only the path of death. Rather than suffering a prolonged misery, I might as well bear all the pain at once."

"Miss Sun," Clark said, "please don't talk like that." He looked her in the eye. "This problem, there has to be a solution." He closed his fist. "Everything arose because of me. I will take responsibility to help you."

"How can you help me?" Xiu-Qing looked at him askance. "You think you can solve this problem because you have money? You're only a mortal person. You can't bring Hong-Lie back to life. You can't change the reality that I'm bearing a child without a father. Even if you give me money to go away from Shanghai and I lie about why I have a child, I can't go anywhere alone as a woman and be safe. The Japanese soldiers are everywhere. You can't help me."

"There has to be a way," Clark said. He wasn't ready to give up, no matter what she said. "Give me time. We can resolve this." Yes, he was sure of it. This was the chance for him to make it up to Hong-Lie. He just needed some time to figure this out. "Miss Sun, don't do anything impetuous. Give me a chance. I promise you I'll do my best to think of a solution. For Hong-Lie, and for his child."

Xiu-Qing gave him a side glance. A trace of uncertainty lingered in her eyes.

Seeing her doubt, Clark asked, "How about this? If I really can't help you, then you can decide your own fate. But for now, let me see what I can do for you."

"Then . . ." Xiu-Qing loosened her arms and looked down.

"You go on home. Get a good rest. Be careful for the baby." He glanced at her abdomen. She wasn't showing any signs yet. "How long has it been?"

"About two months," she mumbled.

"Understood. Don't worry. I will do everything I can." He handed her his handkerchief. This time, she accepted and patted it over her eyes and cheeks. Nonetheless, doubt remained on her face.

Clark let loose a deep breath. He would have to save this woman and her child, no matter what.

The Cadillac slowed down on the lane leading to the Yuan residence's driveway and a man in a dark suit strolled nonchalantly by. His dark sunglasses and fedora hid his face. From the passenger seat, Clark watched him approach the vendor selling used lamps and radios from a cart. The suspicious man examined the merchandise. Was he truly a pedestrian, or was he another member of the Tian Di Hui, the Heaven and Earth Society, sent to keep watch on his house to protect his family? For that matter, was the vendor selling used lamps and radios really a street merchant, or was he a Tian Di Hui member too?

Who else on the nearby streets were actually here to guard and watch over them?

Surely Wen-Ying would know, but she wouldn't tell him if they were. Tian Di Hui operated in secrecy. They wouldn't divulge anything about what they were doing even to their allies.

Regardless, he appreciated the extra level of security. Tian Di Hui would only do this if they believed they could not lose either him or Wen-Ying.

The car pulled into the driveway and the two burly Russian guards waved to his driver. Clark had hired and paid for the armed guards himself. All twelve of them, Russian and Chinese, three posted on each side of the family mansion. In the evening, another twelve would come and take their places to ensure someone was on the lookout around the clock. These ones didn't even include the personal bodyguards he hired for his mother and his youngest sister Mei Mei.

On entering his house, the maidservant came up and offered him a towel and a glass of water on a tray. His mind preoccupied, he waved his hand and refused. "Where's Dashaojie?" he asked for Wen-Ying.

"In her room."

He hurried upstairs to look for his sister. She was the only person he could talk to who also knew the truth about Hong-Lie's death. "Wen-Ying." He anxiously knocked on her door. "I need to talk to you."

"Ge?" She looked up from her sofa. "You've returned? What a coincidence. I need to talk to you too." She tilted her head, apparently noticing the distress on his face. "You first."

Clark closed the door and came toward her. He noticed Japanese propaganda leaflets scattered on her coffee table, but ignored them. "Xu Hong-Lie's fiancée came to my office today."

Wen-Ying put down the leaflet in her hand.

"I can't tell anyone else about this, but she's pregnant."

"Oh no. How long has it been?"

"Two months. She's afraid when people find out, she won't be able to face anyone anymore. She wanted to kill herself, but I stopped her." He slid his hand into his pocket and paced back and forth as he spoke. "I have to help her. Hong-Lie joined the resistance because of me. I must take care of those he left behind." He stopped and turned toward Wen-Ying. "You're a woman too. Do you have any better ideas? What do you think we should do?"

Wen-Ying stood up. "Losing her reputation will be inevitable, but we should be able to take her in. Her livelihood wouldn't be a problem then."

"No." Clark shook his head. "That's not good enough. Hong-Lie made such a huge sacrifice. His child should be able to take pride in his father being a hero. The child shouldn't have to live as a bastard."

"That would be hard. What Hong-Lie did can never get out to the public."

"I know." Clark paced around the room. "I have to find a way to help them keep their reputation. I don't want them to suffer any bitterness and pain."

Wen-Ying crossed her arms and sighed. She thought for a moment. "Ay! Is there any way to find someone to adopt the child?"

"Adopt the child?"

"What if she tells everyone she's been hired by us to care for Ma for a few months?" Wen-Ying tapped her arm with her finger, thinking out loud. "In the meantime, we rent a flat where she can stay until she gives birth. And then, when the child is born, the child can be given up for adoption."

"This solution could work." Clark looked up with hope. "The question is, would she be willing to separate from her child."

"Even if she's unwilling, she wouldn't have any better choice. If she gives birth out of wedlock, her name would be ruined."

"Mmm." Clark nodded. He knew Wen-Ying was right. "What about Ma? You think she'd help us lie?"

"I think she would." Wen-Ying smiled. "Ma's a kind-hearted person. Hong-Lie was one of our most loyal employees. Also, he was Uncle Six's nephew. Ma will definitely agree to save the girl and her child. Our hiring a caretaker for Ma wouldn't be a farfetched excuse either. Ma's spirits are still down."

The mention of their mother brought Clark another bout of grief. "Ma still hasn't shown any improvement?"

"She's been depressed since Ba died. She's like a walking ghost. She's always sleeping. When she's not sleeping, she's praying to the gods and the ancestors. In the past, every time she played mahjong with the band of *tai tai*, the noises and gossip would annoy me. Now, I wish I could hear the mahjong tiles' shuffling clacks. If it were possible, I would suggest she take a trip. But in this current environment . . ." Wen-Ying's voice trailed off and she looked away.

Clark exhaled and hung his head. Their father's sudden death was painful enough. The changes brought about by the invading Japanese forces made it that much harder to help their mother to overcome her grief.

"Mei Mei took her to see a Peking opera a few days ago," Wen-Ying said. "It seemed to have cheered her up a little."

"Really?" Clark rocked back on his feet. "Lucky we have Mei Mei to give Ma more attention. I keep not finding time to be with her." And he felt extremely bad about that. He spent so many hours at work. On top of work, he had to follow through with all the tasks he had to carry out for Dai Li. Too often, he didn't even know what was happening at home.

"You're busy enough," said Wen-Ying. "Ma will get better slowly."

He hoped. "What's Mei Mei doing these days? Is she still with that little twerp Liu Zi-Hong?"

"Listen to your tone." Wen-Ying laughed. "With your attitude, she wouldn't let us know even if she was still with him. But lately, I indeed haven't seen him around. Now that school's out for the summer, she's been taking calligraphy lessons with her female classmates. To be honest, the political situation here is so volatile, I myself have too many other things to worry about." She glanced at the door, then whispered, "I've been secretly monitoring the Ambassador's confidential correspondence." She was talking about the British Ambassador, in whose office she still worked as a translator. Her access to the British mind now was more valuable than ever to the resistance. "The British government's been telling him to yield to the Japanese. They said they need to focus their military resources in Europe because of Germany. They're afraid if they upset Japan in Shanghai, Japan would side with Germany."

"Is that so?" Clark casually raised a brow. "I predicted they would react that way already." He shrugged and tried not to let the news bother him. Still, he felt disappointed.

Wen-Ying was less forgiving. "Of course, they'd make peace even with the devil. The white demons only care about themselves." She walked over to the vase of flowers on her dresser and fiddled with the stems and petals. Her eyes hardly landed on the beautifully arranged peonies an amah had thoughtfully brought in from their garden. "I think if the Japanese demons dare to challenge the Municipal Police and take over the International Settlement, the British troops here will just stand by and let it happen." She turned toward Clark. The stem of the flower she was playing with snapped. It bent and the blossom fell dangling above the dresser top.

Clark met her gaze. He thought so too, but why speak of it? Talking about it made it feel more inevitable. "I hope that won't be the case. If any British members of the SMC express real concerns about Japan, I'll tell you."

She didn't answer. Her worried eyes returned to the flowers. Clark doubted she put much weight into the power of the SMC.

He decided to change the subject. "Didn't you say you need to talk to me about something?"

"Yes." She walked over to the coffee table and picked up several leaflets. "The Japanese are disseminating lies again. They are saying the new provisional government will restore Chinese authority and Japan will help them bring greater prosperity to the Chinese people."

"No one would believe them." Clark smirked.

"Maybe not. But they now run the Wireless Administration and the Post Office. The telegraph administration and other cable offices are under their censors' control. Chinese news reporters and publishers can't publish the truth without risking death." She showed him one of the leaflets. "Look at this. The writing style looks familiar, don't you think?"

He opened it to the first page.

A New Order. China and Japan United for a Prosperous Asia

He frowned and continued reading.

Chiang Kai-Shek did not protect you.

His chest tensed. That wasn't fair. That wasn't the whole story.

Follow Chiang Kai-Shek down a long road of agony? Surrender your future to the Communists' unproven fantasies? Continue to bear the humiliation of being trampled by British colonial lords?

Trust in Japan. Rejoice in the New Order. An Asia led by Asians. Rekindle our friendship with Japan for both countries to rise to new heights.

Clark clenched his jaw. Wen-Ying showed him another one from the stack.

Harmony brings prosperity. Continued strife, prolonged pain.

The warning was followed by the well-known lines of an ancient poem.

After crossing mountain after mountain and flood after flood, all roads appear to lead to a dead end.

But just ahead are shades of willows and blossoms of flowers, behind which is another village.

Wang Jing-Wei and the Provisional Government will bring the country peace and help China flourish.

Clark crumpled the leaflets in his hand. A cynical smile slipped from his face. Only one person he knew had such a smooth way with words.

Tang Wei.

So this was how Tang used his talent now.

He wanted to ask Tang Wei, was it worth it? Did his mind rest at ease when he went to sleep at night?

Relaxing his fist, Clark asked his sister, "Do you think we'll win?" A rhetorical question. He felt like asking anyway.

"I don't know." Wen-Ying stared back at him. "But I tell myself, we can keep up a good fight. Remember our soldiers? They kept the Japanese soldiers out of Shanghai for two months, and they were nothing more than two divisions of thieves and bandits before that. Nobody thought they stood a chance."

She was right. Their soldiers, armed with only guns, rifles, grenades, and left with no reinforcements except desperate men, women, and children in the city bringing them bowls of rice at night, held strong against Japanese warplanes and defended their city for much longer than anyone imagined possible.

Wen-Ying put her hand on his back. "They didn't give up. Neither should we."

6

HELL KNOWS NO FURY

"EDEN," Dottie Lambert said as she approached Eden's desk, "it's noon. I'm heading out to get something to eat from across the street. Would you like to come?"

"No," Eden answered with a quick glance before returning her eyes to her typewriter. "You go ahead. Thanks." Her mind was running, and she didn't want to stop her train of thoughts.

"All right." Dottie slung her purse strap onto her shoulder. "Do you want me to bring back something for you? How about a cheese sandwich?"

Eden looked up again. "That would be great. Thank you."

"Not at all." Dottie waved. Eden smiled and watched her walk toward the elevator. What would they do if they didn't have Dottie to manage everything else while they rushed to meet all their deadlines?

She sat back into her seat. A whiff of floral fragrance reminded her of the small bouquet of five peach roses at the corner of her desk. The blossoms brought her a sweet warmth she had never felt until the first time Clark held her in his arms, when, standing before the statue of the Angel of Peace, they finally understood what they meant to each other.

She brushed her fingertips over the rosebuds. Neil used to send her flowers too. Beautiful ones. But his flowers were always so dramatic, almost like he had to use the flowers to affirm his intentions not only to her but also to himself. Clark's flowers were subtler. They rarely made any bold statements. Instead, they flowed into her heart like water under a gentle wind, slowly enveloping her with the sweet nectar of love.

She paused her fingers on the flowers, then willed herself to return her mind to her article. Someone had stolen the manhole covers on Nanking Road again. The SMC put new ones in just three weeks ago, but junk collectors kept stealing them. The officials at Holt's Wharf reported it was costing them five dollars each day to replace them.

Everyone knew who were the culprits behind the thefts. At court this morning, she was able to confirm it again. The little old Chinese woman on trial gleefully admitted to the judge she'd stolen the manhole covers on Bubbling Well Road to sell to the Japanese junk dealer. He was paying as much as fifty cents apiece. The exasperated judge scowled and sentenced her to a week in jail, but the old woman reacted with neither fear nor shame. Instead, she broke into a huge smile. When Eden asked the court interpreter to inquire with the old woman whether she was happy she received such a short sentence, the old woman said she was happy because now she would be eating three meals a day for a whole week.

Eden didn't blame her. The old woman was only doing what she could to survive. The Japanese were the real ones to blame. They were stripping the city of every piece of scrap iron they could get. Ronin raided abandoned or bombed-out cars, buildings, and factories, stripping metal from every piece of machinery, and even hinges and doorknobs from doors. Their war machine had a hunger for iron and it demanded to be fed.

Her phone rang. The sound jolted her out of her thoughts and she picked it up. "Hello? It's Eden Levine."

"Miss Levine?" A female voice came from the other end. "I hope you still remember me. I'm the nurse at the Hospital St. Marie. My last name is Bai. Do you remember me?"

Bai? Of course she remembered. Bai was the nurse who gave her evidence of Neil's extortion scheme against his business rivals with the help of the corrupt Dr. Green. "Hello, Miss Bai. I do remember you. How've you been?"

The nurse let out a loud sigh. "As good as can be. Very overworked. So many sick and injured people since the occupation."

"Yes. I can imagine," Eden said. "To what do I owe the pleasure of your call today?"

Bai lowered her voice. "I'm calling about the murder of Tsai Tiao-Tu."

"Tsai Tiao-Tu?" Eden's hand froze. "You mean the late manager of *Shen Pao*?"

"Yes," Bai whispered. "The one whose head they hung on the telephone pole. I know who murdered him."

"You do?" Eden held the receiver closer to her mouth. "How?"

"He's a collaborator. He got injured in a gunfight and stayed at the hospital for a few days. I overheard him talking to his people."

"Okay." Eden grabbed a pen and a notebook. "Can you tell me his name?"

"I can, but I don't want to talk about it over the phone. Besides, I've got his picture for you."

His picture? "Where do you want to talk?"

"Can you meet me at four-thirty today at the New Asia Hotel?"

"New Asia Hotel? In Hongkew?"

"Yes."

That was odd. Why pick a hotel in the Japanese district?

"Miss Levine? Will four-thirty work?" Bai asked again.

Eden glanced at the clock on the wall, then at her desk calendar. Her meeting with Charlie would have to wait. "Yes."

"Come to Room 815."

"Room 815?"

"Yes. I can't risk anyone seeing me talking to you."

"Okay." Eden jotted down the room number. Also, she hadn't forgotten. Exclusive scoop came with a price. "How much do you want for this information?"

"Nothing."

"Nothing?"

"The collaborators are traitors," Bai said. "It's good enough for me if you expose him."

"I see," Eden said. What a surprise. The Chinese sellouts galvanized even the mercenary Miss Bai. "In that case, I thank you in advance."

"I'll see you at four-thirty," Bai said and hung up the phone.

Eden put down the receiver. What luck. This exclusive story came by without any effort on her part.

Charlie would be pleased. The entire news community would be too. When the murderer was named on the front page, it would show the Japanese they couldn't intimidate the press.

At four fifteen, Eden arrived promptly at the New Asia Hotel for her meeting with the nurse, Miss Bai. At first glance, this nine-story hotel on Tiendong Road was no different from all the other luxury hotels in Shanghai. Yes, it was new, constructed only in 1935. Yes, it was designed by a British architect. It even had a rooftop garden, with small rabbits and exotic birds. But for anyone who had spent any time in this city, such extravagance would soon become the norm.

She crossed the lobby toward the lifts, passing by the hotel's restaurant on the way. Now, the restaurant might be something worth a visit. It served Cantonese cuisine, a reflection of the hotel owners' Cantonese roots and the mostly Cantonese guests they served. The restaurant, she heard, was the best of its kind.

While waiting for the lift, she watched the guests amble into the restaurant. A few minutes later, the elevator door opened. A gangly man with a square jaw and wry lips, wearing a well-tailored chalk-stripe suit, walked out.

Was that Jack Riley who just came out of the elevator?

Eden turned her head to take a second look.

Yes. That was him. "Lucky" Jack Riley, who owned all the slot machines in Frenchtown, Chapei, and the Western Roads. Since the Japanese chased the notorious Green Gang's boss out of town, Jack Riley had become the big man in the Shanghai underworld. In just a few months, he'd made himself millions. Her colleagues at the *China Press* often talked about him. They'd heard rumors he was an American prison escapee.

Who knew what shady deal he made and with whom to rise so high so fast?

She entered the lift. Actually, the real question was, why was he here at the New Asia Hotel? This hotel marketed itself on its three virtues. No gambling, prostitution, or consuming opium on site. What was a man like Jack Riley doing in a fine establishment like this?

"What floor, Miss?" the lift operator asked.

Eden came out of her thoughts. "Eighth. Thank you."

The lift operator pulled the lever and took her to the top floor. When they arrived, she followed the signs down the hall. At Room 815, she stopped and knocked.

A Chinese man opened the door.

Confused, she drew back her hand. "I'm sorry. I'm looking for Miss Bai. I must have the wrong room." She backed away and checked the room number.

"You're at the right place," the man said. "Come in."

Hesitantly, Eden entered. Bai hadn't told her someone else would join them.

The man closed the door. The room's entryway appeared to open into a suite. Strange. Could Bai afford to book a full suite?

Eden took another step forward. Behind her, the door locked. Instinctively, she turned around. The man who invited her in stood with his back to the door. His blank face gave her a chill. What was going on?

"Come in, please," a woman called out. Eden had heard the voice before, but it wasn't Bai's.

Who? She walked into the living room of the suite. At the center of the room, a Chinese man, about fifty, sat bound to a chair. The ropes crisscrossed around his arms, legs, and chest. He couldn't speak through the handkerchief tied over his mouth.

A Chinese bodyguard stood beside him, his arms crossed behind his back. His face looked colder than ice.

"What is this?" Eden asked. The man bound to the chair moaned. He looked at her, his eyes crying for help.

"Hello, Eden." A woman sauntered in from the bedroom. A trail of smoke flew from the long cigarette holder in her hand. The curly petals of the red chrysanthemums embroidered on her black *qipao* sprung from the fabric like claws. She inhaled a drag of smoke and blew it out. "Long time no see," she said in heavily accented English. "Do you remember me?"

Remember her? Yes. Shen Yi. Clark's ex-fiancée.

Lost for words, Eden stared at her.

"You forgot me already." She smiled, but her eyes widened with a flash of anger. "I'm Betty!"

"Betty, " Eden said, recovering her bearing. "Yes, I remember you." She took a quick check of the room. "Where's Miss Bai?" She glanced at the man tied to the chair. "Who's this man? What are you doing to him?"

"Miss Bai? The nurse?" Shen Yi curled up her lips. "She's not here. She's not a part of this. I paid her fifty yuan to telephone you."

"What?" Eden inhaled a deep, shaky breath.

"This man . . ." Shen Yi shot her eyes at the victim. "His name is Gao Zhen. A very important banker." She sashayed over to him and put her hand on his shoulder. "He is your father's patient."

Eden stared at the man in horror. Her heart began to pump. She looked back at Shen Yi. "What do you want?"

"What I want?" Shen Yi crossed her arms. "What I want, you took away from me." She pressed her lips together into an angry thin line. The victim moaned again, but she walked away from him and came toward Eden. "You know, I almost believed Guo-Hui when he said he didn't leave me for you. He almost fooled me. I thought going to America changed him and turned him into a Casanova. He put on quite a show. I'm very impressed. But then I saw you two love birds at the park, and then I realized, he did that all for you. He lied to take the blame off you."

Eden gripped her purse strap. What should she do? Could she reason with this woman?

She turned around and looked behind her. The bodyguard who let her in was blocking the door. She could not escape.

"It's not fair." Shen Yi blew out an angry puff of smoke. "You two are happy. You don't even remember me. You two don't remember who you hurt."

"That's not true . . ." Eden said.

Shen Yi ignored her and continued pacing back and forth. "I'm married now. I had to do that, you know. Because of you, Guo-Hui almost ruined my name. I'm a good, chaste woman. If I didn't get married, everybody would wonder, why wouldn't Yuan Guo-Hui marry her?" She stopped. "So now, I'll never have a chance to love. But I didn't do anything wrong. I was faithful to Guo-Hui. Why should I lose out on love when you two are the ones at fault?"

"Betty . . ." Eden gathered her nerves and stepped forward. "Let's talk about this."

"There's nothing to talk about." Shen Yi shot her a glare. "It's time you make amends. It's only fair if none of us gets what we want. You will go and tell Guo-Hui you're breaking up with him. If you don't . . ." She walked up to the man tied to the chair. The bodyguard standing beside him stepped back in deference and she touched the victim on the back. "If you don't, this man will die."

The man cringed. He cried out, but the handkerchief tied over his mouth muffled the sound of his voice.

"You can't do this!" Eden shouted.

"I can't?" Shen Yi raised a brow. "Of course I can. Haven't you heard? We have a New Order now." She held open her palm. The bodyguard gave her a short, heavy knife. She poked its tip on the man's back just below his neck. The man cried out again.

"No!" Eden shouted again.

"Yes." Shen Yi put a hand on her hip. "This time, I get to decide our fates."

"No." Eden came closer. The guard stepped up to block her, forcing her to halt. She looked back at Shen Yi. "This is wrong. You have no right to make me leave Clark. You have no right to hurt this man."

"I don't care!" Shen Yi gave her cigarette to the bodyguard. In exchange, he handed her a black notebook. She held it up to show Eden. "Do you recognize this? This is what your father used to keep the names of his Chinese patients. All three hundred and sixteen of them he treated since he came to Shanghai. I got this from his office."

"My father's . . ." Eden's mouth fell open. The break-in! It wasn't a robbery. It wasn't about money at all. Shen Yi staged it to get the names of her father's patients.

"Gao Zhen's only the first one." Shen Yi glanced sideways at him and smiled. "If you and Guo-Hui don't do what I say, I'll kill

SHANGHAI YESTERDAY71

one person on the list every week. One by one, they'll be killed until you two make everything right."

Eden shifted her eyes to Gao. Her palms and back were breaking out in cold sweat. She had to save this man. "Shen Yi, please," she said through short, quickening breaths, "please don't do this. I'm sorry if we hurt you. I'm very, very sorry." She eased her face and tried to show her sympathy. "Please forgive us. Like you said, you're a good woman. I know you don't really want to hurt anyone. I can't believe you mean what you said."

Shen Yi wasn't moved. "You don't believe me. You think I'm joking."

"No." Eden shook her head. "I do! I—"

"This is no joke." Shen Yi held up the knife. "I think I need to show you how serious this is." She returned to the victim and traced the tip of the knife around his ear. "How about I cut off his ear and give it to you to show you I'm serious?"

"No!"

Shen Yi smiled, her eyes clear and her face relaxed. "Ah Long," she barked to her bodyguard and plopped the knife in his hand, then stepped back.

The bodyguard raised the knife. In one quick move, he sliced off the man's right ear. The man shrieked. Blood spattered over his face and dripped down his neck. Eden's knees buckled and she fell to the floor. Her own scream mixed with the man's as she covered her own ears with her hands.

Shen Yi came and stood in front of her. "Go ahead. Scream." She bent and shouted at Eden. "Scream louder. No one can hear you." She swung open her right arm. "Above us is the rooftop. I control all the rooms next to us and the rooms below us. This whole floor and the floor below are now reserved for use by the Empire of Japan, and my husband is in charge. No one can set foot on these floors unless I or my husband say so." She straightened back up and laughed. "So scream. Let me hear you scream."

Eden raised her eyes in horror. The victim's screams stopped. He fainted when the bodyguard slapped a wad of cloth over his wound. The bodyguard picked up the ear and tossed it into a wooden box. Shen Yi motioned for him to come closer. He did as she ordered, holding the open box with both hands.

Shen Yi pointed at the box and asked Eden, "Do you want to keep this?"

Wildly, Eden shook her head. Her heart was pounding out of her chest. The bodyguard held the box in front of her face. The blood-glazed ear made her stomach churn. Gagging, she recoiled and looked away.

Watching her choke, Shen Yi waved the bodyguard away. "Stop crying," she ordered Eden.

Eden sucked in a breath of air. Her eyes felt wet. She looked at Shen Yi, but dared not move.

"I haven't killed him yet," Shen Yi said as the bodyguard closed the box and put it on the table behind the victim. "But whether he lives is up to you. I will give you three days. You stop seeing Guo-Hui. You never speak to him again." She glanced back over her shoulder at the man. "If you do that, I'll let him go."

Trying to keep herself up, Eden pushed her hands against the floor. Her arms, her entire body quaked. She wanted to speak, but no voice would come out through her chattering teeth.

"Oh, stop crying." Shen Yi grabbed a silk handkerchief on the table. "You slob." She bent down and mopped the handkerchief over Eden's face to dry her tears. When she finished, she tossed the handkerchief to the floor and stood up. The security guard gave her back her cigarette and she inhaled a deep drag of smoke. "All I'm asking for is fairness. You can understand that, can't you? Besides, I don't think you want your father's patients to die. If they do, it'll be all your fault." She raised the notebook to show Eden one more time, then handed it back to the bodyguard.

The bodyguard put the notebook next to the box holding the victim's ear.

"Get up." Shen Yi pulled Eden by the elbow and prodded her to stand up. At her touch, Eden flinched. This woman. This evil, evil woman.

"And don't bother asking the police for help. The SMP only protects foreigners. They won't intervene if a Chinese threatens to kill another Chinese. But if you don't believe me, you can try. I don't care, and it won't do you any good. Besides, the Japanese army owns this hotel now. Everything we do in this hotel is official business of Imperial Japan. If any SMP policemen dare to get involved, they'll be interfering with the Japanese army at their own risk. Do you understand me?" She glared at Eden. Her harsh voice slashed the air and Eden bowed her head, fearful that either agreeing or disagreeing would make matters worse.

"I'm glad we're clear," Shen Yi said. "Ah De!" she called the guard standing at the door. *"Guo lai."*

The guard came over. Keeping her eyes on Eden, Shen Yi softened her voice. "This is my bodyguard Ah De. He'll escort you out of the hotel."

Eden shuddered and moved back from the bodyguard.

"Don't worry, he won't hurt you." Shen Yi inhaled a drag, then added, "Not as long as you do what I say." Her smile deepened. "My English is better now, don't you think?" She lifted her head. "I studied hard. And now, no one can look down on me anymore. Do you agree?"

Eden clenched her teeth.

Not hearing an answer, Shen Yi dropped her smile. She ordered Ah De, *"Dai ta zou."*

Ah De dragged Eden by the arm. Still shaking, Eden stumbled along. The door of Room 815 closed behind them. As he led her down the corridor toward the lifts, she glided her eyes from left to right. What was happening behind these doors? Were all these rooms empty? Were more people being held inside against their will? Were other patients of her father in any of them?

A whimper escaped from her mouth. Her legs lost their

strength and she nearly fell. The bodyguard, Ah De, shot her a look. Terrified, she forced herself to continue to walk.

Silently, they waited for the lift. In her head, Eden began counting from one to a hundred. How long? How far would she have to count before the lift would reach this floor and she could run?

The lift arrived. Without uttering a word, they both walked in. Ah De spoke to the operator in Chinese and the operator pulled the metal gate closed. As the lift descended, Eden wanted to scream, but Ah De was next to her and she didn't dare to make a sound. She stared at the floor, afraid to look up in case the lift operator could see the terror in her eyes.

She began counting numbers again in her head.

The lift arrived at the lobby and the operator opened the door. Trembling, she walked out. Ah De walked closely beside her as they made their way to the exit. Keeping her head low, Eden glanced at the hotel staff and guests. Did anyone know what was happening on the eighth floor?

She watched bellboy push a cart of suitcases toward the lifts, and the front desk manager checking in a guest.

Could she alert anyone?

Her heartbeat quickened.

What if they already knew?

Realization dawned on her. Of course they already knew. This hotel was not what it seemed. Its grandeur and virtues were now a facade. Its owners and clientele had all changed. Who were these people around her? Their mannerisms, their speech. These weren't Cantonese travelers and businessmen. On closer look, she could see they were ronin, ruffians, and thugs.

At the hotel's front door, the porter greeted them. Ah De pointed to a taxi and the porter hurried to the curb to wave one down. When the taxi drove up, he asked Eden, "Where are you going, Miss?"

Startled, Eden jumped. She glanced at Ah De. He looked back at her with a cold, expressionless face.

Trying not to stutter, Eden gave the porter her address. The porter spoke to the taxi driver and opened the passenger side door. Warily, Eden climbed into the backseat. The porter slammed the car door shut and walked away. The taxi began to move, but Eden remained stiff. Her chest felt so constricted, she could not breathe.

The taxi drove down the blocks. When it crossed the Garden Bridge and she was back safe on the British side of the Creek, her body collapsed. All the air in her lungs flooded out. Catching her breath, she fell back into the seat. Her body shook, worse than when she was walking out of the hotel.

What should she do?

The taxi driver took a turn onto the road leading to her home.

No! She sat up. She couldn't go home. She had to tell Clark. Shen Yi was holding a man hostage at the hotel. "Shifu!" she called out to the taxi driver. In broken Chinese, she redirected him to Clark's address.

The taxi driver drove to the traffic light and made a U-turn.

Eden held her hands together and looked ahead. She had to find Clark at once. If they didn't act quickly and do something soon, the man in Room 815 would be killed.

7

HER IMPOSSIBLE DEMAND

"A BABY?" The master of the house gawked. "You're asking us if we want to adopt a baby?"

"Yes," Clark said. The man he was talking to, Chen Zhen-Hua, was a distant cousin on his father's side. With a hopeful heart, he waited for Chen and his wife, Shu-Yin, to respond. In so many ways, they were the ideal couple to help. Both were in their mid-thirties, and they had three children of their own. Financially, they were more than capable. Just look at this house. They could easily take in and feed another kid.

"Guo-Hui." Chen rubbed his chin. "We're all one family. You know whatever you ask, we'll certainly help if we can. But when it comes to adopting a child, this isn't a matter to be taken lightly."

"Exactly," said Shu-Yin. "Bringing up a child is a very big responsibility. My three are still small. Adding another one, I'm afraid I won't be able to handle it. Have you tried asking other families? Maybe there are other people for whom this would be easier."

Clark clasped his fingers. "I've asked several. To be honest, there aren't many people I can approach. I can think of some nice families, but they don't have the financial means. The others, I don't feel secure enough to trust them to take good care of the child." He stopped short of telling them that the wealthy families he'd already approached would only agree to raise the child to become a servant when the child grew older. "*Biaosao*," he addressed her in the honorifics for the wife of a cousin, "you have the heart of the Buddha. If you adopt the child, I know you'll definitely treat this child as one of your own."

His praise seemed to have the desired effect. All at once, she became lost for words. She couldn't deny she was a compassionate person.

Chen, though, was not convinced. "Of course Shu-Yin's the kind of person who always looks out for others. But you know, the world situation now is not suitable for casually promising to do good deeds. Today, the International Settlement is still considered safe. Tomorrow, if the tide of the world turns and we have to seek refuge, taking three children plus a baby? Not so easy!" He tossed up his hands to emphasize his point.

"I understand," Clark said. "But—"

"Zhen-Hua's right," Shu-Yin interrupted him. "You also know that if we promise someone something, we would take full responsibility. If by chance something bad happens to the child, how would we answer to his mother?"

"I understand your concern." Clark sat forward. "However, I know the mother would only feel grateful. If something you can't avoid happens, she definitely won't blame you."

"That's easy to say now," Shu-Yin said. She put her hand on her husband's back. "To be adoptive parents, it's easier said than done. Even if we can escape disaster, as the children grow up, people will judge everything we do. If we so much as appear to treat our own children better, outsiders will accuse us of favoritism. When the adopted child grows up, he will resent us. If we need to treat the adopted child better, then I myself am unable to do that. After all, my own children are mine. This situation is very difficult, wouldn't you say?"

Clark felt his hope slipping away. When he came to see Chen and his wife, he had thought they would offer a helping hand. In the past, they'd always been so kind. Their roundabout refusal disappointed him.

Chen commiserated with a deep sigh. "If the young woman needs money, we'd gladly contribute a bit of effort and help. However much she needs, say the word anytime. I, Chen Zhen-Hua, won't hesitate." He sat up and slapped himself on the chest.

Money? Money wasn't the problem. If money were the solution, Clark could resolve this on his own.

He slumped in defeat. He could continue to make a case, but his cousin clearly didn't want to take on this matter. If they accepted now at his insistence and later regretted it, it wouldn't be a good situation for the child either. "Thank you then." He ended his request with a courteous smile.

The Chens, too, seemed relieved. Shu-Yin slowly waved her pink floral oval fan below her neck. "Actually, Guo-Hui, in today's world, to have someone like you who's so willing to help others is extraordinary. I often say, among all our relatives distant or close, Guo-Hui's the most capable and most reliable." She gave him a hesitant look of sympathy. "We're all family. I hope you won't mind me, your *biaosao*, speaking a few words of truth. In any case, my life experience exceeds yours. The way I see it, this young woman probably isn't worth you making such an effort to help her. Of course, her fiancé passing away is a sad tragedy. But in the end, this situation came about all because she didn't keep to moral behaviors. How can a young woman casually give herself to a man before she gets married?"

Clark winced. Her criticism grated his ear. Society judged a woman so harshly when she made mistakes. If he didn't help Sun Xiu-Qing and her child now, who would?

"As to this matter," Shu-Yin continued, "I suggest, why not try to find a less well-to-do family? Given enough financial compensation, some might be willing to take him."

"I agree," said Chen. "With money, you can make a ghost grind the mill. The way I see it, you'll have a better chance if you look for a family that can use more cash."

"Mmm." Clark put on another smile. The Chens were a dead end, but putting Xu Hong-Lie's child into a home that only wanted financial benefits was absolutely out of the question.

"This time, we really have the will at heart but not the ability," Chen lamented. He raised his cup to soothe himself with a sip of tea.

"Thank you," Clark said. "In that case, I'll be taking off."

"So soon?" asked Shu-Yin. "You big, busy person," she joked. "You so seldom come to visit us. Why don't you stay for dinner? I'll tell the kitchen to add more dishes. Afterwards, you and old Chen can play a game of Go."

"Thanks." Clark unclasped his fingers. "Next time. I still have some matters to attend to at home." He stood up.

No. He had nothing at home that couldn't wait. But after the fruitless conversation, he was in no mood for entertainment or games.

The Chens said their goodbyes and Clark left their place. Outside, Huang Shifu pulled up. In the car, Clark tried to think. There were still a few families he planned to approach, but he'd pinned his highest hope on the Chens. From here on, the chances of finding a family to adopt Sun Xiu-Qing's child would only go down.

He gazed out the window up at the sky. Xu Hong-Lie. Was he up in heaven looking down? If he were, could his soul help them find a way?

The dimming sky seemed like a sign saying no, but the gleaming stars urged him not to give up hope.

When he arrived home, Clark's mind was still on how to help Sun Xiu-Qing when Mei Mei came out to greet him. "Ge!"

"I'm back," Clark said to her as the houseboy took his hat and briefcase.

"Good. Eden's here. She came to see you."

"Oh?" The news gave his spirit a jolt. He broke into a smile, but caught himself before he revealed too much. He hadn't told his family yet about his new relationship. Mei Mei probably would be happy for him anyhow. Wen-Ying might or might not approve, but she'd be too preoccupied with matters of Tian Di Hui to pay attention to his personal life. His mother, though, was a different story. His father's death was a big blow. The Japanese invasion, too, brought her much distress. He didn't want to upset her again so soon.

Keeping an impassive face, he asked, "What does Eden want to see me for?"

"She didn't say," Mei Mei said. "She doesn't look well. I asked her to join me to listen to the radio while we wait for you, but she said she wanted to wait for you alone. So I invited her to wait in the small sitting room. She's been here for an hour."

An hour? Clark frowned. "All right. I'll go see what she needs." He straightened his tie and headed down the corridor.

"It's almost dinner time," Mei Mei called out after him. "Shall I tell the kitchen we'll be having a guest?"

"I'll ask her if she wants to stay," he called back out to her.

Coming to the small sitting room, Clark eagerly pushed open the door. "Eden?"

On the sofa, Eden gazed up. Her pale face and haunted eyes confused him.

"Eden, what's wrong?" He closed the door and came toward her.

"Clark!" She jumped out of the seat and threw her arms around him. He could feel her body shaking.

He held her and asked, "Eden, are you all right?"

"No." She clung on to him and shook her head. "Betty, your ex-fiancée—"

"Betty?" Who? He pulled a bit away. "You mean Shen Yi? What about her?"

"She kidnapped a man," Eden said. "She lured me to a hotel this afternoon. She said the man—I forgot his name—she said he's my father's patient. Remember my father's office was broken into last week? She did it. She did it to steal the names of all my father's Chinese patients. And then . . ." Eden squeezed shut her eyes and pressed her face against his shoulder.

Clark thought back to the last time he saw Shen Yi. Could she do such things? He tried to remain calm. "Then what?"

"At the hotel room, the man was tied up. She had two bodyguards there. She told me I have to stop seeing you. She said if you and I don't stop seeing each other, she'll kill the man. And she'll kill all my father's Chinese patients, one for every week we continue to still see each other."

Clark grabbed Eden by the arms. "She can't do that! That's outrageous. She wouldn't. She's only trying to scare you."

"No." Eden shook her head again. "No, she's not. She ordered her bodyguard to slice off the man's ear. And then she showed it to me." She cried. "There was so much blood."

"How could she?" Clark drew back, still holding Eden's arms. Could Shen Yi be this vindictive? Was she really capable of such cruelty?

Eden wouldn't lie to him. "Which hotel?" he demanded to know. "I'll go report this to their management. If she's holding someone there against his will and hurting him, then this is a crime." He grabbed her hand and turned toward the door.

"Don't." Eden pulled him back. "You can't. It's the New Asia Hotel. She said the Japanese army owns it now. She said they're doing work for the Japanese government there. If what she said is true, then reporting to the hotel won't do anything. It'll only put you in danger."

Clark halted. He gripped her hand. "This cannot stand. Japanese or not, New Asia Hotel is still in the International Settlement. She still has to abide by our laws. I'll report it to the Municipal Police."

"She said the Municipal Police won't help. She said they won't care if the victims are Chinese. She also said if they get involved, they'd be interfering with the Japanese army, and there'll be consequences. Regardless, I'm afraid if we report her, she might harm not only that man she kidnapped, but my father's other patients too. She has the names of three hundred and sixteen people. There's no telling what she would do to them if we report her and try to stop her."

Clark stood, trying to think. How dare she? How dare Shen Yi try to break them up? How dare she hurt and threaten to kill innocent people to force their hands?

The full scope of what was happening began to sink into his mind. Thank Heaven Eden got out of there unharmed. If Shen Yi had hurt her too, he didn't know what he would do.

He had to put a stop to this.

He took Eden into his arms. "Listen. At least you're not hurt. So that's good. Let me go find her." He pulled back and looked into her eyes. "She can't do this to us. She can't use other people as a threat. I'll make her stop."

"How?" Eden asked.

"I'll talk some sense into her." He stroked her back, wanting to reassure her. "Everything will be okay."

Eden nodded. Her brave face lessened his worries. What a horrifying ordeal this must have been for her. "We'll stop her," he said. "Go on home. I'll have Huang Shifu and one of my security guards take you back. Try not to worry. Keep yourself safe." He kissed her on the forehead. He dared not tell her how much it frightened him to think she might've been kidnapped and hurt too.

"Maybe I should come with you," she said.

"No. Let me handle Shen Yi. I'll go find her right now. We'll put an end to this. Everything will be okay." He hugged her one more time, more for himself than for her, to make sure she was indeed in his arms and safe.

8

JUSTICE

THE SLOT on the front gate of the Liu Kun's lane house slid open and the eyes of a houseboy peeked out from behind. "Who are you looking for?"

"I came to see Madam Liu," Clark answered, trying to keep his voice calm despite his fury at the woman he'd come to confront.

"What's your name?"

"Yuan Guo-Hui."

"Wait a moment."

The slot slid closed and the houseboy returned inside. A while later, the wooden gate creaked open and the houseboy stood to the side. "Please come in."

Without further formality, Clark marched through the garden and into the house. The houseboy invited him to take a seat in the living room. Clark waved his hand and refused. An amah brought out a tray of tea and fresh fruits. He ignored it as she bowed and retreated back into the hall.

What were all these theatricals? He didn't come here for a social call. He paced around the room. The golden Buddha statue on the shelf against the main wall grinned at him, as though mocking him.

"Guo-Hui?"

He raised his head in the direction of Shen Yi's voice. The sight took him aback. He almost couldn't recognize her face under the thick lipstick and heavy red rouge. He could see her body had filled out, and her black silk *qipao* with golden trim showed off the sensuality of her curves.

The curves of a siren, he thought.

Slowly, she walked in. Smoke trailed behind her from the cigarette in her hand. When did she pick up this bad habit?

Her eyes brightened when she saw him looking at her. "What a rare visitor! How is it you came to see me?"

"Shen Yi . . ." Clark said.

"Eh? Amah brought the tea and dim sum out already?" She walked over to the tray of tea on the end table. "Would you like a cup of tea? This is premium oolong."

Clark frowned. What was she doing? He had no time or interest in playing games.

"Oh, you probably prefer spirits instead." She left the tea and went over to a cabinet displaying shelves of whiskey, scotch, gin, brandy, and cognac. "How about a scotch? It's been so long since we've met up together, we ought to celebrate, right?" She picked out the bottle of Chivas Regal, poured it into two crystal glasses, and offered one to him.

"Shen Yi!" Clark took a step forward, restraining himself in hopes of starting with the right tone. "You know my purpose for coming here."

She arched her brow, then took a sip from the glass she'd offered to him.

"I know I wronged you," Clark said.

She crossed her arms and turned her face the other way.

"Whatever I did wrong, I apologize again. If you're still angry, then no one can blame you. But what good is it to take it out on other people? If you want to blame anyone, then blame me. Everything is my fault. As for the person you're holding, can you lift high your noble hand and let him go?"

"You want me to let him go?" she asked. "That's easy. You stop going with that fox sorceress, and I'll let him go at once."

Clark laughed in disbelief. "Shen Yi, you and I . . . it's all in the past. Even if I leave her, what good would that do you?"

Tilting her head, Shen Yi said, "I'm only asking for justice for myself."

Clark threw up his hands. "Shen Yi, whatever you want is fine. As long as it's within my abilities, I'll definitely do it to make amends. I only ask that your request be reasonable." He looked around the room, at the golden Buddha statue, the high-quality rosewood furniture, and the artful Chinese landscape paintings on the wall. "I see your position now is very enviable. Why are you still dwelling on the past?"

"Enviable?" she sneered. "Do you know how much humiliation you gave me when you broke off our engagement? The whole world was pointing at me, laughing at me. A woman who someone abandoned. I had to marry immediately just to save my name. Even then, I couldn't become a legitimate first wife." She laughed bitterly and downed a gulp of her scotch. "Marrying that old head, and having to pay a huge dowry too. Then I get to idle here every night while he goes out to find his flowers and willows, reveling in his spring dreams with his mistresses and sing-song girls. You say this is enviable?"

Clark lowered his head, not without shame and guilt. "I never wanted to cause you pain. Only feelings can't be forced. Even if I married you, neither of us would be happy. Neither of us would've had luck and blessings."

"Oh? So you left me out to bear the misery alone while you go on to seek happiness?"

"That's not what I mean."

"I didn't do anything wrong. Why should I be the one to suffer bitterness?"

"That . . ." Clark didn't know what to say. He tried apologizing again, "I'm very sorry."

"It's too unfair. Yuan Guo-Hui, you ruined my whole life." She finished the remainder of her scotch. "If I have to bear the misery, why shouldn't you? Let all three of us suffer together. You, me, and the fox sorceress."

Clark stared at her. That wasn't right. He was in an impossible situation too. "What about the man you kidnapped? This matter doesn't involve him. You captured him. You sliced off his ear. How is that fair?"

Shen Yi sneered. "How the world treats me, that's how I'll treat the world."

Clark fell back a step. Her coldness chilled him, trapping him like an ice wall. Madness. This woman, she'd gone mad. "Let that man go." He gritted his teeth. "He's innocent."

"I'll let him go when you break it off with your fox sorceress."

Fox sorceress. Enough. He'd had enough of her throwing this vile insult against the woman he loved. He'd given it a try to bring this matter to a harmonious end. Shen Yi didn't deserve the benefit of the doubt. She didn't deserve his sympathy. Not if she would intentionally harm someone else to get her way. "You're really going to force us?"

"Yes."

"You're going too far."

"I'm only seeking justice for myself."

"You can't do this." He glowered at her. "I won't let you threaten me. Whatever debt I owe you, this is wrong."

"Ha!" She laughed and took a drag of her cigarette. "Try and stop me. What do you plan to do? Report me to the Municipal Police? Tell your British and American friends on the Municipal Council to penalize me? Today, in these times, let's see if you're more powerful, or I'm more powerful."

Clark turned around and started toward the door. He couldn't talk to her anymore.

"Hey!" she called him back. "The person in my hand is Gao Zhen."

Gao Zhen? Clark swung around. The victim was Gao Zhen? The man who had given him the biggest sum of money in red envelopes every Chinese New Year when he was growing up? The man from whom Clark himself had extorted outrageous amounts of political contributions to the KMT? The man who had nevertheless forgiven him and consoled him with kind words and advice when his father passed away during the Japanese invasion?

He clenched his fist. He could hardly breathe. "You venomous woman."

"You made me this way!" She threw up her head. "I have three hundred and fifteen more people on my list. Many are your longtime family friends. Like I told your fox sorceress, for every week you two are together, one of them will get killed. When that happens, don't blame me. It'll be all your fault."

"You shameless woman." Clark turned around once again and stormed toward the door.

Behind him, Shen Yi called out, "Three days! You have three days to answer to what I said."

Clark slightly turned his head. Without answering her, he stormed out. If he stayed any longer, he would say even more that he could not take back.

———

As always, the Angel of Peace gazed out with her welcoming arms in front of the Whangpoo River, just as she had on the day Eden came looking for Clark after she ran away from her wedding. Since that day, Eden thought they had finally overcome all the obstacles that had stood in their way.

Clark had wanted her to go home, but she needed a moment to think through what was happening with a clear head.

On the water, a fleet of Japanese naval vessels flared their lights over the fishermen's boats docked for the night. Junks and sampans must all scatter now to make way for the new lord of the sea. A New Order now reigned in this city. The rules of the right of way no longer applied.

Under this New Order, a new breed of authority had risen. She had seen their ways up close. The cold stares of the bodyguards. The blood running down the kidnapping victim's face. His severed ear in the wooden box. The demand of Shen Yi, Clark's ex-fiancée, and her laughter.

That shrill, icy laugh.

Eden winced. That vengeful, heartless woman. She wanted to separate her and Clark. In this world where so much darkness had already spread, she wanted to take their little corner of happiness away.

How wrong! How unreasonable of her! Clark didn't love her. He never loved her. Why couldn't he be free to love whomever he wanted?

With these thoughts, she walked up to the balustrade. They couldn't give in to Shen Yi's demand. It was wrong!

But what about the Chinese man?

She closed her eyes. The image of his mutilated ear appeared, etched into her memory. Her mind wouldn't let her forget.

It'll be okay, she told herself and opened her eyes. Clark said he'd handle it. He'd rescue the poor man and put a stop to this madness.

But what if he can't . . .

The little voice of doubt nagged at her, sending shivers of fear through her veins.

He can't persuade her to change her mind . . .

The little voice grew louder. She held her breath.

Clark would handle it. She exhaled and rested her elbows on the balustrade. Hunching her shoulders, she tried to shut out the voice. He knew powerful people. He had connections all over the city. He would find a way.

But if he couldn't, what would she do? the voice asked her again. Would she let the victim die? What about the other patients? Would she let Shen Yi kill them all, just so she could be with Clark?

No. No. Of course she wouldn't.

Then what would she do? Given the stakes, what choice would she make?

"Miss, buy flowers?" A little pauper girl came up to her. Her soiled face broke into a smile, revealing the gaps in her teeth. "Buy flowers?"

Normally, Eden would refuse. An underground crime syndicate controlled the community of beggars in this town. She'd learned not to encourage their use of children to run these schemes. Today though, the child's smile tugged at her heart. Her little face reminded her of all the poor people in this country and those living under threat. Meanwhile, she, a foreign outsider, had found a safe haven here and had taken all the advantages this place had to offer.

Was it not enough? Could she add to the sufferings of the people who had given her a new life and a shelter by risking their deaths?

"Buy flowers?" The girl held up a bunch of wilting roses. The girl looked so small, no more than three or four

Eden softened her stance. Who knew who ruled the beggar community now? The Japanese had run Big Ear Du, the notorious Green Gang boss, out of town. Even the criminal underworld had a New Order now. Maybe the little girl was just a child orphaned by the September attack.

"No, thank you," Eden said. She took a piece of candy out of her purse and gave it to the girl. The girl seemed confused by the offer. But quickly, she grinned and grabbed the candy, then skipped away. The waves of pedestrians soon eclipsed all traces and shadows of her tiny footprints, but not the crowds of beggars squatting on the streets. Many of them, no doubt, had ended up here because Japan had destroyed their homes.

Her eyes landed on a homeless man in a torn shirt. He kept scratching his head. His thick, waxy hair looked like it hadn't been washed in months. Surely, he needed immediate treatment for lice.

How could her own misfortunes compare to these people's?

As if he sensed he was being watched, the man stopped scratching his head and turned his eyes in Eden's direction. Embarrassed, Eden looked away and turned around to face the river.

Her father didn't know his Chinese patients were under threat. One had already been harmed. What would he think if he found out they could be killed because of her? He would be swamped with regret. He would wish he had never treated any one of them. And he would stop treating anyone who was Chinese.

What if the power of Japan and their collaborators grew? Would they threaten even the non-Chinese?

Her family was stateless. If Shen Yi had it in her power to threaten her parents, or Joshua, would she?

Eden shuddered at the thought.

It won't happen. She pulled her arms close against herself. It won't come to that. Clark would do everything in his power to put this whole thing to rest.

She had to have faith. She had to believe that before they reached that point, a solution would come to light.

There has to be a way, Clark thought repeatedly on his way home. Shen Yi couldn't possibly get her way. Think! What was the solution? There had to be a solution.

He entered his home, only to discover the repercussions from this crisis continued to mount. In the living room, he found his mother and sisters with Madam Gao, the immediate victim's wife. Her two children, a seventeen-year-old girl and a fifteen-year-old boy, sat crying beside her.

"Ma!" Clark rushed toward them. He didn't have to ask why Madam Gao was here. He already knew.

"Guo-Hui!" His mother called out to him. "Hurry, hurry, come over here. Exactly what happened? Why did someone kidnap Uncle Gao? Why are these people saying Uncle Gao's life is in your hand?"

"Ma . . ." Clark bit his lip. He looked at Madam Gao's red, tear-soaked eyes. He didn't even know where to begin to explain.

"Guo-Hui." Madam Gao lurched forward from her seat onto her knees and grabbed his arm. "Save him. I beg you, you have to save him."

Clark got down on one knee. "Gao tai tai . . ."

"Old Gao's been missing for two days," Madam Gao cried. "Yesterday, when he didn't come home, I sent people all over to find him. When they couldn't find a trace of him, I knew he must've been kidnapped. I was ready to pay the ransom, no matter how much they asked. Then just now, before I came here, my houseboy found a wooden box left at our door. Inside . . . inside was Ah Zhen's ear!" She wailed and bowed over. Mei Mei hurried over to help her back up. Clark looked up at his terrified mother. Wen-Ying eyed him with her own alarmed and questioning gaze.

"There was a note pinned to the ear," Madam Yuan said to Clark while Gao's wife cried. "The people who kidnapped Uncle Gao said if you don't do as they say in three days, they'll kill Uncle Gao. What are you doing outside that would bring on such a huge crisis? What do these people want from you? Why are they using Uncle Gao's life to threaten you?"

"I didn't . . ." Clark vehemently shook his head.

"Guo-Hui." Madam Gao recovered her breath. She grabbed his

arm again. "I believe you. You've always been a good boy. Whatever is the case, you must help my husband. You have to save him. If not, I don't know what to do anymore." Her entire body slumped and she broke down again. Behind her on the sofa, her children cried even louder.

Anger fumed inside his chest. Shen Yi, that demonic girl. How could she? How could she wreak havoc on this innocent family?

"Gao tai tai." Wen-Ying came and helped Madam Gao to her feet. "We will all resolve this matter and rescue Uncle Gao at once." She gave Clark a quick glance. "Let my mother and Mei Mei take you and your children home. If you need, they can stay with you overnight. My brother and I will discuss this. We'll definitely think of a way to help. My brother will do whatever it takes to save Uncle Gao."

Taking her cue, Clark said, "Yes, Gao tai. Don't you worry. I won't let Uncle Gao suffer any more harm. You go home first. Get some rest. Everything else, leave it up to me to resolve."

Relief came to Madam Yuan's face, like she'd found her star of salvation. "Then, Guo-Hui, I'll rely on you for everything."

Her words hung heavily in his heart. He'd made her a promise, but could he deliver?

"Mei Mei," Wen-Ying said to her little sister. "Take Gao tai tai and the children home with Ma. Take good care of them tonight."

"I understand." Mei Mei went to the crying children and tried to comfort them with a smile. "Come on, let us bring you home."

Madam Yuan, too, got up to do her part. "Don't worry anymore," she said to Madam Gao, her tone laced with righteous indignation. "Guo-Hui will take care of everything. He won't let those kidnappers get away with this, right, Guo-Hui?"

"No, I definitely won't," Clark answered. Somehow, he could not look her in the eye. He waited for her and Mei Mei to coax Madam Gao and the children out. When they'd all left, he sat down, took a deep breath, and closed his eyes.

"What happened?" Wen-Ying asked, now that they were alone in the room.

He tried to speak, then propped his forehead onto his hands.

Wen-Ying came closer. "Is this related to something you're doing for Dai Li?"

"No."

"Are you in a dispute with the Japanese?"

"No."

"Then . . . does it have to do with our company?"

"Not that."

"What is the matter then? Tell me!" She stood in front of him and forced him to face her.

Clark looked away to the side. Could he tell her? Wen-Ying had never warmed up to Eden, especially not since she found out he had feelings for her. If she knew the truth about why Gao Zhen had been kidnapped, what would she think?

She would probably tell him to leave Eden to save Gao.

He stood up and moved away from her.

"Ge." Wen-Ying followed him. "Uncle Gao is a lifelong friend of our family. We can't ignore this matter. Whatever difficulties you're up against, maybe I can help. Tian Di Hui will help you if you need."

The Heaven and Earth Society? Clark raised his head. Could he enlist their help? If Tian Di Hui intervened, they might be able to rescue Gao Zhen.

And Wen-Ying might lend a hand, even if she wasn't inclined to do this for Eden. Shen Yi kidnapped Gao Zhen. She sliced off the man's ear. His righteous sister wouldn't let that go unpunished.

Watching him, Wen-Ying nodded. "You know Tian Di Hui swore it would never coexist with the Japanese army and those who support them. If the Japanese army or the collaborators are behind this, you just say the word. We're not a paper tiger like the police force run by foreigners. Tian Di Hui will bring justice for Heaven whereas the Western cowards would only run."

Bring justice for Heaven. Clark felt his blood stirring.

"On July 7th, Tian Di Hui will launch a series of attacks," she told him.

"July 7th? The anniversary of the Marco Polo Bridge incident?"

"Yes. It'll be a message to all our enemies and traitors. We're not afraid. We're not gone. If we can deliver justice, then no matter how great a loss we take, we Tian Di Hui members will never regret it."

Regardless of how great a loss . . .

Clark let the thought linger in his head. No. It wouldn't be a good idea. Certainly, Tian Di Hui was capable of a rescue attempt, but they would be risking their lives. Would he ask these brave men who'd sworn to fight for their country to risk themselves for his own benefit, when he could end this by giving up a woman?

But Shen Yi was a collaborator. She was using her power to inflict harm on an innocent man. That would justify him seeking help from Tian Di Hui, wouldn't it?

Clark put his hands to his waist. The incident was personal, but Tian Di Hui could use this as an excuse to strike back at another collaborator. Warring groups had always used personal conflicts as an excuse to wage attacks.

No. He shook his head. He was trying to justify himself. He wanted their help, but it was for his own reasons, not a greater cause.

And even if they were able to rescue Gao Zhen and escape unscathed, what then? Shen Yi had three hundred fifteen more victims she could kidnap and kill. The problem would never end.

They would have to kill Shen Yi. It'd be the only way to ensure no one else would get hurt, and for him and Eden to go on and live the life they deserved.

But how could he? Yes, Shen Yi was despicable. But if he

intentionally took another person's life to ensure his own happiness, then he would be no less an evil monster than her.

More than anger, he felt shame. Whether he was in the right or wrong, breaking their engagement did cause her to suffer. And now, he would have her killed too? How could he ever bear this guilt?

There had to be another way.

Wen-Ying went to the shelf where the portrait of their father was on display. "Ever since the Japanese took control, all the treacherous thieves have been acting with no bounds on law or morals. If Japan never invaded our country, we wouldn't have this wave of kidnappings. Ba wouldn't have died, and no one would've taken a good man like Uncle Gao. All these catastrophes are the fault of the Japanese. They're demons."

The Japanese? Clark dropped his arms. An idea struck his head. There might be another solution after all.

"No," he said to his sister. "This matter isn't about the Japanese or the resistance. This whole situation came up because of me. I don't want anyone from Tian Di Hui taking any unnecessary risks for me. As for Uncle Gao, he's an innocent bystander too, but I might have a way to save him. Tomorrow, there's a person I will go see. If he agrees to help me, then everything will be resolved."

Wen-Ying stared at him, her eyes asking whether he was sure, but she didn't press him further. "In that case, you keep in mind what's best. No matter what, you have to bring back Uncle Gao."

"I know." He stood up. "I will."

He had one more card yet to play.

9

DAS RHEINGOLD

THE SERVANT HAD BARELY SET down the drinks, but Kenji Konoe couldn't wait to show Clark his latest obsession. "I'm so glad you've come today." He laid the album on the turntable. "I've been listening to this all week. You don't know how frustrating it is to listen to something so extraordinary, only to have no one around me who can understand and appreciate this masterpiece."

Politely, Clark smiled. He hadn't come here to discuss music, and the urgency of the reason why he'd come was burning him inside. But Konoe was his last hope, and he needed the Japanese nobleman's help.

Konoe set the needle on the album. "You do like opera, don't you?"

"Sometimes," Clark said.

"This is Wagner. *The Ring of Nibelung*." He handed Clark the album cover and cranked the handle of the gramophone. All at once, the vibrato of "The Ride of the Valkyries" soaked the room, followed by the brisk, frantic zings cutting back and forth from the violins until the powerful blare of trumpets rose and surged above the multilayers of sounds from the flutes, bassoons, oboes, and French horns.

Clark had heard this piece many times. Still, the cycles of rhythms and rises always roused his own emotions and swept him along.

Across the room, Konoe's face brimmed with excitement. His eyes shone brighter with each wave of melody that exhibited a perfect fusion of instruments. The music was carrying him to a whole other plane.

The orchestral score soared to its dramatic end and Konoe swirled his hand with the closing notes. "That was magnificent, wasn't it?"

"Yes." Clark didn't disagree.

"My country's been in talks with Germany. This will help me gain a better understanding of their psyche."

"Oh?" Clark crossed his legs, forcing himself not to roll his eyes. "Shall I assume you've read *Mein Kampf* too?" he asked, barely able to hide his sarcasm and contempt.

"As a matter of fact, I have," Konoe said.

"You have?" Clark peered at his friend, his curiosity now piqued. "And what do you think?"

"What do I think?" Konoe gave it a mere second's thought, then shrugged. "Nothing more than the ramblings of an idiot."

"Why's that?"

"He contradicts himself. He rambles on and on about the supremacy of the Aryan race, but then he goes on at length about the threat of the Jews, and the conspiracy of the Jews. See, if the Germanic race is so superior, then how can any other race threaten them? His entire thought process is devoid of logic. I'm never impressed by anyone whose mind is devoid of logic." He picked up the bottle of Yamazaki his servant had brought earlier. "Would you like a drink?"

"Sure," Clark said, not interested in the least either way. "So you don't subscribe to the theory of racial superiority?" Did the

Kizoku prince not realize this would contradict his own people's view of who they were?

"Well . . ." Konoe opened the whiskey. "There's no question some races do come out ahead." He poured them each a glass. "It's science. Darwinism. Survival of the fittest. The races most able to adapt and evolve will dominate. But I vehemently disagree with his analysis that the Japanese are inferior to the Aryans. That alone tells me his entire manifesto is garbage. Besides, I still can't understand how Jews and Aryans are different. Aren't they both white? Regardless, if you follow his theory that the Jewish people will ultimately bring about the destruction of Germany and control the world, then one can only come to the scientific, logical conclusion that it is actually the Jewish people who are superior."

Clark raised his glass, a gesture of endorsement to Konoe's own wild thoughts. He had to admit, Konoe had a way of seeing things unlike anyone else.

"Anyway, Germany being led by someone with such a sophomoric level of intelligence as Hitler can only bode well for my country. I'm not boasting when I say this, but, if you look at the facts, the evidence actually points to the Japanese as the winners of the contest of natural selection."

"Oh yeah?" Clark lowered his drink from his lips.

"Look at how far Japan has come in the last seventy years. Our restoration starting with the Meiji reforms brought us into the modern world in ways no other Asian country has achieved. China wasn't the only country forced to open to the West. Japan was powerless too when Commodore Perry came and subjected us to their unequal treaties. But while China lags in its old ways, we in Japan learned from the British how to build our fleet of naval warships. We learned from the Germans and threw away our swords for their guns. We learned from the Americans and industrialized our economy, built our banks, rails, communications, companies. We turned our enemies into allies, realigned the geopolitical imbalances, and ended all the unequal treaties imposed upon us. I'm sorry to say this. China's big, but your people have done none of these things in the same period of time."

Clark kept his calm. What Konoe said was true, but it wasn't entirely fair. "China is much bigger than Japan. Its population's much larger. It's not as easy to enact policies and implement new systems."

"Perhaps." Konoe shrugged. "But I'd say the truth is our people are better at uniting with a single mind to further our own progress. China had its revolution after the Qing Dynasty fell. We had our civil war with the Shoguns. And now, decades afterwards, your country is still fighting a civil war. Meanwhile, we successfully reformed our government, our schools, our social fabric and hierarchy." He returned to the liquor cabinet. "Again, please don't misunderstand me. I'm not saying these things to belittle you or your people, but Japan has proven itself to be the most capable of getting ahead. All the other countries in Asia are at least a hundred years behind us. And that is why Japan is the obvious leader to create a greater, more prosperous Asia."

Clark didn't agree, but he didn't care to debate. The more pressing matter was, how should he bring up the matter of Shen Yi?

Still wrapped up in his own grand theories, Konoe took no note of Clark's silence. He refilled their glasses. "I think, for any race, even a superior race, there are inferior people. Most people are ordinary. Average. Even the ones who are powerful are often unremarkable. They chase after the mundane. Look around at our world now. Everything is just like the chaos in *Das Rheingold*. Gods, demigods, giants, dwarfs. Everyone's motivated by lust and greed. They go to war chasing a cursed ring. Such is this world. This planet. So what difference does it make whether a race of people are gods or dwarfs? It's a shame. To me, what's more important is transcendence. To be one of the selected few who can attain a higher level of existence."

"You told me this before," Clark said. "The first time I came to your home."

"You remember!" Konoe pointed at him. "Yes. To me, supremacy of the individual is a worthier pursuit. Like Siegfried in *The Ring*. He's someone not swayed by earthly desires. He could forge a sword no one else can. He knows no fear, and he wants to explore the greater world. Supreme individuals like this exist in every race. Richard Wagner is such a person. So is Albert Einstein. They're men who exceeded their mortal selves in the pure pursuit of something genius and they became extraordinary. My friend, this is the kind of supremacy you and I should pursue."

Sounds grand, Clark thought, except he had something more urgent to pursue right now than fantastical goals. "Kenji," he gazed down and frowned, "You called me your friend. I came to ask you for your help."

Konoe sat down. "What kind of help?"

"I had a fiancée. Our parents arranged our marriage before we were born. Marrying her wasn't something I wanted to do, so I broke off our engagement."

"You're talking about a woman named Shen Yi?"

Surprised, Clark asked, "You know her?"

"If you'll forgive me. When we first met, I had looked into your background. I was delighted to meet a friend like you, but I had to make sure you were someone I could trust."

"All right." Clark casually raised his brow. He had suspected as much.

"She's now the wife of Liu Kun, the man who gave you some trouble a while back. If you recall, I got him out of your way when you needed to retrieve your equipment from your old factory, and I did it even without you asking."

"You did," Clark admitted. "And I still appreciate it," he said, without mentioning the fact that Konoe had done this to try to recruit him to become a collaborator.

"Tell me about this woman Shen Yi. How can I help you?"

"She's not happy I'm involved with someone. Someone she mistakenly blames for our broken engagement. She kidnapped a man and threatens to kill him unless I stop seeing the woman I'm with. She has a list of three hundred and sixteen people she's threatening to kill if I don't comply. I need to stop her. I can't let her harm anyone because of me. I'm asking you to make her stop."

Konoe's voice turned serious. "Is anyone on her list Japanese?"

"No. They're Chinese."

"Well, then." Konoe reclined back. "It seems to me there's an easier solution. Just stop seeing the other woman."

Clark twitched his hand. "That's not an option."

"No? Help me understand. This business with Shen Yi, it isn't a business or political conflict, but a personal dispute?"

"Yes."

Konoe sighed, then shook his head. "I'm afraid I can't help you."

"Why not?"

"Last time I lent you a hand, at least I had the excuse of salvaging commerce in the city. This matter though? You know Liu Kun and his wife are allies of Imperial Japan. If I turn around and help you to undermine them, how will it look to them? How will it look to everyone in China who is giving Japan their support? What reason would there be then for them to continue to put their faith and trust in us?"

Clark tensed. He squeezed the armrest of his chair. "I thought you valued our friendship."

"I do," Konoe said with all sincerity. "That's why I think there is a way to get around this problem."

"How?"

"Join me." Konoe held out his hand. "Pledge your allegiance to Imperial Japan. My country will lift yours out of its backward past. We'll stimulate and industrialize your economy. We'll reform education, and teach your children good moral values and science." His face glowed with excitement. "Better yet, you and I can work together to engineer a plan to create a Greater Co-Prosperity Sphere of Asia. It'll be more glorious than anything the world has ever seen. We'll dominate the world. You're leagues above imbeciles like Liu Kun and his wife. If you join me, I'll be able to help you any way you want."

"No," Clark said without hesitation. "I can't."

Konoe's excitement broke. He gazed at Clark with sympathy. "That's a shame. In that case, I simply cannot intervene in a private dispute between Chinese."

Clark gripped the armrest. "Kenji, I saved your life once."

"I remember." Konoe flashed him a firm stare. A flicker of real emotion slipped past his face.

"And you can't do me a simple favor in return?" Clark sat up.

"It is precisely because I owed you my life that I won't repay you with something so immaterial. If I do return a favor, it ought to be something of much greater importance, not dealing with a woman acting in an irrational fit of jealousy." He wrinkled his face in disgust. "Women. Everything they do is driven by nonsense. They're obsessed with everything trivial, and always carry loads of histrionics. If you want my advice, you shouldn't even deign to respond to a low-level creature like her. You should extricate yourself from this nuisance at once."

"I would if I could." Clark seethed. Konoe didn't understand at all. What he felt for Eden wasn't immaterial. And trivial or not, he shouldn't have to extricate himself from anything just so Shen Yi could get her way.

Konoe sipped his drink. His eyes twinkled with wonder and amusement. "You love the other woman?"

Clark didn't answer. He remained stiff in his seat.

Konoe put down his glass. "I'm so sorry, my friend." He gave Clark a cautionary glance and picked up the album cover on the coffee table. "In the *Ring of Nibelung*, the hero, Siegfried, knew no fear. He was born invincible, until he fell in love. It always confounded me how Westerners heap praises on this curious concept called love. They write poems and stories, and make movies about it. They say love makes one strong, but in truth, it just makes you vulnerable and gets in the way."

"Or maybe it's something you're too cold-blooded to understand," Clark said. It was the truth.

Konoe didn't take offense. "Let's not have any hard feelings between us. Especially not over something like this." He smiled, then turned serious again. "I haven't forgotten. I owe you my life, and I regard you as a kindred spirit. If you're really in need, as long as it's not something against my country's interest, I will help. Right now, you don't actually have a problem. You're being hassled by a silly housewife. While you might not see it this way, I'm going to save you from going down the wrong path. By not helping, I'm steering you away from this worthless feeling called love. It's only a distraction from greatness. You'll be a better man without it."

Clark stood up. What did Konoe know about love? This whole visit was a waste. "Thank you for not helping."

Konoe put the album cover back down. Without saying goodbye, Clark left. He made his way to the door and walked out. In the garden, the guard bowed and opened the gate.

On the street, Clark stood. What should he do now?

He had only one option left. To save Gao Zhen and to stop her from ruining their lives, he would have to take out Shen Yi herself. If she were gone, she would no longer be a threat to anyone.

Tian Di Hui would help him. They would take out a collaborator.

Could he live with marking Shen Yi to be killed?

He took a step forward.

He and Eden shouldn't have to separate. Shen Yi had no right to make that demand.

That didn't mean Shen Yi should die, did it?

The answer made him shudder. He swallowed to try to absorb the thought.

He wasn't at fault. She brought this upon herself.

Did she? Or was he the one who planted the seed of their feud? This was a woman he had already hurt.

She was a Japanese collaborator! That dark-hearted woman. She tortured Gao Zhen, an innocent man. She could stop all this now. She wouldn't. She deserved what was coming to her.

So many better people had already died. Xu Hong-Lie. Peng Amah and her family. The soldiers who fearlessly defended Shanghai during the Japanese attack. The thousands upon thousands down the coast who were killed in the war.

Who was Shen Yi? A traitor to her own country. An oppressor to her own people. Heroes and innocents had died when they didn't deserve it.

What was one more?

10

EDGE OF EVIL

THE SOLEMN LOOK on Clark's face was not what Eden had hoped to see when he asked her to come to his home tonight.

In his study, he stood without saying a word. She put down her purse and waited for him to speak.

He stared at the floor, his head bowed and his hands hidden in his pockets.

She came closer. In the last two days while he went about trying to find a solution, she had been thinking it through, and she had made up her mind what to say if they had to make a choice.

A burning pain spread through her heart. She realized now, for certain. She loved him. More than anything. No word could describe the pain she was feeling at the thought of breaking up with him.

But their love would come at the price of three hundred and sixteen lives.

She didn't want to let him go, but they had to do the right thing.

Finally, she spoke first. "Well?" She tried to smile but her lips quivered. "Were you able to change her mind?"

"No. She won't listen to reason."

"I understand what you're telling me," she said, trying to cover the pain in her own voice. Let her be the one to say what neither of them wanted to say and ease his pain. "We . . ." She started to recite the words she'd been rehearsing for the last two days, but a sour lump sat in her throat like a rock. Her heart was pulling the words back from her mouth. The speech she'd planned fell by the wayside and all she could do was ask, "Is this the end of us?"

"No!" He turned to face her and grabbed her arms. "It is not."

"It's not?" She gazed back at him. An unfamiliar coldness gleamed behind his eyes. It took her aback. Its trace was barely visible, but its harshness still cut through.

He held on to her, no longer avoiding looking at her. "My sister, Wen-Ying, belongs to a resistance group. It's a secret."

"Wen-Ying? You mean Estella?"

"Yes." Clark nodded. "Do you remember the Japanese commander who was shot on his way to visit the Japanese Consulate a few months ago? You must've heard about it. It was in the news. Her group was behind it. And the car bomb that killed the assistant to Su Xi-Wen, the head of the Ta Tao administration?"

"Ta Tao. That's the new local Chinese administration the Japanese set up to run the Chinese sectors of Shanghai."

"Yes. Her group was behind that too."

"Okay." Eden drew back from him. His tone of voice had turned detached. His expression changed from anguish to one devoid of emotions.

"The man Shen Yi kidnapped and maimed, he's not only your father's patient. He's a longtime friend of my family. He watched me grow up."

"Oh no! I didn't know."

"A person like Shen Yi needs to be eliminated. She poses a

threat to more than three hundred people. On top of that, she's a collaborator. A traitor. Wen-Ying's group can get rid of her."

"What are you saying? . . . You want to kill her?"

Her question made him pause. She could see his conscience wrestling with the cold gleam behind his eyes.

What was happening to him?

"You want to kill her?" Eden asked again. A new fear sprung up in her chest. This wasn't Clark. This wasn't the man she loved. Holding her breath, she waited. She feared he would answer yes.

"There's no other way," he cried. Raw agony choked his voice. His hands still held on to her arms and she knew he would never want to let her go.

She raised her hand and touched his face. To her question, he didn't say yes. He couldn't bring himself to say yes to murdering someone for their own happiness.

And she would never want him to become someone who could. The world had too many monsters already. All around, evil roamed, consuming whatever it could in its path. Now it wanted to snatch Clark into its palm too.

She wouldn't let it.

"You would kill her for me?" She let her fingers linger on his cheek.

He met her gaze and whispered, "I would do anything for you."

The firmness in his answer left her no doubt.

She knew then what she had to do. She could not let his love for her ruin the man that he was. She could not let their love turn into a constant reminder of how ugly they, too, could become.

"Clark," she said. The pain inside was killing her. "If you would do anything for me, then do this. Tomorrow, go to Shen Yi. Tell her you and I will not see each other anymore."

"What?" He gripped her arms. "Eden! We can't let her force us. I can—"

"No." She touched his lips. "If you kill her, you'll regret it. You won't be able to live with what you've done. And we'll never be able to love each other in peace without knowing we would take another person's life for our own sake."

"Eden . . ."

This time, it was she who couldn't look at him. Her eyes might reveal how much she wanted to remain with him.

"Eden," Clark pleaded again, "I don't want to lose you." His words made her heart ache so much more.

"I know," she willed herself to go on. "But this is what I want, and you will do this for me. You said you'll do anything for me. Will you promise to do this for me?"

"I . . ." He looked at her with a crestfallen face.

Holding back her tears, she held firm until he finally answered, "Yes."

She forced out a smile. The coldness in his eyes vanished, even though he looked like he had lost all hope. Gently, she stroked his face. "Clark, you're the most honorable, upright man I've ever known. I'm so glad we've met. I'm so lucky you love me. I'll always cherish what we have together, even if it couldn't last. I'm not asking you to do this because I don't love you. I love you. I really, really love you." She closed her arms around him and softly kissed him one last time.

The sweet sadness wasn't enough. He wrapped his arms around her and planted his own kiss on her lips. In his kiss, a sea of passion engulfed her. Years of yearning which they'd kept in restraint unleashed. She embraced him back, wanting to feel forever the warmth of his embrace, wanting more than anything to never let him go. If only fate would show them mercy. If only life would give them a chance.

He ran his lips across her cheek to her ear. "You know what I wish for?" he whispered. "I wish I could leave all this behind. Everything here's broken. Every day, I run around, trying to patch things up. I can barely keep myself an inch ahead before the seams fall apart." He hung on to her. "I wish I could run away with you. I wish I could take you somewhere far, far away, where it's only you and me. Why can't we have that?"

"I don't know." She rested her head on his shoulder, letting the warmth of his breath caress her skin while her tears soaked his shirt. "I wish we could do that too. Maybe you're meant for something else. Something greater." She drew back slightly and looked up. "You'll have to go on. You can't let this break you. The world is at war. A lot of people who are wicked will try to make things worse. They'll hurt us, and it'll be tempting to fight evil with evil. But your family needs you. Your workers need you, and your country needs you. For them, you have to stay on the side of what is good. Otherwise, if even someone like you would lose his sense of what is right and wrong, there'll be no hope left for anyone."

Clark hung his head. Seeing him this way, her heart shattered, but he remained the man with whom she had fallen in love.

"Remember," she said and kissed his lips again, "I want you to stay good. People like Shen Yi inflict pain. They would hurt, even kill others to get their way. I don't want you to be like that. Never. I want the man I love to always be on the side of what is right. I want him to always act with compassion and mercy. Would you remember that?"

His scowl deepened. Through a strained voice, he said, "Yes."

Against every wish in her body, she pulled back from him. It was time to cut off the lingering threads between them. The longer she stayed, the harder it would be for her to keep her resolve. "Goodbye, Clark."

"Eden . . ." he called out to her once more.

"Goodbye." She picked up her purse and left. She couldn't believe she had to say this word.

She wiped away her tears. In the mad hell which this world

had become, even love could turn into a force to drive someone to evil.

But she couldn't let love drive Clark to evil. Their love had to be a force for something better.

Perhaps in time, he would understand she had asked him to give her up only because she loved him too much.

11

ENMITY'S DUE

"YOU REALLY WILL LEAVE HER?" Shen Yi asked, eyeing Clark skeptically while holding the long cigarette holder between her fingers.

On the sofa in her living room, Clark said again, "Yes."

The stunned look on Shen Yi's face slowly changed to a sneer and she laughed. "Finally, you can see I'm not someone who would come when you wave a hand, and go when you wave me away. Today, it is I who decide your fate."

Clark kept his eyes on the floor. No. She didn't decide his fate. But he didn't bother telling her the only reason he had come to concede was because he promised Eden that he would.

This stupid woman. If it weren't for Eden, she'd be dead.

"Very good." She put her free hand on her hip. "Now you, too, can get a taste of the feeling of lost love."

Lost love. What did she know about lost love? What he and she had wasn't love. He bit back his tongue. "So now you can release Gao Zhen."

"Not so fast," Shen Yi said. She sauntered closer and took a deep drag of her cigarette. "You said you'll leave her. How do I know you're not lying? How do I know it's not a ploy to fool me?"

Clark clutched his knees. He forced himself to contain his anger. "When I, Yuan Guo-Hui, make a promise, I don't back out."

Hearing his strong words, she hesitated, then crossed her arms. "All right. For now, let's say you're speaking the truth. I'll release Gao Zhen tonight. However, this matter isn't over yet. Not until I see proof you and that fox sorceress are really separated."

"Proof?" Clark glared at her. "What kind of proof do you want? We already agreed to your demand. You can't hang this matter over us forever."

"What are you getting so angry at me for?" Shen Yi shot back. "I've said before, I'm only seeking justice for myself. If you hadn't broken our engagement, we wouldn't be here today, and I would've rightly become Madam Yuan. I would've been good to you, and been a good wife. It was you who denied me everything that was mine. It was that whore who stole your soul, altered my destiny, and ruined my fortune. Because you changed your heart, I'll only be the wife of an old head for the rest of my life. What right do you have to be angry at me?"

No! Clark wanted to argue. Shen Yi was wrong. He wasn't the one to blame. It wasn't his choice they were engaged.

Instead, he fell a bit back. It wasn't her choice either. What choice did she have? Hard as it was for him to admit, she had fulfilled every obligation the world expected of her, up until he broke off their engagement.

In his mind, he heard Eden's voice. *Act with compassion and mercy.*

He wouldn't defy what Eden asked of him.

I want the man I love to always be on the side of what is good.

He stared at Shen Yi. She looked like a lone, wounded animal, baring her teeth and lashing out blindly at whatever she felt was causing her harm. If he wasn't the one to blame, then who was? Their parents? Society? The world? The gods in Heaven? What cosmic forces caused his fate and Shen Yi's to cross, and the threads of their love and hate to be all tangled up without an end?

Shen Yi glowered back at him. Resentment stewed in her eyes. Would she have become the hate-filled, terrifying woman she was today if he had never ended their engagement?

But how could he have married her? If he had, it would've been his life that was ruined.

It was an impossible situation. He had few choices. She had even fewer. Maybe none.

"You're right." He clasped his hands. "I shouldn't be angry at you."

His conciliatory tone surprised her and the look of vengeance on her face changed to one of confusion.

"This matter has to end somehow," he said. "If you continue this, you won't be any happier. You want us to share your pain, you got your wish. What can I do to convince you we're giving you what you want?"

Shen Yi flitted her eyes from one side to the other. Clearly, she was expecting a prolonged tug-of-war. She was gearing up for a protracted fight, not their surrender. "What I want . . ."

Clark sat quietly and waited. This vicious woman with a simple mind. She didn't know what she wanted. At least not about anything beyond making him and Eden suffer with her. And now, she didn't know what to say so she could come down the stage without embarrassing herself for having no answer.

She flicked the ashes of her cigarette into an ashtray, then lifted her chin. With a victorious smile, she said, "I want to see with my own eyes definitive proof you two are not getting back together. When your fox sorceress marries someone else, then I'll know your heart will have to die."

His heart will have to die? he thought with a bitter smile. His heart was already dead.

He unclasped his hands and turned up his palms. "How can you make this demand? I can't control when or whether Eden will get married. Are you going to keep three hundred and sixteen people's lives indefinitely under threat?"

Shen Yi twisted her lips. "I don't care. You all want to fool me. Until she marries another man, I won't consider this matter over." She blew out a whiff a smoke.

Clark dropped his stare. Shen Yi was beyond reason now. She only knew she wanted him and Eden to feel hurt like herself and to be deprived like she felt she was.

An unthinkable idea came to him. Its mere thought made him balk. He gazed back up at Shen Yi. His mind slowly came around.

If she wanted this much for him to feel her pain, then let her have it. Eden had already left him. Nothing else could hurt him more than the hurt he already felt. Calmly, he asked, "What if I get married?"

Shen Yi jerked her head. "What?"

"I can't make Eden marry another man just to please you. But if I'm married, wouldn't the result be the same? She will give up on me. Would it be enough for you if I get married?"

"That . . ." Shen Yi said, her mouth falling open.

"Or do you expect me to never get married? Will you threaten to kill people every time I attach myself to another woman?"

Shen Yi scowled and turned her back toward him.

Clark stood up. "How about this? I know you suffered because you had to marry someone you don't love. Let me keep you company in the same predicament. I'll go find someone I don't love and marry her. Whether she's poor, or old, or ugly, I don't care. All the errors, all the consequences of bitter pain, we'll bear the same together. Would that be enough for you to put an end to this matter?"

"You'll do that?" Shen Yi turned back around, smiling as

though amused. "You're not lying? You'll pick a random woman and marry her?"

"If you vow you'll never harm anyone anymore on my account, yes."

Shen Yi laughed. A shrill laugh that screamed the helpless state of the turn of their fates.

When her laughter died down, she wiped a tear from her eye with her finger. "If you had known how things would turn out today, then why bother ending us to begin with? In the end, you're still not with the woman you want." She laughed again, a bitter laugh with no satisfaction or joy.

He watched her laugh, venting her pent-up grievances through a cry wrapped up in a laugh. No, he still didn't regret not marrying her. But yes, life had played a cruel joke on them both.

"Very well." Shen Yi collected herself. "I can't have you, she can't have you. Very well, Yuan Guo-Hui. I married an old head I don't love. If you marry a woman you don't love too, then I'll deem our debts to each other cleared by one deed."

"Fine. I'll make it happen immediately," Clark said. "But I warn you. Don't think I'm afraid of you, or I don't have any other way to make you stop. This time, consider it a payback. If you don't hold up your end of the bargain, I won't be so courteous next time." He looked firmly at her to let her know he was serious. The smugness on her face ebbed. She stared back at him with uncertain eyes.

Without saying more, he started toward the door.

Behind him, Shen Yi yelled, "Then I'll wait for your wedding invitation. You appreciate free love so much, I'll take a good long view and watch how you'll cope with being denied free love too for the rest of your life."

Clark halted his steps. "Shen Yi." He turned his head slightly around. "If your heart is so dark, you'll never have happiness and peace."

Shen Yi winced. Defiantly, she held up her head. "We'll see about that as we go."

TWO BIRDS, ONE STONE

IN THE CAR, Huang Shifu asked, "Where to now, Young Master?"

"Two thirty-five Edinburgh Road," Clark said and looked out the window. He felt drained. His soul had left him. Without Eden, his life had no color anymore.

For himself, nothing mattered anymore. Whatever happened to him from now on, he really didn't care.

But he was still a man, and a man had responsibilities. If Shen Yi had to insist on her outrageous demand, and Eden chose to leave him, then all that was left for him was to forget his own life and do what he could for everyone else who depended on him.

Maybe this was what his life was meant for. Forget his own happiness. Give his life to ensure the well-being of those for whom he was responsible. Do everything in his power to win back the country so traitors like Shen Yi wouldn't be able to continue to do whatever they wanted without regard for morality or the law.

He touched the car window and traced an invisible circle on the pane with his finger.

The ring of wu. The circle of emptiness.

The sphere of no self.

The building at 235 Edinburgh Road was just an ordinary residential apartment where hard-working Chinese lived together in close quarters. It was the type of housing where the dwellers would often get into one another's way as well as one another's business.

But what it lacked in luxury and privacy, it made up for in community. When the lift operator opened the door to let Clark and an amah out on the fifteenth floor, Clark could hear the sound of the popular actress Zhou Xuan singing on the radio from the unit on the right. Farther down in another apartment, the clacks of mahjong tiles commingled with voices of the people playing the game inside. Across the corridor, an elderly man came out of his home, swinging a birdcage in his hand.

The amah who had gotten off the lift on the same floor greeted the man. "Uncle Wang, going for an early evening walk?"

"Yes," the elderly man returned her greeting. As he passed them, he smiled and nodded at Clark too, his flip-flops dueling with his canary's whistles and tweets.

Clark stopped and watched him walk down the hall. The life in this building gave him a jolt.

Since leaving Shen Yi's house, he thought his soul was dead. But seeing these ordinary people, a trickle of strength returned. The lives of people like the ones here were all that was left of Shanghai's way of life. Was this not the world he'd been fighting to keep alive? If even this small community collapsed, there would be nothing left.

No matter the pain, he could not wallow in his own heartbreak. Turning his grief and anger into power was the only way to fight back for what he'd lost. He still had much work to do.

The first thing he needed to do was to make things right for those whom his dear friend Xu Hong-Lie had left behind. He owed it to him.

At the end of the corridor, Clark pressed the button and rang the doorbell. The shuffle of footsteps came toward him. Sun Xiu-Qing opened the door. "Young Master Yuan? What are you doing here?"

"Miss Sun." Clark took off his hat.

From within the apartment, someone called out, "Who is it?"

Xiu-Qing turned around and answered, "A friend from work." She looked back at Clark.

"Can you come out for a moment?" Clark asked. "I have something I need to discuss with you."

"I . . . " She gazed back inside, then nodded. "Please wait a moment." She closed the door. A few minutes later, she came out. She'd put on her shoes and taken her purse.

Clark stepped aside to give her room. "Sorry to bother you."

"No problem," Xiu-Qing said and followed him to the elevator.

Outside, Clark strolled with her along the tree-lined sidewalk. After two blocks, he asked her, "How've you been?"

"Scared," she said. "I know you want to help me. I'm very grateful. But I already accepted my fate. This world has no place for an unmarried woman with an illegitimate child. I won't be able to support myself and my kid. Even if I'm willing to face the shame and do hard labor to bring the child up, nobody will hire me. That day, you should've let me die. Now, I'm just afraid I won't be able to find the courage again to do what I have to do."

"Miss Sun," Clark stopped. "You don't have to walk the path of death." He took one step closer to her. "You can marry me."

Xiu-Qing drew back. She widened her eyes. "What?"

"No, not marry me for real," he quickly explained. "I have no inappropriate intentions toward you. It's the truth. We will only bear the name of husband and wife, not the substance. But if you would agree to go through the formalities of marrying me, then nobody would ever know. This secret will be between the two of us, and I can take care of you and your child."

"Young Master Yuan." Xiu-Qing dropped her mouth. "How . . . I cannot possibly ask you to do that."

"You don't have to ask me. I'm offering."

In shock, Xiu-Qing raised her hand to her heart.

"Of course," Clark said, "you and your child will have to accept some grievances. You'll be bound to me for life as a wife of the Yuan family, or at least until your child grows up. Maybe you're not willing to do that. Also, your child will have to take my surname instead of his father's. I regret that. However, he will have a secure, comfortable life. You will too. You can focus on raising him. You won't have to worry about anything else."

Xiu-Qing's lips quivered. Tears welled up in her eyes. "What about you? Wouldn't you want a wife of your own? And your own children?"

Clark slumped with a bitter smile. A searing pain shot through his heart. Who would understand?

He gazed out at the road. "Right now, the country's in a huge chaos. Hong-Lie already told you about the kinds of activities he and I were involved in. I have a lot of things I still need to do. I have no time to attend to my own personal matters. I don't have the heart to either."

"What about in the future?" she asked.

The future? When he looked to the future, all he could see was an endless passage shrouded in gray.

"Things in the future, we'll deal with them in the future," he said. "Don't worry so much. The most important thing now is for us to figure out the best situation for your child. You just need to trust me that, no matter what, I'll take good care of you, both mother and child. This is the least I can do for Xu Hong-Lie."

The tears Xiu-Qing had held off fell and she wiped her hand down her face. "Young Master Yuan, you're too nice a person."

Clark swayed back. He didn't feel particularly nice. He only felt hopeless for himself.

That being the case, he might as well do what he could to give hope to others.

"Think about my proposal," he said. "If you agree, then in a few days, you can come to my home and meet my mother. And if your parents have no objections, we'll go through with our plan."

Xiu-Qing bit her lip, unable to stop crying.

He gave her a handkerchief from his pocket. "Also, don't call me Young Master Yuan anymore. If we want people to believe we want to get married, it won't do for you to keep calling me young master."

"Yes." Xiu-Qing patted her eyes with his handkerchief. "Thank you, Young Master Yuan."

Clark chuckled. He watched Xiu-Qing slowly calm down her emotions. For her at least, he was able to make something better. It gave him a bit of comfort.

"You go home first." He tipped his head at the direction from which they'd come. "Get some good rest. Problems can always be solved."

A smile broke through on Xiu-Qing's face. She clutched his handkerchief and thanked him with her eyes, then slowly walked away. Clark watched her return home and thought about her question again. What about the future? Would he want a wife of his own?

He watched the chickadees jump on the pavement and thought of Eden's last kiss. In the depths of his heart, he knew he would never love another woman the same way again. So no. He did not want a wife simply to have a wife. For him, it would always be only her.

THE VOICE OF SHANGHAI

How DID everyone navigate this traffic on a bike!

Just as Eden swerved to the left to avoid a woman and her child crossing the street, another bicycle zoomed past her on the right, nearly knocking her down from the side.

After two years, she thought she'd gotten used to the chaos of the Shanghai streets. She didn't realize riding a bicycle would be this difficult.

She steadied the wheels, determined not to give up. She'd already given up Clark. She wouldn't let a small problem like traffic stop her too. And she was on her own now. No Neil. No Clark.

No Clark.

She clutched the handlebar and pumped the pedals with her feet. It hurt. The fresh wound inside her hurt so much. The searing pain would not go away.

She had to go on. If Clark knew how upset she felt, it would be that much harder for him. If she couldn't stay strong and walk away, he might doubt the conviction of her choice, and he might rescind his promise. For him, and for the three hundred and sixteen lives at stake, she had to go on, alone.

The headwind pushed against her face and a tear stinging her eye was about to drop even though she was trying her hardest to hold it back. She pedaled faster ahead. Enough of scooting this way or that to avoid an accident. Everyone else could get out of her way.

"Miss! Miss!" someone shouted over the noise of motor vehicles, vendors, and pedestrians. The shout came from somewhere behind her and she paid it no attention.

Vroo-vroom. A mechanical buzz rode up beside her, followed by two piercing beeps of a horn. Eden gasped and came to a halt.

"Miss!" shouted the man on the dark red Indian Scout motorcycle slowing down to her speed. Eden looked at him, confused. The man stopped. "You're about to ride into the manhole." He pointed at the spot about a meter in front of her.

"Holy smoke!" she cried out. She hadn't even seen it. Of course, someone had stolen the manhole cover. Her wheel would've fallen right into it and she would've tipped over face down onto the ground.

"That was a close call." The man on the motorcycle flashed her a dashing smile. From his speech, she could hear his distinct American accent. His voice, deep and forceful yet smooth and warm, sounded so familiar. Where had she heard it before?

"Yes, it was." She glanced at him, trying to think who he might be. "Thank you."

"You're welcome," the man said. "Always a pleasure to rescue a pretty lady." He pushed his rider's goggles up to his forehead over his leather cap. His eyes unabashedly held her gaze.

Eden looked away. What a forward fella. She got off the bike and pulled it to the sidewalk.

"The name's Alex." The man drove his motorcycle beside her. "Alex Mitchell."

"Alex Mitchell?" Eden swung her handlebar back toward him. "The radio news reporter?"

Alex winked, in a cheeky way that nonetheless did not make her think he was bragging. "What's your name?" he asked her.

Normally, Eden would have declined to answer, or given a false name, thanked him again, and continued on her way. No woman in her right mind would strike up a conversation with a random man on the street. But this was Alex Mitchell! She couldn't possibly miss the chance to add him to her contact list. "I'm Eden Levine of the *China Press*."

"The *China Press*?" Alex looked at her anew. "Yes. Miss Levine. Of course. I've read your articles."

"You have?" That was a surprise. And he remembered her name?

"Yes." Alex grinned. "I like the last one you wrote. It's good someone's pointing out Hitler's repatriating his army officers from China. Your paper's articles are syndicated overseas. The Americans need to understand those Krauts are allying themselves with Japan. I've been telling the people in Washington this is a wake-up call. It's terrible. No one there wants to do anything about Europe. In their minds, China's about as important as Mars. Then there's that sonofabitch von Weigand singing Hitler's praises, saying everything opposite of what I'm saying. Excuse my language."

"It's okay." Eden dipped her head. Karl von Wiegand was a star U.S. reporter for the Hearst Press based in Shanghai. He had literally written he thought Hitler had "the earmarks of a leader" and a potential for a "great movement."

"Say, Miss Levine," Alex said and stared up the block. "My studio is right over there in the Christian Literature Society Building. If it's not inconvenient, would you mind coming with me? I want to ask you about what you said in your last article about Germany pulling their ambassador from Chungking."

Oh, that. Eden turned her head sideways. Clark had fed her that piece of information. He gave her a series of inside information other news reporters weren't privy to. It looked like she had lost that privilege now too.

"I have another half an hour before I go on the air at six o'clock. It'd be great if we can chat a bit before then. How about it?" Alex cocked his head.

An invitation from Alex Mitchell himself? "If I come, could I stay for your broadcast?"

"Why, of course!" Alex grinned. "I'd be delighted to have you there. You can give me an evaluation afterwards."

Eden gave him a side glance. "I doubt you need my opinion."

"All right then." He pulled his goggles back over his eyes. "It's 128 Museum Road. I'll meet you on the street out front. There's an attendant who can keep watch on your bike." He stepped on the engine. Another loud vroom later and he was gone.

Eden got back on her bike and pedaled over. At the bottom of the building, Alex was already waiting. He led her through the main entrance to the radio station on the second floor to his own office. There, a short, pudgy man looked up from behind one of the desks. His roundish face didn't tame his stern demeanor in the slightest.

"Mr. Mitchell!" The short man glanced over the top of his dark-rimmed glasses. "Oh, good! You remember to come back. I thought someone had kidnapped you and taken you to Timbuktu."

"Lucian, you give me too little credit. When have I ever missed a scheduled broadcast? When?" Alex replied, then turned to Eden. "This is Lucian, my assistant."

"You were supposed to be back here three hours ago!" Lucian drooped his mouth. His thick, graying mustache drooped too, pulling down his face.

"Sorry! I got held up," Alex said. He tossed his cap and goggles onto an empty chair and said to Eden, "He's just worried about me. He thinks the Japanese are going to capture me and kill me."

"That's no laughing matter!" Lucian put down the papers he was reviewing. "They hate you. They can stop the newspapers from circulating out of the foreign districts, but they can't stop the airwaves, and they hate it that everyone can hear you. Even their own soldiers can hear you. You should seriously consider wearing a bulletproof vest."

"A bulletproof vest?" Alex gawked. "That thing weighs forty pounds! How will I ride my iron carrying forty extra pounds?"

"You should stop riding that thing. It puts you too much out in the open."

Alex rolled his eyes and motioned for Eden to join him at his desk. Eden walked over and noticed the huge piles of letters lying on top. Several had been opened.

What is your middle name and how tall are you? . . .

Could you please send me an autographed picture? . . .

I'm writing again to tell you how much I enjoyed your show last week . . .

Looked like fan letters.

Lucian continued to glare at Alex. "You were supposed to return Cornell Franklin's call this afternoon, and the call from the President at the Shanghai Waterworks. I'm running out of excuses why they haven't heard back from you."

"I'm a busy man, what can I say? I was chasing a lead. I'll call them."

"The *Shanghai Evening Post and Mercury*'s looking for you. They want to know if you have time to write another piece for them."

"No, I don't have time," Alex said. "Maybe next week. By the way, Lucian, this is Miss Eden Levine from the *China Press*."

A smile finally came to Lucian's face. A welcoming one too. "How do you do, Miss Levine?"

"I'm good, thank you," Eden said. "How do you do?"

Before he could answer, Alex interrupted, "Lucian, why are all these letters still on my desk? I asked you to look at them to see if there are any we need to respond to."

"Well, I would've done it if I hadn't spent all day fielding your calls." Lucian snorted. "Bah." He threw up his hands. "I can't take all the fawning over you anymore. Find someone else to do it."

A young man in a white shirt and suspenders entered. "Alex, it's almost time for your show. Are you ready?" He handed Alex a folder.

Alex looked at the clock on the wall. "Is it six o'clock already? Jeezes! Where did the time go?" He took the folder and said to Eden, "I'm sorry. He's my show producer." He pointed at the young man. "Looks like we'll have to do my newscast first. Do you mind?"

"No." Eden smiled. "Not at all." Hearing him broadcast live was the reason she wanted to come anyway.

"Good. Let's go to the studio."

Eden followed him to another room where the crew had set up the transmitter and microphone. The show producer brought them each a glass of water and Alex invited her to take a seat beside him. Before he began, he said to her, "Ovaltine's now one of my sponsors. They signed the contract last week." He showed her a colored Ovaltine ad from his folder.

"Very impressive." Eden leaned closer and took a look. She meant that too. Alex Mitchell was the first newscaster in Shanghai who had convinced private companies to give him financial support.

He gazed into her eyes. She could see why he was the Pied Piper to all his female fans. If his voice and wit on the radio didn't charm them in person, he would definitely win them over. She had barely known him for an hour, and already, he was making her feel like he only had eyes for her.

It was just a play for her amusement, she knew. Not real and not serious. His every action carried an air of jest, as if they were both in on a joke.

The producer counted down the seconds with his fingers, then Alex spoke into the mike. "Good evening, this is Alex Mitchell reporting from XMHA. Before we start, a word from our sponsor, Ovaltine." He drew back from the mike and the producer played a pre-recorded commercial touting the cocoa-flavored malt beverage. When the commercial ended, Alex took to the mike again. When he did, his face turned somber. He spoke like a completely different person. "Earlier today, there was bombing at the Chinese Hui De Primary school. Sixteen students and two teachers were injured. Five students and one administrator were killed. The police are still investigating, but from what I've heard from witnesses, they believe it was a retaliation against the school for refusing to teach the doctrine of Asia for Asiatics required by Imperial Japan."

Eden listened in awe. At first, she thought he was adapting his tone to add dramatic effect. But sitting near him, she could see his veins throbbing on his temple.

"What kind of lowlife would attack children? Children? I do hope the authorities in charge will pursue this and bring those responsible to justice. Or will the figureheads sitting on their rears at the SMC continue to play nice with the Japs because they're too afraid to rock the boat?" He furrowed his brows and checked the notes before him. "I'm obliged to report that the Japanese consular police have said they had investigated the matter and found no Japanese involvement with this incident." He snickered. "No Japanese involvement. Well then, if the SMP discovers anyone else who would have a motive to bomb a Chinese primary school, I'll let you know." He exchanged a look with Eden. She didn't miss the sarcasm in his voice.

And then, the outrage on his face disappeared. A casual indifference took its place. "But there is sad news for Japan too," he said, his voice sounding anything but sad. "Following the explosion at Hui De Primary School, a shoot-out ensued and claimed two Japanese victims. Lance Corporal Jiro Himura, and a Mr. Yoshi Sakai, his occupation unknown." He turned his face toward Eden and mouthed the word "ronin." Eden threw back a look to show her agreement but stifled her smile to keep herself from accidentally making any noise.

"According to police reports, the two men were escaping the scene when they were hit by gunshots," Alex continued. Eden raised her fingers over her mouth to hide her chuckle. He almost sounded impartial, but his face looked like he was gloating. "The police have not yet found the person or persons who fired the shots. They're suspected to be Chinese resistance fighters. What an unfortunate turn of events. My heart goes out to Japan."

Eden couldn't look at him anymore. If she did, she would burst out laughing at his exaggerated tone of voice and his face pretending to mourn. He was clearly not sorry at all.

"What were these two men doing loitering around a Chinese primary school? Anyway, we definitely don't want any more Japanese men getting hurt. For their own safety, they're advised to stay away from all Chinese facilities. Yes, if they stay away, it would definitely help save lives."

Eden squeezed her shoulders. She was trying hard not to laugh. His tone of delivery warning the Japanese to stay away added just the right touch.

He noticed her reaction and opened his hand with an innocent shrug. "Next, we have the Chinese and international bulletins. Let's see. My good friend Mr. Yamato's been badgering me about not giving sufficient air time to reports in the Japanese bulletin, so I'll start with their main story today. At 2:00 p.m. tomorrow, there will be a demonstration at the border of the International Settlement at North Szechuan Road to protest British occupation of Shanghai." He held up the bulletin and read the next sentences with one roll of the tongue. "The demonstration is supported by the new Ta Tao Government of Shanghai and their good neighbor Japan for the Chinese people to voice their opposition to British rule and to call for an end to Western oppression in the East."

When he finished, he tossed the bulletin to the side. He spread his elbows on the desk and clasped his hands. His face turned serious again. "Mr. Yamato, thank you for your country's support for Chinese freedom and giving the Chinese people a chance to speak their minds. Now perhaps Japan will also step in and put a stop to whoever's been launching the terrorist attacks against the Chinese press. Since last November, the *Shen Pao* daily's office has been bombed three times. The newspapers *Ta Mei Wan Pao* and *Hwa Mei Wan Pao* have also been bombed. I'm sure they would greatly appreciate your help to make that stop."

In her seat, Eden wanted to applaud. The Japanese's use of violence to censor the press struck her especially hard. She had many friends in the business, and she still remembered the horrific murder of *Shen Pao*'s manager, Tsai Tiao-Tu. Not to mention, the threat was coming too close to the foreign press's doorsteps.

Alex moved on. "Now, some entertainment news from the SMC bulletin. Tomorrow sure is a day full of performances. What do you know? The Edinburgh Children's Theater will be performing the puppet show *Pinocchio*. Showtime begins at 2:00 p.m., the same time as the Ta Tao Government's demonstration. All are invited to come and see this classic tale of the boy who loves to lie."

By now, the producer could barely contain his laughter and left the room. Alex glanced at Eden and made a gesture of pulling his nose. Eden had to look away. He was practically calling the Japanese liars.

The producer returned and pointed at his watch. Alex acknowledged with a thumbs-up. "And this concludes my report for the evening. Once again, a word from our sponsor, Ovaltine."

A second Ovaltine advertisement recording began to play and

Alex switched off the mike. He swiveled his chair toward Eden. "How did I do?"

Eden laughed. Her feedback was superfluous at best. "You were brilliant."

"Thank you. I try." He relaxed and rested his arms on his chair. "So, we still haven't had a chance to talk. How about we go to dinner? There's a very good Hunan restaurant not far from here. They have the best cumin roasted ribs."

Dinner? With Alex Mitchell? How tempting to say yes. If only her parents hadn't already invited Isaac over tonight. The Weissmans were now on a waiting list for a ship again and nothing was certain. Her mother had made a special dinner for Isaac to cheer him up. "That sounds lovely, Mr. Mitchell—"

"Alex," he interrupted her, "call me Alex, please."

"All right, Alex. I wish I could, but I already have plans. I would love to talk to you some more." She gave him her business card from her purse. "Why don't we make another appointment?"

He held the business card up and turned it from front to back. "If I call you, would you only accept a business call? Or would a social call be welcomed too?"

"Excuse me?" Eden asked. His question confused her. Now she wasn't sure if he was still joking. Not with the serious way he was asking her.

Thankfully, he saved her from having to give him an answer. "I'll call you then." He put her business card into the pocket of his shirt. "Thank you for coming here nonetheless. It was a pleasure having you here. Let me walk you out."

Eden rose to her feet. "The pleasure's all mine."

At the front of the building, Alex stayed with her while the street attendant went to fetch her bike. While they waited, an Asian man in a dark suit came up to him. "Mr. Mitchell?"

Alex turned around. His body was still at ease, but his voice changed. "Yamatosan," he greeted the man. "What are you doing here?"

Yamato gave Eden a quick side glance. Instinctively, she stepped back. His stare made her skin crawl. So there really was a Mr. Yamato.

Yamato did not bother to extend her any other sort of acknowledgment. "Mr. Mitchell, the head of Japan radio control board, Major Azano, would like to have a word with you. Would you please join him for a drink? He's waiting for you at the bar at the Ristorante Fiore across the street."

"Ristorante Fiore?" Alex asked. He held his hands to his waist. "I have my heart set on Hunan food tonight."

"Ah, so. But Major Azano would like to speak to you," Yamato repeated. His voice sounded cordial enough. "It would be best if you go to Ristorante Fiore."

Eden wondered if she should intervene. Alex and Yamato seemed to be testing each other's line. Perhaps she could give Alex a little help and ask him to take her home? She took a step closer to him. From the corner of her eye, she saw two men moving in toward them.

Ronin.

Alex noticed them too. He gave them a quick glance, and they kept their distance. Still looking calm, Alex said, "Miss Levine, I'm afraid I'll have to take my leave of you here. I've got a little business to attend to."

"Alex—" she started to protest, but Alex smiled and subtly shook his head.

"I'll call you tomorrow. I promise." He waved goodbye and followed Yamato across the street.

When they were gone, the ronin retreated too. She could no longer find them.

Left to herself, Eden had nothing more to do but to go home. She tipped the street attendant who retrieved her bike and proceeded on her way.

Alex Mitchell sure had some nerve.

The Japanese's intentions didn't look too friendly.

She hoped he would call her tomorrow. If he didn't, she would call his station herself. That way, she could make sure nothing bad happened to him.

14

DAUGHTER-IN-LAW

"How long has this been?" Madam Yuan asked. She switched her gaze from Clark to Xiu-Qing, then back to Clark.

On the couch across from her, Clark stole a sideways glance at Xiu-Qing and braced for his mother's reprimand. He had warned Xiu-Qing in advance his mother might think them an utter disgrace. He hoped he'd prepared her well enough to withstand the scolding. If they could get through this, everything else would work out.

The poor girl. Her face was burning red. She couldn't raise her head to look at anyone.

He saved her the humiliation and answered his mother, "Two months."

"Two months!" Madam Yuan's jaw dropped open. Clark exchanged a look with Wen-Ying. His sister was the only other person who knew the truth. She nodded to show her support. Beside her, Mei Mei hunched her back and waited for the storm to unfold.

To his surprise, the storm never came. Slowly, his mother's face eased. "You young people. Always acting on impulse. But I don't want to blame you either."

Clark didn't dare to move. The whole room was waiting for his mother to give her final verdict.

"Of course, if this kind of thing were passed on to the public, it would be very shameful to hear. But since it already happened, and Guo-Hui is already grown up, it's pointless for me to badger you about the how's and why's. Guo-Hui should've started his own home and family much sooner. If you two really feel the same way about each other, I won't object."

"Ma!" Clark breathed a sigh of relief. "Thank you." He looked encouragingly at Xiu-Qing. This was the toughest part of this scheme. He wasn't sure if his mother would accept a daughter-in-law from a working-class family. The pregnancy added even more complications. He didn't think his mother would give her approval so easily.

"Ge, congratulations." Mei Mei broke into a smile. Wen-Ying, too, smiled, but it was the smile of someone who knew a secret.

"Thank you, Madam Yuan," Xiu-Qing whispered, still not daring to raise her head.

"What does your father do?" Madam Yuan asked.

"He's a supervisor at a fabric dye factory."

"And your mother?"

"She's a buyer for electronic merchandise at the Sincere Department Store."

"Mm." Madam Yuan nodded. "And you met Guo-Hui at our company?"

"Yes." Xiu-Qing twiddled her fingers. Her face turned red again.

Clark jumped in to try to help. "After the Battle of Shanghai, we were shorthanded. Xiu-Qing's a bookkeeper. She came to do some after-hours work for us. She's been a great help."

"Then you two must've worked a lot of evenings together," Madam Yuan said. "How come you never brought her home for dinner?"

"That, uh . . ." Clark scratched his neck.

Thankfully, Wen-Ying came to their rescue. "Ma! You ask such private questions, other people would be too embarrassed to answer you."

"I just wanted to know why I haven't met my future daughter-in-law earlier," Madam Yuan replied. Still, Wen-Ying's comment did enough to convince her to stop. "All right, never mind. At this stage, we shouldn't delay anymore. It'll be best to arrange the wedding as quickly as possible." A sparkle came to her eyes, which had shown only grief in the last nine months. "Since your father passed away, this house has felt like it lost all its air of life. Now, we finally have a jubilant event to counter it." She smiled at Clark and Xiu-Qing. "If the baby is a boy, then our Yuan family will have an heir. Your father's spirit in Heaven could rest in peace and be happy."

Clark smiled back but avoided her eyes. A phony marriage was one thing. An imposter heir felt like a betrayal to his own ancestors and family.

Xiu-Qing, too, kept her eyes down. This lie must weigh on her conscience.

"I'm embarrassing you both again," Madam Yuan said. "All right, we'll talk about something else. Guo-Hui, you can see about when to invite the in-laws over for dinner. Xiu-Qing, come see your father-in-law. We'll light incense for the ancestors."

Xiu-Qing gave Clark an uncertain glance. Clark encouraged her with a nod and she rose to her feet. Madam Yuan grabbed her hand to lead her out of the room to the family altar.

Sharp-minded as always, Wen-Ying eyed Mei Mei and tossed her head at their mother. Catching the cue, Mei Mei left to make sure their mother wouldn't put Xiu-Qing in a difficult spot.

When they were the only two let in the living room, Wen-Ying said to Clark, "This, too, is a solution."

"I'm just glad you don't disapprove," Clark said. Wen-Ying

didn't normally take so easily to outsiders. If she objected, this plan wouldn't have gone through so smoothly.

"Xu Hong-Lie sacrificed himself for the country. If we can save him from more losses, it's something we should do."

"I think so too." Clark thought of his friend with some comfort. "By the way, how's Uncle Gao? Have you heard any news?"

Wen-Ying's face dropped. "Not well. Whoever abducted him truly had a cruel heart and a searing hand. His ear was sliced off. The wound will heal, but his mental well-being? It's hard to say. He wouldn't tell anyone what happened. Gao tai tai is still terrified. She's afraid someone might still come after them."

Clark's eyes fell. "If you can, tell her there's no need to worry anymore. They're safe now." He would tell them himself, but the Gaos refused to see him.

"You're really not going to tell me what this matter was all about?"

No. He didn't want any more people involved. "I handled it. It's over."

Wen-Ying waited for him to say more. When it was clear he wouldn't change his mind, she turned her gaze to the doorway where their mother led away Xiu-Qing. "I hope she'll have a girl."

"Why?"

"We can help others, of course. But in the end, an heir to our family can't be someone else's son."

Clark clasped his hands behind his head. His parents should've had more sons.

"Maybe you can take a second wife in the future," Wen-Ying said.

Clark dropped his arms. "I truly don't understand you. You're an educated woman. Polygamy, preferences for sons. These are horrible traditions. Why are your perspectives always so backward?"

"This isn't a matter of my perspectives," she said. "Whether something is traditional or progressive, I don't care. I only care about protecting the welfare of our family. Only you can safeguard our family's future."

Yes. He didn't need the reminder. "I'm not talking to you about this anymore." He got up and went to join his mother and the others.

At the family altar, Xiu-Qing had just finished setting the burning sticks of incense in front of the portraits of his late father and grandparents. Clark joined her and bowed his head. He said a silent prayer to apologize for lying and asked for their forgiveness. When they finished, Mei Mei stepped up. "Xiu-Qing jie, let me show you the rest of the house." She linked her arm around the woman she assumed to be her future sister-in-law and walked her out to the backyard.

When two young women were out of their earshot, Madam Yuan came to his side. "When you suddenly told me there's such a girl like Xiu-Qing, I almost didn't know how to handle it. Nonetheless, this girl Xiu-Qing has clear eyes and graceful brows. Her temperament seems quite gentle and docile. Even though her family background is a bit poor, she herself went to school. She also worked in a foreign company, so she has seen the bigger world. For me, I'm pretty satisfied. What's more, she's Chinese. I really have to thank heaven and earth for that."

That last comment grated on Clark's ear and he winced.

"Actually," Madam Yuan sighed, "after all that has happened, I don't ask for much anymore. As long as you children are healthy, and our family can live happily and peacefully, other things don't matter much."

Clark smiled. She was his mother after all. He couldn't be upset with her for long no matter what.

"From now on, you be good to Xiu-Qing. Understand?" Madam Yuan asked, not a question but an order.

"I understand," Clark reassured her.

Pleased, Madam Yuan left to look for Mei Mei and Xiu-Qing. Clark hadn't seen her look so happy since his father died.

What a joke life was playing on him. His mother wanted this. Xiu-Qing needed this. Shen Yi demanded this. Now everyone got what they wanted from his life, except him.

15

SWEET TEMPTATION

THE MOTORCYCLE ZIGZAGGED around the cars on the left and the buses on the right. As the bike tilted, Eden pressed her legs against the passenger seat and squeezed her hands to hold on to Alex's jacket. She wouldn't fall off, would she? He was going so fast!

She'd hardly finished her thought when the motorcycle picked up its speed and zoomed into the gap between two trucks.

"Ahhhh!!" she screamed. She squeezed her eyes shut. Never mind modesty. Never mind propriety. This was life or death. She wrapped her arms tightly around him and pressed her body against his back.

The fumes from the vehicles ahead of them stung her nose and her hair was flying every which way. She had no idea how many blocks they'd gone before he finally slowed down. When he stopped and put on the brake, she opened her eyes and found themselves at the entrance of the Garden Bridge.

"What'd you think?" Alex turned his head around.

Eden released herself from him. "I had no idea when you invited me for a ride, you meant you would bring me to the brink of death."

"Brink of death?" Alex stepped on the pedal and the engine vroomed. "I was only going at half my normal speed."

She didn't doubt that. He wasn't wearing his goggles and helmet, so this must be an easy ride for him today.

He pushed his sunglasses up and let them rest above his forehead. "What's the fun in riding a motorcycle if you're gonna be stuck in traffic?"

"What use is it to talk your way out of troubles with the Japanese only to tempt fate with a motorcycle crash?"

"You worry the Japanese might harm me?" Alex laughed. "They wouldn't dare yet. There's a price to pay for harming an American journalist."

"What did they want with you anyway? That Yamato gave me the creeps."

"Oh, the usual. They said I was breaching American neutrality. They complained I was demoralizing their soldiers. I told them to beat it. Look." He pointed at a group of Asian students in high school uniforms on the bridge. "Over there. See all those kids holding cameras? Who do you think they are?"

Eden looked toward their direction. "They look like they're on a school trip. Are they tourists?"

"Tourists?" He raised his brows. "Maybe. One thing I'm sure, they're also Japanese spies."

"Spies? But they're only kids."

"That's how they all get away with it. Every Japanese person here is working for the Mikado. Soldiers, school students, old people, shop owners, businessmen, housewives. Their whole population's working in concert to expand their empire. You can't trust a single one of them. Look to your right. The couple over by the bridge are snapping photos of the commercial ships entering Shanghai ports today. They're taking pictures of British naval and American marine activities. They're spying on the whole city under the pretense of being tourists."

"Are you serious?" Eden gazed at the students again. "You're sure you're not being paranoid?"

"I'm not paranoid. Next time you need to buy film, go to one of the Korean or Japanese camera stores. Watch how the Japanese customers never have to pay for film or anything else they buy. You see, the Japanese government already paid for all their film. When they come back to get their film developed, they'll get to keep the photos, but the store keeps the negatives. The negatives will be sent to the Japanese War Office." He lowered his voice. "I got this straight from a Korean source where I buy my camera supplies."

Eden took a second look at the couple. "That's an ingenious way to get people to do the army's work."

"Yes, it is," Alex said. "You know what though? I think the Japs would spy for their government even if the film and development weren't free. Free is a bonus, but the Japanese are fanatically loyal to their country. They're patriotic to a fault. They believe their emperor is a god. They really believe Hirohito is a descendant of their gods, and his bloodline goes back more than two thousand years. Their army and the people in power use this legend and turn their country into an imperial cult."

Eden squinted at the students, who were now passing by the Japanese soldiers guarding the bridge. "I think I understand," she said. That was how things were back in Munich. The Nazi rallies. Their frightening display of national pride. The unquestioning embrace of Adolph Hitler and the doctrines he sprouted. "That's what's happening in Germany. It's fanatical."

"Maybe," Alex said. He looked out to the Japanese vessels dominating this part of the creek. "The difference is, the Germans are brazen about it. They're not even trying to hide how great they think they are. It's obvious Hitler wants to take over the world. With the Japs, you don't know anything. They're outwardly polite, but they'll bite you like a snake when you turn your back. They don't show you their feelings. They'll work quietly against you and let you show your hand while you're trying to appease them. But make no mistake, they want to rule the world, and they think they're superior too. The difference is, unlike the Germans, they don't need anyone else to acknowledge it."

"Those are very strong words," Eden said.

"Just telling it like it is." Alex shrugged.

Over on the bridge, the Japanese students turned their cameras in their direction. Quickly, Alex flipped his sunglasses back down. He turned his face and said to Eden, "Look the other way."

Eden did as he said, but asked, "Why?"

"Don't ever give them a chance to get a photo of you. We're reporters. Whether you write about them or not, they're keeping score. And you have written about them, so you're marked too. If they can identify who you are, you'll never be safe."

Shaken, Eden let her hair fall over her face. She'd never considered that spies might be photographing her.

"Let's get out of here." Alex released the brake. "What do you say we go for some of that Hunan food we missed last time?"

"All right." She wrapped her arms around his waist. "Can we please ride slower this time?"

"Not a chance." He stepped on the gas and zoomed back onto the street.

———————

Arriving home late that afternoon from her outing with Alex, Eden opened her purse to search for her keys. While she was looking, the door of the next apartment opened.

"Eden?" Her neighbor, Keiko Dupre, stepped into the hallway. "I was just coming to look for you."

"Keiko." Eden gave her a warm reply. "How've you been?"

"I'm good," Keiko said. "A friend of mine returned from Japan two days ago. She brought me some excellent sweets and we're about to have our afternoon tea. Would you like to join us?"

Eden smiled. She was still full from the big Hunan meal with Alex, but she didn't want to be rude. "Oh, I'm not hungry, but I would love to join you for a cup of tea. Shall I ask my mother to come too?"

"No." Keiko waved her hands. "Your mother's not home. She took Joshua and Hiroshi to a Chinese acrobats performance."

"She did?" Eden hesitated. "In that case, all right." She dropped her keys back into her purse.

"Good, good." Keiko bobbed her head. She led Eden into her apartment to the table where a woman already sat waiting. "Eden, this is my friend Hina Kato."

Hina stood up to greet her. She was almost beautiful, but not quite. The contrast between her jet-black hair, red lips, and ivory skin looked so striking, it made her face look severe. Her eyes, though bright, cut too sharp.

Nonetheless, Eden greeted her as she would any new friend. "How do you do?"

"Good." Hina blinked. "I've been looking forward to meeting you." The way she spoke reminded Eden of Alex's Mr. Yamato.

Eden shook it off. She must be imagining this. She sat down with the two women and unfolded the napkin onto her lap. "Keiko said you just came back from Japan?"

"I did." Hina opened her hand above the plate of delicately shaped confections on the table. "These are *wagashi*. I brought them back from Kyoto, my hometown. Traditionally, we serve them so the sweet would counteract the bitterness of tea. Which one would you like to try?"

"I don't know," Eden said. The colorful sweets molded into shapes to resemble white peaches, orange persimmons, green leaves, and pink sakura flowers all tempted her appetite. "They're so pretty."

"How about this one?" Hina asked. Using a sugar cube tong,

she served Eden a red piece carved in the shape of a flower. "It's my favorite. It's filled with plum paste. Try it."

"All right." Eden put the piece into her mouth. The soft, gooey paste of the plum filling slowly dissolved on her tongue. Its flavor —subtle, mild, even, and not too sweet, made it a pleasant experience of both sight and taste. "It's delicious."

"I'm glad you like it," Hina said. "Have as many as you want. They're all meant for your enjoyment."

Eden paused. What did she mean by that? They'd never met until now.

"You're a news reporter?" Hina asked and leaned in closer to the table.

"Yes."

"I'm in the news business myself."

"Is that right?" Eden asked. In her mind, her caution kicked in, but she kept the tone of her voice warm and unchanged. "Are you a reporter as well?"

"No," Hina said. She eyed Keiko and signaled her to pour the tea. "I work for the Ministry of News and Media of Imperial Japan. I'm a public relations specialist."

Eden glanced at Keiko. Keiko smiled back and nodded, then turned her eyes to Hina.

"My government is very impressed with your work," Hina said. As she talked, she kept on smiling. "We would like to work together with you."

"Work together? How?"

"There are so many false reports out there. Sometimes, it is better for honest reporters to make sure the truth is told."

"I don't disagree with that," Eden said, carefully choosing her words.

"You're an honest reporter. Why don't you help us give the facts to the people?"

Eden paused. "I'm not sure I understand. How can I help you?"

"Easy. For example, we can send you information about all the wonderful things our government is doing to help make Shanghai a prosperous city. So many people don't know the Chinese Provisional Government and Japan are working together. With the new Chinese leadership, the relationship between our two countries has never been better. You can help by telling all the foreigners here and elsewhere about this." She put her hand on Eden's. "The New Order is working. So, the Chinese in inland China can stop fighting us now. Everything will improve once they stop. The occidental countries should recognize this too. The countries in Asia want to determine their own destiny. The countries in the West need to stop interfering and let us take the course that will best benefit us. If you help us, you'll be helping to ensure every country will proceed in the direction of peace. And, you'll be handsomely rewarded."

Eden looked back at Hina. The Japanese wanted her to become their mouthpiece?

She wanted to pull her hand back, but that wouldn't be a wise move. She returned a cordial smile to Hina. "It's not that simple. Everything I write has to be approved by my boss."

"So convince your boss." Hina closed her hand around Eden's. "I've read all your articles. You're very persuasive."

Eden's breath shortened. "Thank you for thinking so highly of me. But when I write my articles, I don't rely on anyone else to provide me the facts. I like to investigate everything myself."

"Of course." Hina let go of her hand. Eden quickly drew it back. "What we want is to help, and that includes investigations too. We can show you topics that would be relevant to your readers. Whatever details or facts you need, we will provide them for your review. Whoever you want to interview, we will arrange it. We can make your job so much easier."

"Really?" Eden laughed. "That's a very generous offer." She glanced at Keiko again. To her disappointment, Keiko nodded in agreement with Hina.

Alex Mitchell was right. The Japanese were united in their cause. Even their housewives.

Hina took a sip of her tea. "I know this is a very unexpected proposal. Perhaps you need to think it over. How about I come back in two days? You can discuss this with your boss. Then, you can give me an answer."

Two days? Eden bit the inside of her lip.

Hina picked up the sugar cube tong again and put a piece of *wagashi* on each of their plates. "Sweet things are good, aren't they?" She smiled at Eden. "The Western countries don't share many sweet things for stateless people in China. We Japanese are not like them. We want to share. We'll work with people who don't belong anywhere and treat them well. Whatever you want to sweeten the deal, all you have to do is ask."

Eden stared at the *wagashi* on her plate. Sweet thing, that little piece of delight sculpted like a white rabbit.

Sweet and poisonous.

WEDDING DAY

"GE, CAN I COME IN?" Mei Mei knocked on the door.

"Yes," Clark answered. He looked into the full-length mirror and straightened his bowtie.

His youngest sister entered his room. "Everyone's waiting downstairs."

"I'm ready." Clark turned around.

Mei Mei gave him a once over. "You always look so handsome in a tuxedo."

"Thank you. You look beautiful yourself." He watched her blush. The color of her rose-pink chiffon dress suited her well. Every day, his little sister grew even prettier.

"Today, it's not a matter of whether I'm beautiful. The most beautiful would be Xiu-Qing jie."

"Right." Clark flitted his eyes to the side.

"You forgot to put on your boutonniere. Let me help you." Mei Mei picked up the single bud of calla lily on his dresser and pinned it to his lapel. "It would've been so great if Ba was still here. If he saw you starting your own family, he'd be so happy. Ma's overjoyed. Her only complaint is the church is too small.

She said your wedding will look dingy when we take photos after the ceremony."

Clark laughed. "Well, it's the only church we were able to book on short notice. Tell her when you get married, we'll have an even more lavish wedding at the biggest church we can find in Shanghai."

Mei Mei lowered her gaze with a quiet smile. "I don't want a church wedding." She smoothed out the fabric around the boutonniere.

"Why not? You're not thinking of going back to wearing a *gua* wedding gown and praying to heaven and earth like the old days?"

Mei Mei shrugged. "I'm not a Christian."

"It doesn't matter. Xiu-Qing and I aren't either. Most people getting married in churches aren't. It's only a ceremony."

"A church is still a place that advocates religion. And religion . . . it's a kind of opium."

Opium? Clark's smile vanished. "Where did you hear of this?"

"Nowhere." Mei Mei stepped back. "I think this way myself."

She was lying. This was a Marxist thought. Someone was feeding her these nonsense ideas. "Wen-Li. Are you still together with Liu Zi-Hong?"

Mei Mei swung around to turn her face away from him. "I know you don't like him, and he lost your trust too." She held her hands behind her and gazed up. "Actually, Zi-Hong and I have grown apart. After you terminated him from his job at your office, he started putting distance between us. Maybe you won't believe it, but he feels regret toward you too. He told me that himself. I think that's why he feels too ashamed to be around me. Plus, he's been spending a lot of time on things he considers important than personal matters. If I see him, it's only when I run into him in school." She dropped her head. Her words drizzled with heartache.

"Mei Mei." Clark touched her on the shoulder. "Maybe it's

best not to be fixated on one boy. You're a wonderful girl. You'll find someone else."

"Like you found Xiu-Qing jie after you got over Eden?"

Clark snatched his hand back. No. He couldn't simply get over Eden and find someone else.

Mei Mei abruptly stepped away. "Let's not keep talking anymore. It's time. We have to leave, or else we'll be late." She grabbed his arm and led him toward the door.

Throwing all other thoughts behind him, Clark braced himself for playing the part of the groom for the rest of the day ahead.

At the altar, the priest recited the traditional wedding proclamation to the guests. Doing his part, Clark stared forward and listened, all the while feeling removed from everything around him. The church, the priest and the children's choir, the flowers, and all the guests in suits and formal dresses. They all felt like props on a stage.

His life wasn't his. His wedding was all but a show to redeem for the losses he had caused.

"Mr. Yuan Guo-Hui and Miss Sun Xiu-Qing, you are now husband and wife. From now on, the two of you will become one. . ."

From now on, as far as he was concerned, his only purpose was to fulfill his promises. His promise to Xiu-Qing, his promise to Shen Yi, his promise to Eden. These were his real vows.

The ceremony concluded and the organ music prompted him to continue with this script of his phony life. With the flower boys and girls leading the way, he offered Xiu-Qing his arm and walked her down the aisle and out of the church. Sounds of applause from the guests surrounded them. Were their cheers a sign from God commending him for doing the right thing? Or was it Fate taking a sinister pleasure in mocking him for having to live a life of lies instead of the life of his dreams?

Outside, on the church's front steps, the photographer dashed forward, shouting for the family, bridesmaids, and groomsmen to line up to pose for photos. The crowd of guests who were tossing confetti and rice at the bride and groom made way. As the photographer cheerfully shouted for everyone to smile, Clark gazed out to the roof of the lane house two streets over. The photographer's camera popped. But a much louder boom supplanted it. The side of the lane house exploded and a geyser of gray dust spurted up.

Laughter turned to shrieks. All at once, Huang Shifu raced forward and hustled Clark and Xiu-Qing into their Cadillac while their other driver rushed his mother and sisters away. Before Clark left, he turned his head and glanced back at Wen-Ying. As calm as ever, she gazed at him, her eyes gleaming with victory. This was one of the six bombings the Heaven and Earth Society had set out to launch today on the anniversary of the Japanese's attack at the Marco Polo Bridge. That house where the bomb had just gone off belonged to a former KMT lawyer who now advised the Japanese.

If all had gone as planned, the traitor himself was inside and he should be dead.

The sudden attack threw the wedding guests into a frenzy. Everyone scrambled for a taxi or rickshaw to get away. In their own car, Huang Shifu slammed on the gas pedal and sped away while sirens wailed behind them.

"My father and mother!" Xiu-Qing cried out and looked back through the rear window.

"They'll be fine," Clark reassured her. He saw them being rushed into a car by one of the two dozen security guards he had hired. And while he didn't know for sure, he suspected dozens more Heaven and Earth Society members were patrolling near the church. One thing he did know, some of them were posing as taxi drivers to help take their guests away from the scene. Wen-Ying told him this two days before the ceremony. Tian Di Hui wouldn't risk her safety or his, and the wedding of the head of the Yuan Enterprises nearby provided too good a distraction for their plot.

The attack didn't deter anyone from attending the wedding banquet. Bombings and gunfights were now the norm in Shanghai. They no longer stopped anyone from continuing on with their daily plans and routines. Two hours later, their guests arrived at the banquet hall. One after another, they consoled him with flowery words to recast the bad omen of a terrorist attack on his wedding day in a positive light. This was a sure sign of Chinese strength, they said. A sign of China rising from defeat. They congratulated him for having two joyful events landing at his door, a celebration of a wedding and a takedown of a treacherous dog.

Clark accepted their toasts of good intent. The wine soon clouded his head and he joined them in their boisterous laughter. No one would blame the groom for getting drunk. Let the alcohol numb his senses. Perhaps then, the sting of heartache inside him would disappear. Heartache for the chaotic state into which his country had fallen. Heartache for losing all hope of ever being with the woman he loved.

Through the thick, drunken haze of his mind, he glanced at Xiu-Qing. His mother was loading the best pieces of chicken and prawns onto his phony bride's plate. When no one was looking, Xiu-Qing threw him an apologetic glance. He gave her a subtle nod to help her go on.

This was hard on her too. Xiu-Qing's life wasn't hers either. She would never have the life she wanted with Hong-Lie. Now she must live with the burden of guilt for lying to those who saved her and showed her such genuine affection.

This day finally came to an end. On their ride home, Clark kept the car windows down. The night air started to clear his head and the feeling of detachment returned. In his life, what was real? Not this fake marriage to Xiu-Qing, not his stormy affair with Ekaterina Brasova, not his betrothal to Shen Yi, which he'd never accepted in his heart. Only Eden was real, except she, too, was but a broken dream.

At home at last and in his room, he and Xiu-Qing dropped their facade. While the family was celebrating at the banquet earlier, the staff had changed their bedding and replaced them with brand new red ones embroidered with the golden dragon and phoenix customary for newlyweds.

Behind closed doors, Xiu-Qing stood anxiously by the dresser.

"Come on in." Clark walked over to the bed. "This is your room now too." He picked up one of the pillows. He knew this would be an awkward moment for her, and he'd already decided before the wedding day how to put her at ease. He tossed the pillow onto the couch, then went to the closet and pulled out an extra blanket. "Take the bed. I'll sleep on the couch."

"No." Xiu-Qing came to the couch. "Guo-Hui Ge, the bed is yours. Let me sleep on the sofa."

Clark unfolded the blanket on the sofa. "Don't fight over this with me. How can I sleep well on the bed if I let a pregnant woman sleep on the sofa? You go sleep on the bed."

"But I feel really bad." She held her hands tightly against her chest.

"How about this? From now on, you help me fold away the blanket and put my pillow back on the bed in the morning before amah comes to make up our room."

Xiu-Qing hesitated. "Then . . ."

"Let's just do that." Clark went to his drawer and pulled out his pajamas. He didn't really need her help. He only made the request to give her a way to lessen her feelings of guilt. "I'll go out and change. You can get ready for bed. Don't think too much about anything else."

Now more at ease, Xiu-Qing looked around the room. Clark took his pajamas and went to the door.

"Guo-Hui Ge," she called him back. "Thank you."

Clark smiled. He grabbed the doorknob, then paused. "You looked very beautiful today. The one who should've been with you today was Hong-Lie. If he'd seen you, he would've been so happy."

She returned a bittersweet smile. Clark opened the door and left the room. In the hallway, he could still hear the laughter of his mother and sisters from his mother's room as she recounted everything that happened earlier at the ceremony and during the banquet. He threw a casual glance at their direction and went downstairs to the study. Before he turned in, he had one more thing to do.

In the study, he made a call. The phone rang on the other end and a woman's voice answered, "Hello?"

"Ming Zhu?" Clark asked.

"Young Master Yuan!" Pearl said. "Today's your big day. Congratulations. July 7. Very meaningful. If you'd chosen July 7 of the lunar year calendar instead, it would've been the holiday of the Seventh Sister. You know the foreigners call that holiday the Chinese Valentine's Day. I'd say, you picked a date with good omen."

Clark smiled. He raised the receiver closer to his mouth. "How'd it go?"

"All smooth. Tan Shao-Yu got cleaned up by us tonight."

A fitting end to the thief who sold out his country. Wen-Ying and her Heaven and Earth Society had their plans. Juntong and Dai Li had theirs. Tan Shao-Yu belonged to them. No one who was waging a war of resistance would miss the chance to send a message on this fateful day of July 7.

Now this traitor would never become head of the puppet Chinese government as the Japanese wished.

"What a waste," Pearl said. "He fought in the revolution with Sun Yat-Sen. He served in official posts with the KMT. In the end, he actually chose to be the Japanese demons' running dog."

While Pearl talked, Clark noticed a package addressed to him on his desk. He picked it up and opened it. Inside, he found a black notebook and a note.

Guo-Hui, congratulations. A working-class girl. You chose well. Consider this my wedding gift to you. Even though you think my heart is cruel, I didn't make a copy. See? I also kept my word. From now on, consider the debt between you and me is canceled by one deed.

Clark half sat on his desk and flipped open the notebook. Indeed, Shen Yi kept her word. These were the names and addresses of Dr. Levine's patients.

On the phone, Pearl was still talking. "So many people are hungry, and he was still in the mood to buy antiques. Really, even Heaven couldn't let his treachery pass its eye. He was admiring the porcelain statuette of the war god Guan Gong when he got axed in the back of his head."

Clark closed the notebook. Pearl was right. Tan Shao-Yu knew too much. Juntong had to eliminate him. Dai Li would never let him turn to collaborate with the enemy. How unfortunate. He chose to ruin his own legacy at the last stage of his life.

"What happens to the delivery of antiques now?" Clark asked. "Juntong paid big money for them. Don't tell me they left them at Tan's home."

"Of course not." Pearl laughed. "I suppose we'll resell them. The best thing would be to resell them to foolish Japanese buyers at an outrageous price, then use the money to fund more attacks against the traitors."

Clark unlocked the top drawer of his desk and put the black notebook inside. "Can you do something for me?"

"What?"

"Can you send the Guan Gong statuette to Madam Liu Kun tomorrow? Send it anonymously with a note and tell her Tan Shao-Yu sent her this gift from hell."

"As you wish, Young Master Yuan."

"Thank you." Clark hung up. By tomorrow, all the collaborators in Shanghai would've heard the news about the assassination of Tan. A delivery of Guan Gong, the bravest and most loyal army general from the Han Dynasty in the third century, ostensibly from Tan, should send Shen Yi a clear message that someone was watching her.

He locked the drawer, turned out the light, and went to the bathroom to change. When he returned to his room, Xiu-Qing was already in bed. The comforter covered the lower half of her face. Quietly, Clark turned off the dim lamp by the door. He lay down on the sofa and pulled the blanket over himself. The spongy cushions gave his back little support. He tossed and shifted, trying to find a tolerable spot. It was futile. He closed his eyes and did his best to ignore his discomfort until weariness finally brought him much-needed sleep.

17

ALL THAT COULD NEVER BE

ALL MORNING, Eden fidgeted at her desk, waiting for Charlie to arrive. Her afternoon tea with Hina Kato was no small matter. She dared not speak to anyone about it until she could discuss it with Charlie first.

As soon as he came in, she went to his office. "Charlie?"

"Good morning." Charlie hung his hat on the coat rack and went around behind his desk.

She closed the door behind her. "We have to talk. An agent of the Japanese Ministry of News and Media approached me yesterday."

Charlie stared at her. He pointed at the chair across from him.

Eden took a seat. "Her name is Hina Kato. She approached me through my neighbor. My neighbor's a Japanese woman. A housewife married to a Frenchman."

"What did they want?"

"She asked me to work with them. They want me to be their mouthpiece and write their propaganda articles. She even tried to bribe me. She thought she could persuade me. She gave me two days to think it over."

Charlie crossed his arms. "What did you tell her?"

"Nothing yet," Eden said. "I don't intend to work with them at all. I need to figure out how to tell her no."

"I know." Charlie rubbed his chin. "This is tricky."

"Do you think I can tell her it's just not our policy to work with an outside party? Maybe I can use this as a chance to show they can't influence free press? I'll do it if you support me on it."

"No." Charlie shook his head.

"No? Why? Aren't you offended they try to interfere with your paper?"

"Sure I am," Charlie said. "But I don't want to reject them outright. I don't want us to appear blatantly hostile. I have a responsibility to our staff for their safety."

"You think they'll really harm us?"

"We've seen what they've done to the Chinese news reporters. The only thing protecting us is our foreign status."

Eden looked away. She loathed the idea of cowering to their threat.

"You'll have to decline them in a way that won't make them lose face," Charlie said. "Here's what we'll do. When you see this Hina Kato woman again, tell her you've been reassigned. From now on, you'll report on society and entertainment news."

"Society and entertainment news?" Eden bolted upright. "You can't be serious."

"I am serious."

"I don't want to write about trivial things."

Charlie gave her a look of reproach. "First of all, that's not a very respectful way of looking at your colleagues who do report on society and entertainment news, and I have as much regard for them as all the other reporters."

"I'm sorry," Eden apologized. "I don't mean to belittle what they do. But reporting hard news is what I do. I want to open people's eyes, tell them about current events, not indulge them in gossip and entertainment."

"Eden." Charlie propped his elbows on the desk. "You're not only my employee. You're my friend. I'm doing this for your own safety."

"I don't want to be silenced."

"No. But I care about you, and I won't risk anything happening to you, or your family. Would you risk something happening to them? What if they threaten to harm them too if you don't do what they say?"

Eden twitched her lips. "What if they approach another one of our reporters? You can't keep reassigning them to avoid the problem."

"No, but some of us are more vulnerable than others. You're not like most of us. Take me, for example. I'm an Aussie. I have a government that will protect me. And if that's not enough and someone really threatens me and my family, I can always pack up with my wife and kids and go back to Melbourne. But you? You're stateless. Who will protect you? Where would you go? If you ask me, I think that's why they approached you. They see that you have a weakness."

Eden frowned. "This isn't fair."

"No. But it's for the best." He gave her an encouraging smile. "Don't look at it as a downgrade of your job. It is not. Yes, it's important to report the hard news, but it's also important to give people something to escape from pressure and stress, especially now when fear and uncertainty is everywhere. We need to keep people's spirits up. If everything is doom and gloom and there's nothing else, they'll all want to leave. Give them something normal and something they can enjoy, and you'll give them good reasons to keep fighting for this place. So I need good, dedicated reporters even for what you call trivial news." He looked her in the eye. "Besides, I think you'll do a good job."

She looked back at him. "Now you're trying to sweet talk me." She groaned, but broke down and smiled.

Charlie sat back and clasped his hands behind his head. "Take the day off. You can start fresh tomorrow. For now, let the others do the fighting for free speech. I promise the *China Press* won't become a propaganda machine for the Japs. Not under my watch."

Eden got up and returned to her station. Society and entertainment news. She still felt disappointed.

At her desk, she grabbed her purse.

"Going out?" Dottie asked as she walked by.

"Charlie gave me the day off. I'll see you tomorrow." Eden waved goodbye and headed for the exit.

Where should she go? She didn't want to go home yet. Her mother was home, and she wanted to think through how to explain to her parents what happened.

She could go see Alex Mitchell. He would understand. The Japanese had been pressuring him too. Maybe he would have a thought or two about this.

―――――――――

"Eden Levine!" Alex Mitchell eagerly greeted her at his office at the XMHA studio. "To what do I owe this pleasure?" He invited her to take a seat.

"I've joined your ranks," Eden told him. "A Japanese government agent approached me yesterday. She works for their Ministry of News and Media. She said they want to work with me."

Alex's face turned serious. He held a pen to his chin. "Did she threaten you?"

"They did not. She tried to bribe me though. She hinted her government might offer me protection from being stateless, and she told me I can ask her for whatever I want."

"What are you going to tell her?"

"I was going to tell her no. I'm not going to become a tool for

Japan. But it's all irrelevant anyway. I told my boss, Charlie, what happened, and he reassigned me. From now on, I'll be reporting society and entertainment news."

"Society and entertainment news?" Alex laughed.

"It's not funny!" Eden glared at him.

"All right, all right. I'm sorry." He stopped laughing. "Looks like you have your own Mr. Yamato now."

"Yes, and I don't like it one bit."

Alex flipped his pen. "Your boss sounds like a sap. Is he that afraid to say no to the Japs?"

"Charlie's not a sap. He just feels responsible for protecting the staff, and he's looking out for me and my family. He doesn't want anything to happen to us." She dropped her eyes to the only photo he kept on his desk. It was a picture of his dog, a Labrador that had died two years ago. He told her that last time she visited. "I wish I could be like you and say anything I want without a care."

Alex studied her with a half-grin. "Maybe you can. Where there's a will, there's a way."

Eden gave him a side glance. "What do you mean?"

"Come work with me. We'll give you a pseudonym. You can investigate and report on anything you like. I'll broadcast your reports to the world. I'll even credit you to your pseudonym. Here's a name that'll get those Japs all steamed up. Matthew Perry."

"Matthew Perry?"

"Yeah, you know, the commodore who forced them to open their ports to the outside world in the 1850s? He brought them to their knees with guns and cannons when they were still fighting with swords. That'll make their blood boil. Wouldn't you like that?"

"I don't know . . ."

"Or better yet, Apollo. Apollo Perry! Those jackasses think

they're the source of the sun. We'll stake our own claim on the sun. That'll irritate them to no end. What do you say?"

Eden lowered her eyes. "I'm not sure."

"We should do it," Alex urged. "If you're worried about your safety, I'll take careful measures to not expose you. You can trust me on that."

"That's not the problem. I trust you."

"Then why hesitate?"

"I like working for the *China Press*. I don't want to abandon Charlie."

"That's too bad," Alex said, not hiding the disappointment in his voice. "If you change your mind, I'm right here."

Eden gave him a noncommittal smile. He didn't push her further but held her gaze. The tender curiosity in his eyes caught her off guard. She looked away to the mountainous stack of fan mail on his desk. "I should go. It looks like you have a lot of letters to get back to. Thanks for breaking your day to talk with me." She rose from her seat.

He threw a disinterested glance at the letters and stood up. "Anytime." His gentle tone of voice, so unlike how he spoke when he was on the air, felt a little too intimate. Quickly, she walked to the door.

"See you." She hurried off without waiting for his response and didn't slow her pace until she got outside.

What was she doing? She thought as she got on her bike. She was probably reading too much into everything. If she told anyone she thought Alex Mitchell might be interested in her, they'd laugh.

Even if it was true, getting involved with someone would be the last thing she wanted. From all appearances, she looked fine. Nobody knew a wound was still bleeding inside her. Blood no longer spilled from this wound, but it dripped. It'd drained all her emotions, and she had no more energy or love left for anyone else. The only thing she wanted now was to concentrate on her work and do something important with her life. Thanks to Hina Kata, now she couldn't do that either.

———————

Back at her building, Eden rang her neighbor's doorbell. From inside the apartment, Keiko looked out from the peephole, then unlocked and opened the door. "Eden?"

"Hello, Keiko, can we speak?"

"Sure." Keiko stepped to the side. "Come on in."

Eden entered and looked around. "Are Hiroshi and Thierry home?"

"No. Thierry's still at work. Hiroshi went out with his friends. Can I get you something to drink? A cup of tea? A glass of juice or Coca-Cola?"

"No, thank you. I came to give you a message to pass on to Hina."

Keiko stood and folded her hands.

"Can you please tell her there won't be any need for her to come and talk to me tomorrow. I won't be able to work with her and her Ministry."

"You won't?" Keiko furrowed her brows. "Why not?"

"I didn't bring this up yesterday because the decision wasn't finalized yet. You see, I won't be covering current events anymore. I'm being reassigned to report on society and entertainment news. I won't be able to help Hina in that position."

"Ahhh! I see." Keiko bobbed her head. "That's too bad. Hina will be very disappointed."

Eden responded with a cool smile. Actually, the one who looked genuinely disappointed was Keiko. It made her wonder. "Keiko, there wouldn't be any ramifications against you because I turned her down, would there?"

"Against me?" Keiko waved her hand. "No, no. Why would there be?" She smiled at Eden with her round, innocent eyes.

The smile looked too sweet. What was Keiko's real role in all this? Was she a pawn too? Or was she truly a willing participant? "Keiko, I just want to make sure Hina won't be upset at you because I said no."

Keiko cocked her head. She pursed her lips as if Eden had just told her something she'd never thought of. "Umm, thank you."

Thank you? That wasn't even an answer.

Sweet, demure Keiko. Who knew? It never occurred to Eden one could deflect people and deny her own accountability by embracing the role of a dumb woman.

She put on her own artificial smile. "Anyway, I'd appreciate you passing on the message."

"Of course." Keiko bowed and saw her out.

Back at her home, Eden took off her shoes and went to find her brother in his room. "Is that a new jigsaw puzzle?"

"Yes." He filled a piece in the center.

She sat down across from him on his bed. "Joshua, I know you and Hiroshi are very good friends."

"Yes."

"You know I like Hiroshi too."

"Yes?"

"You're aware China and Japan are at war."

"Yes. So?"

"I'm worried that Hiroshi might be used by other people."

"Used by people? Who?"

"The Japanese government?"

"What would they use him for?" Joshua made a face. He looked at her as though she had gone mad.

"I don't know," Eden said. She did know, but she didn't want to say too much.

"Hiroshi's fourteen. Why would anyone want to use him for

anything?" He picked up another piece of the puzzle and connected it to the edge.

"All the same. Be careful what you say around him. Don't tell him too much about yourself, or Papa and Mama, or me. Would you do that?"

"Okay." Joshua rolled his eyes.

Eden returned to the living room. Her mother came out of the kitchen. "We're having lamb for dinner tonight." She began to set the table.

"Sounds good," Eden said. "Mother, I've been thinking. Remember I told you Ava Simms left me the keys to her apartment? I think I'll take advantage of it and stay overnight there sometimes."

"Oh?" Mrs. Levine put down the plates. "How come?"

"I've been reassigned at work." Eden shrugged, covering herself with a casual smile. "I'll be covering society and entertainment news from now on. I expect I'll be staying out late sometimes. This way I won't be waking you all up if I come home after you've gone to sleep."

"Reassigned at work?" Mrs. Levine frowned. "What's that all about? And a single woman spending the night out alone? I'm not sure."

"Mother! I'll be at Ava's apartment, that's all. I won't be doing anything improper. Her apartment building is one of the most desirable properties in town. There are doormen twenty-four hours a day. You can always call there and find me if you want."

"Even so. How late would you have to stay out at night? Would it be safe? Will anyone be escorting you? Isn't it too much for your paper to assign a woman to do work where she has to run around at night?"

"I'll be fine," Eden said. "I'll be going to very exclusive social functions and public events. A lot of people would pay tons to get into the places I'll be going to."

Mrs. Levine hesitated, then grudgingly picked up the utensils. "I don't like this, but—ask your father."

"Thanks, Mother!" Eden gave her mother a hug. Her father was the easier one to convince. And if only her mother knew. With Keiko and her fellow Japanese next door, she'd be safer and better off if she was somewhere else.

Mrs. Levine gave her a feigned look of reproach. "Finish setting the table. I'll get the food ready." She returned to the kitchen.

The apartment door unlocked and Dr. Levine entered. He took off his hat. "Is everybody home?"

"Papa," Eden greeted him.

"Smells like lamb chops." He sat down at the sofa and opened his briefcase on the coffee table. "Look what I got." He pulled out a black notebook. "It's the notebook I use to keep records of all my Chinese patients."

Eden's heart nearly stopped. "How'd you get it?"

"Clark Yuan sent his clerk to bring it to me today."

"He did?" Eden asked, trying to conceal the tremble in her voice.

"Did you ask him to help us find the culprits?"

"I might have mentioned something. I don't remember." She busied herself setting the table so her father wouldn't see her hands shake and her lips quiver.

"His clerk said Clark was able to retrieve this. He didn't tell me how. Clark's on the SMC, isn't he? He must've gotten the higher-ups at the police department to help. He also sent me a note telling me to lock the address book in a safe place."

"Did he?" Eden asked. "You should listen to him then." She laid down the spoons. So Clark didn't only convince Shen Yi to end her threat and release the man she was holding hostage. He got her to return the notebook.

And what a steep price they had to pay.

"Did you know Clark got married?" Dr. Levine asked.

"Married?" Eden swung around.

"Yes. I asked his clerk how Clark and his family are doing. He said Clark got married and he had a huge wedding. Even the office workers and household staff were invited to the banquet. The guy wouldn't stop talking about the banquet. He said employers don't usually invite the whole staff to the celebration."

All the pain Eden felt when she left him came flooding back. What did Clark do? How could he get married so soon? "Who's the bride, did he say?"

"A Chinese girl. The clerk said she's very pretty. He said she and Clark look very good together."

"Really?" Eden squeezed her shoulders. "I'm very happy for them then." She took a deep breath and rubbed her forehead. "Papa, I'm not feeling very well. I feel a headache coming on. I'm going to my room to lie down."

"Are you all right? Do you need any medicine?"

"No. I just need to lie down." She lowered her hand from her forehead to cover her face and went into her room.

Once in her room, she locked the door and fell on her bed. The tears she was holding back came rushing out. Had he forgotten her already? How could he put their feelings for each other behind him so quickly and marry another woman?

Did his mother put him up to it? No. It couldn't be. All this time, he adamantly refused to marry Shen Yi because it wasn't his own choice. He defied his parents then. Why would he change now to bend to his mother's wishes? He wouldn't. His marriage had to be something he wanted.

Perhaps he rushed into a marriage because he was too heartbroken? Maybe getting married was the only way he could forget about her.

Eden laughed at herself. How she wanted to think that was the case. But Clark wasn't irrational like that. If Clark made a decision to marry, then there was only one reason. He decided to move on.

She brushed away her hair that had fallen over her face and dropped her hand on the tear-soaked pillow. Why was she upset? Either way, they could no longer be together, and she was the one who made the decision for them to separate. What did it matter whether he moved on now or later?

But it did matter, because now, it felt ever more real that they were truly over. All that they could have had together would never, ever be.

Lying still, she let her tears fall. If she shed enough tears, maybe they would wash her pain away.

18

THE WHITE FOX

BACK WHEN CLARK got his father a seat on the Shanghai Municipal Council, better known to people as the SMC, the Council was more a gentlemen's club than a typical government body. From the way his father talked about it, their meetings sounded more like a social gathering of men from the city's list of who's who. Aside from setting local policies for the International Settlement, the meetings were where the city's richest and most powerful hobnobbed and rubbed shoulders with each other to get things done.

Of course, only the wealthiest Shanghailanders could ever hope to join the Council, and only the ratepayers who owned and paid taxes on land had the power to decide who would rule the Settlement when election time for the Council came around.

"Could the system be any different?" Clark's father once discussed this with him in an idle chat.

"No. Not currently. I don't see how," Clark remembered saying himself. This city had three million people, and a large number of them were transients. They couldn't give the right to vote to people who had no vested interest in the city. Many were also illiterate. They wouldn't know who to vote for or even how to cast a vote.

An argument could be made that the ratepayers' right to vote was only fair since they were the only ones in the International Settlement who paid taxes, and their tax dollars funded public services for everyone in the city. But fairness was never a real concern, or else why would the make-up of the Council be fixed by nationalities to guarantee that power would remain in the hands of the West? The British and the American interests were often aligned. The interests of the Chinese and the Japanese never were.

Still, they all shared the fundamental need of protecting their wealth, and no serious disagreement ever got in the way of everyone's desire to make a profit.

All that had changed now. The SMC meetings Clark attended never felt anything like a social gathering. They felt like a game. The balance of powers teetered on the brink. Beneath the surface, everyone was always testing the ground to see where the line stood.

In the chamber of the SMC, Clark sat seething as the Japanese Council member Hayashi Yukichi said again he would not vote for the proposal to create a jobs program for the Chinese refugees who had fled into the International Settlement. His compatriot, Okamoto Izamu, the other Japanese representative on the Council, backed him on every point. Okamoto always did that. All he ever did was to support Hayashi with a second vote.

There wouldn't have been so many jobless and homeless refugees in the International Settlement in the first place if Japan hadn't attacked the city. And now, these fiends wouldn't even let the Council dole out a little cash to ease their plight.

Clark raised his hand to speak. "Hayashisan, fifty thousand dollars to create jobs to clean the streets and fix the roads isn't a huge amount. Even if you don't care about the people in dire need of making a living, our city's environment's taken a toll. We can all benefit from the extra help."

The seventy-year-old man sat calmly. The white hair of his eyebrows didn't even twitch. "These people are not our responsibility. If we use our funds for them, we might have to raise taxes later. The ratepayers in my people's sector would not like that."

"And you don't think we should try to make the Settlement a safer and more sanitary place? You all live here too."

Hayashi sat unmoved. "It would be better if the refugees went back to where they belong. The incident from last year is over now. The new Chinese Provisional Government has restored order. If these refugees would go home, everything in the International Settlement would return to normal and there will be no need to add new jobs." He glanced at his younger compatriot, who was closer to Clark's age. "Okamotosan, don't you agree?"

"Yes, yes," Okamoto answered like a parrot.

Clark flashed them a look of contempt. These two with hearts of wolves and lungs of dogs. "Hayashisan, Okamotosan, you both know very well why the refugees won't return to their homes. Your suggestion is preposterous. You said the ratepayers in your sector are worried about a tax increase. Are you sure you want to talk about that? Because by my count, half of all the Japanese ratepayers have defaulted on their taxes this year. Shall we put it on our agenda to go after them? Maybe if they all pay what they owe, we'll have more than enough to fund the jobs program."

Hayashi shot him a glare.

Undeterred, Clark glared back.

"Gentlemen," said Cornell Franklin at the head of the table, "let's stay on topic. We're not here to discuss relocation of the refugees or tax collection today."

"That's right," Tony Keswick, of the Jardine Matheson Group, chimed in. Though only thirty-five years old and not the official head of the SMC, the young tycoon wielded the most influence on how things were run. His family's wealth and close ties with the British government gave him real power. "I don't see any good reason for us to get into a disagreement on this issue. How about this? I will personally contribute fifty thousand dollars to back this program. Will that solve the funding problem? Can we then vote on approving the program?"

Clark waited to see the two Japanese members' reactions. Tony Keswick shouldn't have to offer up his own money. His company was taking huge losses this year too because of the Japanese's war on China. How annoying it was to watch even him tiptoeing around the very people who were the root of everyone's problems.

The Japanese had only two votes anyway. They could easily outvote them. Yet, an unspoken agreement seemed to have taken hold. All the non-Japanese members were now always careful not to cause Hayashi and Okamoto to lose face.

Slowly, Hayashi turned his eyes to the tycoon. "Sir Keswick, if we have extra funds, then we need to use it to address a more pressing concern."

"Yes? What concern?" Keswick asked.

"Last month, the Council agreed the Shanghai Municipal Police would promote two Japanese inspectors to chief inspectors. We also agreed there would be four promotions of Japanese at the inspector levels, and ten Japanese constables to sergeants. None of this has happened. Why is the SMP dragging its feet?" Hayashi asked.

"I don't think they are—"

Hayashi interrupted him. "Crime is getting out of control. People don't feel safe."

"I couldn't agree more," Clark said. How nice of Hayashi to acknowledge they had a crime problem on their hands, given that the rise in crime was the Japanese's own doing. Their invasion of

Shanghai destroyed order in the city and opened the floodgate of drug dealing, kidnapping, and robberies.

Hayashi ignored him. "And the bombings on July 7."

Clark raised his eyebrow.

"Seven bombings in one day. Two Japanese civilians were killed. This was a blatant attack against Japan." Hayashi gave the entire table a stern look. "The Japanese people need better protection and assurance of security. The SMP's shoddy performance is shameful. They're clearly incapable of stemming terrorist attacks. Since they can't do their jobs properly, they need to promote and hire the Japanese personnel we requested immediately. Their delay in doing what the Council has promised is unacceptable."

"Hayashisan," Cornell Franklin answered. "I know Commissioner Bourne is working diligently to strengthen the police force."

"Kenneth Bourne isn't doing what he should to look out for the safety of the Japanese residents. In fact, considering the current state of affairs, I can only conclude the SMP is harboring Chinese terrorists against innocent Japanese people running stores and shops, and people who are peacefully going about their lives."

"That's not a fair claim," Clark raised his voice.

"Gentlemen." Franklin held up his hands. "Hayashisan, I assure you Commissioner Bourne is fully committed to protecting people of all nationalities within the International Settlement, including the Japanese. He has an impeccable record. I can personally vouch for him the SMP is not harboring terrorists, nor would they let criminals go unpunished."

"Then as I said already, he's incompetent. He's overwhelmed. It is imperative that the SMP follow through with the promotions as we've agreed. Going forward, they should hire more Japanese police."

"Hire more Japanese police?" Clark asked.

"Yes. To ensure that the police force is acting fair and without bias. We're ready to recommend a slate of applicants from our gendarmerie to help expedite the process."

Clark tried to catch Franklin's eyes. Franklin had to know this was a ruse. Hayashi was trying to stack the SMP with his own recruits. Franklin couldn't accept this.

"Thank you, Hayashisan," Franklin said earnestly. "Your offer to help is much appreciated. However, to pass a resolution to hire more police today would be premature. We really ought to get Commissioner Bourne's input first. I assure you again, he's doing everything he can. Let me speak to him. If there is a need to hire more police, we will see to that."

"Very well," Hayashi replied in a more conciliatory tone. In no way was that a concession. Clark knew that. When Hayashi said "very well," all he meant was that it was very well for Franklin to think that way. That was how the Japanese side-stepped open conflict. This matter was not over.

Hayashi turned to Keswick. "Sir Keswick, if we do expand the police force, I think the money you proposed to contribute would be better spent on salaries and equipment for that purpose."

The room turned silent. Everyone gazed at Keswick to see what he would say.

Thankfully, Keswick still had some backbone. "I'm sorry, Hayashisan. My offer is only for creating temporary new jobs for the refugees. If the SMP needs to expand, perhaps we will have to consider a tax increase."

"Or collect all the unpaid taxes," Clark added.

Hayashi and Okamoto both glared at him, but he didn't care.

"All right." Franklin looked around the table. "If there's nothing else then, shall we cast our votes? All who are in favor of the work program for refugees, raise your hand and say 'aye'."

Everyone except Hayashi and Okamoto raised their hands. The Council's secretary, Godfrey Philips, recorded the votes into his notebook.

"The resolution passes," Franklin said. "Meeting is adjourned. Thank you for coming, gentlemen."

Clark got up, ready to leave, but Keswick called him back. "Can we please talk for a minute?"

Clark nodded and followed him to a private room in the chamber.

Keswick closed the door. "I noticed the animosity between you and Hayashi."

"Just me? Tony, they're trying to push you around too."

"I know."

"Then why don't you push back? They don't deserve the courtesy you're giving them."

"No, but I'd rather not test their resolve."

"Seriously? Are you afraid of them? You and all the Britons have so much at stake here. If anyone can take a stand in Shanghai, it's you."

"Me? Take a stand? With what?"

"Certainly your government would back you. I don't believe Chamberlain would send their troops to save us Chinese, but how could he not come to your aid? Your family's been here for three generations. Your company is your country's gateway to the East."

"Unfortunately, they won't," Keswick said. He slid his hands into his pockets. "Things have changed even from a few months ago. Chamberlain's got his hands full with Germany. He's meeting with Hitler next month in Munich. It is expected Hitler will be asking to annex part of Czechoslovakia. We've been watching the German troops mobilize along their western borders. If we don't agree to his demand, Europe will break out in war. If that happens, my country will direct all its resources to defending Europe."

Clark put his hands on his hips. "What do you think Chamberlain will do? Will he go to war with Hitler?"

"The word I hear is that he will make whatever concessions

are necessary. He will work to maintain peace at all costs, and he will do the same here."

"So that's it?" Clark asked. "The great British Empire will simply capitulate to anyone who decides to use force to take over the world?"

With his silence and the solemn look on his face, Keswick admitted as much. "This is only between you and me. My government's given me a clear directive. If Japan exhibits any sign of aggression against us, we're not to resist. We only have two battalions here. There will not be any more. This city is indefensible unless the Americans decide to step in."

"The Americans?" Clark's heart sank. He had long given up on that. Joseph Whitman, his friend and one-time liaison at the U.S. Consulate, had affirmed again and again the Americans had no intention of being drawn into any war overseas.

"I'm on your side," Keswick said. "I have as much to lose here as anyone if the International Settlement does not hold. We need to at least keep up a front. We can't test the status quo. As long as the Japanese believe there's a risk of Western retaliation, we'll still have some influence over them, and we can still make them play by our rules. We'll hold on this way as long as we can. Hopefully, if the problems in Europe can be contained, I can try persuading my government to give us more support."

Clark dropped his shoulders. An ironic smile slipped from his lips. All this Western glory displayed here for so many years. In the end, everything was a mirage.

"Work with me." Keswick moved a step closer to him. "We haven't lost everything yet."

They hadn't? Clark swayed back. "I'll see you at the next meeting." He opened the door and walked out.

With a heavy heart, Clark left the SMC building and returned home. When he arrived, a crew of men was delivering a new bed into his room.

"What's going on?" He sidestepped the ropes and plastic wrappings on the floor and the men leaving the room.

Wen-Ying turned around. Next to her, Xiu-Qing stood shyly with her eyes down.

"Ge," Wen-Ying said, "you're back."

Clark walked to the new piece of furniture tucked along the side of the room. "What's all this?"

"I arranged to buy you a new bed." Wen-Ying tipped her head at the couch. "That isn't a long-term solution."

Clark eased. Nothing ever got past his smart sister. He glanced at Xiu-Qing, who was still too embarrassed to look at him. "How did you explain this to Ma?" he asked Wen-Ying.

"I told her you toss and turn too much at night. You're disturbing Xiu-Qing's sleep. I told her we should get you another bed until the child is born. As soon as she heard you're disturbing her grandchild, she hustled me to hurry up and solve the problem."

"Good thing you thought of it." Clark chuckled and scratched his head.

"Actually," Xiu-Qing spoke up, "Guo-Hui Ge needs to sleep well. He goes to work so early in the morning. All these nights he had to sleep on the sofa, I really feel awful."

"No need to say that." Clark waved his hand.

"Really, Guo-Hui Ge, Wen-Ying, I don't know how to ever thank you both."

"At least you two's little charade is making Ma happy," Wen-Ying said. "Poor Ma. Before you came here, she couldn't stop being depressed. Ba's death hit her very hard. She was afraid to leave the house too. For one thing, she's terrified it's unsafe, with all the new beggars, ronin, and Japanese soldiers on the streets. Another thing is, after so many people died from the Battle of

Shanghai, she truly believes there are thousands of ghosts roaming around. But now? For her grandchild, she has no choice but to go out and make plans."

The crew returned to pick up the bits and wrappings. In the hallway, Madam Yuan's excited voice came ringing out, "Xiu-Qing! Xiu-Qing!"

"Speaking of Cao Cao," Wen-Ying glanced at the door and laughed when Madam Yuan entered.

"Eh," Madam Yuan exclaimed, "you're all here. Xiu-Qing!"

"Yes, Popo," Xiu-Qing answered.

"Come, come. I just got back from Wing On with Mei Mei. We bought two dozen baby outfits. All made in France. Come and take a look." She grabbed Xiu-Qing's hand.

"Yes." Xiu-Qing gave Clark and Wen-Ying an apologetic smile and left with their mother to go downstairs.

When everyone was gone, Wen-Ying surveyed the room. "The new bed does make everything a little tight in here, but at least you can sleep better."

Clark nodded. "Thank you."

"Want to come try out your new mattress and see if you like it?" She lightly slapped the mattress's top.

"Maybe later."

"Yes, we should have the maids come and put new sheets on it first." She picked up a pillow and tossed it onto the new bed. He walked toward the dresser and loosened his tie.

"Ge?" Wen-Ying furrowed her brows. "Are you okay? Why are you so glum?"

"I just came back from an SMC meeting," he said. "Remember you told me the British government has been telling Ambassador Kerr to yield to the Japanese? John Keswick told me privately after the meeting the British won't be sending any troops here, not even to defend their own people."

Wen-Ying listened. The news didn't rattle her the way it upset him.

"He said his government's too tied up dealing with Adolph Hitler."

Deep in thought, Wen-Ying ran her hand along the edge of the new bed. "I never considered relying on the Western countries to save us as a solution. Chinese land must be defended by Chinese people. If those of us who are committed to fighting stay united in our spirits, we can still win."

"I hope so."

"Also, Western aid doesn't necessarily have to come from their governments. Sometimes, we can rely on those who would help us because they're our friends."

Friends? That was a change in tune from her. Wen-Ying had never spoken well of foreigners before. "Who are you talking about?"

"Do you remember Greg Dawson?"

"The American pilot? Yes, I remember him." When Clark was still working for the KMT, Dawson used to help him fly supplies to the Chinese army.

"After the war broke out, Greg joined up with a former American army captain named Claire Chenault. They formed a band of American pilots in Hankow called the 14th Volunteer Bombardment Squadron. They've been retaliating against the Japanese air force ever since. When the year began, they bombed out the Japanese troops in Loyang. Sadly, the squadron disbanded in March when most of their planes were shot down. He's still there though. Sometimes, the KMT hires Soviet bombers for air defense and he'd join up with them. Other times, he's in Kunming training Chinese pilots."

"How do you know all this?" Clark asked. "Do you still keep in touch with him?"

"I do." Wen-Ying smiled. "He writes to me."

"Wait. You know he likes you." He squinted at her. "Have you decided to give him a chance?"

"What are you talking about?" Wen-Ying retorted. "Of course

not. I keep in touch with him because we might have a use for him someday. He also sends me news about what's going on out west in Xinjiang. I know you've always been more open to trusting Westerners than me. I only wanted to tell you, you're not entirely wrong."

He appreciated her good intentions to brighten his spirits, but he worried about Greg. The American pilot was a straight, simple fella. He was no match for his sister. "Wen-Ying, Greg's a good man. I hope you won't do anything to take advantage of him."

She lowered her stare. "I won't if it's not necessary."

Clark started to argue, then shook his head. "You yourself be mindful to do what's right then."

"I will." She came closer to him. "However, looking at our situation now, sometimes it's hard to say what's right and what's wrong. The International Settlement and the French Concession are all surrounded by hostility. We're living on a lone, isolated island. Japan is only waiting for its chance. To save what we still have, we have to fight fire with fire. It's our only path left. We'll take down their leaders. We'll eliminate any traitors who help them. We can't spare anyone. Do you understand that?"

He looked into the mirror beside the dresser. "Yes."

On this lone island, they were on their own.

19

SMOKE SCREENS AND SILVER SCREENS

EDEN COULDN'T REMEMBER BEING LESS enthused about a work assignment than the one she'd been given today since she started working for the *China Press*. How did she, in two months' time, go from reporting on rapes, murders, war, and politics, to interviewing a movie starlet?

How could she take her assignment seriously anyway? She'd been waiting for over an hour, and the starlet wasn't even here. The tea that the amah brought her had turned cold, and she was tired of staring at the four pastel walls. The only sign of the actress was her giant poster on the wall.

Eden got up and found the actress's personal secretary in the den listening to the radio. "Excuse me."

The secretary, Ines, a Eurasian of Portuguese descent, lowered the radio volume. "Yes?"

"Would you please tell Miss Ye I'm leaving? I'm going back to my office."

"You want to leave?" Ines jumped up. "You can't leave. Miss Ye's a big star. If she comes back and you're not here, she'll be very angry."

"Will she?" Eden smirked. "That's too bad. I'm not sitting here waiting all day."

"If you leave, she'll never grant an interview with your paper again."

"Is that so? Fine. That will be her loss." Eden turned around. Charlie would have to do without this one. Coddling celebrities wasn't her forte.

Just then, the front door opened. Ye Ting, dressed in a gold *qipao* embroidered with small red camellias and red trim, sauntered in. Behind her, a Chinese man in round-rimmed glasses and a Western suit directed two runners in concierge uniforms to take the loads of shopping bags to the back.

Ye Ting gave Eden a quick, disinterested glance, then plopped herself onto the sofa and called for her amah in Chinese. The man in the Western suit came toward Eden. "You must be Miss Levine! I'm Michael, Miss Ye Ting's agent. Thank you for coming this afternoon."

"The afternoon's almost over," Eden said.

Michael laughed. From the kitchen, the amah brought out a tray of tea and roasted watermelon seeds. Ye Ting picked up a cup and blew the surface of the tea before taking a sip.

"Please, come sit down." Michael invited Eden to the sofa.

Eden flicked her eyes. She truly was ready to walk out. Only her sense of professionalism steered her back. She sat down across from the actress and took out her notebook. "Hello, Miss Ye."

Ye Ting smiled. Her smile was surprisingly sweet. Sweet enough that even Eden herself felt half her annoyance dissipate.

Michael said to Ye Ting. "This is Miss Eden Levine from the *China Press.*"

"I know." Ye Ting put down her tea. Up close, she had a very appealing face, youthful and innocent. Almost vulnerable, except she wasn't. Her eyes glinted like a wildcat's, unbridled, alert, and untamed.

She offered Eden the plate of watermelon seeds. "Want some?"

"No, thank you," Eden said.

Ye Ting shrugged. She put down the plate of seeds. Eden opened her notebook. The actress's profile said she was twenty years old. Born in Suzhou and grew up in Shanghai, she was a rising star currently under contract with the Jinxing Film Company. Her upcoming movie, *Song of Peonies,* would be released next month in October. Her publicist claimed this would be the best Chinese movie of 1938, and this was her first time interviewing with an English press agent.

"Shall we begin?" Eden asked.

"Okay."

"Miss Ye, where did you learn to speak English?"

"I took private lessons." Ye Ting smiled. She picked up a watermelon seed, cracked it between her front teeth, then spit the shell into an empty bowl. "One day, I want to become a Hollywood actress. That's why I learned English." She washed the seed down with a gulp of tea, then sat back and crossed her legs. "I studied very hard."

"Uh-huh," Eden moved her eyes from the seed to Ye Ting's feet. Considering the way the actress was jiggling her foot and dangling her shoe from her toes, Eden didn't see how she could sit still and study.

"I watch a lot of American films too. I have friends in the U.S. Marines. They take me to see movies."

The Marines. Eden held the tip of her pen to her chin. That was how Ye Ting picked up her English. Ye Ting probably worked as a taxi dancer or sing-song girl before she became an actress.

No point in digging out the girl's less than glorious past. "How did you get into the movie industry?" Eden asked.

"When I was seventeen, a friend introduced me to Lianhua Film Company. Lianhua was a shitty company. They didn't give me good roles. When my contract expired, I joined Jinxing.

Jinxing treats me much better. As soon as I signed with them, they put me in a starring role. Good thing I did too. Lianhua closed down when Japan attacked China." She opened her sandalwood fan and fanned herself. "I'm hungry. These watermelon seeds are too dry. I want some macarons. Amah!" She called out to the maid, who came hurried in. Ye Ting spoke to her in Chinese, but the maid kept repeating "mei you," which Eden recognized to mean "don't have" in Chinese.

Pouting, Ye Ting shut her fan. "I want macarons." She pointed her fan at her agent. "Michael, go buy me some macarons."

"Me?" Michael pointed at himself. "Why not let Amah go?"

"Amah doesn't know how to buy French desserts. She doesn't know what I want. I want the French lemon-flavored ones, and mimosa. From Cafe Palais."

"But Miss Ye," Michael said, "I promised Mr. Luo I would be here for this interview. He'll be furious if he finds out I'm not here."

"I want macarons!" Ye Ting crossed her arms. "If you don't go get them for me, I will tell him you mistreated me. I'll tell him I want you fired."

"Okay, okay." Michael held up his hands. "I'll go. I'll go now."

"Hurry!" Ye Ting glared. Quickly, Michael jumped to his feet. He tugged his suit and went out the door.

On the couch, Ye Ting watched him leave with a wry smile. When he was gone, she asked Eden, "You think I'm a bitch, don't you?"

Eden balked. The words that came out of this girl's mouth!

Ye Ting opened her fan again. "He's an ass head. You should see how mean he was to me when I was still a nobody. But now, he needs me, so he follows me like a dog."

Eden rested the tip of her pen on her notebook. "If you don't like him, why don't you fire him?"

Ye Ting held her fan against her chest. Ever so slightly, Ye Ting's mouth twitched. "Many things aren't in our control anymore," she muttered. "He's boring. Let's not talk about him. Ask me another question."

"All right." Eden scanned the actress's profile again. Her eyes stopped at the name Luo Ce-Xi, Ye Ting's boyfriend. Financier. Supporter of arts and films. Son of the new Minister of Finance of the Provisional Government of China.

Provisional Government? Eden looked up. Ye Ting's boyfriend's father was a collaborator? Was he also a collaborator? Was Ye Ting?

Keeping her expression neutral, Eden asked, "Michael mentioned Mr. Luo just now. Was he talking about Mr. Luo Ce-Xi, your boyfriend?"

"Him? Yeah," Ye Ting said. The mention of Luo's name elicited no particular reaction from her. "Oh no, I almost forgot. I have to go with him tonight to have dinner with those *riben gui*."

Riben gui? Japanese demons?

Before Eden could ask her follow-up question, Ye Ting called out, "Ines!"

Her secretary rushed in. "Yes, Miss Ye."

"Has the tailor delivered my dress for tonight yet?"

"No, Miss Ye."

Ye Ting scowled. She checked her watch. "They're late. Can you go and pick it up?"

"Yes, Miss Ye. I'll go immediately." Ines bowed, then hurried back to retrieve her purse and left.

"Can't rely on anybody nowadays." Ye Ting fanned herself. "What were we talking about?"

"Mr. Luo, your boyfriend," Eden said, careful not to reveal her own thoughts. Her reporter's instinct detected a story. "Sounds like you two are having dinner with your Japanese friends tonight."

"Friends." Ye Ting arched her brow. "Yeah. They're the people who financed my next movie."

"The *Song of Peonies*?"

192

"That's the one. Do you know what it's about?"

"No." Eden hadn't even heard of it. The movie was made for a Chinese audience and would be shown in Chinese. "Can you tell me?"

"Oh, yes." Ye Ting bared her teeth with a big, exaggerated smile. "It's about a handsome Japanese doctor who came to work in China. His name is Haru. Haru's here to help modernize Chinese hospitals. I play Fen, a nurse whose brother is a resistance fighter. At first, Fen didn't want to work with Haru, even though Haru started pursuing her. But then, she saw how much he cared about the Chinese patients, and she had a change of heart. They started to fall in love, but she was afraid to openly admit her feelings because her brother and her family would be enraged if they knew. One day, her brother was injured from gunshots when he and his gang got into a fight with the Japanese soldiers. He was brought to the hospital, and Haru worked all night and saved his life. After that, Fen and her brother realized continuing the violence would only hurt many more people. They decided to work with Haru to spread peace through the country." Ye Ting stopped. She crossed her arms. "They're going to ruin my career."

Eden paused her pen. "What do you mean?"

"Sorry. I made a mistake. I shouldn't have said that. I should say, I hope this movie will help bring a message of peace, friendship, and harmony to the Chinese and Japanese people." She wrinkled her nose as she smiled.

"You're not fond of this movie, are you?" Eden asked.

Ye Ting pursed her lips. The wild glint in her eyes was pushing to break out.

Eden decided to push her limit. "This movie sounds like Japanese propaganda to me. Was it your choice to do this role? I can't imagine the Chinese audience will be very happy when they see this film."

Ye Ting uncrossed her arms. "What do you want me to say?

I'm not stupid. You're a reporter. If I say something like that and you put it in print, those sons of bitches will kill me."

"All right." Eden tried another tack. "But let me guess. You're a rising star. The Japanese see that the Chinese audience likes you. They decided to take advantage of you and use you to spread their propaganda. Your boyfriend's father is a Japanese collaborator, so to assist them, you have no choice but to go along. Am I correct?"

Ye Ting let slip a smile and held a finger over her lips. "Maybe. Maybe not. Either way, I don't have anything more to say about that." She tilted her head and studied Eden. "You're just like everybody else, aren't you? You think I'm stupid too. You're trying to trick me into saying bad things about them so you can print it in your newspaper. I won't fall for it."

Eden lowered her pen. "I don't think you're stupid. I think you're being put upon to do something you don't want to do. I don't think that's fair, and I sure wish I could help you tell the whole story because I don't think it's right what the Japanese are doing to your country. If I can report the truth of all the harm they're doing here, I would."

"You would?" Ye Ting asked. A mischievous smile came to her face. "Maybe I can help you with that."

"What do you mean?"

"I can't say anything bad about my movies, or why some people are making or funding them if it puts them in a bad light. But I know all the other shit they're up to. Luo Ce-Xi talks about it all the time. He likes to brag, that dirty fink. When he gets drunk, he would brag to his grease-ball friends about all his dirty schemes right in front of me. They don't even care if I know because they all think I'm just a bimb. If you don't let it on that I'm the one telling you all about their shit, I'll tell you everything I know."

"Seriously?" Eden asked, dumbfounded. "You're not worried you might get Mr. Luo into trouble? He's your boyfriend."

Ye Ting laughed. "Yeah, he's my boyfriend, officially. And no, I'm not worried. He deserves to eat shit for all the crap he put me through. By the way, in your article about me, why don't you write that we're growing apart because of my busy film schedule. Let him sweat a little." She giggled. "A hint about a breakup is always good publicity."

"Okay." Eden opened her notebook again. She narrowed her eyes at Ye Ting. "You really trust me?"

"Why wouldn't I?" Ye Ting asked, twirling a lock of her hair. "Look at your face. You're salivating. You want to know what I know. You wouldn't want to lose me as a secret source, would you?"

Eden stared at her, wide-eyed. This girl was much smarter than anyone thought. "No, you're right. I wouldn't."

"So, before we continue with the rest of the interview, how about I tell you about all about Luo Ce-Xi's counterfeit money scheme with the Japs." Ye Ting lowered her voice and began to tell Eden the lowdown of a racket no one at the *China Press* had ever heard about.

Eden scribbled as fast as she could. What an extraordinary turn. Her detour into entertainment reporting had just given her a direct line into Japan's criminal operations with the Chinese collaborators. Now all she had to do was to convince Charlie to let her return to reporting hard news.

Thanks to Alex Mitchell, she had just the right idea how.

THE WHITE DRUG

THE CHAMBER of Golden Clouds was still blocks away. But already, the lower-rung prostitutes were stalking the streets. Keeping a casual pace, Clark checked out the Chinese ones in their raggedy *qipao* waving their fans and batting their eyes. On these blocks surrounding the Great Western Road, information was currency, and anyone could be watching him.

This was what this area had become. The hodgepodge of bars, opium dens, casinos, and dancehalls had all opened only this year. Not even Blood Alley could compare to this place, which now had its own notorious name, the Badlands.

"Hello, darling." A white Russian girl walked past him and pulled her already short skirt up another inch.

Clark flicked his eyes at her thigh and moved away. These girls were getting bolder. They felt no shame if they openly hawked their wares.

At the intersection, a peddler ran after him. "Boss! Boss!" He flashed in his hand a packet the size of a piece of Wrigley's chewing gum. "Ten cents."

Clark quickened his steps. The man followed, matching his pace. "Ten cents. Ten cents."

The man wouldn't relent. Clark tipped his hat lower over his face and scooted into the first pub he saw, a hole-in-the-wall joint where men ran their own private poker games and huddled with their honeys of the hour.

Casually, he walked over to the bar. At the other end, the two men smoking cigars on the stools paid him no heed. The bartender poured them each another shot as the voice of Alex Mitchell ranted on the radio.

Let me tell you, it is a travesty! An absolute travesty what Chamberlain did this week in Munich. He calls that agreement he signed with Hitler a symbol of Anglo-German desire for peace. I call it a sellout. He sold out the people of Czechoslovakia to appease a beast. He betrayed their trust, and the trust of everyone around the world who believes in freedom and democracy . . .

Clark glanced at the door. Outside, the peddler had gone to hustle someone else.

It wasn't the hustling that prompted him to seek escape. He had to make sure the man was only a peddler and not an informant following him in disguise.

On the radio, Alex Mitchell continued his tirade.

So Chamberlain said, and I quote him here, 'This settlement of the Czechoslovakia problem which has now been achieved is, in my view, a prelude to a larger settlement in which all Europe may find peace.' What a bunch of bunkaroo. Does he honestly believe that? It really depresses me when someone in his position can be so naive. He thinks giving away a little piece of land in Czechoslovakia is going to satisfy the man who calls himself the Führer? I guarantee you not. Hitler, with his band of Nazis, is cancer. This cancer will continue to spread. Mark my words . . .

Cancer, Clark thought as he watched a rickshaw coolie hand his coins to the peddler in exchange for the packet that he himself had earlier refused. A cancer was growing right here and now. As if all the opium dens sprouting up in this area weren't bad enough, now this white drug—heroin—was flooding the streets. On every corner, someone was peddling this poison, and hardworking laborers like that coolie were succumbing en masse to its promise of a quick hit that would jolt their energy and ease their aches.

The Kuomintang wasn't perfect. With their hands bound to the local drug lords, their efforts to control drugs had limits. But still, they tried. When he first returned to China two years ago, the problem was contained. Addiction was subsiding. And now, what little they did achieve, the war had completely obliterated.

"What would you like?" the bartender asked Clark.

"Nothing, thank you." Clark left the pub and continued on his way to his appointment with Pearl.

In a narrow alley, a lone woman in a dirty, skimpy dress held out her hands. A prostitute on the verge of destitution. Her bony frame rocked left and right as she came forward. Clark moved farther away. She stopped and pushed back the clump of hair falling over her face, revealing her sallow skin and sunken cheeks.

A dope peddler on the corner noticed her and went toward her. They spoke for a moment. He handed her a small packet and they disappeared into the depths of the alley, where shadows veiled those who were left to rot.

Clark winced and walked on. Only when he reached the Chamber of Golden Clouds did he feel a temporary respite. In a private chamber away from the vices he'd just seen, he lamented, "I feel like every time I come here, this place degenerates even more."

"It is that way indeed," Pearl said. "Don't you know? The more crimes infest this place, the more money the Japanese demons can suck out of us. Last night, Nakano, the head of the Shanghai Supervised Amusement Department, came and paid me a visit."

"Shanghai Supervised Amusement Department?" Clark asked. "What is that?"

"It's a branch of the Japanese army. I sent my best girls to sit and drink with him and his men all night. He said this area's fostering too much crime, and his new department was set up to keep us safe." Pearl sneered. "So now, for our own protection, I have to turn a third of my profits over to them. A third from me, a third from the casino next door, a third from the nightclub across the street. When you add up a third from every nook and den, it becomes a hefty stash of cash, isn't that right?" She poured more Chinese yellow wine into their glasses. "Of course, crime won't stop. His branch depends on crime to thrive, so they'll have an excuse to continue to collect money from people like me."

Clark shook his head. "And yet shops like yours keep opening up."

"That's because they opened most of the new ones. They own all the new opium dens. You wouldn't know it though. They use Koreans as their fronts, and they make them do all their dirty work. When people complain, they'll just say it's the Koreans' fault."

"You're saying the Japanese are the ones feeding the white drugs to the market?"

"Yes. Up north in Shanhaikwan, they've set up hundreds of narcotic factories. That's where all the white drugs are coming from. They're all hidden in small houses on back streets. As soon as Juntong brings one down, those Japanese demons build another one up."

Clark sipped his drink. So that was how the Japanese raked in their cash. They sold drugs. They sucked money from their victims this way to fund their army, and a nation of addicts wouldn't have the strength to fight back.

Cancer.

Pearl lit a cigarette. "I have no choice but to pay up. Maybe now the ronin and Kenpeitai will quit coming around demanding I pay them protection money. We'll see if Nakano can at least stop them. Or is that my wishful thinking?"

Clark smiled. Of course they would still come. She didn't need him to tell her that.

"That Japanese lout," Pearl said, flicking off ashes from her cigarette into the ashtray. "After drinking all my wines and keeping my girls the whole evening, he and his thugs didn't pay the bill. He even shorted the girls. He tipped them with yen."

The yen, of course, were worthless. Neither Britain or the U.S. recognized the Japanese currency. In China, even the Japanese merchants themselves wouldn't take it.

But why worry about the yen when they could use drugs as their new currency?

"Never mind," Pearl said. "Let's talk about more serious matters. Dai Li has a job for you."

"What is it?"

"He wants to recruit a new cadre of resistance fighters in Shanghai. He wants me to bring in former Green Gang members, and he wants you to identify prospects outside of this area. A lot of war refugees have been thrown out of work. He wants you to advertise and post notices for job openings. When people come to your company looking for jobs, he wants you to pick out the ones you think would be most suitable to be trained to join Juntong's action squads."

"Action squads? You mean assassins?"

"Yes. Find the ones who won't be afraid to shoot a gun or toss a grenade. Young graduates who are quick-witted, healthy, and hot-blooded would be good candidates. Gather their information and let me know who they are. Juntong will investigate them and recruit them to be their new trainees."

Young graduates. This was the future waiting for their strongest and brightest.

Clark hardened his heart. He closed his hand around his glass of wine. "Understood."

From the soulless streets of the Western Roads, Clark returned to the haven of his home. Eager to leave the weight of the Badlands behind, he joined his mother and Xiu-Qing when the maid brought out a tray of special broth.

His mother took a bowl from the tray and gave it to him. "I told Wu to make this black-boned chicken and mountain yam soup today. Black-boned chicken nourishes life, and mountain yam can calm fetuses. Here, Xiu-Qing, you should have more." She handed a fuller bowl to Xiu-Qing.

Xiu-Qing took the bowl with both hands. "Popo, you're too kind to me."

"No need to say that. We're one family," Madam Yuan told her, then griped to Clark, "Wu asked to resign today."

"Our cook wants to resign?" Clark lowered his spoon. "Why? He's been working for us for six years." He was a darn good cook too.

"He said a Japanese colonel wants to hire him. That colonel offered to pay triple what we pay him. I had to agree to match his pay to convince him to stay. I tell you, if we weren't about to have a child, I would've told him to go and go fast. I don't want to retain someone with no loyalty either."

Clark put down his bowl. "How could he want to go work for the Japanese? And why would they want to pay so much to hire him?"

"Because he cooks well. He makes dishes as good as restaurant chefs. That's what we get for paying all that money for him to take cooking classes. These Japanese are pillaging our best workers. Madam Kong's driver got hired away by a Japanese company director. People now have no loyalty. They're only loyal to money."

Clark sighed. He didn't contradict his mother. Although, could they blame the workers? The price of everything was tripling. Quadrupling. How much longer could they continue if they couldn't make enough wages?

"Never mind," Madam Yuan said. "Let's not talk about unpleasant things anymore. Why don't we talk about what name we should give the baby? It would be so much better if your father was still here. I thought about this back and forth. I still can't think of a good one."

Clark glanced at Xiu-Qing. What an oversight. With so much occupying his mind, he hadn't even thought about a name.

Xiu-Qing smiled at him. His heart softened as she laid her hand lightly on her abdomen. The child wasn't his, but the responsibility of being his father was. He needed to remember that.

The child's name though . . . he hadn't even thought of himself as someone entitled to give the child his name. "Ma, we still have time. We'll think of one slowly."

"All right." Madam Yuan folded her hands. "We also need to start planning for the child's full-month banquet."

"That would be good," Clark said. Planning the traditional banquet to celebrate the baby reaching one month old would keep his mother busy and happy.

The doorbell rang. A houseboy opened the door and brought in an unexpected guest. Clark immediately stood up and went to the front entrance. "Zhou Ke-Hao!"

"Young Master Yuan," said the police officer. Two years ago, Zhou, who worked in the Old City in the Chinese sector before the Japanese occupation, helped save Eden from being charged after street scammers falsely accused her of harming a child.

Clark warmly shook his hand. "We haven't seen each other for so long." Since Japan took over Old City, they had lost touch.

"So sorry to bother you at this late hour."

"No problem," Clark said. "Come on in. My mother and wife are here." He pointed to the living room.

"No." Zhou held up his hand. "Young Master Yuan, I came to speak with you alone."

Clark noted his friend's solemn face. "Of course." He glanced over his shoulder at his mother and Xiu-Qing. "Come with me."

He led Zhou to their smaller sitting room, then closed the door and invited Zhou to sit. "I'm so glad to see you again. I've been so worried about you all along. All the old administrations are gone. I didn't even know how to find you."

"After the Battle of Shanghai, my band of brothers at the Public Security Bureau became virtually homeless. Some escaped south with their families. Others disappeared. When things calmed down, a group of us gathered to talk about what to do. We're all hot-blooded men. We cannot accept what Japan has done. Rather than suffering humiliation to survive, we decided we must resist. We formed a covert group. We call ourselves the Whangpoo Special Task Brigade. These last six months, we've been coordinating attacks against the enemy's side."

"How many of you are there?"

"Thirty-two people. We salvaged all the firearms we had and acquired whatever weapons we could get our hands on. We've got Mauser pistols and hand grenades stored in a secret location." Zhou looked down at his loosely clasped hands. "This is the reason I've come. We're running short on ammunition. We barely have money to feed ourselves. When we could find odd temporary jobs, we gave over most of our money to help the Brigade, but it's not enough. I hope you can give us some support." He looked at Clark, his eyes filled with desperation and hope.

"Zhou," Clark said. "You should've come to me sooner."

Zhou sighed with relief.

"Actually, I'm also working with Juntong to resist Japan," Clark told him.

"You too?" Zhou's face brightened.

"Yes," Clark said. He thought back to his talk with Pearl earlier in the evening. "Juntong is expanding its operations in Shanghai. Under them, a new national salvation movement is underway in Occupied China and Free China. If you really want to succeed, you ought to ally with them. That way, you'll not only have my financial support, but also more efficient means of obtaining arms and access to intelligence."

"Really?" Zhou sat up. But then, a shade of doubt came to this face. "Juntong is a branch of the KMT. One of our members belongs to the Communist Party. I'm afraid Juntong won't accept him, and he won't agree."

Clark frowned. "Zhou, at this time, how can we continue to let party divisions hinder us? Even Chiang Kai-Shek himself has publicly said he'd unite with Mao and the Communist Party. If you can persuade your brother, I will handle Juntong on my end."

"Then . . ."

"Don't hesitate anymore. The resistance needs help. The people in the city need help. To have the help of elite fighters like you would be even better."

"All right," Zhou said with a firm nod. "I trust you. I'll go talk to him. If we can strike at the enemy's side, then everything would be worth it."

21

APOLLO EIRENE

"WHAT IS THIS?" Charlie asked when Eden put the two articles she wrote on his desk. Ignoring the one she had written which profiled Ye Ting, the next queen of the Chinese silver screen, he picked up the one titled "Blinders Over Western Eyes."

"It's an article I wrote about how the Japanese are running a racket selling counterfeit money," Eden said.

"Eden." Charlie dropped the article back onto the desk. "I thought we agreed. You're not to put yourself out there reporting hard news."

"I know. That's why I used a pseudonym."

He held up the article again and read the byline. "Apollo Eirene?"

"Yes." Eden smiled and lifted her head. Apollo, the Greek sun god, like Alex Mitchell suggested. "Eirene" was the Greek goddess of peace.

Charlie read the beginning of the article. "How did you find out about this?"

"Since you asked," Eden said and enthusiastically took a seat, "when I was interviewing Ye Ting, I found out she knows everything about the Japanese's racketeering activities. Their

Chinese collaborators are deep in on it too. Luo Ce-Xi, her boyfriend and movie producer, is a key person in the scheme. He's flushing the market with fake cash."

"Ye Ting told you about this?" Charlie looked at her with his eyes askance. "Why would she expose her own boyfriend?"

"They're not really going with each other. They were, but not anymore. Their relationship is only to give her fans something to gossip about."

"Still, I don't understand. Why would she tell you all this?"

"Because she wants to get back at Luo. Luo's forcing her to make propaganda movies for Japan. She doesn't like that because that makes her look like a traitor to her fans, but she has no choice. This is her way of taking revenge. She doesn't even care if he gets arrested and thrown in jail. If she's freed of him, she can sign with another studio and make the kind of movies she really wants to make."

"Huh." Charlie ran his eyes down the first page of the article again. "I don't know . . ."

"Charlie," Eden pleaded, "I know you worry about my safety. I've found a way to get around that now. And you need me. Ye Ting's too good a source to lose. Luo and the goons he runs with think she's a tomato. They don't take her seriously and they think no one else would either, so their lips are loose around her. But she's a lot smarter than they think. With her in our corner, we're going to have a lot of juicy stories to tell."

Charlie crossed his arms and scowled. "I'm not comfortable with you using a pseudonym. It goes against our credibility. When we put our name on something, we stand behind what we said. We hold ourselves accountable. A pseudonym . . . anyone can make an allegation if they don't have to deal with the consequences."

Eden tightened her lips. "I know what you're saying. But Charlie, look at all the propaganda circulating around us. What's a pseudonym compared to that? Who's holding those liars accountable? We're living in a very dangerous time. We have a chance here to expose those who are destroying this city and hold them accountable. Do you really want to lose that chance because of a pseudonym? Besides, if the article is published by the *China Press*, wouldn't that already be a sign of accountability?"

Charlie picked up the article again. "So the Japanese are circulating fake money through casinos?"

"Yes. How it works is, a Japanese person would come to China and pose as a tourist. He would bring the counterfeit money with him and exchange it at a cheap rate to Luo and others like him. Luo would disseminate the fake money through his casinos and gambling houses. When someone wins a game, he would pay the winner with the fake money. Of course, if the house wins, the gamblers would be paying with real cash. This way, the house would lose nothing but would gain everything. At the end of each month, seventy percent of all the profits go back to the Japanese. Luo himself gets to keep thirty percent. The Japanese use the profits to buy oil and iron for their army."

"That's terrible." Charlie flipped the page and continued reading. "Unbelievable. The Chinese are funding their own enemy's war against them."

"I know," Eden said. "It's awful."

"And everything you said in this article checks out?"

"Oh, yes. One night, Ye Ting took me to one of Luo's higher-class casinos. You should've seen the crowd. She caused an uproar when she walked in. We played a few hands of blackjack. Since we were women and seemingly not the type who gambled much, the dealer let us win several hands to amuse us. The next day, I took the money we won to the bank. The bank officer said the bank notes were bogus. We went back to that casino a couple of times. She took me to two of his smaller gambling houses too. Every time, the same thing happened."

Charlie raised his brows. "What about the Japanese connection? Where's the proof Japan is the culprit behind this?"

"Ye Ting has proof. Luo Ce-Xi lost interest in her quite some time ago. He's only keeping her around because the Chinese movie audience adores her and the Japanese want her to make pro-Japan movies for them. But she knew she had to get herself some insurance against him. One of her brothers is a security guard at Luo's casino. Her family depends on her and she got all her siblings jobs when she signed with his studio. Her brother secretly took pictures of the casino manager buying counterfeit cash from a Japanese crook named Hirata. She showed me the pictures. Hirata's been charged with presenting fake money at the Standard Chartered Bank in the past. This was before the war broke out. The SMP would have records of this."

Charlie reread her article, more closely this time.

"The Japanese have been running this gambit long before they started this war," Eden said. "They're not just fighting the war on battlefields. Their entire occupation was planned to ruin this country inside and out."

"Right under our noses." Charlie finished reading. "Those pictures you saw, can we get copies?"

"I can ask. So what do you say? Can I return to reporting hard news? Under my pseudonym?"

Charlie swiveled in his chair. He smiled. "Let me think about it."

"Come on, Charlie." Eden's shoulders sagged. "You know you won't give up a story this good. Besides, she has many more."

Dottie pounded on the door. "Charlie! Charlie!"

"What is it?" Charlie asked.

"I just got a phone call. The XMHA station's been bombed."

"XMHA?" Eden cried out.

"When?" Charlie asked.

"An hour ago," Dottie said.

Eden grabbed the armrest. "Charlie, that's Alex Mitchell's station."

"I know," Charlie said, his face pale. "Everyone said this

might happen, but I didn't think anyone would really have the gall to bomb a Western news office."

Eden stood up. "Alex Mitchell's my friend. I have to go see if he's okay."

"Go." Charlie nodded. "Be careful. Take Emmet with you. I want him to cover the story."

———

From the outside, Eden could see that the grenade had left a large hole in the second-floor wall at the spot that was once Alex's window. Along with Emmet, she walked over the scattered debris on the street. The shock had dissipated, and gawking pedestrians were starting to disperse. A medic closed the door of the ambulance and drove off without the siren. Eden caught one of the policemen returning to his car. "Sir, were there any casualties?"

"No," the policeman said. "They were lucky this time. No one got hurt."

Emmet followed up with the cop. "Sir, we're reporters with the *China Press*. Can you tell us what happened?"

The policeman began to recount the explosion. Eden took one look at him and Emmet, then left them and went into the building.

In the XMHA studio, Eden found Alex and his assistant Lucian surveying the wreckage of his office.

"Eden!" Alex gave her a big smile as soon as he saw her. "Fancy seeing you here."

Eden entered the room. "Thank goodness you two are all right."

"Thank goodness is right," Lucian said and bent down to pick up a stack of papers covered in dust. "No thanks to this one." He pointed the papers at Alex. "I don't know why I keep letting you talk me into staying here. If I don't get murdered as collateral damage, I'll die from a heart attack."

"This isn't my fault." Alex threw up his hands. "I'm the target victim here! What do you want me to do?"

"Maybe tone down your bragging? Try not to gloat to people who already hate you."

"I don't brag!"

Lucian glared at him.

"Okay, maybe I sounded a little too excited this morning. But can you blame me?"

Lucian muttered under his breath and returned to salvaging the typewriter and telephone on the floor.

Eden came closer to Alex. "What happened? Do you know who did this?"

Alex grinned. "The Japs sent their calling card, I guess."

"Why? Why now? Did you say something extraordinarily offensive?"

"What happened was our station is now operating on shortwave. That means many more people in cities and countries outside of Shanghai will hear my broadcast. Even their own soldiers fighting in Free China, and all the foreign embassies in Tokyo. The Mikado isn't happy at all about that."

Eden frowned and looked around the room. Alex's desk was destroyed. His chair was broken to pieces, and the side of the bookcase next to the window had been blown apart. "I can't believe they would attack a Western news outlet. Is no one safe?"

"We're safe," Alex said. "Everything's fine. No one was in this room when they hurled that grenade. They didn't even do anything that would stop me from broadcasting. All my recording equipment and my transmitter are in the back. Besides, we're insured. The damage here is minimal."

"Minimal?" Lucian plopped the typewriter onto the chair by the door. "Look at this mess. And the wall. Now we can't work in here until it's fixed."

"Yeah, that's inconvenient." Alex scratched the back of his head. "Eden, since you're here, why don't we go down to the gym at the racetrack and play a game of Jai Alai?"

"What?" Eden asked. "You want to go play Jai Alai? Now?"

"Yeah. Have you ever played?"

"No."

"It's a Basque game. I tried it last week for the first time. It's so much fun. No wonder it's becoming all the rage."

"You can't leave," Lucian said. He slapped the layer of dust on his pants, trying to clean it off.

"Why not?" Alex picked up his goggles and leather helmet, which escaped damage as they were left on top of the cabinet by the door away from the window. "You already said we can't work in here until this room is fixed."

"You gotta help clean up this place!" Lucian flapped his hand at the office items mixed with rubble and scraps of paper.

"But you'll do such a better job than me. I'll just add to the mess. What I ought to do is get out of your way. And Lucian, hire a couple of Chinese boys to help ya. They can use the money, I'm sure. Eden," he said and swung his arm around her waist, "come on, doll. Let's blow."

"But I'm not properly dressed—"

"You can watch then. It sure will be a lot more fun than watching Lucian here clean up."

Lucian opened his mouth and protested, "You're not going to—"

"I'll be back in time to go on the air at six." Alex waved goodbye. He pulled Eden out of the room and closed the door. "Ready for another motorcycle ride?"

22

KRISTALLNACHT

EARLY IN THE MORNING, Clark sat down at his desk. Another stack of contracts waited for his signature and approval, but those weren't the priority on his mind. He was expecting a call.

At eight o'clock sharp, his phone rang. Pearl was on the other line. "Good morning, Young Master Yuan."

"Good morning. You sound tired. Did you sleep last night?"

"Sleep?" Pearl laughed. "My night just ended. I'll be going to bed after this phone call. I needed to tell you Chen Lu is indeed planning a secret trip back to Shanghai over Chinese New Year to see his family."

"You're sure?" Clark turned with the receiver to face away from the door. Chen Lu was the minister of foreign affairs of the puppet Reform Government which now nominally governed the occupied regions in the North. For someone as high profile as him, coming back to Shanghai at all was a dumb move.

"Yes. One of his bodyguards turned. He'll be giving us Chen's itinerary and schedule when he visits in February. This is a big job. Are you sure that Whangpoo Brigade can execute?"

"I trust them," Clark said. "They're experienced policemen.

We'll have a better chance of success with them than relying on new Juntong trainees."

"Let's hope you're right." She hung up the phone.

A knock came on the door. "Come in," Clark said.

"Young Master Yuan." His secretary entered and bowed. "This gentleman said he urgently needs to see you." She stepped back so Clark could see the man behind her. Clark had never seen him before.

"Counselor Yuan." The man took off his hat. "I came here on behalf of Consul-General Ho Feng-Shan in Austria."

Ho's title immediately caught Clark's attention. He stood up from his desk. "Please come in." The man walked in. Clark said to his secretary, "Close the door."

The secretary left, and Clark invited the man to sit. "May I please ask your surname?"

"My last name is Yao. Ho Feng-Shan is my *ganqin*."

Ganqin. A family friend so close that he was considered related. Since Yao looked no more than twenty years old, Ho must be his gan father, a nominal parent who Yao's own family had chosen to be Yao's guardian and additional parental figure by ceremonial rite. "Pleased to meet you."

Yao gave him a quick smile. The grave look of concern, however, never left his face. Clark asked, "How can I help you?"

"I received a telegram from Consul-General Ho this morning. Counselor—"

Clark stopped him. "Regrettably, I'm not a foreign affairs agent anymore."

"Mm." Yao nodded in deference. "Nonetheless, my gan father hopes you will still honor your previous role and fulfill your duty if called upon to do so."

Clark searched his memories of the time when he worked for the foreign affairs office. "I'm not very well-acquainted with Consul-General Ho. I met him once when he visited the city before the Battle of Shanghai. But of course, if he needs my help with anything—"

"He does. Not only him, but perhaps thousands more. Last night, huge riots broke out all over Germany, Austria, and the Sudetenland. Hundreds of synagogues were vandalized and destroyed. German stormtroopers broke into Jewish homes and ransacked Jewish stores. The rioters assaulted the Jewish people they caught. The German police did nothing. They stood by and watched. The riots are still going on."

"I've heard nothing about this." Clark sank back into his seat.

"The news is coming out," Yao said. "By tonight, everyone around the world will know about this. It will be front-page news everywhere tomorrow." He handed Clark the telegram he'd brought with him. Clark started reading the message. It was more or less what Yao was telling him. "My gan father called me long-distance in the middle of the night last night. It's total chaos there. The rioters are not only beating up the Jewish people. They're arresting them and sending them to concentration camps. My gan father can't watch and accept this."

"No. If I were him, I wouldn't be able to either." He clutched the telegram and thought of Eden. Had the news reached her yet?

"The Jewish people are terrified," Yao continued. "Some of them came to him for help. They need to get out of their country." He paused and lowered his voice. "This is strictly confidential. We're placing a lot of trust in you for what I'm about to tell you. We don't want to alert the German authorities to what we're doing. We also don't know if Ambassador Chen in Berlin will approve our plan." He paused again and waited for Clark's reaction.

"Go on," Clark said.

"My gan father is going to issue visas for anyone who comes to him who needs to escape. They won't need a visa to enter China, but they need one to exit. If they can find a way to leave with a Chinese visa, Shanghai is where their ships will dock.

When they arrive, they'll need help. You used to work in the foreign affairs office. You're a member of the SMC. Can you help arrange for the refugees to settle here?"

"Certainly." Clark sat up. "How can we watch people's lives being threatened and not help? Besides, I understand very well what it's like to be under attack when no one outside would do anything to help. At least this time, I can offer a little bit of support."

"Very well then." Yao smiled with a sigh of relief. "My gan father said he's always heard from his colleagues you're a trustworthy person. He doesn't have wide contacts in Shanghai. In Vienna, he'll do whatever he can. Here, we'll be relying on you for everything."

"I understand." Clark took a piece of notepaper and wrote down his phone number at home and at work. "Please tell the consul-general to call me. I want to tell him myself he doesn't have to worry about the situation on this side."

"Thank you." Yao accepted the note.

Clark saw him out, then called for his secretary to come in. The first thing he needed to do was to instruct her to contact all the synagogues in Shanghai. After that, he'd have to get in touch with Cornell Franklin. The people arriving would need to be registered, so they could be documented to receive help. They would need housing and information about this city. But before all that, there was one important thing he needed to do.

He needed to go see Eden.

Why? His inner voice asked.

Because she'd want to know. She still had friends back in Munich.

She'll hear about it without you breaking the news to her.

It'd be better for her to hear about it from him than to find out by news wire.

Why? So you can console her? Comfort her? Is it still your place?

He tried to shake off the voice.

She was part of the Jewish community. If she knew what he and Ho Feng-Shan were doing, maybe she could find more ways to help.

Or maybe you're just looking for an excuse to see her.

No. He wouldn't let his thoughts go there. He wouldn't think about this. Not now. There were lives at stake and he had more urgent things to do.

He shut his inner voice from his mind and began explaining to his secretary what he needed her to do.

With the news pouring in from Berlin, Vienna, and the Sudetenland, and the entire office buzzing to try to grasp the scale of what was happening, Clark showing up at the *China Press* office was the last thing Eden expected.

"Can we talk?" he asked her. "It's about the riots in Germany last night."

"Yes." She shifted away her eyes. The clack of typewriters behind her made it so hard to think. "This place is too loud. Why don't we take a walk?" She led him toward the door. She didn't want to talk to him in front of everyone in the office.

He followed her, and they strolled down the street. Her heart was beating too fast and her breath was running too short. The months that they hadn't seen each other should've put a distance between them, yet the pull she'd always felt hadn't gone away. The closeness between them still felt so real.

The cool November wind brushed past her face, reminding her to act with a clear head.

"It's been a long time. How are you?" Clark asked.

"Good." She pulled the wool scarf around her neck closer to her face. The soothing sound of his soft voice warmed her all over. She could use a bit of that warmth for comfort right now.

"It's terrible what's happening in Germany," he said. "I have no words to say how sorry I am to hear about it."

"I'm heartbroken. A lot of reports came into our office this morning. The Nazis were burning houses and synagogues, smashing front windows of stores and looting the shops. I don't know what's going to happen to all the people who lost their homes and properties."

"That's actually the reason I came to see you. The consul-general of China in Vienna contacted me. He wants to help. He'll be issuing visas to Jewish people to come to Shanghai. He asked me to help the escapees settle when they arrive. I had my secretary contact the synagogues this morning. Later this afternoon, I'll go see each of the rabbis to find out what else I can do to help. Maybe the SMC can work with them. Horace Kadoorie is on the Council. I'm sure he would want to help." Kadoorie was one of the wealthiest Sephardi Jewish tycoons in Shanghai.

"Thank you. There will be many who will need help for sure. I know Rabbi Hirsch at the Ohel Rachel very well. I'll talk to him too."

"That would be great," Clark said. For an awkward moment, they stood. There were so many words she wanted to say, but couldn't. She could feel the deep emotions behind his gaze.

She broke her own gaze away and continued walking.

"Your friend Isaac, has he heard from his parents yet?" Clark asked.

"I don't know." Eden shook her head. "I don't think so. I told my mother about the riots as soon as I heard this morning. She went to the hospital where he works to find him, so she could tell him about it. I'm so worried. If something happens to them, he'd . . ." She couldn't finish the thought. The Weissmans were like family. If something happened to them, she would be as upset as anyone else.

"If he does hear from them, let me know. I can put them in touch with the consul-general. Maybe he can help."

"I'd appreciate that." She gave him a grateful smile. "My family and I are so lucky we came two years ago. Things were bad then, but who would've known it would get this bad. I can hardly believe this is happening."

"If only this city was a better place." He scowled at a flyer pinned to a telephone pole. She couldn't read the Chinese text, but from the Provisional Government's five-color flag below the text, she gathered it was a piece of propaganda.

He turned his eyes from the flyer to the traffic. "All the people trying to escape are looking for a safe haven. I'm afraid what they find here won't be much better. The Japanese are ruining this city. Every day, there are robberies and kidnappings. Behind the scenes, they're pushing drugs, gambling, prostitution, and no one would hold them accountable. They hide their tracks so well, it's hard to even prove they have a hand in all the vices bringing down this city. Then they come to the Council meetings demanding to be treated with respect like their hands are clean." He said the last words through gritted teeth.

"I have proof," she said.

"You do?"

"My paper's about to run an article. We're going to expose how Japan is disseminating counterfeit money into China. We've found out one of the people they work with is a casino manager named Roy Bain. I can send you copies of the information we have."

Clark looked surprised, but pleased. "Okay. I don't know what I can do with that information, but I'd like to know everything about it."

"Of course."

They came to the end of the block. Should she go any further? She was now quite far away from her office for a short break.

Another awkward moment rose between them.

"I heard you got married." The words came out of her mouth before she could catch herself and retract.

He gazed at her, his eyes full of anguish. "Yes. I . . ."

She shifted her eyes from his face. "Congratulations. I'm happy for you."

"Eden . . ."

"I should get back to work." She checked her watch. "See you." She turned around and hurried away.

With brisk steps, she weaved through the pedestrians while watching her own footsteps.

How he found a woman to marry so suddenly, why he chose to marry her, and why Shen Yi would allow that marriage, none of it mattered. The answers wouldn't bring back what they once had.

She looked up to the view ahead. A lot of people who would need help would be arriving. It was no time to mourn a love that could never be.

23

SAFE HARBOR

WHY ARE YOU REALLY HERE? Clark asked himself as he walked up to the Embankment House, the large apartment complex north of Soochow Creek.

It was Saturday afternoon and he knew Eden and Isaac Weissman were there, volunteering to help the refugees arriving from Vienna and Berlin.

Why, of course, he'd come here to deliver the good news. Consul-General Ho Feng-Shan had gotten in touch with Isaac's parents. He was making arrangements to get them out of Germany.

He could've telephoned Isaac and told him the news. He didn't need to come here.

But it was a good opportunity to see for himself how the refugees were settling in.

Walking along the river, he'd twice almost turned back. Why did he come here? He had so many excuses. All so valid. None fully convincing.

He couldn't stay away. When he saw Eden again at the *China Press* office two weeks ago, everything that happened since the summer faded away. The time before they separated and the time they saw each other again linked back up, and the time they could be in each other's presence was all that mattered.

He went into the building's lobby toward the table where Eden was passing out blankets, pillows, and bags filled with soap, toothbrushes, and toothpaste to a line of new arrivals. Isaac was doing the same alongside her. People were moving all around and she didn't notice him coming.

"Eden," he called her from behind.

She recognized his voice right away. Her body stiffened before she turned around.

Her eyes. Those eyes with a soul that captivated him all along. Did she know how much he missed her?

"Clark." She smiled.

Isaac came closer and greeted him.

"I have good news," Clark said in a casual, cheery voice. "I spoke with Consul-General Ho. He got in touch with Mr. and Mrs. Weissman through the Chinese consulate in Munich. He renewed their visas to depart the country."

"Thank you!" Isaac shook his hand. This was the first time Isaac had shown him such genuine warmth. "I don't know how to thank you."

"That's wonderful," Eden said. "We can finally stop worrying."

Clark swayed back and lowered his eyes. This was all he wanted, to see her happy and to be able to do something for her. "The Consul-General and his friends will do everything they can to help. When Mr. Weissman's health recovers, they'll see what they can do to put them on a ship."

"Thank you," Isaac said. "My father was a very robust man. These last two years took a toll on him. A few months ago, he was beaten badly by a group of Hitler Youths. If all these things hadn't happened, he wouldn't have caught pneumonia so easily."

He looked at the lines of refugees. "My mother said it was a cold night, and they broke all our windows."

Eden touched him on the arm. "He'll get better."

"The assistant of the Chinese consul in Munich offered to take them in when Mr. Weissman gets out of the hospital," Clark said. "The SA won't harass them as long as they're guests of Chinese diplomats. They'll be safe."

The worried lines on Isaac's forehead eased. He gave Clark a bright smile. "We owe Consul-General Ho for giving us all a way out. Look at all these people here. We registered four hundred arrivals today, and more are still coming. Some of them already bought ocean liner tickets to leave before the riots, but they couldn't get a visa to any country. Once they got the Chinese visa, they switched their tickets to a China-bound ship."

"That's good to know." Clark put his hands into his pockets. He didn't want to tell them Ho was already receiving pushback. Ambassador Chen in Berlin was worried his attempt to help the Jews might sour Chinese relations with Hitler. So far, Ho had refused to bend.

A little girl passed by with her mother and she waved at Isaac. Isaac smiled and waved back. His face dropped after she left. "No one feels safe in Germany anymore. Even children aren't spared. The ones who are here are lucky Consul-General Ho opened the door for them. They said he's issuing visas to everyone who asks. If it weren't for him, who knows what would happen to them. He even cut the normal application period to three days. They said he's been issuing more than a hundred visas a day since the riots. He has such a big heart to help so many people."

Or maybe he was issuing as many visas as he could before the higher-ups forced him to stop. But Clark kept that thought to himself.

"Victor's converting the lower floors of this building into temporary housing for the new arrivals," Eden said.

"Victor? You mean Victor Sassoon?" Clark asked. "You stayed in touch with him?"

"No." She looked out to the lobby and all around. "We got back in touch only because of this crisis. He's a good man. He doesn't hesitate to do his part when other Jewish people are in need."

"It's not only him," Isaac said. "The Jewish committees and groups in America, Hong Kong, and Singapore are all sending donations. It's very heartening to see so many people reaching out to help."

Eden picked up a pamphlet on the table and showed Clark. "Look. Isaac's starting a Jewish Refugee Society. He's organizing volunteers to help the arrivals find new homes and schools."

"I just want to do my part," Isaac said. He drew back with a humble glance. "When we came to Shanghai, we traveled first class. We knew we had enough to start a new life here. The people who are coming now, they have nothing. Those damn Nazis made them give up all their money and property or they wouldn't let them leave. This is the least I can do to pass the blessings around."

"Eden," someone called out. A man in a leather jacket, unzipped, strode over. He looked to be in his mid-twenties. If Clark had to guess, he'd say the man was American. He had that air of open, friendly arrogance.

Eden looked surprised but happy to see him. "Alex."

"Isaac," Alex greeted Isaac with a wide smile.

Isaac's eyes dimmed. He shook the man's hand with an obligatory smile and returned to giving out pillows and blankets.

Without prompting, Alex held out his hand to Clark. "Hi, I'm Alex Mitchell."

Clark shook his hand. "Clark. Clark Yuan."

"Nice to meet you."

"Likewise."

Eden moved a step closer to Alex. "Alex is the host of XMHA's radio news."

"That Alex Mitchell?" Clark gave him a second look. "I listen to your broadcast now and then."

"Why, thank you. I hope you like what I have to say on the air." He opened the newspaper in his hand and showed it to Eden. "Apollo Eirene?"

Clark closed his hands in his pocket. The cozy way Alex squinted at Eden and his teasing tone of voice chafed him.

The way Eden subtly shook her head while stifling a smile, like they were sharing a secret, didn't sit so well with him either.

"Can we talk about this later?" She pushed the newspaper down.

Alex shrugged. "Sure! How about over dinner. It's six o'clock. Time to eat. There's a homey little Korean barbeque joint I found a few streets from here. You should come try their bulgogi. I guarantee you'll like it. Maybe you can give them a write-up and bring them more business."

"Me? Do a write-up?" Eden laughed. "If you want to bring them more business, all you have to do is give them a plug on the air."

"Since you suggested it, I'll do just that." He agreed with a toss of his head. "So, shall we go?"

Eden looked at Clark. Her face cooled. An invisible wall rose between them. She said to Alex, "Okay."

"Great." Alex rolled up the newspaper. He looked at Clark and asked, "Would you like to join us?"

Clark smiled. He wasn't so dense as to think that Alex really wanted him to come along. More importantly, Eden didn't want him to go with them. He felt sure of it. "Thank you. No. I've got somewhere else to be this evening."

"Thank you for coming by and giving us the news," Eden said. "We'll see you around?"

"Sure." Clark took a step back. A sinking feeling began to bear down on him.

"Let's go get my coat," Eden said to Alex. Alex gave him a wave goodbye and they left.

Clark watched them walk away. It'd been almost half a year since he and Eden separated. Since that time, he himself had married another woman. Why shouldn't she leave the past behind and begin seeing other men?

But Alex Mitchell?

He went up to Isaac. "I don't mean to pry, but. . . are Eden and Alex together?"

"You're asking me?" Isaac laughed. "She never tells me anything."

Clark gazed across the lobby. At the exit, Alex opened the door and led Eden out.

Isaac resumed a more serious tone. "They probably are. If not yet, they will be."

Clark thought so too. He said to Isaac, "Being close to someone like Alex is risky. His radio broadcast rallies a lot of people. That's good. What's not good is the more he exposes and humiliates the Japanese, the greater the risk they'll look for ways to make him stop."

Isaac picked up another pillow. "What are you saying?"

"Nothing." Clark shook his head. "Just watch out for her, will you?"

"If she lets me," Isaac replied. He sounded almost annoyed, but then he softened his voice. "Of course I will."

Yes. He would try. Clark believed that. It was obvious Isaac loved Eden too. His feelings were written all over his face.

Some things just weren't meant to be.

"Take care." Clark slipped his hands into his trench coat and left for the exit.

Outside, he strolled idly along the river. It was pointless to dwell on his own sadness. If Eden could find happiness, then he ought to take comfort in knowing she was well. As long as no danger came to her, he would wish her well from afar.

———————

Three blocks away from the Embankment House, Eden asked Alex, "We're not taking your motorcycle?"

"You want to ride my bike?" He feigned disbelief. "I wish I'd known. I didn't think you'd want to ride behind me if you were wearing a coat."

He said that as a matter of fact. Eden smiled and let it slide. That was considerate on his part. The carefree daredevil Alex Michell wasn't one known for being attentive to others.

Or, to state it correctly, he was being attentive to her. She'd noticed that for a while now, and she'd be lying if she didn't admit she felt flattered.

So why didn't she drop hints to encourage him? Like now. She could make a little joke and point out he was looking out for her.

She knew the answer to that too. A person only has so much love to give. And for a long time, her heart was still with Clark. A raw wound remained open. Like a lamp that had burned out, she had no more oil left to reignite the flame.

Seeing Clark again over these last two weeks only made things worse. All the heartache she had laid away, concealed even from herself, came rushing back.

She sensed this was the same for him too. He hadn't changed the way he looked at her.

It wouldn't do to stay at this standstill. In her mind, she knew. If they continued to dance around this knot, neither of them would be free.

"I see you decided to take my suggestion after all," Alex said.

"What suggestion?" Eden came out of her thoughts.

"Are you going to tell me more about Apollo Eirene?"

"Oh, that. Yes. You gave me the idea, and I used it to talk my boss into letting me go back to reporting hard news. So thank you. Although I'll still have to keep my cover and write society and entertainment news."

"You used my suggestion but you didn't come work with me? Why?" He stopped and clutched the newspaper in his hand, his joking face half dulled by disappointment.

Eden walked to the lamppost near the river. When Alex proposed she work with him, her mind wasn't ready. If she and Alex became more than mere acquaintances, she would have to dig up all the feelings she had buried to understand where her own heart stood.

Life, though, had its own way of forcing one to confront fears. The world ahead had opened up. Two paths lay before her.

"You're Alex Mitchell. I'm just a newspaper reporter. You don't need me." She tried to make light of the subject.

"It's not a matter of need," he said. "I want justice in this world. I want to call out those responsible for inflicting oppression, and I want to shame those in power who could do something but won't. You want the same thing too. I can tell from everything you've written. There are people who would sit back and let things pass. The world crumbles around them and they keep their heads down and do nothing. Not you and me." He came closer to her. "We make a good team."

"Perhaps." She stared away toward the water. He was right. They did have that in common. And standing so near him, she had to ask herself if she wasn't letting something good slip by.

"I mean it. We'd be good together, in more ways than one." He raised his hand and tenderly lifted her chin toward him.

Under the lamplight, she gazed back into his eyes. While she was holed up in the shell of her mind, the ray of sunlight that was Alex Mitchell had seeped in. His uplifting gaiety stood in stark contrast to the never-ending web of hard decisions and dilemmas that followed her and Clark at every turn.

"What if we're more than a team?" he whispered against her

ear. His soft breath brushed against her face. Her heart sprung open.

The haze of a future that could never be began to slide into the distance.

It was time to set herself free. She closed her eyes and yielded to the caress of his lips on her own.

YEAR OF THE PREY

THE NEW YEAR'S fireworks blasted along Avenue Joffre as Clark made his way to the Dongchang Hotel. For once, the pops and cracks of firecrackers replaced those of grenades and guns.

At the hotel's entrance, two large red scrolls hung in the front to welcome their guests and the arrival of the year of the rabbit.

Year of the rabbit. An apt sign of the time. The first day of 1939 had begun, and everyone in Shanghai could fall prey. Those within the foreign concessions were themselves as good as rabbits in a trap. But the predators outside of the trap weren't safe either. The hunters, too, were being hunted because even rabbits could turn rabid. When the rabid bunnies struck, their bites could be just as deadly.

Like the takedown of the puppet government's foreign minister Chen Lu last night. Zhou Ke-Hao and his band of brothers opened the new year on their first job attempt. This group of former Chinese police who called themselves the Whangpoo Brigade had combined their forces and joined Juntong at this most crucial time.

Chen's assassination wasn't all. Yesterday, a second Juntong action team attempted a hit on Koyanagi Jiichi, an official Japanese army photographer, plus another Japanese man and two Japanese taxi girls who were lunching with him. They didn't take down Jiichi but wounded the other Japanese man and one of the girls.

Too bad that mission didn't succeed. Even worse, one of the assassins, a sixteen-year-old boy named Mo Hai-Sheng, got caught.

Juntong would have to deal with that problem later. At least they kept up the running threat of terror. Japan could have no peace here.

Clark entered the hotel and discreetly walked to the elevator, careful not to draw the attention of the hotel staff and the guests. The reception desk had plenty of candy, peanuts, and roasted melon seeds to keep them busy.

He rode the elevator to the second floor and knocked on the door of the room where Zhou had been told to hide till tomorrow.

Zhou peeked through the peephole, then opened the door. "Young Master Yuan."

"*Gong xi fa cai,*" Clark greeted him with the customary new year wish for him to get rich.

Zhou laughed and said the same back to Clark. Getting rich was hardly their top priority.

"I brought you a new year rice cake." Clark gave him the gift he'd brought. "It's the new year holiday, and you're holed up in here. I feel really bad."

"Don't say that." Zhou accepted the rice cake. "Thank you."

"Also, this." Clark handed him today's newspaper and showed him the top headline "Chen Lu Assassinated" below the date of February 18. "You did well."

Zhou laughed. "All thanks to my group of brothers." He sat down on the bed. "The six of us took different routes to the Broadway Mansions. I came by the No. 1 double-decker bus, and the others came by car and rickshaw or on foot. We met up at six o'clock. We couldn't go inside right away. There were still too many people in there."

Yes. Clark could guess. The Broadway Mansions wasn't only a living accommodation. The puppet government's Foreign Affairs Bureau operated on its fourth floor. Zhou and his friends took a huge risk to execute their plan.

"We went to a bar across the street and waited. At seven o'clock, a heavy rain started to fall. We thought that was a good time. We went back to the Mansion by Yu Yuen Road and had the place surrounded. Lucky for us, there was only one bodyguard standing watch. There should've been two, but one sneaked off somewhere. We surprised him when we approached and took his gun before he could react. Four of us then went into the Mansion through the kitchen. Inside, Chen Lu and his wife, plus their two guests, were waiting for dinner to start. Chen was on the sofa with the male guest. One of my brothers, Ren Tian-Ming, walked in and fired three shots at Chen point blank."

Clark's eyes fell to the newspaper's black and white photo of the traitor lying dead on the floor. "What happened next?"

"Chen collapsed," Zhou said. "His wife flew over to him and their guests rushed out to escape. I was standing in the hallway. I watched them leave and entered the room myself. Chen was still breathing. I emptied my pistol and killed him with a shot to his head. After that, I threw the scrolls down." He picked up the newspaper and stared at the traitor's dead body in the photo. "I threw one on his body." He stared at the scroll covering the torso with a message in large black letters, *Death to Collaborators. Long Live Generalissimo Chiang Kai-Shek.* "The other one, I threw on the sofa." He pointed at the sheet over the couch with the message, *Resistance will bring victory. Establishment of the country will succeed. Protect China's land and soil forever!* "I wanted to make sure those thieves who sold the country would see what's coming."

Clark gazed at the scrolls. The messages were signed *Chinese Iron and Blood Army*.

Zhou continued. "We then left and regrouped outside the Mansion. We let go of the bodyguard and departed separately. I took a taxi and came back here."

"Good thing you came back unscathed," Clark said. "We really have to thank you all this time."

"If we can give our efforts for the country, we won't mind anything." Zhou put down the newspaper with a satisfied smile. "Young Master Yuan, there is something my brothers and I want you and Juntong to help us with. We think you would agree with us too."

"What's that?"

"We want to get rid of Xi Shi-Tai, the secretary of the puppet government's police commissioner."

"Oh?"

"Before, the Public Security Bureau was our territory. To watch the dog thieves taking it over and not being able to do anything about it, we can't swallow this anger. Moreover, he works for the Japanese military press. We can't accept it that this lying mouthpiece for the shorties is the voice of the Chinese police. Whether you and Juntong will back us, we will still make this happen. It would just be better if we have your help."

Clark nodded. "Since that's the case, I'll talk to Juntong's side. There shouldn't be any problem."

"Thank you."

"I'll go now to report back to Juntong." Clark stood up. "You take good care."

"You as well." Zhou got up and let him out.

Quietly, Clark left the hotel. On the street, a group of small children ran by. Neighborhood kids out playing tag.

He thought of Xiu-Qing back at home, playing with her baby who was wearing the new outfit she'd made for him to celebrate the new year. In the end, she took his suggestion and named the boy "Fu", a word to signify *fu guo*, meaning restoring the country. He hoped his late, old friend, Xu Hong-Lie, the boy's actual father, would agree.

WAR WITHIN THE WAR

IN THE CHAMBER of the SMC, Clark checked his watch while Hayashi Yukichi rambled on with his complaint about the Shanghai Municipal Police. Today was only the fifth day of the Chinese New Year holiday, and he did not appreciate being dragged here to attend an SMC meeting, much less one that was called solely to appease the Japanese.

"Chen Lu was a friend of Imperial Japan," Hayashi said to the rest of the Council members. "He was a valuable member of the new Provisional Government. Koyanagi Jiichi is an army photographer. The attempt against his life is an open act of war. These threats against Japan and those who collaborate with us in good faith cannot continue. The Japanese consul-general, the Japanese Military Police, and the Japanese government have voted for the following resolutions. I bring forth these resolutions, and I urge you to take these actions immediately. We shall make the same request to the consul-general of France."

He held up a piece of paper and glanced at the men sitting around the table. Clark remained still. He did not intend to give Hayashi the faintest hint what was on his mind.

Hayashi cleared his throat. "First, the SMP will establish

special units of agents appointed by Japan and the new Provisional Government to investigate anti-Japanese elements."

Clark slightly raised his brow. This was just another way for them to stack the SMP with their lackeys.

"Second," Hayashi continued, "the Council will allow Japanese authorities to exercise free police rights within the International Settlement, including the right to investigate and make arrests. The same rights shall be extended to the officers of the Provisional Government public security bureaus."

A grumble broke out among the members. Municipal Police Commissioner Bourne, who Cornell Franklin had invited to join the meeting, raised his hand. "That's unprecedented. No foreign concession has ever allowed police forces of another jurisdiction to claim authority within their own territory."

Hayashi ignored him. "Third, the SMP shall suppress all Chinese anti-Japanese associations."

Clark propped his chin on his fist. No. He would not agree to any of this.

"Fourth, the punishment for members of anti-Japanese associations shall be death."

"Bullocks!" Director Dong yelled out. Clark had never seen the elderly magnate lose his composure, let alone use such language in English among Western company.

Hayashi kept on. "Finally, all criminals arrested now or in the future for anti-Japanese terrorist activities shall immediately be handed over to Japanese police authorities and shall be tried by the Japanese tribunal."

"No!" Clark said. The SMP had arrested Mo Hai-Sheng, the young Juntong assassin who took part in the attempted assault of the Japanese army photographer Jiichi. This would put Mo's life in jeopardy. "This is unacceptable. They'll never get a fair trial."

Hayashi glowered at him. "The trials are unfair now. All the judges in the International Settlement mixed courts are KMT appointees. They think these terrorists are patriots. They don't hold the terrorists accountable."

"Please, please, gentlemen," Cornell Franklin interjected, "let's calm down and discuss this."

"Mr. Franklin." Commissioner Bourne raised his hand again.

"Yes?"

"I strongly object to the proposal for giving outside forces police power on our grounds. This would lead to utter chaos. We would have our police teams and other police teams concurrently investigating the same crimes. Who would get to keep the evidence during an ongoing investigation? What would be the chain-of-custody of any evidence we found? If there's an arrest to be made, and more than one squad shows up, we'd get into each other's way. This simply will not work." He glanced at Hayashi. "And if you don't mind me saying, if police forces from other jurisdictions can come and go and exercise their powers as they please, it would infringe on our police sovereignty. It would undermine the authority of the SMP in the public's eyes. I find this demand completely disrespectful."

Hayashi half closed his eyes. "If the SMP had been doing its job properly, we wouldn't be making this request."

"Excuse me," Bourne said, "I will not stand to have my staff unfairly criticized this way. Our police force was one of the most competent in the world until the Battle of Shanghai. Since then, crime has increased tenfold. Our district absorbed tens of thousands of refugees, and the Badlands area is out of control. We deal with all of this in addition to politically motivated kidnappings and attacks between the Chinese and the Japanese every day. My force is working around the clock and we're stretched to the max. Given the challenges, how can anyone fault us?"

"Are you saying you and your men can't manage the Badlands?" Hayashi asked. "The area actually does not fall under British jurisdiction. Out of respect, my government hasn't pressed for your units to withdraw from that area. But as you just admitted yourself, that area's out of control. Perhaps you and your force might like to step back and let the Japanese and Provisional Chinese police take over?"

Bourne winced. From where Clark sat, he could see the veins throbbing on his temple.

He glanced back at Hayashi. What a weasel. The rackets in the Badlands were perpetrated by the Japanese's minions. Bourne knew it. Hayashi himself knew it too.

The other Japanese council member, Okamoto, spoke up. "Commissioner, based on what you just said, I think our proposal for establishing special units should be a very good solution."

Bourne tightened his mouth. Tony Keswick, who had been silent so far, raised his hand. "I agree. That is something we could consider."

Clark frowned. Keswick wasn't thinking of giving in, was he?

"I second that," said Franklin. "Commissioner Bourne made a very good case why we can't allow foreign police to exercise authority within our jurisdiction. Maybe what we can do is establish a task force dedicated to investigating and preventing anti-Japanese activities by the Chinese."

Clark sat up. Franklin too? Were they all colluding on this?

"The special unit will have to be staffed by appointees of the Japanese and Chinese authorities," said Hayashi.

"That is an option."

Clark couldn't hold his voice any longer. "Pardon me. We can establish a task force, sure. But why can't Commissioner Bourne decide who he wants to appoint? Why should the Japanese and Chinese authorities have any say in this?"

Hayashi crossed his arms. "Because it is our people who are the victims of the actions of these so-called National Salvation Movement terrorists."

"Clark," Keswick said to him, softening his face,

"Commissioner Bourne will still be the chief of the SMP. No matter who the appointees are, they'll all still be subject to him and will have to follow his orders. This would preserve the sovereignty of our police force, which I think is of utmost importance and cannot be compromised." He stressed the last sentence with a forceful tone and eyed Clark to signal him the point.

"Hayashisan," Franklin said. "Why don't we agree to this? We can't let Japanese and Chinese police infringe on the authority of the SMP, but the SMP will establish a new task force comprised of Japanese and Provisional Government appointees, who will be under Commissioner Bourne's control."

Hayashi didn't say yes expressly. He uncrossed his arms. "We have forty-five candidates standing ready to fill the positions. We also need to follow through with our previous request for adding thirty-three more recruits to the Japanese branch of the SMP, and senior Japanese officers at the superintendent and inspector levels."

"Commissioner?" Franklin looked over to Bourne.

"Fine," Bourne grudgingly agreed.

"And the SMC will be responsible for covering the expenses for the new hires?" Hayashi asked.

Franklin and Keswick exchanged a glance. "Yes," Franklin answered.

Clark shook his head. The Japanese and the puppet police were infiltrating the SMP, and the Council would be providing the funds to help them.

"What about all the Chinese anti-Japanese associations? The SMP has to make it an agenda to shut them down."

"I object to that," Clark said. "People within our district are entitled to the freedom of speech and the freedom to associate. We can't take these rights away from the Chinese people if they haven't done anything wrong."

Hayashi snorted. "These are terrorist cells. They manufacture discontent. They fan violence, even if they don't engage in violence themselves. They must be terminated."

"This isn't fair," Clark replied. "Not—"

"Clark," Keswick interrupted him. "Political violence is in fact a serious public safety concern. We do need to start finding ways to curb the constant political attacks. I understand there are Chinese people who feel grievances for their own reasons. We all understand politics." He tried to make it a joke, but no one laughed. "Politics aside, it is our job to keep the Settlement safe for everyone. Don't you all agree?"

No one answered. Franklin asked, "Why don't we put this to a vote? The Council can adopt a regulation prohibiting anti-Japanese associations as a safety measure."

"I second that," Keswick said.

"Okay. Those in favor?"

"Aye." Hayashi and Okamoto raised their hands. When Keswick raised his, the other five British members followed. Seeing the Britons close rank, the three Americans, including Franklin, cast their votes yes.

Only the five Chinese members remained. Two timidly raised their hands. One of them, Shao Ping, looked away when he met Clark's gaze.

"Those who oppose?"

Clark raised his hand. The cause was already lost, but he couldn't in good conscience vote yes.

Director Dong, too, raised his hand.

The last Chinese member took a deep breath and puffed up his chest. "I abstain."

Franklin clasped his hands. "Resolution passes."

Clark looked away as the Council secretary, Godfrey Philips, noted the resolution in the minutes.

"We haven't discussed the criminals arrested for anti-Japanese activities," Hayashi said. "Can we agree they will be turned over to the Japanese authorities to be tried by Japanese courts?"

"How can this be acceptable?" Clark knocked the table. "The Japanese courts have no jurisdiction over anyone who's not Japanese. It's outrageous you even ask."

Hayashi gave him a side glance. "You say so, Mr. Yuan, but what you really want to do is to give the pro-Chungking loyalists protection, isn't it?"

"That is not the case."

"No? Well, I'm finding that hard to believe. Your insistence on refusing every request we've made has me wondering if you might even be part of the National Salvation Movement yourself."

Clark stared at him. "Are you accusing me?"

"You were a KMT official once. Maybe Chiang Kai-Shek's regime is behind all this."

"You're out of line," Clark shot back.

Cornell Franklin chimed in, "Hayashisan, please. We're all friends here. Let's not make rumors and innuendos without any basis. We all know Clark. He's an upright businessman. He's got a lot of investments in the International Settlement just like us. It's absurd to think he's a part of any terrorist organization."

"I agree," Keswick joined in. "We're veering off topic. Let's get back to the real issues at hand."

Still maintaining his calm demeanor, Hayashi held up his nose. Clark forced himself to bite back his tongue. He didn't fear the old fox, but bringing suspicion upon himself out of anger would yield him no gain.

"Very well," Hayashi said. "Do we have an agreement then?" He turned his eyes to the police chief. "Commissioner Bourne, are you currently holding a suspect in custody for the attempted murder of our army photographer Koyanagi Jiichi and the shooting of his friends?"

Not expecting Hayashi to address him, Bourne blurted out, "Yes, a sixteen-year-old boy."

"You will turn him over to our authorities?"

Bourne widened his eyes. He turned his shocked face to Franklin and Keswick.

"Hayashisan," Franklin said. "You're putting us in a very difficult position. This is an international jurisdiction matter. My government, as well as the British government, would not condone us turning our accused over to a foreign power without giving the accused a fair trial."

"An international matter indeed," Hayashi said. "My government takes the security of our people very seriously. They're ready to press the case if the Council decides to harbor Chinese terrorists against Imperial Japan. Such an action would be tantamount to an act of war." He gave Franklin and Keswick a grave look. "As a Council member myself, I advise you all to make your next decision very carefully. Are your countries ready to declare war on Japan?"

Clark held his breath. The stakes were now laid open. No one in the room dared to speak.

Bourne was the one who broke the silence. "Hayashisan, about your army photographer, my officers have been looking into the case. We think it was not an anti-Japan terrorist act at all. We believe the conflict came about because of one of the women accompanying Jiichi was a girlfriend of a man in a Chinese gang."

A woman? A Chinese gang? Clark eyed the Commissioner. Mo Hai-Sheng, the young assassin, couldn't have come up with this story. Of all the people in this room, Bourne was the one trying to save the boy.

"So even if you and the rest of the Council decide to allow Japanese courts to try Chinese terrorists, in this case, it wouldn't be appropriate." Bourne opened his palms on the table. Nothing on his face indicated he was lying.

Hayashi remained unmoved. "Jiichi is part of the Imperial Japanese Army. The suspect attempted a hit on him. Regardless of reasons, that makes it a potential anti-Japanese terrorist act." He switched to a more cordial face. "Of course, if our court finds that in fact it was nothing more than a case of jealousy, we'll promptly return the suspect to you."

Return Mo? Clark kept his eye on the old fox. They never would. Once Mo was in Japanese hands, he would never get a fair trial. He'd simply be tortured for information, then killed.

Franklin looked up with a grim face. "All right. We will proceed as you wish. Tomorrow at 2:00 p.m., Commissioner Bourne will arrange to transport the suspect from his cell to a facility you designate."

The urgency now bearing down, Clark raised his hand. "Cornell, I have to object. This is grossly unfair to the Chinese."

"I am thinking of the Chinese too," Franklin said. "Tony is right. Political violence is endangering this whole city. They're straining our resources to a breaking point. If the instigators realize they would be turned over to Japanese authorities, maybe they'll stop resorting to violence. And if the violence would stop, it would be safer for everyone all around."

Clark clenched his fist. Safer? What about the attacks instigated by the Japanese? Who did Franklin think was behind all the kidnappings and murders of pro-KMT Chinese and all the bombings against the press?

"I'm glad we've come to an agreement." Hayashi smiled. "My government looks forward to our continued cooperation."

No one responded. Franklin took a closing look around the room. "If there's nothing else, the meeting is adjourned."

The two Japanese got up. The other Council members followed. Clark sat back and watched Okamoto shake hands with the American and British members. What a phony display of friendship. These were the countries the world was looking to for upholding the virtue of freedom? All it took was a little island country like Japan to make a threat, and down they all went on their knees.

Standing behind his chair with his cane, Hayashi stared at him. Silently, Clark stood up. No. He would not be intimidated.

He made it a point to walk past the old fox on his way to the door. As he passed, Hayashi said, in a low voice only he could hear, "You have no idea what you're up against."

Clark halted. He stared back at the man.

"Don't think the ones with real power haven't considered you a target. All your wealth, and your status. Rather than challenging me, young man, you'd do yourself and your people a favor if you get them all to stand down. You won't win."

We shall see, Clark thought.

Hayashi turned around and took off.

This was what the Westerners didn't see. All this talk about crimes and terrorism. They were the mask of the continuing war still raging between China and Japan. The Battle of Shanghai never stopped. Only now, soldiers weren't the ones fighting. Japan was pushing into the foreign concessions with drug dealers, gamblers, ronin, and yakuza on the outskirts and penetrating the hearts with their police. The Chinese resistance was fighting back.

One by one, the Council members filtered out the door, including the Chinese members who did not vote to support their own. The last of them, Shao Ping, came up to Clark. "I have no choice. I can't openly contradict those shorties. It's too dangerous. I have to look out for my wife and children. You understand?"

"Do you understand?" Clark retorted. "If Japan has its way, your family won't ever be safe."

Shao shook his head and left. Only Franklin, Keswick, and Bourne remained, along with Director Dong, who still hadn't left his seat.

"Clark, Director Dong," Franklin said apologetically, "what just happened, I know you feel it wasn't right. We don't either. Believe me, our sympathy is with the Chinese."

"You had a hell of a way of showing that," Clark said. "You gave up a sixteen-year-old boy like a lamb to be slaughtered."

Franklin dropped his head. Keswick stepped forward. "Our hands are tied. Yesterday, Admiral Darnell of the British Royal Navy had a private meeting with us. He made it very clear. If Japan launches a full-scale attack against us, they will not try to stop them. The Admiral himself had explicit orders to surrender in that event and seek asylum with the American Marines."

"Surrender? You mean they wouldn't even come to save you and all the British nationals?"

Keswick shook his head. "They will not divert military resources here. Not with Hitler's threat looming."

"What about the Americans?" Clark asked Franklin.

"There have been no firm words from the higher-ups," Franklin said. "You can look at it to mean there's still hope, or you can take it as there's no firm commitment."

"We are on your side," Keswick said. "I can leave Shanghai. So can Cornell, and Commissioner Bourne. But we're still here. Despite how bad it looked to you at the meeting, the truth is, we are staying because we know we're the only ones who can still hold this area safe for the Chinese. We're the only ones who still care to try. But we can ride this out only if we can keep up the front. Negotiation is the only bargaining chip we have."

Clark slumped. He stuck his hand on his waist and swiped the other across his forehead. In his seat, Director Dong listened with a sullen face. He could guess what Director Dong was thinking. These Westerners couldn't care less what happened to the Chinese as long as they could keep themselves and their properties safe.

Franklin came closer. "Giving up the boy is a decision that will haunt me for the rest of my life. Why did I do it? Because I had to give a reason from our side why we would concede to that outrageous demand. And now, they got what they demanded, but our official reason is not because we're afraid of them. Our official reason for turning over Chinese attackers is that I made it an imperative to put a stop to political violence in our territory.

This is the only thing I can do to show we haven't ceded any ground."

Clark grimaced. "What about the boy?" He never even met the kid. He was only sixteen.

Keswick put his hand on his shoulder. "We can't save him, but as long as the Japanese are afraid to test our limits too far, we can still protect the Chinese in our district. Look, we didn't agree to give them free rein to send their police in to harass and arrest people. Commissioner Bourne is still in charge. As long as the SMP is under his watch, it'll be his call whether a violent crime is an anti-Japanese terrorist act or a personal dispute. So, while we agreed to let their courts try the suspects of terrorist acts, this will rarely happen. The SMP will make sure of that."

Clark let out a bitter laugh. "Do you know what real terrorism is? It's surrounding us with their military. It's unleashing a wave of crime past our borders and making all of us unsafe. When they take over the police force, their real control of this district will be complete."

Keswick pulled back his hand. Commissioner Bourne looked Clark in the eye. "As long as I'm here, I'll do all I can to make sure that won't happen. I will do everything in my power to make sure no one will be given over to the Japanese and be denied a fair trial."

Clark blew out a frustrated breath of air. The earnest look on the policeman's face was the only thing that stopped him from giving up entirely on these men.

He paced a few steps in front of the table. "If you want Hayashi and his people to continue to believe you're still a force to be reckoned with, you'll need to show you still mean business." He raised his head. "Are you all aware Japan is behind a racket that is pouring counterfeit money into the city?"

"I read about this." Bourne stroked his mustache. "The *China Press* reported on this. I wanted to investigate it, but they wouldn't let us speak to the reporter who wrote about it. We made some inquiries but got nowhere."

"I have inside information on someone who's helping them perpetrate this scheme. His name is Roy Bain. He's a British national. He's the casino manager mentioned in the *China Press* article, although the article didn't give out his name. I can tell you everything I know for you to conduct a formal investigation."

"If we can find sufficient evidence, we can charge him."

Keswick, too, had now caught on. "We can put him on trial. It'll send a message we won't tolerate illegal activities and racketeering."

"Exactly," Clark said.

"I like this idea." Franklin smiled. "Considering the compromises we made, this will send a counter-message."

"Yes," Keswick said. "That'll help us keep the Japanese guessing."

At the conference table, Director Dong, who had remained quiet throughout, stood up and put on his hat. "Good day, gentlemen." He tipped his hat at them and took his leave.

"Director, I'll walk with you," Clark called out after him. He nodded at Franklin and the rest, then followed the old man out.

On the steps in front of the building, Director Dong stopped. He turned to Clark. A tranquil smile crossed his face. "If your father were still alive, he would be proud."

The compliment took Clark by surprise. In deference, he bowed his head.

Dong clasped his hands behind his back. The skirt of his *tangzhuan* flowed with the wind over his legs. "I, Dong whoever, have lived to this age. What else do I have to be scared of? Certainly not Hayashi. Even if those rotten people from Japan invade this place, at worst, I'll just clash against them with my old life. My life isn't worth much anymore. But yours? Take utmost caution for every step you take. The future of this country, it'll all depend on those like you."

"Director Dong . . ." Clark watched the dignified senior. Dong wasn't just a whoever or a nobody. He was the living reminder of the Chinese's long history and heritage in which they could all take pride.

Dong gazed up into the sky. "When the National Day comes in May, I will hang the flag of blue sky and white sun on the door of my home and every store and office I own. Not because I hold unwavering loyalty for Chiang Kai-Shek, but because this is Chinese land. On Chinese land, the Chinese flag is the flag that should stand."

The old man kept his proud smile as he walked away to his car and chauffeur. After he left, Clark looked up to the sky himself. Could he, too, look at the heavens and find the strength he needed to fight on?

The white clouds floated away, unmasking the sun. The sun's rays warmed his chest and face, as though comforting him and assuring him he would be forgiven for the next thing he was about to do.

When he arrived home, he made his way to the study and closed the door. He had to make an urgent call.

The phone rang on the other line and Pearl answered, "Hello?"

"Ming Zhu?"

"Yes?"

"It's me. Yuan Guo-Hui. Bad news. The SMC made an agreement with the Japanese to hand over Mo Hai-Sheng."

Pearl fell silent on the other end.

"The Municipal Police will transport him from the station at Connaught Road tomorrow. Two o'clock."

"So soon?"

"Yes. This transfer cannot happen."

Pearl paused for a moment. "Understood." She hung up the phone.

Clark replaced the receiver and slumped back against the

desk. That poor boy. He'd be dead by tonight. They could not risk him divulging any information.

Hopefully, whoever Pearl would pay to handle the job inside the prison cell would take the least painful way to end his life.

Whichever way he took, one thing was sure. It would be much, much less painful than what the Japanese had planned.

YOU MUST COME WITH US

NOTHING GOT BETTER.

More than a year had passed since Japan invaded Shanghai. Everything kept getting worse. Japan claimed they respected the foreign concessions as neutral territories, but Eden didn't believe any of it.

How could she when the *China Press* office itself was now guarded like a fortress?

At the corner of the block to her office building, the guard carrying a machine gun waved at her. Out of courtesy, she slowed her bike and waved back. He was one of Charlie's hires. In fact, he'd hired a machine-gun-toting guard at every corner around their building, plus the bullet-proof Oldsmobile sedan parked across the street. All of them stood ready to shoot anyone who might try to attack her or any one of their own.

Charlie's worries weren't unfounded. It all started with the bombing of Alex's radio station last year. After that, it was open season against the Western free press. The British-owned *North China Daily News*. The American-owned *Shanghai Evening Post and Mercury*. All who spoke out against Japan came under attack. The *China Press* itself wasn't spared. Those terrorists, presumably under Japanese order, had tried to bomb their office dozens of times.

The Chinese newspapers and press, of course, were always frequent targets. The opponents of free speech and free press did not discriminate.

Eden stopped her bike and locked it against the rack next to a row of parked cars. The attendant came and she gave him a coin for the fee. One of the security guards standing at the building's front entrance rushed over to her. "Good morning."

"Good morning," she returned the greeting. She gazed up at the building's exterior wall, now covered with steel netting to shield the staff from grenade attacks. What neutrality? She was part of the war.

She proceeded inside, ready for another day's battle. The security guard followed her until she was safely inside and out of sight from the streets.

At her desk, she sat down and focused her mind on her latest article. There was no use thinking about the dangers. If she was that scared, she could quit.

No one else had quit, and neither would she. She spent the next hours drafting and reviewing her work.

The phone rang. She picked up the receiver. "Hello?"

"Eden?"

"Yes?" She dropped her arm down a bit. "Clark?"

"I spoke to General-Consul Ho Feng-Shan just now. I have some news."

"What's that?"

"The Weissmans will be leaving Germany. They got tickets for the MS *St. Louis* to depart on May 13."

"The MS *St. Louis*?" Eden asked. She didn't recognize the ship's name. "It's bound for Shanghai?"

"No. It'll be heading to Cuba."

"Cuba? Why are they going there and not here?"

"It's the first ship they could get on. A lot of people are

desperate to leave. There are only a few places they can go. All the ships to China are booked out till July. The Cuban officials in Munich are selling visas for entry into their country. The Weissmans have the option to leave for Cuba in six weeks or wait till they could come to Shanghai in July. They decided not to wait."

Eden flipped her desk calendar to the month of May. No, they shouldn't wait. They'd been trying to get out for two years. The Nazis were now arresting Jews and deporting them to Poland. Every day they delayed, they risked their safety even more. "Thanks for letting me know. Have you told Isaac yet?"

"No. I will. I thought I'd tell you first."

Tell her first? Why?

She knew why. He couldn't help himself.

Their conversation came to a stop. She held on to the phone. What still lingered between them, it was like a wilting flower in a desert, dying under the scorching sun. A heavy downpour of rain, rather than reviving it, had beat its stem to the ground. It'd be hopeless to think it could survive.

Finally, she spoke, "Thank you then."

"You're welcome. I'll call Isaac."

"Okay." She hung up the phone. Her hand still held on to the receiver like it had a mind of its own. She felt an urge to snatch it back up.

"Eden!" Alex's voice snapped her out of her thoughts. He came toward her desk like he had not a care in the world.

"What are you doing here?" She stood up.

"I was in the area," he said. "Thought I'd come and see if you want to have lunch with me."

"Lunch?" She looked up at the clock on the wall. It was well past noon.

"Yeah. I got my iron with me. We can zoom over to that little restaurant where we had *dan dan mian* last time?" He meant the Szechuan dish with soft, thin white noodles served in a spicy broth with chili oil with chopped peanuts and ground pork. He never thought much of the imitation version of soggy noodles smashed with peanut butter paste they served in America. Only when he came to China did he realize how the Chinese actually cooked this dish. And now, he couldn't get enough of it.

"I'd like that," Eden said. She put away her work. Alex came at just the right time to rescue her from her own doleful thoughts. "Good thing I wore pants today." She grabbed her coat.

"Maybe you were hoping I'll take you on a ride," he put his arm around her and whispered.

On his Indian Scout, Eden held on to Alex as he cruised past the traffic. He always drove too fast and the headwind was blowing her hair into a mess. But she didn't care. She leaned forward against his back. Let the wind take her wherever it wanted her to go. Alex knew how to drop all worries and enjoy life as it was. If she stayed with him long enough, she might catch a whiff of that.

They turned into a quieter side road. Suddenly, a black car cut in front of them and blocked their path. Alex slammed on the brake and came to a full stop. Eden jerked back but held on.

Two Asian men exited the car. The driver remained in his seat.

"Alex Mitchell?" asked one of the men who had gotten out of the car. He wore a Japanese army uniform with the collar patch of a lieutenant, the one with gold and red stripes bearing one star.

Alex didn't answer.

The lieutenant squinted. "Are you Alex Mitchell, the radio news reporter?"

Alex still wouldn't answer. From behind him, Eden couldn't see his face.

The lieutenant and his cohort exchanged a glance. The other man checked the photo in his hand, then raised his cold eyes at Alex. Eden pulled Alex closer and whispered, "What's happening?"

Alex shook his head to signal her to be quiet.

The man holding the photo nodded at the lieutenant. The lieutenant came closer. "You are Alex Mitchell. Yes, we think so. So sorry, you must come with us."

Cautiously, Alex got off the motorcycle. Eden got off too to get out of his way. Her pulse started to race. Was he actually going to go with them?

The man in civilian clothing stepped forward. The open collar of this shirt revealed a glimpse of his muscular chest. Alex glanced at the photo he was holding. "Can I see that please?"

The man raised his hand to show him the photo. As he did so, Alex grabbed his forearm. Caught by surprise, the man widened his eyes and struck out his other arm. His movement was quick, but Alex was even quicker. He blocked the man and swiped his arm away. Before the man could react, Alex shot out his other arm and sliced his hand against the man's throat. The man yelped.

Where did Alex learn to hit like that?

Not taking a chance, Alex swung out his leg sideways and kicked the man on his lower back. The man howled and fell forward face first onto the ground.

Eden gasped. With those boots Alex was wearing, that kick had got to hurt.

The lieutenant's face burned red. He reached for the gun in his holster.

"Alex!" Eden shouted.

Alex turned his head. The lieutenant tried to raise the weapon, but Alex slapped his forearm down. He pushed his other hand forward and smashed the bottom of his palm against the lieutenant's nose. Blood splattered out from the man's nostrils as he fell backward and dropped his gun.

Stunned, Eden took a step back. Alex jumped back onto his motorbike. "Eden! Get on!"

Quickly, Eden climbed back onto the seat behind him. Alex slammed his foot on the gas. The motorcycle vroomed and they sped away in the direction from which they had come. As they rode, Eden squeezed her eyes shut. Her heart hammered against Alex's back. She didn't know how long they had ridden before he slowed down and came to a stop on the side of a wide and busy avenue. Still hanging on to him, she opened her eyes.

Alex turned his head around. "Are you all right?"

"Yes." She took a deep breath. "Who were those people?"

"I don't know."

"Where did they want to take you?"

"Beats me." He shrugged.

A frightening thought came to her mind. "Those men wanted to kidnap you, didn't they?" she asked, almost afraid to say the words.

He didn't answer. That meant he was thinking the same thing.

Real fear sank in. Her body started to shake.

"We got away." He flashed her a quick smile. "That guy holding my picture was a judo fighter. I could tell from the way he moved. Too bad for him. My Wing Chun moves were better."

"Wing Chun?"

"Yes. It's a form of Chinese martial arts. I've been taking lessons for more than a year. It helps me focus my mind. Never thought I'd actually use it for self-defense though."

And a good thing it came into use. Knowing he could fight like that, her mind felt a little more at ease.

But perhaps it wasn't enough. Instead of making another wisecrack, Alex said, "I'm taking you back to your office."

"Why? We still haven't eaten yet."

"I don't feel comfortable taking you around like this right now. I need to sort some things out."

She started to tell him she was fine, but the quiet look on his face gave her pause. She'd never seen him look so serious.

Without another word, he started the motorcycle again and drove until they returned to the *China Press* office. A security guard from the building came toward them and she got off the bike.

"I'll call you tonight." Alex turned the handle and rode off.

The security guard greeted her, "Good afternoon, Miss Levine."

"Hello," Eden said. She looked down the street but Alex was already gone.

"Did you have a good lunch?"

Eden didn't know how to answer, so she smiled. No, she did not, but she'd lost her appetite now anyhow.

Slowly, she left the street and let the guard escort her back inside.

7

OUTFOXED

AT THE CAFE SAMBUCA, Clark made his way to the bar. Zhou had already arrived, nursing a drink. Discreetly, Clark took a seat on the barstool beside him, but kept enough distance so it would appear they were both there by themselves.

Zhou gave no sign of acknowledging his arrival. He swirled his glass, then raised it and took a sip. A bartender came over and asked Clark what he would like. Clark ordered a martini and waited for him to walk away before he spoke. "Too spectacular," he said, praising Zhou and his team. Their assassination yesterday of Xi Shi-Tai, the puppet government's police commissioner in Shanghai, was the Whangpoo Brigade's most daring achievement yet. When Xi came out of his backdoor in the morning, Zhou stepped out from the shadows and opened fire at him point-blank, killing him on the spot.

Luckily too, the getaway car whisked Zhou away before he got caught. The cracks of the gunshot brought a police constable to the scene. A watchman at Xi's house tried to retaliate. But in his haste, he fumbled and failed to pull the trigger.

"Thank you." Zhou smiled. "That needle in the eye. My brothers and I wanted to get rid of him long ago."

"A drink to victory." Clark raised his glass.

Zhou did the same. "A drink to victory."

Clark put down his martini. No doubt, Hayashi would raise hell again with the SMC. Let him then. The SMC at this point was no more than a theater where everything was done only for show. For Clark himself, the show on stage now was Roy Bain, the pathetic tool of Japan's counterfeiting schemes. The SMP had put together enough evidence against him to issue a warrant for his arrest. When Bain went on trial and began to spill on everything the Japanese had been doing, it would be beyond delightful to watch Hayashi lose face in front of Keswick, Franklin, and the rest.

But Bain wasn't even the main attraction. That was still to come. In June, Juntong would strike from within the Japanese Consulate. An agent, a sous-chef, had been planted in the consulate's cooking staff. Two months from now, when Vice Minister Shimizu of the Japanese Foreign Office came for his visit, a pack of high-ranking Japanese officials, along with the dogs serving as their collaborators, would meet their date with death. A potent poison from the kitchen awaited them.

The waiter came over, a bottle of gin in his hand. "Want another one?"

"Please." Clark tapped the bar top. Zhou held up his glass to signal he wanted another one too.

While the waiter mixed their drinks, the owner of Sambuca, Mauricio Perez, whose connections extended throughout the Shanghai underworld, walked up to Clark. His somber face put Clark on high alert.

"Bad news," Mauricio said under his breath. "Sergeant Wylie tried to arrest Roy Bain an hour ago. Bain ran into Hongkew and now they can't touch him."

Clark frowned. How did Wylie let him get away?

"That's not all." Mauricio shifted closer as he darted his eyes at the people near them. "Wylie ran into Hongkew during the chase and the Japanese gendarmerie arrested him."

"Arrested Wylie?" Clark asked. "For what?"

"They said he's been selling arms to the Chinese."

"Wylie? Selling arms to the Chinese? That's ridiculous!" That was a lie. If Cliff Wylie were selling arms to the resistance, he would know.

"Not your kind of Chinese," Mauricio said. "The Chinese on the other side. The collaborators."

"What?" Clark nearly choked on his drink. "That's got to be a joke."

"No," Mauricio answered in all seriousness.

Clark couldn't believe it. Never mind the accusation was outrageous. Even if it were true, it would mean the Japanese were accusing someone of aiding their own running dogs.

"They're turning Wylie over to the SMP. Of course, you know Wylie's an American. It's against American law for U.S. citizens to sell arms to foreigners."

"I don't believe it." Clark took a large gulp of his drink. "Wylie wouldn't do this. They're making this up. They'll make up fake evidence against him, I'm sure, but their accusation is false."

"Actually . . ." Mauricio lowered his eyes. "I have a reliable source telling me it's true."

"No." Clark slammed down his glass. "Why? Why would he do that? Mauricio, please tell me no."

"I wish I could. Crimes in the Badlands are out of control. He tried to leverage help from some of the opium houses and gambling dens. The deal was, he would supply them guns if they would keep some of the robberies and kidnappings down. He thought it'd be a win-win to help those places protect themselves."

Stunned, Clark froze. Mauricio called the bartender over. "Would you like another drink? I'll get you one on the house."

"No thank you." Clark took a bill out of his wallet and put it on the bar.

"Good luck," Mauricio said.

Clark got down from the barstool. He'd need plenty of luck all right. This would be a hell of a mess to clean up.

Zhou gave him a quick glance, then looked away and returned to nursing his drink. Without acknowledging him, Clark waved goodbye to Mauricio and left.

At the SMC meeting, Clark sat stone-faced while Hayashi laid out the evidence against Sergeant Wylie on the table. The sworn statements of collaborators and various miscreants could be questioned, but the photos were beyond dispute.

Up until last night, Clark thought he had the winning hand. He'd been savoring the idea of watching Hayashi stew when they caught Roy Bain. Instead, here he was now, watching Hayashi gloat.

However frustrated he felt, Commissioner Bourne looked even worse. Hayashi now had an excuse to blame the SMP and hold them directly responsible.

"I trust the American authorities will take proper actions." Hayashi pushed the witness testimonies toward Cornell Franklin.

Franklin had no choice but to concede. "We will certainly look into this."

"This just goes to show, American police are not above reproach when it comes to ethical standards."

"No. Of course not." Franklin rubbed his temple. "If Sergeant Wylie is found to be guilty, my government will hold him to the highest degree of accountability."

Clark dropped his arms to his side. It was painful watching Franklin shamed by the old fox.

Hayashi turned his attention to the police chief next.

"Commissioner Bourne. How could you let this happen? You said you had the SMP under control."

Bourne's face turned deep red. "Yes. This was my oversight. My understanding is, Sergeant Wylie elicited outside help when he felt his squad couldn't keep the area secure on their own. Nonetheless, it's no excuse. What he did was wrong, and it happened under my watch. I let you all down. I'm sorry." He kept his head high and looked them all in the eye.

What a shame. He'd been trying so hard. Clark wished he could say something in his defense. Even Wylie shouldn't be blamed. It was a foolish move. But if the Badlands hadn't turned into such a cesspool and the police hadn't been so overwhelmed, would he have done what he did? And now, he would personally suffer the consequences. In all likelihood, he'd go to jail.

"At least now we can admit fault comes from all sides." Hayashi sat back and crossed his arms. "Rather than laying blame, my government wanted you all to understand we desire nothing more than for all of us to work together. That's why our gendarmerie will be turning Sergeant Wylie over to you. We understand Sergeant Wylie committed a grave crime that violated American law, and he should properly be tried by an American court."

Clark gave him a side glance. That old fox was couching another message in his words.

"We hope you'll take this as a gesture of goodwill from us." Hayashi held his hand out calmly around the table. "Commissioner Bourne, perhaps you will now see the value of adding even more of our recruits to your force. I have a new slate of candidates for you to consider." He handed him a sheet of paper.

Bourne thinned his lips. With great reluctance, he said, "I'm open to discussion."

"Good." Hayashi nodded. "Mutual cooperation. That's how we can stamp out crime. Would the Council agree?"

"Yes," Keswick said, saving his compatriot from further embarrassment. "Mutual cooperation has always been our goal."

Watching them talk, Clark squeezed his fist. There was no hope for Keswick to take a stand to try to salvage their plan. He would have to do it himself. "Hayashisan."

The old fox raised an eyebrow.

"Since we're talking about cooperation, what about Roy Bain? Sergeant Wylie was trying to catch him before he ran into Hongkew."

"Roy Bain? Ah, yes. The casino manager passing off counterfeit money. Such a dishonorable person."

"That he is," Clark said. "He's in your sector now. Would your government help us catch him so we can bring him to justice?"

"Of course we would," Hayashi said. "The only problem is, we don't know where he's gone. If our gendarmerie catches him though, you can be sure we'll let the SMP know at once and turn him over."

Clark looked down. He shook his head and smirked. "What about his conspirators? We know he was working with someone named Hirata."

"Yes. I've been told." Hayashi threw him a glance. A trace of annoyance flickered, but Hayashi kept his composure. "I will inquire with our gendarmerie and ask them to look into this. However, these allegations are all hearsay at the moment. We don't even know who Hirata is. No one on our side has ever heard of him. But if the SMP would like to give us all the information they have found about him, it would go a long way to help us investigate."

The cunning old man. If the SMP turned over their files, the Japanese would immediately erase every trail and evidence they had on Hirata.

Thankfully, Commissioner Bourne saw through this too. "Police bureaus from different jurisdictions sharing information is not standard practice. While in this case, it might be helpful, I don't recommend we go down that road. It would open the door for similar requests by every other jurisdiction in the future. That could compromise ongoing investigations. I'm sure the Japanese gendarmerie would feel the same way if the request for information came from us."

"Very well." Hayashi shrugged. He didn't push the matter any further. Then again, he didn't need to. Pretty soon, the SMP would be overrun with Japanese, and all he'd need was to ask any one of his spies whenever he wanted to know what International Settlement police were up to.

The old fox smiled at the table, assuming the air of the one presiding the meeting. "If there's nothing else, shall we call the meeting to a close?"

Taken aback, Cornell Franklin stuttered, "The meeting's adjourned."

Hayashi stood up. The rest of the Council members followed and filed out of the room. Dejected, Clark waited for Franklin and Keswick. They all understood that their plan to use the trial against Roy Bain as a public show of force was ruined.

Before he left, Clark pulled Franklin aside. "What will happen to Sergeant Wylie?"

Franklin said with a straight face, "He'll need a very good lawyer."

28

VOYAGE TO NOWHERE

EDEN HAD BARELY SAT down at her desk after arriving at work when Charlie called her into his office. On his radio, the announcer of the international evening news broadcast spoke from the United States.

> *As of 4:00 a.m. this morning on May 27, the MS* St. Louis *from Hamburg has arrived at the Havana Harbor. However, President Brú has refused to let the ship dock. All passengers on board have been denied entry into Cuba, including the ones with entry visas issued by the Cuban embassies.*

"Denied entry?" Eden frowned and looked up. "What does that mean?"

Charlie shook his head, indicating he didn't know either. The radio announcer continued.

> *By Decree 937, the Cuban government has declared that all permits and visas issued before May 5 are officially invalid.*

"That's outrageous!" Eden slammed her hand on the desk. "They have all the right papers!"

Charlie held up his pen to halt her so they could hear the rest of the radio announcement.

Captain Gustav Schröder is in negotiations with the Cuban officials. We will continue to monitor the situation and keep you up to date.

The news report ended and music replaced the announcer's voice.

"How can they do this?" Eden asked as soon as Charlie turned off the radio. The Weissmans were on board that ship, and they were holding Cuban tourist visas. They paid $150 U.S. dollars each for them!

"They changed their immigration law," Charlie said. "It's terrible but I'm not surprised. The whole immigration problem's been festering for some time. There are allegations Gonzalez was illegally selling visas and permits." Gonzalez was the Director General of the Cuban immigration office. "The Depression is hitting the Cuban economy hard. A lot of people there are complaining about immigrants taking away whatever jobs that are left."

"Or they just don't like the Jews, and they don't care what would happen to them."

Charlie hung his head. He tossed a copy of the newspaper to the side of his desk.

"I have to find my friend Isaac and tell him." She walked toward the door.

"Things might turn," Charlie said. "Maybe they'll be able to negotiate something and work it out."

Maybe. But what would she say to Isaac now?

———

At the office of the U.S. Consulate, Eden tried her best to remain patient as Joseph Whitman explained the situation with MS *St.*

Louis. Once again, Clark was giving them a direct line of contact with someone who might have the means and ability to help the Weissmans. She was grateful, and she didn't want to appear otherwise.

"What does it mean, Mr. Whitman, that the passengers must wait their turn like all other immigrants before they could be admitted into the United States?" Dr. Levine asked. "It's been six days since that ship arrived in North America. How long would the wait be? How long do you all think the passengers can remain on that ship before it's their turn?"

"That's the State Department's official line," Whitman answered. When Cuba refused to accept any passengers except for four Spanish citizens, two Cuban nationals, and twenty-eight others who had U.S. visas, the ship's captain, Gustav Schröder, sailed the ship to Miami, hoping the United States would take them in.

"We have immigration quotas," Whitman explained, "but that would not be a concern for you, I promise." He looked over at Isaac. "Mr. Weissman, if the ship eventually docks at our harbor, I have friends standing ready to issue visas to your parents, regardless of what the government's official position is."

Isaac scrunched his face. "They're so close. They're off the coast of Miami. Isn't there any way you can send a dinghy or something to pick them up?"

Whitman stared at his hands. "It's not that simple."

"Mr. Whitman, can you tell us the truth?" Dr. Levine asked. "There's no chance the U.S. would accept these passengers, is there? After all, your Congress wouldn't even pass a bill to add more Jewish children to your quota. If they won't even save the children, what's the chance of them taking these passengers at all?"

"That's right, Mr. Whitman," said Mrs. Levine. "We do appreciate everything you're trying to do for us. I know you're only one man, and there's only so much you can do. But please allow me to say this. It's not only our friends the Weissmans who need help. Our people are being persecuted in Germany. Our very lives are at stake. The whole world knows that after what happened last November. These people on the ship are desperate. Your government is in a position to help. Why won't they? We're only talking about nine hundred and seven people. We have thousands arriving in Shanghai. Surely a big country like the United States can take a few hundred."

"Yes." Whitman rubbed his nose. "From a humanitarian standpoint, I absolutely agree. Unfortunately, back in Washington, things are more complicated."

"What's so complicated?" Mrs. Levine asked. Eden could see her mother felt angry, and her mother rarely got angry. "I respect that you have laws, and I understand your government might be concerned about more ships coming with passengers to seek sanctuary. But can't the people in charge come up with plans on how to deal with that later? These people on the *St. Louis* are already there. They can't go back. They'd be imprisoned and sent to concentration camps. How can everyone stand by and do nothing?"

"Mrs. Levine—" Clark said.

"Mother," Eden interjected. As frustrated as she felt, she didn't want to jeopardize Clark's goodwill. Or Whitman's either. It wouldn't help to put him on the spot.

"I understand your point," Whitman said. "Again, I don't disagree. But convincing the people back home isn't so easy. This last week, the Germans have been claiming in their press the passengers are Communists."

"That's ridiculous!" Isaac tossed up his hand. "That's a lie. Those Nazis are only trying to make themselves look justified."

"Of course. You must understand though, the people in my country . . . xenophobia is a serious problem."

And anti-Semitism, Eden thought, although she didn't say it out loud. Anti-Semitism was everywhere. Why else would so many countries turn a blind eye to their plight? Besides Cuba, every Latin American country had said no.

"Xenophobia is driving many Americans to remain isolationists," Whitman said. "When people fear something they don't know, they believe all sorts of rumors. Such as German Jews being Communists, or worse."

"Worse?" Isaac asked. "Like what?"

"Like allegations that the Jewish passengers on board the *St. Louis* are Gestapo spies."

"Gestapo spies?" Isaac laughed. "That's absurd! The Nazis hate us. Why would they trust any Jews to spy for them? Why would any Jew work for them?"

"I know. But these are the fears motivating some people to argue against letting the passengers in."

Isaac's mouth fell agape. Then, his expression calmed. For a moment, he seemed to have retreated into his own thoughts. Mrs. Levine put a hand on his back. "Mr. Whitman, whatever people may believe, your president can't possibly think this is the case."

Whitman tightened his shoulders and clasped his hands. "I believe my government is doing its best to find a solution. There are ongoing negotiations with several other countries, including Cuba. We might be able to convince President Brú to change his mind."

Eden dropped her stare to the floor. The government was doing its best. None of it sounded convincing.

Isaac straightened up in his scat. Eden thought he wanted to complain. Instead, he gave Whitman a grateful smile. "Thank you, Mr. Whitman. Whatever happens, I really appreciate your help."

Whitman twitched his lips and tried to smile back, but couldn't.

"Clark," Isaac said and turned to him, "thank you for bringing us here."

"Of course," Clark said. "Anything I can do to help. I hope everything will work out."

Whitman stood up from his desk. Isaac got up too. Eden watched as the two of them shook hands. Isaac had never looked more dignified. The back of her throat soured and a sting pinched her eyes. The whole world was casting his parents aside. Somehow, he'd found the strength to still carry himself with respect. She felt so proud of him.

As they got up to leave, she glanced over at Clark. Their eyes met. This time, he was the first to look away.

She watched him say goodbye to Whitman and Isaac, then her parents. To her, he merely waved from a distance, and then he left.

Standing back, she felt as though an anchor had slipped away. In the ocean now, she would have to find her own way out.

Sitting by Alex's side in his studio, Eden listened as he railed about the plight of the MS *St. Louis*. Four days ago, Captain Schröder decided to sail back to Europe. The story became old news and other agencies had moved on, but Alex would not let the controversy drop.

> *Horrendous! This is a horrendous turn of event. Two weeks. That ship was stranded along the Miami coast for two weeks, and not a single country in all of North America has the mercy to take those people in. There are children on board, for God's sake. How can the U.S. government stand by and watch this ship go back to Europe? Where is Roosevelt? Why hasn't he said anything? He knows what Hitler would do to these people if they go back. At this point, we're as bad as the Nazis.*

Alex waved his finger in the air as he spoke, his strong voice giving her the only sliver of comfort. Amidst the silence from all those in power, Alex's voice was the only one shouting out to the world the pent-up anger she felt inside. And he was never one to mince words.

He picked up a paper with his notes and ranted again into the microphone.

I think Canadian Minister Blair summed up what those in charge think. So here, listen to this. This is a direct quote: "No country could open its doors wide enough to take in hundreds of thousands of Jewish people who want to leave Europe. The line must be drawn somewhere."

He slapped down the paper.

So because no country could take in hundreds of thousands, that means all countries must shut their doors right now and take no one? There are nine hundred and seven desperate people on the St. Louis. *All the countries on the entire American continent couldn't come up with a plan to grant asylum to nine hundred people?*

Eden listened with a grim face. Nine hundred and seven was just a number. The Weissmans were not a number. They were real people. What would happen to them now?

Draw the line? We're drawing the line on saving human lives? Where is our moral conscience? Why can't we draw a line and say enough is enough, and we must not allow discrimination and violence against the Jewish people to continue? If he truly worries that hundreds of thousands of Jews would show up at the harbor in Halifax, then this is what he should be talking about. I want to know, how do these "world leaders" sleep at night?

While speaking, Alex reached out and stroked her back. A fog of sadness overtook her.

We'll see now if the leaders in Europe will do better. Captain Schröder
vowed he won't take the ship back to Germany until every passenger finds
landing somewhere else. There are limited food and supplies for these people
on the ship. If no one helps them, then for these people, it'll be the end.

He let out a deep sigh and glanced over at Eden. She gave his
hand a gentle squeeze and he returned to his mike.

On another note, I have some good news to report today. Oh, sorry, I mean
bad news. More bad news.

He made a face that indicated he was not sorry. Eden smiled.
This piece of news came from the actress Ye Ting. Ye Ting heard
it from the group of puppet officials she was lunching with earlier
today, and she called Eden afterward to give her the tip.

I got this exclusive from my good friend Apollo Eirene of the China Press.
Yesterday, June 10, the Japanese Consul-General Miura gave a dinner in
honor of Vice Minister Shimizu of their Foreign Office. At the dinner was
Shanghai Garrison Commander Lieutenant General Yamada, and the head
of the Chinese Reform Government Liang Hong-Zhi and his underling
Mayor Gao from Nanking. According to sources, after dinner, everybody fell
ill. So ill, in fact, General Yamada and two of his attachés died. Mayor Gao
is still hospitalized. Was this a bad case of food poisoning?

A smirk came across his lips. He made it a point to emphasize
and enunciate the word "poisoning." No listener could miss the
clue now. Someone, most likely the Chinese resistance, had tried
to kill these people with poison. The men who Ye Ting dined with
believed this was the case too.

Curious. There's been no official report of this from the Japanese bulletins.
Three people died, including a high-level military official. Now, I would've
expected the authorities to investigate whether foul play was involved.

Strange how they seem to be covering this up. Or maybe not. If this wasn't simply a case of bad food poisoning, then it'd be hugely embarrassing for them to have to admit to their own soldiers that someone from their opposition had succeeded in infiltrating their consulate.

Anyway, my sincere condolences to Emperor Hirohito and all of Japan. I'm sure it was just a bad case of food poisoning. How sad to hear a mighty military general has been taken down by an amoeba. My heart goes out to him and those who have fallen. Not on the battlefield, but killed by an amoeba.

At this, Eden covered her mouth and chuckled. The Japanese hated to lose face, and Alex was once again poking their sore spot.

He wrapped up his broadcast and turned off the mike. She beamed at him and clapped her hands.

His producer came into the studio. "Eden, there's a phone call for you."

"For me?" Eden asked. Who would call her at Alex's studio?

She followed the producer and Alex back to his office and answered the phone.

It was a woman on the other line. "Eden? This is Dottie."

The secretary at the *China Press*? "Dottie?"

"You said you'd be at Mr. Mitchell's studio tonight during his broadcast. Well, I just want to tell you, I was trying to listen to it on the radio earlier, and I couldn't hear anything he said."

"What do you mean?" Eden frowned.

"All I heard were statics. My neighbors in the apartments next door said the same thing."

"Statics? Dottie, can I give you over to Alex? I'm not sure what you're saying." Eden handed the phone to Alex.

"Yes?" Alex answered. "Umm-hmm . . . huh . . . Is that right?" He glanced at her. "Thank you, Mrs. Lambert. I appreciate it." He finished and hung up.

"What was that all about?" Eden asked.

"Jamming." He fell into his seat and slid down, stretching out his legs. "I've been getting reports from listeners about this. The Japs are trying to jam the radio signal so people can't hear me when I'm on the air. It started last week. Mr. Yamato's got transmitters set up all over Soochow Creek trying to disrupt my radio frequency."

"That's terrible."

"Yeah. In some parts in the city and some areas outside, my show's blotted out." He looked at Eden. The brashness on his face softened. "Don't worry, doll. Their transmitters can only interfere with the local reception. I'm now on shortwave. The whole world can hear me." He pulled her onto his lap. "They can't stop us," he said and allayed her worries with a reassuring kiss.

29

HITLER'S FIRST MOVE

WITH THE BAG OF DATES, jams, and apples dipped in honey in her hand, Eden rang the doorbell to Isaac's apartment. It was still more than a week till Rosh Hashanah, but the gifts might cheer him up.

He looked surprised to see her. "Eden? Come on in."

"I brought these for you." She handed him the gifts. "Something sweet to start off a new year?"

"Thank you." He closed the door and opened the bag.

On the radio, BBC London was repeating the broadcast of Neville Chamberlain's full speech.

This morning, the British Ambassador in Berlin handed the German government a final note, stating that unless we heard from them by eleven o'clock that they were prepared at once to withdraw their troops from Poland, a state of war would exist between us.

I have to tell you now that no such undertaking has been received, and that consequently, this country is at war with Germany.

Isaac turned off the radio. Yesterday, Britain declared war on Germany. France immediately followed.

The Weissmans were now in France.

When the MS *St. Louis* sailed back to Europe, Captain Schröder worked out an agreement with Britain, Belgium, the Netherlands, and France to each take a number of passengers. Isaac's parents were among the two hundred twenty-four who landed in France.

"I got a letter from Ma and Pa yesterday." Isaac served her a cup of tea.

"What did they say?"

"They said they're settling in fine in Paris. A lot of Jewish groups have reached out and helped all the *St. Louis* passengers find homes and new jobs. Pa took a clerical position at a local school. Of course, they sent that letter four weeks ago, before all this." He pointed at the radio.

"I'm sorry."

"It's all right." Isaac flashed a cheerful smile. "The world is what it is. We just have to take it in stride. Anyway, my parents got out. They're in France now. That's much better than where they were two months ago. Besides, now that Britain and France declared war on Hitler, maybe all the Nazi craziness will stop."

"I hope so."

"Say, I got some mooncakes. Would you like some?"

"Mooncakes?" Isaac bought mooncakes? Since when did he celebrate the Chinese Mid-Autumn Festival? And he never cared for Chinese snacks and delicacies.

"Yes. I got some with red bean paste, and another kind with lotus seed paste and salty egg yolk. Which one would you like? They'll go well with your tea."

Eden's jaw nearly dropped. "The lotus seed paste with salty egg yolk will be fine."

He got up and went into the kitchen. Moments later, he returned with a plate of small wedges of mooncakes for them both.

She picked up a wedge and took a bite. "Isaac, you've changed."

"Changed?" He raised an eyebrow. "How?"

"You're more optimistic."

"Am I?" He threw a wedge of mooncake into his mouth. "I guess I came to realize, there's no point dwelling on things I can't change. Even if my own situation is bad, there are always people who have it even worse. Look what happened to the Chinese two years ago when the Japanese came and leveled this city. I'm here. I'm making a living because of what they could give me. If I can give others a little support, then why wouldn't I?" He grinned and finished another wedge of mooncake. "If everyone would give to each other instead of hurting each other, our world wouldn't be such a mess."

Eden finished the rest of her wedge. She felt better now. Isaac was not wallowing in sadness and self-pity.

"Anyway, when France and Britain put Hitler in his place, maybe I can move to Paris and join Ma and Pa."

"You want to go back to Europe?"

"I'd like to be back with my parents. Besides, you can see for yourself. China isn't exactly the safest place to be either. Who knows how long their war with Japan will go on?"

That was true. If her family had somewhere else to go, they might want to leave too.

"I'd invite you to come with me," Isaac said. He looked straight at her. There was no concealing what he meant. His directness took her off guard. He'd never been so forthright about his feelings for her.

"Of course, you already have different plans. You'd be heading to a different continent. Maybe America." He smiled and beamed at her. This was so unlike him. She didn't even feel annoyed as she always had.

He finished his tea and wiped his mouth with a napkin. "Did

your parents tell you? I started a work training and job placement group for Jewish refugees."

"Yes." She picked up another wedge of mooncake. "They mentioned something about that. Tell me what you're doing."

"We've been working with foreign companies to keep a tally of job openings where we can send applicants. Of course, things are difficult here for the new arrivals. Most of them can't speak anything but German and perhaps Yiddish. I'm working with some colleagues at the hospital to teach them basic English and French. If they can master that, they can replace the foreigners who left."

Right. Many foreign expats had departed the city since Japan took over the Chinese sectors. "That's wonderful. I'm sure a lot of people would appreciate what you're doing. Do you mind if I tell Charlie about it? Maybe he'll run an article about it."

"Sure. As long as the article doesn't focus on me. The more important thing is to let employers know there are people who need jobs, and if they can work with us, they could give these people a lifeline." He gave her a wry smile. "Maybe Apollo Eirene could write the article."

Eden jerked up her head. "You . . . How'd you . . ."

"Come on, Eden! How long have we known each other? You can fool other people, but you can't fool me."

The doorbell rang. He gave her a quizzical look. "I wonder who that is." He got up to open the door.

A man in a blue sport coat and gray pants stood outside. He looked to be around their age. "Isaac!"

"Jacob," Isaac greeted him. "Come on in."

Jacob entered. When he saw Eden, he took off his hat. He didn't wait for Isaac to introduce them. "Isaac, we've got a serious problem. Sixty-three people we helped placed in jobs just got fired."

"Fired?" Isaac asked. "Why?"

"All their employers are British companies and French companies. They said their countries are now at war with Germany, and German Jews are German, so they can't hire them anymore."

"You're joking!"

"No. They're all at the Jewish Community Center now. There's also a group of men who run their own businesses. The French government revoked their business licenses. They were told they could no longer operate in Frenchtown."

"That's madness!" Isaac exclaimed. "Germany doesn't even recognize us as citizens." He turned to Eden, "I'm sorry. I have to go. I have to go see what's going on."

Eden got up. "I'll come with you. Charlie will want to hear about this."

Isaac nodded. He picked up his keys and they followed him out.

In the courtroom, Clark sat in the back while he waited for the judge of the United States Court for China to declare the verdict. From the side door, an SMP officer brought in former Sergeant Cliff Wylie with his hands in cuffs.

Across the aisle, Hayashi Yukichi sat, his hand resting confidently on the top of his cane. Aside from them, only reporters and friends of Wylie from the SMP had shown up. No American officials wanted to be associated with Wylie in any way.

Clark turned his attention back to the front of the courtroom. To his surprise, Eden came and sat down beside him. She gave him a soft smile, then looked up at the front of the courtroom at the judge.

The officer brought Wylie to the defendant's podium.

On the bench, the judge announced, "Having regard to the

totality of the evidence presented in this matter, the decision of this court is the following. First, on the count of violation of Section One of the Neutrality Act prohibiting the export of arms, ammunition, and implements of war to belligerent countries, the defendant is found guilty."

Clark slumped back. Over on the other side, Hayashi's mouth twitched up.

The judge continued, "Second, on the count of attempted export of arms, ammunition, and implements of war, the defendant is found guilty."

Beside him, Eden whispered, "I'm so sorry."

He was too. What should've been an opportunity for the SMC to show the Japanese the West still had teeth had completely backfired.

At the podium, Wylie hung his head. His entire career had been destroyed, and that wasn't the worst. The judge continued, "I hereby sentence you to five years of imprisonment for each count, to be served concurrently. You will be deported back to the United States to serve your time as soon as arrangements can be made."

The officer led Wylie away and Clark stood up. Hayashi glanced at him, not a friendly salute but not outright antagonistic either, then walked out.

Still, Hayashi made his point. Japan had won this round.

Along with the other trial spectators, Clark and Eden left. Outside on the courthouse steps, Clark said to her, "I'm the one who should say sorry. You gave me a good lead. We made a mess of it."

"You tried."

"Does it matter?" He gazed out to the flags of all the nations still fluttering on top of the buildings lining the Bund. "Do you still keep the same dreams?"

She came a step closer. "Yes."

He turned to face her. Did she? Really? Or was it only the right thing to say?

Her firm voice left him no doubt. "Yes, my dreams haven't changed. There are still people only you and I can help. Last week, almost two hundred Jewish refugees lost their jobs because their British and French employers said they were at war with Germany and they couldn't hire Germans anymore. They said the German Jews were German. I wanted to believe it was an honest mistake, but when we talked to some of the managers at the companies where they worked, it was obvious some of them were using the war as an excuse to dismiss the Jews."

Clark frowned. "That's ridiculous."

"I know," Eden said. "It's a cruel world. People like you and me, we're the last line of defense. For those refugees who were dismissed, we eventually got through to the right people and sorted out their situation. Isaac went to every company and demanded to see the top person in charge. One of our reporters wrote a scathing article condemning what happened. Anyway, if we hadn't been there for them, those refugees would be destitute. When we help them, we make the world a little better, and a little part of my dreams comes true. For you, I think you're also doing what you can to save people. They can go on because you are here to stand guard to protect them. And I dream that you'll succeed in the end."

Clark stared out at the laborers loading cargo at the dock. He wanted to be convinced, but deep down, he doubted.

She touched him on the arm. "You already sacrificed so much."

Sacrificed? He looked at her. Indeed, he had. They both had. The biggest sacrifice being one of which they could never speak. Not thinking, he touched her hand.

Startled, she pulled hers back. Did she still feel something for him? Had Alex Mitchell not erase him entirely from her mind?

He shifted his eyes away from hers. He didn't want to find out. Best not to come any nearer to the truth.

"Make it all worth something," Eden said. She took one more look at him and hurried down the steps. He stood, hanging onto those words. Those words could be all he had to keep him from giving up.

30

FOUL PLAY

THE BUTLER CAME AROUND to each of the guests and filled their wine glasses. At the head of the table, Tony Keswick, the newly elected chairman of the SMC for the next two-year term running from 1940 to 1942, sat up in his seat. "Gentlemen, thank you for coming this evening." He smiled warmly at the members of the Council. "It is my honor to have you all at my home. I hope our dinner tonight will mark a successful start to our joint effort to serve the International Settlement. May I propose a toast?" He raised his glass. "We're now entering a new year and a new decade. Here's to the continual growth and prosperity to all of us in Shanghai."

The guests raised their glasses and drank their wine. Clark swirled his after the toast and quietly observed the new chairman. Given how Japan was swallowing up the International Settlement around its rims, the Western coalition of the Council thought it would be best to put Keswick at the top. Franklin was only a lawyer. Jardine Matheson was the leading trading firm in the whole Far East. That gave Keswick a lot more clout with the Shanghai business community. Keswick wanted the appointment too. With the vast amount of assets his company held in China, he had a lot more at stake.

With Keswick at the helm, would the Japanese feel more restraint?

Franklin thought so. He raised his glass the highest when they made the toast.

"Sir Keswick." Hayashi gave him the most pleasant smile. "Our Consul-General Miura wants to congratulate you for your new position, and so do we. As such, we've brought you a little gift." He eyed Okamoto, the younger Japanese representative on the Council.

Okamoto took a large bottle out of the bag beside his seat and brought it to Keswick. "This is *daigingo jumei* sake produced by the Tagaki Shuzo brewery in the Yamagata prefecture. It is the premium sake of Japan. The brewery's been around since 1615. Their sake is rare even in our own country. This particular bottle is best served chilled."

"Thank you, Okamotosan." Keswick stood up and accepted the gift. "Thank you very much, Hayashisan, and Consul-General Miura too." He held up the bottle and admired the label. "I look forward to enjoying this, as I look forward to working with all of you as head of the SMC."

Okamoto bowed and returned to his seat. The butler began to serve the soup.

"Since we're on the topic," Hayashi raised his palm and pointed at Keswick. "We have a proposal we'd like to bring up regarding the next SMC members election in the fall."

"Yes?" Keswick answered. "And what might that be?"

"This is something we have raised with Mr. Franklin in the past. Japan currently has two representatives on the Council, myself and Okamotosan. For the next election, we would like to propose an additional three more candidates for Japan."

Keswick's spoon stopped in midair. "Three more? You mean five Japanese candidates?"

"Yes. The number of Japanese nationals residing in Shanghai has increased greatly in the last two years. It would make sense to add more balance so their needs and interests wouldn't be overlooked."

"I see." Clearly caught off guard, Keswick straightened his back. Clark watched him intently. So the Japanese did not feel restraint at all. They were still testing the limits. What would Keswick do?

Keswick cleared his throat. "Balanced representation certainly is important. It's probably too important to discuss casually over dinner. The next election is many months away. We will definitely put this on our agenda for future discussion and consideration."

"Very well." Hayashi took a sip of wine.

Clark circled the spoon in the soup bowl. Everyone kept their heads down. No one wanted to openly confront the old fox. The Japanese had all but taken over the Municipal Police. Now they wanted to control the Council.

If the Japanese gained three more seats, the British and Americans would lose three seats. Except for Clark himself and Director Dong, the other three Chinese members would always vote with the Japanese out of fear. That would give the Japanese eight votes on all matters while the British and American block would have seven. Japan would effectively control the whole Settlement.

The servant collected the empty soup bowls and brought them the next course of poached salmon. The butler went around the table and refilled the wine. Hayashi picked up his glass. "I'd like to propose another toast."

The members turned their eyes to him. "I'm pleased to announce Imperial Japan has finalized negotiations with former Chinese Premier Mr. Wang Jing-Wei to return power to the Chinese people. Under President Wang's leadership, the current regional government administrations will all consolidate into the new Reorganized National Government of the Republic of China."

Clark threw him a side glance. Wang Jing-Wei? That traitor? So all the rumors were true. That arch-rival of Chiang Kai-Shek who defected from the KMT regime in Chungking was working with Japan to make himself king.

"In regards to the occupied parts of China," Hayashi continued, "It's always been Japan's policy to never demand land, to never demand reparations, and to cease military activities within two years. My country is now making good on that promise. We respect China's right to govern itself. We want to assist China to become independent, so we can mutually support each other as friendly neighbors in economic cooperation and to oppose Communism."

Mumbles broke out from the table. Clark silently smirked. How the old fox could speak such outright lies baffled him. Across the table, Director Dong's face darkened.

Hayashi ignored their murmurs. "I believe our respective governments will all achieve much, much more with President Wang. Therefore, I would like to give a toast to Mr. Wang and wish him success."

The Council members eyed each other. Finally, Keswick raised his glass. "Cheers."

The others followed suit, except Director Dong, who remained still with his arms folded. Clark held his glass in his hand and did not take a sip.

There was no way Japan would relinquish control. Wang Jing-Wei would be nothing more than another puppet. How shameful it was for someone like him to sell out his country this way. He once fought in the revolution with their national founding father, Sun Yat-Sen. Now, he was lending his name to the Japanese to give them legitimacy.

While Clark stayed quiet in his own thoughts, Keswick steered the conversation to the latest opera performance of *Le*

Nozze de Figaro he saw at the Lyceum Theater. The butler began serving the third course of steak. The chef had skillfully prepared the dish, but Clark had no appetite.

Hayashi, on the other hand, had appetite aplenty. He sliced through the meat as though he was slaughtering the weak. He turned his eyes to one of the Council's American members sitting across from him. "Mr. Sutton."

"Yes?" Sutton looked up from his plate.

"I hear business is going well for the egg industry."

Sutton wiped his mouth with a napkin. "Not too bad."

"You're being modest," Hayashi said. "I can see from the Shanghai Stock Exchange your company turned in a very impressive profit last year. Congratulations."

"Thank you." Sutton smiled nervously and shifted his eyes between Hayashi and the others looking at him.

"It's not just your company, but all the American and British egg companies. You all must have some magical formula for how to raise chickens."

"I don't know about that." Sutton laughed. He took a sip of wine. "Agricultural science has developed over the years. We strive to learn so we can provide the best products to our customers."

"You're right. Nowadays, farming isn't all about an idyllic field with shepherds and milkmaids. Which brings me to my point. You're the chair of the Foreign Refrigerated Eggs Packers' Association. The president of Mitsui wants me to ask you if his company could have the honor of joining the Association."

Sutton nearly spat out his wine. "Mitsui?"

Mitsui was one of Japan's largest trading companies.

"Yes." Hayashi cut into his steak. "He greatly admires the quality of eggs produced by Western companies. He would like to bring the same to the Nipponese market. This would be a wonderful opportunity for our businesses to work together, wouldn't you say?"

Work together? Clark sipped his wine. The Japanese didn't have a record of ever working together with anyone. Hayashi's proposal was their way to openly steal the Western egg companies' trade secrets so they could directly compete with the West.

"That . . . uh," Sutton stammered, "a membership is not entirely out of the question . . . it's . . . I would—"

"Of course, we wouldn't seek your grant of a membership without offering something in return. The conflict between Japan and the KMT has made it very difficult to operate businesses in inland China. I heard all the skirmishes are disrupting your company's egg packing plants in Central China. Mitsui has the Nipponese government's full support. If Mitsui is one of your Association's members, we will send our military to protect the plants of all of Mitsui's fellow Association members. Better yet, if any Association member would consider entering into a joint venture with Mitsui, we'll ensure the joint venture safe passes and transport of their products into Shanghai for shipment overseas as well. This will be a great way for us to cooperate for our mutual benefit."

His face flushed, Sutton sat with his mouth open.

"I think it's a splendid idea," Keswick said from the head of the table. "How about it, Sutton?" He turned to Hayashi. "I'm sure something can be worked out. I'm delighted to see our businesses working together and supporting each other."

Clark sat back and let the servant take away his plate. He watched Sutton put down his knife and fork. Keswick just threw Sutton to the wolves.

Silently, he gazed into the wine in his glass. He didn't doubt that Keswick wanted to protect the International Settlement. He had enough reasons to do so out of pride, principles, and to protect his own vast fortune in Asia. But when push came to shove, Keswick couldn't be counted on to stand by anyone's side. He bowed too quickly to the Japanese.

Clark put down his glass. Going forward, he'd have to remember this about the new chairman. And as soon as he had a chance, he had to have a good talk with Keswick to make sure he wouldn't actually jeopardize the power structure of the SMC.

After dinner, Keswick invited all the men to his library for cigars and brandy. Clark wanted to excuse himself and leave, but Keswick privately asked him to stay behind. When everyone had left except for him and Franklin, Keswick opened a new bottle of XO cognac and poured them each a glass.

"Well, dinner was delightful." He walked away from the liquor cabinet.

Clark wasted no time bringing up his immediate concern. "Tony, you can't let this happen. You saw what Hayashi was doing. You can't allow them to have five seats."

Keswick held up his hand. "I know. That's what I want to talk to you both about." He inhaled a puff of his cigar. "I also have unfortunate news. The British government's considering withdrawing our troops from Shanghai. It could happen any time this year."

"Withdrawing the troops?" Clark lowered his glass. "Why? Why now?"

"Hitler's taken over most of Poland. The Soviets annexed the rest, and all the smaller countries around its border. Finland's the only holdout, and that's not likely to last. The way things are going in Europe, the British government's not going to expend any more efforts to protect whatever interests they have in the East. If we're to defend what's left here, we'll have to do it on our own."

Clark looked at Franklin. "What about the Americans? Cornell, is the American government planning to withdraw too?"

"I haven't received any indication of that yet," Franklin said. "Although, I don't expect they'll send in troops to defend us either. I'll be honest, the Fourth Marine Regiment alone won't be enough to fight a war with Japan. Even if they join forces with Shanghai Volunteer Corp, it'll still be a losing battle."

Franklin was right. The SVC, the International Settlement's own citizen militia, had just two thousand men even when fully mobilized. If the British withdrew their troops, Japan would know they could take the International Settlement by force.

"We need to think of a way to hold on to power," Keswick said. "If they propose five candidates, we need to make sure their three additional candidates won't get enough votes so we can keep the status quo."

"That will be difficult," Franklin said. "I've been wondering about the influx of Japanese nationals into the Settlement. I thought this was happening because of the Japanese occupation. But now, I'm thinking they're bringing more people to register them as ratepayers so they can increase their number of voters."

"This was planned then," Clark said. "They must've been working on this plan for years. How many Japanese are there now who are qualified to vote?"

"I don't remember exactly. From the tax records, I think there are about ten thousand. In comparison, the Occidental ratepayers only number about nine thousand."

"So that's it?" Keswick asked. "The numbers are against us."

Clark deepened his frown. "We'll have to increase our number of votes. We can't import people into Shanghai, so . . ." He paced from the bookcase to the couch. "What if we subdivide the estates owned by non-Japanese?"

"What do you mean?" Keswick asked.

"Right now, each voter's entitled to one vote for each parcel of land they own. Say there's a large parcel of land. If we subdivide it from one parcel into smaller parcels according to land regulations, then the owner of the estate could have tens, hundreds, even thousands of votes."

Franklin's eyes lit up. "That could work. Practically, it'll be ballot stuffing, but it would work."

"You're the lawyer," Keswick said. A smile spread across his face. "If you say it'd work, then I trust your word." He raised his cigar at Clark. "That's a brilliant suggestion."

"Thank you." Clark gave a modest nod.

"Desperate times call for desperate measures. It's legal ballot stuffing, but if the Japs are playing the system, then so can we." He raised his brandy. "Gentlemen, now this is worth a toast."

⸺

It was already past ten when Clark arrived home from the dinner battle at Keswick's. He thanked the maidservant for the glass of water she brought him, and went straight to the study to check if anyone had called and left him phone messages.

As he scanned the names and numbers of the callers the houseboy recorded in a notebook, Wen-Ying came in. "Ge, you've returned."

Clark put down the notebook.

"I heard some news." She closed the door. "Wang Jing-Wei will be the president of a new consolidated puppet government."

"I already know."

"Tang Wei is now a high official. He'll be named the secretariat for the Shanghai Propaganda Department when Wang Jing-Wei is inaugurated later this month."

"Is that so?" Clark asked. Nothing about Tang surprised him anymore.

"You know Tian Di Hui won't make any exception for old friendships. Whoever the collaborator is, he'd be on our blacklist."

"In my eyes, Tang Wei has long ceased to be a friend."

The patter of footsteps and voices came from the hallway. The door to the study pushed open and a toddler waddled into the room, followed by Madam Yuan and Mei Mei.

"Ay! Little Fu, Little Fu, you're running too fast. Nai Nai can't keep up." Madam Yuan bent down and grabbed the giggling toddler by the waist.

"Little Fu." Clark smiled. "It's so late. How is it you still haven't gone to bed?"

"He overslept during his afternoon nap." Mei Mei jiggled the boy's tiny hands. "Now he's still bursting with energy."

"Where's Xiu-Qing?"

"She's not feeling well. She has a slight headache and went to bed early."

"Hope she's not catching a cold," Madam Yuan said.

Clark crossed his arms and leaned back against the desk. In the time he and Xiu-Qing had been "married" and living together, she'd become like a younger sister, and he treated her as such unless the situations called for them to act otherwise.

Lost a good brother, gained a good sister, he tried to console himself.

Little Fu walked forward and pointed his finger at him, "Ba Ba!"

Madam Yuan and Mei Mei squealed. "Ay-yah! Little Fu! Guo-Hui, did you hear that? He just called you father," Madam Yuan exclaimed. She picked up the child and brought him to Clark. "Say it again? Say 'Ba Ba.'"

The child only laughed. Clark softened his eyes and stroked Little Fu's cheek. The boy's face resembled his father's so much. Looking at him was like seeing Xu Hong-Lie again.

Clark's heart wrenched. The hardest part of this charade was the lie to this child. He could live with deceiving everyone, except Little Fu. He had no right to claim the name of father to him.

"Little Fu, you won't call your father again?" Madam Yuan bounced the boy lightly in her arms. "All right, let's go tell your mother." She turned around toward the door.

"Ma!" Wen-Ying called out after her. "Xiu-Qing's asleep. Don't wake her."

Madam Yuan kept on walking. "Little Fu just called his father

'Ba Ba'! How can his mother not know this? Come, Little Fu. Let's go tell your mother." With a big smile on her face, she left the room. Mei Mei beamed at Clark and Wen-Ying, then followed their mother out.

Next to him, Wen-Ying said, "That kid will thank you when he grows up."

Would he? Clark crossed his arms again. In this world, there was no telling what would happen tomorrow anymore. He didn't need gratitude. As long as the kid could grow up at all, it was all he could hope for.

FRANCE FALLS

"FRANCE FALLS!"

The newspaper headline blazed out in huge type at the top of the page when the evening edition of the *China Press* went to print. Hours later, details of the French surrender were still pouring in. At the office, Eden stayed as long as she could to gather as much information as came in, hoping at least something positive would show itself. But nothing.

Yesterday, Charles de Gaulle told the world he would form a government in exile to lead the fight for the French. His announcement still felt surreal.

Two months. Two months was all it took for Hitler to bring down France. This was France, the country that gave its people Charlemagne, William the Conqueror, Louis IX, Napoleon, and Joan of Arc. How could France, with its history of military might, crumble as soon as Hitler launched his first strike?

Frantically, she waded through the latest international bulletins. When her phone rang, she still hadn't found anything positive to bring home.

It was her mother on the phone. "We're going over to see Isaac now. I'll bring dinner. We'll meet you at his place?"

Eden checked her watch. "Yes. I'm coming now."

"Good. We'll see you there."

Dejected, she hung up the phone. It was almost eight o'clock, but the staff was still bustling around the floor. Reporters and commentators alike were planning to stay all night to try to make sense of what had happened and what it meant for the war in Europe, as well as what it meant for the French nationals here.

She took another glance at the bulletins on her desk, then grabbed her purse. Maybe tomorrow would bring some good news. Maybe tomorrow, Franklin Roosevelt would heed the desperate call of Paul Reynaud, the French Prime Minister who stepped down two days ago, and send a wave of planes to France.

For now, she had to join her family and go to Isaac.

Riding down the streets on her bike, her eyes teared up. Last week, when the French government declared Paris an open city, the Weissmans had sent a telegram to let them know they were fleeing south. That was the last time they'd heard from them.

Did they make it out of Paris? Where were they now?

What would the Nazis overrunning France do to them?

She came to Isaac's apartment feeling hollow, worried, and lost. Her parents and Joshua had already arrived. Poor Isaac. He sat by the table, his face pensive as he listened to the announcer on the radio. The CBS news broadcast had just come on.

According to a united press dispatch from Berlin, the armistice will probably be signed tomorrow . . . Hitler will be there in person. There is still no official information as to the terms, but the general belief is this will only be a preliminary to a general peace to be concluded at the end of the war, and that meanwhile, France will be totally disarmed, and at least parts of the country occupied, with the Channel ports to be used as basis for the attack on England.

"Oh," Mrs. Levine cried. Standing beside her, Joshua put his hand on her back. Eden exchanged a grim look with her father. No place in Europe was safe anymore.

The Italians will apparently conclude a separate armistice, which will have to wait for the appointment of the French commissioners and the fixing of a time of a meeting by Mussolini.

"I can't believe this. France just gave up," Mrs. Levine said. Dr. Levine patted her shoulder, trying to comfort her. In his chair, Isaac crouched forward, his forearms resting on his knees. Eden bit her lip. How could he look so calm? Her heart broke for him.

The rest of the broadcast brought no more clarity as to what would happen to those who were now at Hitler's mercy. When the report was over, Isaac turned off the radio. Eden crossed her arms, hugging herself. She hardly knew what to say. Her parents didn't seem to know either.

Isaac sat up. "Not the news we want to hear, is it?"

Mrs. Levine reached out and took his hand. "Isaac, don't lose hope."

"I won't." He gave her a brave smile. That made Eden feel even more sorry for him.

"Hopefully, Yosef and Hadassah found a way to safety and will contact us soon."

"Of course." Isaac nodded. He smiled again. "I know you're all worried about me. I'm okay. I'll be okay. We need to focus on what's happening here. If Hitler is occupying most of Europe, then all the Jewish people in Europe will be running. They're in the same danger as my mother and father. If they can make it here, I'm going to do whatever I can to help. That's what I'll focus on."

Mrs. Levine took out a handkerchief from her pocket and wiped away her tears. Eden's own eyes smarted.

"Is that dinner?" Isaac got up and opened the paper bag on the table.

"It's sauerbraten," Joshua told him. "And potato salad. And nut cake."

"Mmm. Nut cake. Would you like some?"

"I already had some," Joshua said, but looked sheepishly at Mrs. Levine, who was still dabbing her eyes.

"You can have more if you want," Dr. Levine told his son.

Isaac took the food out of the bag. "Eden. You haven't eaten dinner yet either. Do you want some too?" He looked at her and smiled.

How could she say no? She swallowed the sourness in her throat and smiled back.

He went into the kitchen and brought out the plates and forks. While Isaac served the meat, Dr. Levine speculated on the prospect of American support to Britain, and the various scenarios if the Americans got involved with the war. Eden shifted her eyes away from her father. Who knew what kind of help Roosevelt would extend to England, or if he would extend any at all? Her father was only trying to find something positive he could say to give them all hope. And especially, to give Isaac hope.

Isaac caught her gaze. The knowing look on his face told her he was thinking the same thing. He put a plate of food in front of her. With her heavy heart, Eden didn't want to eat. Still, when he sat down, she smiled at him and took a big bite. He smiled back. She felt so proud of him. After four years in Shanghai, he'd grown into a strong man of character. If his parents could see him today, they'd be so proud too.

In the seclusion of Keswick's home library, Clark leafed through the pamphlet the Japanese were disseminating all over Frenchtown.

Chinese Corps for Riddance of Britons.

He turned the page. In the seat opposite him, Cornell Franklin flipped through another copy.

RAF, RN members: Consider the odious situation of your own country. Better withdraw from Shanghai immediately. Otherwise, you will involve yourself in annihilation.

Clark closed the pamphlet. By the liquor cabinet, Keswick poured himself more brandy. "It's already started. The open campaign to get rid of us."

"They've been disseminating anti-British propaganda for years," Clark said. "It's nothing new."

"The difference is, they used to print those for the Chinese. Now, they're speaking directly to our people. With France no longer a threat, they think they can scare us enough to make our troops leave. And they're right."

Franklin put down his copy and lit a cigar.

"Frenchtown is in limbo." Keswick came toward them and sat down. "Even the French living there are arguing among themselves whether they want to support de Gaulle or Pétain. Do we even have an ally in France? Ambassador Cosme's a pleasant enough fella, but he doesn't have the backbone to rally their people in China to stand behind de Gaulle. As for the new consul-general who's coming to take over the job, his name is Roland de Margerie. I don't trust him either. Who's he answering too? The Vichy? de Gaulle? The Nazis?" He looked at Franklin. "Given what just happened in France, Admiral Darnell told me the Royal Navy would remain here if America would guarantee to send troops here to back us up."

Franklin tossed down the pamphlet. "Military involvement is still a tough sell. Believe me. Roosevelt wants to take action. He needs time to build support from Congress and the people." He bent forward with his hands clasped and looked up. "He got Congress to pass the Export Control Act last week. That'll cut off the Japs' oil and iron supply."

Clark kept still, showing neither gratitude nor displeasure. He'd danced this dance before. He wouldn't expect the British or the Americans to intervene in any substantial way. At this point, Franklin and Keswick were strategic partners, not true allies.

"There is good news." Franklin smiled and sat forward. "We now have enough votes to keep our seats on the Council. I got the report from our Rate Assessment Committee this week. Before the subdivisions, our block had about nine thousand registered ratepayers. With the subdivisions, we now hold almost fifteen thousand votes, as opposed to the Japanese's ten thousand. There's no way the Japs can win three more seats even if all of their ratepayers cast their votes. Heck, Norman Allwood alone will have eight thousand votes now." He laughed.

"That's if all our ratepayers turn out to vote," Keswick said. "We've never had strong election turnouts, but that never mattered before. This time, we need every vote. We can count on the Japs sending every one of their lackeys to the voting stations. The Shanghailanders . . ." He sighed and shook his head. "Look at the crowds at the racecourse. Everyone's still betting and partying like there's no tomorrow. They think they're colonial lords and the Japanese won't dare to touch them. How do we convince them that this time, they have to get out and vote?"

Franklin crossed his arms tightly over his chest and rubbed his chin. "We'll need to campaign. We'll have to make them understand what's at stake. We should work with the press. The local newspapers can get the message out and warn them what would happen if we lose the Council to the Japanese."

Keswick took a sip of his drink. "The *Northern China Daily News* has enough pull to make people listen. I'm good friends with their editor-in-chief. I'll give him a call. And I know enough people over at the *China Weekly Review* and the *Oriental Affairs*. I'll ring them too."

"I'll reach out to my contacts at the *Shanghai Evening Post and Mercury*," Franklin said. He often leveraged his relationship with that American-owned paper to influence public views on the SMC's positions on local matters.

"I'll contact the *China Press*," Clark said. No one knew the *China Press* was still funded by the KMT, even though it was registered as American-owned. He was the one who arranged the setup, although his own involvement with the newspaper had diminished since he stopped working for the government. His ties with the newspaper also ended when he separated from Eden.

Was it a good idea for him to offer to contact the *China Press*? Wasn't it better to not see her again if he could help it?

But he couldn't help this. Getting help from the *China Press* was a matter of utmost urgency.

Did he have to contact her? Couldn't he contact someone else there instead?

"That's a good start." Keswick interrupted his thoughts. "The press might get people to pay attention. But still, people are fickle. Is there anything pressing enough that would make them feel compelled to go out and vote on election day?"

"What about the Jewish vote?" Clark asked.

A curious look came to Keswick's face. "What do you mean?"

"The Britons and Americans might not feel like they're in the hot seat. It's not the same for the Jews. They have nowhere else to go. Japan's an open ally of Hitler. They've got to be worried if the International Settlement falls to Japan. I think we can rally the Jews to vote."

Franklin and Keswick exchanged a glance. "That's not a bad idea," Franklin said. "How do you suggest we go about that?

"I have friends in the Jewish community," Clark said. He dropped his eyes. He'd just found the reason why he had to see Eden.

"All right. Let's give it a shot," Keswick said.

Clark clasped his hands. "I will."

———————

Along the Bund, Clark strolled beside Eden. It'd been nine months since they last saw each other. She looked as radiant as ever. So well, in fact, he could only surmise she had gotten over whatever remnants of feelings she once had for him.

Time could do that. Time could diminish all passion and ardor until all traces of what one loved once were forgotten.

Why then did time not show him a little mercy? Time continued to pass. His own feelings had not wavered.

He dared not look directly at her. He dared not let on any sign of how he still felt.

"If we don't win this election," he said as they walked, "life as we know it in the International Settlement will end. Every Chinese person in here will be in danger, and the Jewish people could lose their rights. Keswick thinks even the British and the Americans are at risk. Most people don't understand how dire their situation is."

"I understand what you're saying," Eden said. "I'll do what I can. My mother and father will help. My mother's on the board of the Ladies Auxiliary Committee. My father knows all the doctors at the Jewish Club. Many of the doctors are ratepayers." She smiled. "Isaac will help too. He's been very active helping the Jewish refugees. A lot of people consider him one of the leaders of our community now. It's wonderful how much he's changed. He takes new arrivals on tours of the city on weekends. He organized a football league for their children and coaches them after work. If only his own parents could be here. We haven't heard from them since France surrendered."

"I'm sorry to hear that. I wish they had waited for a later ship to China instead of taking their chance on the *St. Louis*."

"We can't second guess their decision. If they had waited, the Nazis might've gotten to them and they might have never made it out. I just hope we'll hear from them soon."

Clark slowed his steps. So much was beyond their control.

"I'll talk to Charlie too," Eden said. "I'll ask him to assign someone to give full and regular coverage to the election."

"He can't know about the land subdivisions," Clark warned her. "If this becomes public, the Japanese will get the same idea and do the same thing. We can only assure all the voters if they go and cast their votes, we will win."

"I know." She lifted her head. "Don't worry. Charlie trusts me. He'll appreciate it that you're my source too. Nothing trumps an inside scoop from a Settlement Council member."

He smiled. But suddenly, she stopped. Her airy voice turned silent and he looked up. They were coming upon the statue of the Angel of Peace.

Memories of the day she deserted her wedding for him came rushing back. He risked a timid gaze at her. Her face stiffened, and she shifted her eyes away. "I should go. My lunch hour's almost over."

"Of course." He stepped back. "Thank you for coming out. We appreciate your help."

"I'll always help if you ask," she said. They stood for an awkward moment. Abruptly, she gave him a quick smile and said goodbye before she walked away.

This was a mistake. He lowered his head and continued to walk. His asking her to meet him made her feel uneasy. Seeing her depressed him too as all it did was to bring back the tide of emotions he'd hidden even from himself. Watching her walk away, he felt his own soul slipping away.

He reached the steps before the memorial of the Angel of Peace. The angel's wings spanned out from above, like a promise she'd lift them up, up and away before all the calamities inflicted by men ruined this earth.

What price would he have to pay before the Angel delivered her promise? If he lost his soul, would peace still be enough to keep the wreckage of what was left of his life?

3 2

SHADES OF FIRE

THE WIDE VIEW of sunset illuminating the garden unfolded as their car entered the grounds of the glorious Arcadia Cabaret. Ahead of them, hundreds of well-dressed guests wandered with drinks in their hands. All had gathered here to watch the highly touted and much anticipated 1940 Miss Shanghai Pageant.

In the car's backseat, Eden glanced over to Alex. "Are you sure you should come to such a high-profile event?"

"Why not?" Alex grabbed her hand. "The damn Japs want to scare me. This is the best way to show I'm not afraid."

She raised an eyebrow and let him be. Alex could boast all he wanted, but he knew he couldn't flout their threats so recklessly anymore. He never talked about it openly, but after the kidnapping attempt, he stopped riding his motorcycle. Since then, he'd been traveling in the bullet-proof car they were riding in now, with a hired driver taking him to places while he kept his eyes alert to any potential danger. She didn't ask him about it, but she knew it was killing him to have to give up his bike.

What worried her wasn't just the kidnapping. Earlier this week, the puppet Reorganized National Government headed by

Wang Jing-Wei released a blacklist. Or rather, a death list. It named eighty-seven journalists as targets for assassination. Seven of the names on the list were foreigners. Alex was one of them.

The announcement of the list came with a stern warning for all seven foreign reporters to leave the country if they knew what was good for them.

Lucian wouldn't let a day go by now without nagging Alex to wear a bullet-proof vest. As always, Alex dismissed his fuss.

Then again, it would be such a shame if he was wearing a bulky bullet-proof vest tonight. He looked as handsome in a tux as he did in a motorcycle jacket.

And she was glad he came here with her. With the fate of the Weissmans still unknown, and the future of Shanghai uncertain, the last thing she wanted to do was to cover a beauty pageant, even if it was the premier social event of the season and it was her job as an entertainment reporter to keep their readers informed about all things trivial. At least, Alex was coming along to keep her company. Being around him always made her feel safe, like nothing in the world could truly ever beat them down.

She told Charlie she didn't want to cover this event. He insisted. He said it would do her good to be around happy people.

Perhaps he was right. She could use a reprieve.

Perhaps, the Arcadia itself made it worthwhile too. This Russian entertainment venue, owned by famed restauranteur Nikolai Aleksandrovich Plotnikov, rivaled the Canidrome. It boasted the largest dance floor in the city, and hosted fantastic ballet performances by the likes of Luibov Khazankina and Nina Antares, accompanied by an orchestra conducted by the much sought-after Serge Yermolaev and N. Feoktistov. There were also burlesque performances by Anna Ganina, and cabaret by the dance duet Knyazevs, plus sell-out concerts featuring singer Alexander Vertinsky. These days, Arcadia was the hottest place to be. And no one who enjoyed a good time would miss out on the

Miss Shanghai Pageant, which ballet master Edouard Eliroff began hosting here every year in July since 1937. Six hundred guests were expected to attend this spectacle tonight.

The car stopped in front of the luxurious three-story building in the middle of the garden. An attendant in a white top and black pants opened the car door. They climbed out and followed the path to the outdoor seating area under the canopy. Eden showed her press pass and the waiter took them to a long table with wicker chairs near the stage. A group of reporters had already arrived. Lea Blumenfeld, the gossip columnist, greeted Eden with delight.

"Eden Levine! Long time no see." Lea stood up. "My goodness, Mr. Alex Mitchell!? You're at my table?"

Eden laughed. Alex extended his hand. "Call me Alex, please. And pardon me, your name is?"

"Lea Blumenfeld. I'm with the *Shanghai Jewish Chronicle*. We met once at the fundraiser for the Boy Scouts."

His face went blank. Still, he shirked it off with a smile. "Pleasure to meet you again." He took a seat and Eden sat down between him and Lea.

"I never thought I'd see Alex Mitchell at an event like this," Lea cooed. "Will he be talking about this on his broadcast tomorrow?"

Eden twisted her lips and stifled a chuckle. "I doubt it." Alex wouldn't have been here if she didn't have to come.

At the far end of the table, her colleague, the photographer with the *China Press*, waved hello. She gave him a friendly wave back.

A waiter filled their glasses with water. Behind them, a familiar voice called out her name.

"Eden!"

Eden turned around. It was Victor Sassoon. Quickly, she stood up again. "Sir Victor!"

"How have you been?" He gave her a friendly kiss on both cheeks.

"I'm well. Thank you. And you?"

"Good. Good." He smiled. Despite all that had happened with Neil, Sir Victor had never said anything critical about her or done anything to make her feel awkward when he saw her. In her heart, she still felt a warm spot for the Baronet.

Sir Victor pointed his hand at the man next to him. "Allow me to introduce you to Mr. Alexander Vertinsky."

Eden gasped. "Mr. Vertinsky. How do you do?"

"Very well, thank you," said the renowned Russian singer. His round, pallid face looked exactly like his image on his album covers.

"Eden's a good friend of the Sassoon family," Sir Victor said to him. "She works for the *China Press*. Perhaps you can give her an exclusive. Her pen can make you famous beyond the four seas."

"Oh, you're exaggerating." Eden laughed. "But I would love to have an exclusive interview with you, Mr. Vertinsky."

"Certainly! I'll have my assistant get in touch." The singer winked.

Sir Victor leaned closer to her ear. "Vertinsky's the head of the jury for the pageant tonight."

"Is that right?" Eden dropped her eyes to the juror's ribbon on Vertinsky's lapel. "I don't envy you," she said to him. "A lot of girls are going to be upset with you after tonight."

The singer shrugged and ducked his head. "There can only be one winner."

"Are you going to introduce us to the gentleman you came with?" Sir Victor looked at her with a twinkle in his eye, then glanced at Alex.

"Of course," Eden said. She did feel a little awkward, but Alex gallantly stood up. She put her hand on his back. "This is Alex Mitchell. He's a radio news reporter for XMHA."

"Pleasure to meet you." Alex shook hands with the men.

"The pleasure's all ours, Mr. Mitchell." Sir Victor raised his cane. "I'm a huge fan of your broadcast. Shanghai needs people like you. Keep up the good work." He gave Alex a serious and encouraging look before moving on with his friend.

When Eden and Alex sat back down, Lea said to her, "You're bringing all the celebrities to our table."

Eden smiled and pulled in her chair.

Lea huddled closer. "You know, Vertinsky had an affair with Marlene Dietrich when he was in the United States."

"Did he?" Eden opened the menu to check out the food. Besides its lavish entertainment, the Arcadia was known for the exquisite cuisine served by its venerable chef, Ivan Efimovich Vasyalin. "What a spread!" She ran her eyes down the list of courses. Piroshki, blini with red caviar, pickles, vareniki dumplings, chicken tabaka, shashlik, fried meat, a long selection of seafood appetizers and vegetable salads, and so many varieties of pickles. Plus Napoleon cake for dessert.

Alex waved down a waiter and ordered them each an Ewo pilsner.

"My God, look who's here." Lea shook Eden by the arm.

Eden gazed in the direction Lea was pointing. A man in a lounge suit was walking toward the bar. Eden didn't recognize him.

"That's Gerhard Kahner," Lea stared at the man. "He's the new Gestapo chief in Shanghai."

Alarmed, Eden took a closer look at him. She didn't know if it was her own perception or the truth, but to her, Kahner had a menacing face. "How you know it's him?"

"I keep my ear and eye out for these things."

Alex overheard them. He looked over to the bar, then back at Eden.

"He arrived two weeks ago," Lea said. "Reinhard Heydrich himself appointed him."

Eden's blood chilled. Heydrich was the chief and the architect of the SD, the Nazi's intelligence agency. In Germany, his men could arrest and imprison anyone at any time for any reason. Blackmail, torture, death—nothing was beyond Heydrich. The Jews who arrived in recent months said he helmed the night of the broken glass last November. In Poland now, his death squads were rounding up Jews and forcing them into ghettos.

A group of people passed by the bar in front of Kahner and blocked him from sight. Lea craned her neck to keep her eyes on him. "I heard he's a sadist."

"Of course he is." Alex snickered. "He's with the Gestapo. They're all sadists."

Eden couldn't crack a smile. Here in Shanghai, sometimes it was easy to forget the Nazis were still here, still watching.

Why did Kahner come tonight? To keep track of the Germans and the Jews in Shanghai and their movements and activities?

The orchestra's light, playful tunes suddenly switched. Their trumpets roared and drumrolls followed. On stage, the emcee in a white tuxedo jacket and black pants took to the mike. "Ladies and gentlemen! Welcome to the ninth annual Miss Shanghai Beauty Pageant . . ."

Eden applauded with the audience. The arrival of Kahner spoiled what little enthusiasm she had for this event. Alex noticed her mood and stroked her back.

One by one, the beauty contestants came out. The Russian girls elicited the loudest hoots and cheers. The Italians, Americans, and Britons were far behind. The few Chinese girls fared even worse.

Eden duly noted the names of the ones the audience most favored.

The beauties lined up on the stage and the emcee directed everyone's attention to the men and women sitting at the table in front of him. "And may I present to you our judges for the evening. Like last year, we once again have the honor of Mr.

Alexander Vertinsky as head of our esteemed jury." Vertinsky stood up and the crowd applauded. "Next, we have Professor Eugene Abram, head of the physics department at Aurora University . . . We also have Sir Elly Kadoorie, one of the Orient's most successful industrialists, who has come all the way from Hong Kong to help us determine the final outcome of tonight's contest . . ."

"An esteemed jury indeed," Alex whispered to Eden. "All the titans of the Orient have finally come together to brainstorm the single most important decision for the future of Shanghai."

Eden nearly burst out laughing. She slapped him lightly on the shoulder. But then, his remark struck her. She looked around the garden, from the hanging lamps under the canopy, to the emcee and beauties on the stage, to the well-dressed guests at the tables, and the band behind the bar. Outside of this illusory shelter, the world was burning. In inland China, Japan was still waging their war. Their pilots were raining bombs over Chungking. Germany had bulldozed over Belgium, Luxembourg, the Netherlands. Even France had capitulated. The Luftwaffe was now closing in on Britain, and the Soviets were swiping up all the Baltic states. Yet here they were. Hundreds gathering to drink and revel, and waiters serving silver platters of food. This whole evening felt ever more like a farce.

As though he'd read her thought, Alex said under his breath, "People need a release. It's good to remember silly, ordinary things still exist."

"You're right." She took a bite of her Napoleon cake. They all could use a semblance of normalcy.

The emcee walked to the center of the stage. "Now, before we move on to the next round, I want to remind everyone the ballot boxes will remain open until 11:00 p.m. For a dollar, you can buy a token to cast a vote for any of the contestants. You can drop in as many tokens as you like for your favorite young lady. The girl with the highest token count will be declared winner at midnight. All proceeds from the sale of tickets and tokens tonight will be donated to a fund for a welfare canteen, and to provide free beds for patients in need at the Feodor Chaliapin Hospital . . ."

Alex leaned closer to the table. "Wait, you can buy tokens to vote? Why bother having judges then, and what's the point of voting? If someone wants to win, she can just buy her way to the crown."

"Or someone can buy the crown for her," Lea said. "You just wait till it starts. Last year, the boyfriends of the winner and the vice-winner almost broke out into a fight."

Alex made a face. Eden chuckled and asked, "You going to buy a vote?"

"Buy a vote?" He scoffed. With a tender smile, he picked up her hand. "Why would I? The most beautiful girl in the room is sitting right here next to me. How do I vote for her?"

His soft voice warmed her within. She closed her hand around his and held it as the emcee invited the contestants individually to the microphone.

Beside her, Lea began her own running commentary on the girls. "That one's paid for by that fat Chinese." She pointed at a corpulent man at a table to their left. "He owns five exchange offices on the Bund. He's making a killing with everyone trading in their Chinese yuan for American dollars and gold." When the next girl took her turn, Lea balked. "Ugh! That hideous dress. Hope no one votes for that floozy." She pushed her glasses up the bridge of her nose. "Not with that face. She looks like a goblin . . . Oh dear, that one cackles like a duck . . . Look at her strut. I suppose she thinks she's going to win. Well, the Bond Street Salon is her sponsor . . . This one's pretty. Too bad she's Chinese. The Chinese girls never make it to the second round . . . No, no, not a chance. Too mousy . . . Yes, this one. This one might win. Not that she's a raging beauty or anything, but one of the sons of the Khardunov dynasty is sweet on her. Oh, look, there he is now. He's going to the ballot table. Goodness gracious, will you look at that stack of cash he just whipped out of his pocket?"

Eden watched the man Lea was going on about and scribbled down her comments. If she toned down what Lea was saying, her commentary would be enough to make a full article.

The arduous night finally came to an end. At midnight, the emcee announced a pretty girl named Galina Soldatenko as the winner, and the previous year's winner put the crown and prized sash on the new queen of Shanghai. "This contest was close!" the emcee gushed. "We have so many beautiful ladies competing this year. We received over a hundred thousand votes for the top thirteen contestants and our winner won by a margin of two thousand. Congratulations, ladies . . ."

Another round of applause. By now, all the food on the silver platters had been eaten and the waiters had taken away all the plates. Only a drooping bouquet of flowers lay on the table. Lea stood up from her seat. "I'm going over to get the inside scoop. I'll see you both later." She waved goodbye and left to join the dozens of photographers stumbling over each other snapping photos of the winner and the finalists.

Eden pushed away her empty glass. Alex put his arm on the back of her seat. "Aren't you going to go with her to join the fun?"

"Fun?" Eden looked at the chaotic scene on the stage.

"You don't have to get a quote from the winner?"

"Fight that crowd just to get a quote from a beauty queen? I think not. I'll call Lea tomorrow. She'll spare me a few quotes."

Music once again filled the air. The cabaret's multicolored lights, the first of their kind in Shanghai, beamed across the outdoor dance floor. Guests rose to their feet and took to the floor. The women's gowns swayed to the changing red, blue, and green lights flickering to match the tempos and melodies of the

"Blue Danube" waltz. Alex looked at Eden over his shoulder. "Want to dance?"

"No. I'd rather get out of here." She swept her eyes across the garden. "Maybe we can come back another time. I wouldn't mind watching a ballet. I heard the ballet performances here are the best."

"You got it." He took her hand and led her away. At the cabaret's entrance, the attendant signaled and the driver brought their car. On their way home, Eden gazed out at the dark, quiet streets. For a moment, everything felt so peaceful. The buildings were empty. The lanes were deserted. Only an occasional car and its hums added pulse to the city under the haze of the street lamps.

Everything was peaceful except for those Nazi banners. The long red cloths marked with swastikas hanging in front of the German tennis club broke the tranquility of the night.

"What's wrong?" Alex asked.

Eden pulled her eyes away from the window. "Did you see those Nazi banners we just passed by?"

Alex sneered without looking behind them. "Eyesores."

"The Japanese raise so much hell when the Chinese put up their flag. Even in the International Settlement, the Chinese can't put up their flags for more than eight days a year. And when they do put them up, their shops get vandalized. They could even get assaulted. So the Chinese can't put up their own flag, but the Nazis can wave their flags and banners everywhere every day?" She turned to look at him. "Japan and Germany are allies. If the foreign concessions fall to Japan, would the Germans here come after the Jews?"

"That won't happen," Alex said. His grave face betrayed his own doubt.

"How could you know that?"

He stared ahead. "You're right. I don't." But then, his face eased. "I know one thing though."

"What?"

"Who said the Nazis can wave their flags and banners everywhere every day?" He tapped his driver on the shoulder and told him to turn around.

"What are you doing?" Eden asked.

"You'll see," he answered with a mischievous grin.

The driver slowed to a stop in front of the German tennis club. Alex opened the car door and held his hand out to Eden. "Come on."

"Why are we here?" she asked but gave him her hand. They climbed out of the car and he took her to the club's gate. With one pull, Alex yanked the banner on the left side to the ground.

Eden started laughing. "Oh no! What if someone sees you?" She looked about her, relieved to see no one else was around.

"So?" Alex asked. He grabbed the edge of the banner on the right side and pulled that one down too.

Bowing over, Eden couldn't stop laughing. She'd never dare. No one she knew would dare!

But why not? They weren't in Germany!

Alex picked up the banners and bunched them in his hands. "Come on. Let's roll."

"What are you going to do with them?" Eden hurried after him.

"We'll take them back to my place and burn them."

"Are you serious?"

"Yes!"

Indeed, he was. The driver took them back to his building. Before going inside, he led her to an alley next to his building. From the pile of garbage, he grabbed a large, rusty tin box. He dumped the banners into the tin box and lit a corner of one of the banners with his lighter.

Eden laughed again. She'd never played a prank like this. Not even when she was a schoolgirl.

The red banners shriveled as the fire grew, charring the edges until the swastikas melted into flames. Dark smoke rose like a veil of death. For once, she could watch the symbol of Hitler burn. Let all that vileness masquerading as strength burn away, never to come back again.

The fire dwindled as the monstrous banners withered into a sorry pile of ashes. Alex found a lid nearby and covered the box to put out the dying flames.

The smell of burnt cloth dissipated. She imagined the night air chasing it away. "Thank you."

"Don't mention it." He wiped the soot off his hands. "Want to come upstairs? Let's have a drink and celebrate."

"All right."

Laughing, they returned to his flat. Alex washed his hands and poured them each a glass of wine. She thought he'd crack a joke with a toast. Instead, he put an album on the gramophone. The smooth, alluring tunes of Glenn Miller's "Moonlight Serenade" coaxed her to come closer. She put down her wine. What was Alex holding?

"This is for you." He showed her a long velvet jewelry box. "I was going to give it to you tomorrow but"—he glanced at the clock—"it's tomorrow now."

What was he up to? She looked at him quizzically and opened the lid. A platinum lavalier necklace lay inside. The artfully designed pendant's crystals and emeralds shone back at her.

"I'm not good at buying gifts," he said, his voice a bit unsure. "But tomorrow—today—is two years from the date we first met. I want to give you something to remember it by."

She lifted the pendant. "This is beautiful!"

"Not as beautiful as you." He smiled with relief.

"Can I put it on?"

"Of course! Here, let me help you."

She gave him back the pendant in the box, then turned around and lifted her hair. He put the delicate necklace around her neck and closed the clasp. His hands lingered on her shoulders. The soft rhythm of the music, slow and steady, melded with her rising heartbeat. The subtle caresses of his fingers stirred within her a curious spark. His warm breath on her skin as he bent down to kiss her neck kindled the flame. She closed her eyes and let the sway of the tempo take her to a different plane.

He glided his fingers from her shoulder to the bottom of her neck. Gently, he pulled down the tab of her zipper.

Startled, she swung around. His yearning eyes gazed back at her. The passion of his touch rose, its glow a sign of a line ahead which, once crossed, she could never return.

Was this what she wanted? She grabbed his hand.

What did she want? A proper wedding? A love bound by the rules and customs of society and expectations of people both important and irrelevant?

How pointless. She already had a chance for that. She made a choice to walk away. In this world where nations were breaking all rules of honor and human decency, and human lives and dignity could be tossed to the winds, what did it matter if she lived up to some lofty ideas of proper conduct? The whole world was already burning.

Her guard began to fall.

I want you to know that I love you. I've always loved you.

Her heart tensed. Clark's words flashed in her mind.

Why? Why did she think of him now? Her feelings for him were buried in the long-ago past. Why should she even remember what he said?

Somewhere, in a chamber of her heart which she'd long deserted, a light still flickered. Its fire had waned, but its flame had never gone out. She dared not come near it.

No, she shook off the thought. She was with Alex now. How could she be thinking of anyone else? They were in love.

Were they?

He glided his lips across hers. Waves of emotions passed

between them as the sound of the music swelled to its next height.

They had to be in love. How could it be anything else?

He pulled her into his arms and she let her body sink. Being in Alex's embrace was all she wanted tonight.

3 3

A CORNER OF RESPITE

THE FRAGRANCE of the tea soothed his nose before Clark had taken the first sip. He'd tasted a wide variety of teas from all over the world—Chinese, Japanese, Indian, and British. How did it happen that he'd never tried this exquisite wonder Pearl was serving him in the tiny teacup?

This tea was one of the reasons why men flocked to this place. The Chamber of Golden Clouds offered more than beautiful girls. In this private sanctuary, drinking the rarest fine tea, one could find respite. What a remarkable make-believe world of intimacy Pearl had created. Step inside. Have your every whim met. Hear only words sweet to your ears. Share those innermost secrets you're burning to spill. Ears of sympathetic confidantes were here to relieve you of all your mental anguish—for a price.

Even for him, this was now the one place where he could find respite. Only he didn't come here to seek those comforts. Pearl's private chamber was the only place he could shed his mask, and it was so tiring to always wear a mask. At home, at work, at the SMC, at everywhere.

He put down his cup and sunk into the plush cushions of the sofa.

"This tea is called Big Red Robe." Pearl rinsed the *gaiwan.* "It only grows on Wuyi Mountain." Wuyi was a region in the Fujian province. "This tea was very hard to buy even before the occupation. It's known for its doleful, subtle orchid scent. The scent lasts for a long while."

"How did you get ahold of this?" Clark asked. "Even black-market sellers would have a hard time bringing such a rare item into Shanghai."

"I got it as a gift." Pearl refilled his cup. "I run a high-end establishment. Our clients go out of their way to bring us gifts commensurate with my house's reputation."

"And only to end up with the gift benefitting me." He picked up his second cup and inhaled a deep breath of the fragrance rising with the steam.

"Benefitting you?" Pearl laughed. "The KMT is the side getting all the benefits. They're always short of supplies. Without you, they'd be even more desperate."

Clark shrugged. "The problem is, my ways of forwarding shipments to them are shrinking. With France's defeat, the shipping route via Indochina is closed."

Pearl adjusted the teapot. "I don't understand why even the European countries would go to war," she said. Intelligent as she was, she knew little about the West. Like so many Chinese, she held the erroneous impression of Westerners being more advanced and sophisticated in their ways than people in Asia. But at heart, humans everywhere are all the same.

She offered him a small plate of sweet red dates. He held up his hand and refused. "I fear, if Japan takes over all of Shanghai, the supply route from here will be totally blocked."

"There's still the supply route in the west in Kunming," she said with a firm nod. The determined tone of her voice gave him a jolt of strength.

She then changed the subject. "There's something you need to know."

"What?"

"Wang Jing-Wei's government received the land records and title deeds of the entire Chinese sector of Shanghai."

"Oh?" Clark looked up. The puppet government had been demanding the SMC to turn those records over since early last year. These records contained the names and identities of all the people who owned land in the Chinese-controlled districts before the Battle of Shanghai. Wang's people wanted to know exactly who owned property in the areas they now nominally ruled, so they could identify the Chinese who owned properties there and terrorize them with extortion.

"How did they get them?" he asked. The only copy of those records was locked away at the office of the SMC. Before the Battle of Shanghai, the KMT had entrusted the SMC with these records for safekeeping.

"Tony Keswick gave the records to them."

"Keswick?"

Pearl blinked, slowly and assuredly, to leave him no room for doubt.

Clark held his breath, then exhaled with a cold sneer. "What a headless turtle. The Japanese haven't fought their way to his door yet, and he's already holding his arms up to surrender. He probably thinks this would get him on the Japanese's good side."

"The biggest taipan in Shanghai is this gutless?"

"Yes." And two-faced too. As much as Clark didn't like to think it, Keswick had given the Chinese up to keep his vast business empire in China running. He was proving that white people would hurt the Chinese if it would help themselves.

Clark shook his head. The world was divided along racial lines no matter how much he wished it wasn't.

"As for Wang Jing-Wei," Pearl said, "here are his latest exploits." She unfolded a hand-drawn map on the table. "These are the locations of the new opium dens and gambling houses.

The ones owned by Wang Jing-Wei and his running dogs are
marked."

Clark studied the map. "So many." The marked houses and
buildings spread out like locusts chomping away at the Western
Road.

"Wang Jing-Wei's regime has no money," Pearl said. "The
Japanese said they'll give him control of China, but they don't
give his regime any financial support. He has no one to collect
taxes from. The lands he inherited are all bombed out, and Japan
took over all the remaining money-making enterprises. Gambling
and selling opioids are the only ways for his administration to get
funds."

A government of rackets. The KMT was rotten enough. Now,
Wang Jing-Wei was creating something even worse.

"Wang Jing-Wei doesn't shortchange himself though," Pearl
said. She picked up a translucent piece of the osmanthus cake and
served it on Clark's plate, careful not to let the gelatinous dessert
slip through the chopsticks. "Japan pays him five million yuan
every month."

"Five million yuan?" Clark looked up. So that was the price
for the lives and freedom of everyone in the country.

He put down the map. "What's our next step?"

Pearl opened the silver cigarette case beside the plate of cakes
and showed him the three business cards inside. "Zhou Ke-Hao
should pay them each a visit."

The new hit list. Clark accepted the cigarette case and put it in
his jacket's inner pocket.

"The next step is for you to have a taste of this." She opened
her hand and pointed it at his plate. "Nowadays, osmanthus isn't
something you can buy just because you want it."

Clark relented. Who knew if tomorrow, the Japanese wouldn't
swarm in and overtake the rest of the city? If they did, he might
never have another taste of this exquisite dessert made with
flowers grown only in Guilin.

He put the piece into his mouth. The delicate fragrance of the osmanthus petals, harmoniously fused with the subtly tart sweetness of the crystal yellow gelatin cake, melted on his tongue.

"No one leaves the Chamber of Golden Clouds without a sweet and beautiful experience," Pearl said, playfully ending their meeting with a honeyed voice she must have used countless times to coax the most vital information they needed to slash down their enemy.

Back on the street, Clark walked along, blending in with the other pedestrians while keeping his highest alert to everything happening around him. Two weeks ago, the British cabinet announced they would withdraw all British troops from Shanghai. Just as Keswick had said, without the backing of the American military, Churchill had chosen to abandon China.

Since then, Japan had claimed police power over half of the sector of Western Road that the British soldiers used to patrol. The Shanghai Volunteer Corps assumed guard of the other half.

For a Chinese man like him, defense by Japanese police meant no defense. In the Badlands, any slip of caution now could be deadly. A kidnapper would not think twice to attack. A robber would not hesitate to kill. Whenever he had to come to see Pearl, he made sure to dress down, and he kept his hand free to reach the gun in the holster on his belt.

He came to the beginning of Bubbling Well Road where his car was parked. Obeying his instructions, Huang Shifu no longer opened the car door for him. That trivial custom only added delays. When he needed to go places in his car now, he only wanted to get inside as quickly as possible and move on.

"To the factory," he told the driver.

The car took them north to Nanking Road. On the Bund, a strange new view appeared. For the first time since the British gained territorial rights in Shanghai, the entire British naval fleet had left the Whangpoo River.

What would their forebears think if they knew that on this solitary August night, the HMS *Peterel* would be all that remained of their glory in the East?

THE JEWISH VOTE

SATURDAY MORNING. Eden finished making her bed and went into the kitchen. She didn't often sleep late, and everyone had already gone out. Relishing the quiet time alone, she helped herself to the bread and a pear her mother had left for her on the kitchen counter, and brought the food out to the dining table along with a fresh pot of tea.

She opened the morning edition of the *China Press* her father had left on the table and took a bite of the pear while she turned to the page where her own article appeared. She'd written it under her pseudonym, of course. It was about the closing of the refugees safety zone set up by Father Jacquinot de Besange. When the Japanese army invaded Shanghai's Chinese sectors three years ago, the French Jesuit priest created this zone to shelter the masses of people fleeing into the foreign concessions. Last month, his church summoned him back to Europe, and the displaced Chinese lost even this little corner of peace.

Father de Besange didn't want to leave. He'd been in China for twenty-seven years.

Her article was out. She'd done her best to give a human face to the nineteen thousand residents in the zone who would now have to fend for themselves. Would her words serve to remind everyone why the refugees were left in this predicament in the first place?

The apartment door opened and Mrs. Levine walked in.

"Good morning," Eden greeted her mother.

"Morning? It's almost noon." Her mother brought in the bags of groceries. She looked at the clock. "Oh dear, I'm running late. Eden, would you mind running an errand for me?" She pointed at the stack of old children's shirts, trousers, and dresses on the sofa. "Those are used clothes I collected from our building. I'm supposed to bring these to the Jewish Community Center to donate to the new arrivals. I won't have time today. Would you take them there?"

"Sure." Eden closed the newspaper. "I can go now. I'm free this afternoon."

"That would be very helpful." Mrs. Levine took the groceries into the kitchen. "The Meyers are coming over for dinner tonight. I invited Isaac too. I've got to get the house ready." The Meyers were their old friends from Munich who had finally found their way here this summer. Sadly, they had to give up everything they owned to the Nazis to come here. Her parents had lent them money to help them settle.

While her mother continued talking, Eden finished her tea and dabbed her lips with a napkin. She put the children's clothes into an old shopping bag and put on her shoes. "I'm leaving now," she called out to her mother and grabbed her purse.

In the hallway, she turned the key to lock the door. A suspicious shuffling of footsteps from the apartment next door made her pause. Someone was behind her neighbor's door. She was sure of it.

The footsteps stopped, but no one came out and she didn't hear any sound of someone returning inside.

She glanced up at her neighbor's peephole. She couldn't say for sure, but she had a strong, unsettling feeling someone was watching her. Who was it? Keiko? Her husband Thierry? Their son Hiroshi?

One, both, or all of them had been spying on her since France fell and their regime changed. Every time she left or returned home, she heard those shuffling feet.

Thierry couldn't take Keiko and Hiroshi back to France now. Not with the Germans occupying his country. Their better option now lay with Keiko. Her Japanese nationality would ensure they would remain safe.

Alex always said, all Japanese were agents of the Mikado. Eden hadn't forgotten that. Would Keiko spy on her to curry favor with her government? Would Thierry too? And their son?

She snatched the key from the doorknob and shoved it into her purse. Time to take a leave again and stay for a while at Ava's apartment.

How she hated feeling watched in her own home.

Saturdays at the Jewish Community Center were always an uplifting way to spend the afternoon. Sports games for the children, book clubs for the ladies, and chess for the men. So many people, both old guards of Shanghai who'd been here for generations and newly arrived refugees, came together for the company and the myriad of activities it offered. For all the changes in the city in the last few years, the Jewish community still thrived.

On the way in, she passed by a group of boys playing handball. How good it was to see them running around carefree on a breezy October day. One of the girls jumping rope next to the hopscotch waved to her. The girl's mother was in the Ladies Auxiliary Club with her mother. Eden waved back. Before she walked inside, she made a mental note to stop by the outdoor kosher food market on her way out.

The Center did more now than offering games and entertainment. For the flood of new European refugees, this place was their lifeline for starting over. Those who could help them didn't hesitate. Like her mother, who collected clothes, toys, and food to donate every week.

With the bag of children's clothes, Eden entered the foyer. At a table in front of the library, Lea Blumenthal was talking energetically to the people gathered around her. Beside her, an Asian woman stood, smiling and nodding while Lea spoke. Curious, Eden came closer.

"Miss Sasaki wants you to know Japan stands ready to offer humanitarian relief to anyone who is their friend and ally," Lea said to everyone. "As some of you may know, there are people who aren't happy with so many Jews coming to the International Settlement. They say our friends and relatives fleeing for their lives are straining the resources of the city. I say it's good old-fashioned anti-Semitism. That is why we can't rely on the Britons, or the Americans, or the French." She turned and pointed her hand at Sasaki. "The Japanese have never discriminated against the Jews. They admire the Jews for all their achievements. And now, here's the good news. Japan is offering to provide housing in their sector for those of you who need a new home, if you will vote the right way in the upcoming SMC election."

Eden scowled. What was happening? Japan was giving Jewish refugees homes in exchange for their votes?

The people around her buzzed. The offer of a new place to live struck a chord. The woman named Sasaki spoke to her interpreter. The interpreter translated what she said to Lea. Lea listened and nodded.

She held up a leaflet on the table. "These are the five Japanese candidates who will need your vote in the election. Their backgrounds and qualifications are all in here for you to read. If you're a ratepayer, then vote for them, and the Japanese government will remember to look out for your interests. If you need a home, they will give you one and you can then become a ratepayer and vote for them." She waved a finger in the air. "This city has become very, very dangerous. The Settlement Police can barely rein in the crimes. At this most challenging time, Britain decided to pull out all of their troops!" She sharpened her eyes, huffing with indignation. "If you help the candidates of Japan get elected, they will give you protection. Unlike the British, the Japanese troops will not depart. They will remain here and help restore law and order."

Eden's mouth dropped. Without thinking, she cried out, "Those are lies!"

Surprised by her sudden outburst, everyone around the table shushed.

"Japan will protect us? That is the biggest load of lies I've ever heard!" She snatched one of the leaflets on the table and shook it in her hand. "These people are not our friends. The International Settlement is the last safe place for us, and they're trying to take it over. If they do, no one would be left to protect us. No one!" She looked at the people around her. They stared back with hesitant, doubtful eyes. Sasaki appeared taken aback, but remained poised. Eden threw her a cold glance. "For heaven's sake! Japan signed the Tripartite Pact with Germany last week. Last week! Are you all going to trust a country that makes deals with Hitler?"

The men and women around her mumbled. The interpreter rolled out a series of words to Sasaki. Eden glared and pushed her way in front of Lea. "Lea. How could you? I'm so disappointed."

Lea straightened her stance and clasped her hands. "I'm doing what I can to help our people."

The interpreter held his arm out to Eden. "Miss, you've got it wrong. Miss Sasaki here said the Tripartite Pact is strictly a military agreement. It has no relevance to Jewish people in Shanghai."

Eden gave him another dirty look. She turned away from him and spoke to the others watching them instead. "Some of you were here when Japan invaded Shanghai. You saw what they did to the Chinese. Can you still trust them after that? You can still see how their soldiers treat the locals. It's no different than how the Nazis treated you in Germany. Will you really vote to give them more power?" She pointed at Sasaki. "This woman is not here to protect you. Her people don't care about you. They won't do anything for you."

More men and women had crowded around them to see what the spectacle was about. Lea remained firm and held up her head. "And what has Britain or America done for us? Nothing. They won't even let us into their countries. At least Miss Sasaki is here now, speaking to us. Face it, Eden. No one cares about us Jews. We have to take care of ourselves and choose our friends. France already lost. Britain has left us for dead. The Americans will do the same. We're better off siding with Japan now. It's for our own survival." She looked past Eden to the people behind her. "I'm speaking the truth. You all can go home and think about what I just said, my stateless friends. When the cowardly British and Americans are gone, would you want to be allies with the only power remaining? Or would you want to be their enemy?"

The people around them mumbled again. Fear and uncertainty filled their eyes. Several of them approached the table and picked up the leaflet of Japanese candidates. One of them wiggled past Eden. "Just taking a look," he said sheepishly and reached out his hand to grab a copy.

Lea gave Eden a quick glance. "Once again, Miss Sasaki is here to answer any of your questions." Standing there with a distant expression on her face, Sasaki nodded. Lea held up a leaflet again. "Take one of these. Please take one of these."

The onlookers muttered among themselves and milled around the table. "Excuse me," said one of the women, pushing past Eden. She wouldn't look Eden in the eye.

Lea returned to speaking individually to those who approached her. Sasaki and the interpreter carried on, greeting everyone who came to them asking questions.

Eden slumped and took a step back. What about all those articles Charlie published warning of the dangers of a Japanese takeover? What about all the other foreign publications stressing the urgency of maintaining British and American control? Did none of it get through to these people?

Dejected, she continued on to drop off her donation of children's clothes. As she walked, she began to fume. When she was done, she went straight to the Center's main office.

Fine. Lea and Sasaki could have their say today. Next Saturday, she would come here herself. She'd get Isaac to come too. After all the efforts he'd put in to help the community, Isaac would have much more sway than Lea the gossip columnist. People would listen to him. They'd set up their own table. They'd snuff out these lies. Yes, they would.

Coming home, Eden still felt besieged with anger when she turned the key to open the door. What? Those shuffling footsteps again. She glared at her neighbors' door. Couldn't they let up at least once?

She shoved her door open.

Inside, her father was cleaning a bruise on Isaac's forehead. Isaac's friend Robbie was there too. Her mother was icing red welts on Robbie's back.

"What happened?" Eden kicked off her shoes.

"They got attacked by ronin." Mr. Levine soaked a piece of cotton with alcohol and dabbed it on Isaac's wound.

"What?" She rushed over to them.

Isaac winced at the touch of alcohol on the small gash on his skin. "We were pinning up campaign posters in Little Vienna."

He pointed at the stack of posters calling for votes for the British and American candidates. Little Vienna was the Jewish neighborhood in Hongkew, the sector of the International Settlement governed by the Japanese. It was in the same part of the city where the Jewish Community Center was located. "They told us to stop. I told them no. They came back with clubs and threatened us. One thing led to another and we started to fight."

"That's outrageous!" Eden sat down next to Isaac. "Are you two okay?"

"We're fine," said Robbie. "Isaac's a whole head taller and bigger than they are. They were no match for me either, but I was worried they might have guns. Good thing they were only carrying clubs. We gave them a good beating back."

"I can't believe they would do this."

"I can. The ronin and Japanese soldiers are bullies. That's how they intimidate everyone."

"They're not going to stop us this way," Isaac said. "If anything, they've convinced me we've got to keep urging people to vote to keep them from getting the run of this place."

Eden dropped her hands on her lap. "But I don't want anyone to get hurt."

"Don't worry." He smiled and jokingly pushed Robbie on the arm. "We know how to take care of ourselves."

His reassurance didn't make her feel any better. And while Isaac might not feel scared, a lot of other people would.

How would they keep rallying the others, if thugs were threatening assault?

At the XMHA office, Eden slipped into the studio. By now, the staff here knew her well, and they didn't mind her coming in when Alex was on the air.

Alex noted her presence and continued talking into the mike.

The fact that Japan signed the Tripartite Pact should send an alarm throughout Washington. We've got Hitler spreading his forces over all of Europe, and we've got the Mikado spreading his forces over all of Asia. We're now talking about half of the world. Is that not frightening to anyone?

He shook his finger forcefully in the air.

Now, I know the folks back in America think whatever's happening in the rest of the world doesn't concern them. Let me explain. What happens here in Asia is as important to Americans living in Peoria or Sioux Falls as it is to the Orientals living here. We own a lot of factories in Asia, and we have fellow Americans here facilitating international trade. When they sell our factory products to the people of Asia, they keep the payrolls running at home. They're also working diligently to ship our products back home to make sure we have all the essential products we need. Like rubber for our tires, and hemp for ropes and cords, and tin for our cans of pork and beans. Every day, there are huge cargoes of every type of American-owned products leaving from Shanghai for San Francisco and Seattle, and on to Texas, Chicago, and New York. Some products are more abundant in Asia but less so in America. Camphor, tung oil, coconut oil to name a few, and we have access to them because of our own foreign direct investments. So I tell you, isolationism is a delusion.

He looked up at Eden. She gave him an encouraging smile.

So it is time for Congress and our President to take serious actions. Economic sanctions are not enough.

He stared at the bulletins next to his mike, and his face eased.

No. Economic sanctions are not enough, although it is having some unintended consequences. Let me tell you about something funny I saw today. This is a story of how desperate the Japanese are for metals because we've stopped supplying them metals.

He flashed Eden a grin. Eden crossed her arm. What mischief was he up to now?

So I was driving along with a group of executives from the Shanghai Power Company last week. For those of you who don't know, the Shanghai Power Company is an American company. So we were taking a tour of Kiangwan and the executives were showing me how the Japanese engineers were stringing new copper cables in that area to carry the electric current to their people. Everything was business as usual. Nothing exciting. After a while, we drove on back to where the engineers had started stringing the cables, and about three miles down the road toward Woosung, there was a band of ronin.

Alex's lips twitched. He tried to hold back a laugh. Eden exchanged a puzzled glance with the show producer.

They were tearing down the cables! They tore down and cut up the cables their own engineers had strung not even an hour ago. See, what happened was, those ronin were junk collectors. They were out to collect copper that day and they thought they were stealing American cables. Their engineers hung those cables and their own thieves came and carted the cables away and took them to the junk yard. Those cables must've cost several million yen. It was hysterical!

Alex started laughing. Eden smiled and covered her mouth. Alex regained his composure and calmed his face.

Sadly for the ronin, the episode didn't end there. The Municipal Police constables told me later about fifty ronin were arrested and put before the firing squad. And so, with swift efficiency, the Japanese authorities had

resolved the crime and reassured the public those ronin would never steal
again.

Eden watched him talk. The mocking tone he used to deliver the last line added just the right touch.

Anyway, if you folks in America are listening, call your congressman. Call
the White House. Tell them we need to do more, for democracy, and to keep
our nation great. This is Alex Mitchell from Shanghai, and a final word
from our sponsor, Ovaltine.

The producer switched on the radio advertisement and Alex turned off the microphone. Eden walked toward him, clapping her hands. He took off his headset and stood up. "Hey, doll."

"Hello." She let him peck her on the forehead. "Are you done for the night?"

"Yes. Let me grab my jacket in my office." He led her out of the studio. "I'm starving."

"Where are we eating?"

"The American Club." He looked away from her. He answered casually enough, though it didn't mask how he had changed. Alex used to love eating at local Chinese haunts that served unfamiliar but delicious food. He loved taking her to noodle shops and joints most Westerners didn't know about. Now, he only went to exclusive places like the American Club, where he could be sure he was safe.

She touched him on the back and wondered. Had any other incidents happened besides the time the Japanese tried to kidnap him? They must have tried to threaten him again. Alex wouldn't have given up so many things he liked for one attempted assault.

If they'd tried to harm him again, he never told her. Pride, probably. He wouldn't admit it if the Japanese had forced his hand.

He felt her touch and turned to give her a smile.

In his office, he tidied up several bulletins and put them into the file cabinet. As always, a messy pile of fan mail was scattered across his desk. Eden picked up a few of the unopened ones. "Indiana." She flipped through the envelopes and read out loud from the senders' addresses. "California. New Jersey. Sidney. Singapore." She looked up at Alex. "You're gaining quite an international following."

"Am I?" He closed the cabinet drawer.

She put the envelopes back down. A photo of a young woman in the pile caught her eye. The woman was reclining seductively on her bed, wearing nothing but her negligée. Eden picked it up. Behind that photo, she found another one of a woman sitting with one bent leg on a rug next to her bed. Her skirt fell back to her hip, revealing her smooth thighs and garters. Eden pushed that photo to the side. Several more photos of the same sort exposed themselves.

Eden held up the photo in her hand. "She's pretty."

Slightly taken aback, Alex grabbed the photo from her and tossed it back on the desk. "Crazy fans."

She slid her eyes to the photos and he tossed a few letters over them to cover them up. The rubbish bin was right there, but he proceeded to put on his jacket. Eden decided not to say anything more, although the edges of the photos still stuck out, making them more than an eyesore.

He put his arm around her. Not intentionally, she recoiled back. "What's the matter?"

She changed the subject to something that bothered her even more. "Remember Lea Blumenthal? She sat next to us at the Miss Shanghai Pageant?"

"Yes?"

Eden recounted to him what happened at the Jewish Community Center, as well as how Isaac and Robbie got assaulted.

Alex scowled. A look of injustice rose to this face. "That's outrageous. What a disgrace."

"That's what I said too."

"Why didn't you tell me about the SMC?"

"I . . ." She fell speechless. She didn't have a good reason she could think of. Only that she felt awkward talking to Alex about Clark, and Clark was the one who told her everything and asked her to help.

"I can't stand by and watch the Japs step all over everyone," Alex said. "They want to play tough? All right. I'll tell every Shanghailander to vote against them. I'll wage a campaign for all the British and American candidates on the radio."

"You'll do that?"

"Yes! Besides, it's not just Chinese lives and British power at stake here. If the Japs control the Settlement government, it'll be the end of free press and free radio. They'll shut me down. I can't let that happen."

She hoped not. Alex was the most influential voice coming out of Shanghai. They couldn't afford to lose him.

And if he could add his voice to the campaign, they just might have a chance to win.

ELECTION NIGHT

"WHAT IF WE LOSE?" Eden asked, trying to keep up with Isaac as he strode down Ward Road in the Hongkew district of the International Settlement. She'd avoided this question for the last three months, holding on to every strand of hope. Today, the outcome of the SMC election could change everything, and she finally said out loud the one thing she feared.

"We won't lose," Isaac said. "Not if everyone goes out and votes." He quickened his steps. His haversack, which held the flyers with the call to vote and the addresses of the voting stations, was weighing him down, but he forged ahead. "We still have time."

Eden hustled up and followed. This was their last chance to convince the ratepayers to vote. Noon was a good time to reach the voters who'd be out for lunch, and Isaac had his friends spread out throughout Little Vienna as well the Bund for a final campaign push.

She entered the Cafe Central behind him. The owners, a Jewish couple who often joined her mother to collect donations and supplies for the European refugees, waved at her. They'd been staunch supporters of the campaign to keep the International Settlement out of Japanese hands.

The problem was with the ratepayers. From one table to the next, Eden spoke to the diners, leaving behind a flyer or two and urging them to vote. The diners were receptive enough, always responding with an interested smile, followed by a polite nod and a noncommittal promise to visit the voting station later. Their tones never entirely convinced her.

And this was the reaction she'd been getting all morning. She didn't doubt people would vote for the British and American candidates—if they would make an effort to go to the voting stations. But they had to go to work, or to the matinee movie, or the silk market, or take their children to school, or meet their friends for afternoon tea.

On the radio, the familiar opening tune of Alex's broadcast came on. Immediately, the chatter in the room subsided. The diners perked up and the restaurant owner turned up the volume.

Alex's voice carried from the speaker.

Good afternoon, everyone. No, actually, this is not at all a good afternoon. I just received the latest report from the SMC. So far, the Council has counted just two thousand one hundred twenty votes for our British and American candidates. Well, I have to say, I'm disappointed. Where are all our voters? We're on the brink of—

A loud burst of static interrupted the broadcast. The diners muttered to each other and the cafe owner adjusted the radio dial.

—voters' apathy—

The static interfered again. The cafe owner tried adjusting the antenna.

"Not again!" someone cried out.

Another diner said, "It's Japanese jam!"

"Goes well with bread." A balding man held up his baguette.

—*handing to the Mikado*—

The static cut off Alex's voice. A cacophony of clings and clanks came on, drowning out the signal from XMHA. The Japanese naval ships had been using noises of pots and pans to disrupt Alex from reaching the listeners near Soochow Creek.

The annoyance of the diners grew. They looked at the radio with disapproving faces as the cafe owner tried to recapture the signal in vain.

"Damn the Japs." A woman threw her napkin down on the table. "Enough of this. I'm not handing anything to the Mikado, least of all Alex Mitchell's broadcast. They don't like him telling people to vote against them? Let them watch me do exactly that right now." She put several dollar bills and coins next to her plate and left. Her female companion lifted her chin in defiance and followed her.

One by one, the indignant diners followed. They paid their bills and took off. All of them said they were heading to the nearest voting station to cast their votes. Some of them now earnestly asked Eden and Isaac for directions. The ones who casually brushed them off earlier began to take a serious look at the flyers.

Within a half-hour, the cafe cleared out. Only the Chinese diners remained.

"I'm so sorry," Eden apologized to the cafe owner. "Looks like we chased all your customers away."

The cafe owner laughed. "No worries. I hope we'll win. I voted this morning." He grinned as he cleared and wiped the tables.

"Your boyfriend saved the day," Isaac said to her.

"Maybe." She glanced at the radio. "Do you think it might have been better if people were able to hear his whole message?"

"Who knows?" Isaac put the flyers back into his haversack. "Let's finish our route. Then we'll go check on the voter turnout." He headed toward the door and waved for her to follow.

From the moment they arrived at the racecourse, Eden felt her hope revive. The line of ratepayers waiting to vote extended beyond the lobby into the corridor. There were two hours left until the voting station closed, and voters were still arriving.

With Isaac, she went to the long table where Dottie Lambert, the secretary of the *China Press*, was helping to collect the ballots. Dottie had taken the day off to help at the polls.

"You won't believe what's happening," Dottie said as soon as she saw Eden. "A flood of voters started coming in four hours ago. They all said they came when the Japs jammed Alex's broadcast. That infuriated them." She turned and thanked a voter dropping his ballot into the box.

"I guess I was wrong," Eden said to Isaac. "I thought it would hurt our chances when people couldn't hear what Alex had to say."

"Either way," Isaac said. "Whatever works to get them to come out here."

She looked at the queue again. For the first time since their campaign began, she knew they'd win. She held her hands against her heart, and held on to hope.

In his living room, Clark slowly sipped his brandy as the radio continued to speculate on the election results. It surprised even himself how calm he felt. Was his mental state one of calm before the storm? Or was it what the Chinese called the light of life reflecting backward, the terminal lucidity that gave a person a brief moment of clarity shortly before his death?

His mother, blissfully unaware of the threat he was working so hard to forestall, whirled the toy airplane above Little Fu's head. "Look, look!" She laughed. "Popeye's flying away."

On the floor, Little Fu abandoned the colored wooden blocks and pushed himself up. "Give me. Give me." He stretched out his arms. Xiu-Qing chuckled and put down her cup of sweet cloud ear mushroom and red date soup. Madam Yuan teased the boy, keeping the toy pilot just out of his reach.

To say his mother was ignorant of what was happening in Shanghai would be unfair. The other day, he overheard her telling a houseboy to buy extra bags of rice. She instructed the houseboy to divide the extra rice and give them to each of the maids and servants.

Prices of goods continued to rise. Inflation was plaguing the city's economy with no end in sight.

His own company was feeling the heat. The year was coming to an end, and their business barely squeezed out a profit. If he took into account his contributions to the resistance, he would have to record this year as one in the red.

The distant sound of the phone ringing echoed from the study. Clark glanced at his watch. The election result should be coming in any time.

A houseboy answered and came to find him in the living room. "Young Master, phone. Speaks English."

"Coming." Clark put down his glass and went to the study to answer the call. "Hello?"

"Clark," Tony Keswick greeted him on the other line. "Good news. We won."

Clark let slip a smile.

"We defeated the Japanese," Keswick said. "I wanted to give you the news before it goes public."

"Thank you." Clark picked up a pen and doodled the Chinese word "ghost" on the notepad beside the phone. If Pearl heard this phone call too, she would say Keswick had a ghost in his heart. The man's conscience must be eating at him knowing he'd turned over to the puppet government all the land records and titles deeds of the properties identifying the Chinese landowners in the occupied sector of Shanghai outside of the International Settlement. And now, he felt the need to call here first to relay the good news to allay his guilt.

"I'll see you tomorrow," Keswick said. Clark could hear the strain to sound positive in his voice.

"Goodnight." Clark hung up the phone. For now, they'd weather the storm. But another one was soon to rise, he was sure. Hayashi wouldn't be pleased when he found out the election results. What would that old fox do next?

HAYASHI'S REVENGE

THE FIRST RATEPAYERS meeting of the year at the racecourse brought a high turnout just as Clark expected before he came. Whenever their wallets might get hit, people always showed up, and the new forty percent surcharge on land the SMC was proposing to levy had prompted the slew of Japanese ratepayers to show up today to cast their opposing vote. At a glance, Clark estimated at least two thousand people were in attendance. More than half were Japanese, and they were all sitting together in one block.

Nobody wanted a tax increase, but what other option did they have? The runaway cost of operating the Shanghai Municipal Police had been eating into the Council's reserve funds since the war with Japan broke out. Last year, the SMC's budget went into deficit, and this was with an eight percent pay cut to the police. The fiscal crisis wouldn't have happened in the first place if Japan wasn't fanning the crime wave behind the scenes.

All the other ratepayers understood that. They gritted their teeth and dealt with the burden for the sake of keeping some form of law and order. Only the Japanese ratepayers were here to kick up a stink.

Of course, there was also the matter that they were still sore from losing the election last November. And today, they were certain to be outvoted again too, again due to the land subdivision scheme that led to their election defeat. Some of the British and American voters in attendance here held thousands of votes.

Judging from the crowd, the Japanese ratepayers meant to be heard, even if they would lose. Clark could feel their agitation stewing as he walked into the stands.

He nudged past the men and women straggling in the aisle and down the steps toward the front row reserved for SMC members. At the bottom, he found himself face to face with Hayashi Yukichi.

"Mr. Yuan," said the old fox.

"Hayashisan," Clark returned the greeting.

The old fox stared at him. Clark kept his face blank. The old fox wasn't swayed. "You think you all have won one over me. You enjoy watching me be humiliated, failing in my job to secure advantages for my people."

Clark didn't answer. He had no intention of letting on to the old fox what he thought one way or the other.

"I assume full responsibility for our losses in the election, and it is obvious how the municipal ratepayers meeting today will end. However, I'm not at all in despair. I am willing to come and display a spirit that is worthy of the true Japanese." He smiled and tightened his gnarled hand on his cane. "There must be a limit to forbearance on our part. We may be obliged to meet violence with violence. I am willing to become a stepping stone for our future advance. I shall attend the meeting today joyously and courageously." He flipped his wool scarf over his shoulder and walked away.

Was that a warning? Clark kept his observing eye on the old fox. Or was it the ramblings of a sad, old man?

A chilly waft of wind blew past. Clark turned his attention away from Hayashi and went to take his seat.

On the tracks, Poul Scheel spoke into the microphone on stage and called the meeting to order. Scheel wasn't even a Council member. He was the consul-general of Denmark, but Denmark wasn't even a sovereign nation anymore as Hitler had taken it over. Right now, Scheel was nothing. Clark looked over at Keswick, who had lowered his head to read the notes in his hand while seated in the front row with the rest of the Council members. As chairman, Keswick should be convening the meeting. Why did he arrange for Scheel to chair instead?

Was Keswick that afraid of the wrath of the Nipponese?

Feeble man. All that Jardine Matheson prestige. In the end, it was nothing but a hollow name.

Scheel began with an opening speech introducing the terms of the amendment to impose the new levy, which was already printed out in the flyer left on everyone's seat. At the end of his speech, he said, "The land surcharge, as well as the ancillary special rates, will apply retroactively to January 1, 1940." He swept his eyes over the auditorium. "We will now begin the vote. Those in favor, please say "aye" and raise your hand when we call your row."

The room bustled with mumbles and he began the count. Godfrey Philips, the Council's secretary, dutifully called out each row of people sitting with the block of Westerners and counted their votes. When they finished, Scheel announced, "We have a count of nine thousand and fifty-five votes. The amendment passes—"

The whispers of the Japanese voters erupted. One shouted. "What about the nays?"

Scheel stood with his stiff lips. The Japanese broke into an uproar and stamped the bleachers. "Order! Order!" Scheel shouted into the microphone.

Hayashi stood up. The Japanese crowd quieted. Everyone

turned their eyes to the old fox. Slowly, he walked to the stage and spoke into the mike opened for the attendees. "Mr. Chairman, I have a counter-proposal."

Scheel lifted his hand. "Please, go ahead."

Hayashi took a piece of paper out of his pocket. He unfolded it and stared out into the audience. "The proposed amendment as it currently stands is unjust." His angry tone took Clark by surprise. "The problem of funds can be resolved by loans. There are certain banks ready to meet the requirements of the SMC on a commercial basis."

Pockets of Japanese voters shouted out to concur, but Hayashi's claim was nonsense. The SMC had already been taking out loans for the last three years to cover the rising police expenses. No banks would extend it any more credit.

Hayashi's face flushed. He continued to read the terms of his counter-proposal from the paper in his hands. "Should the important recommendations I hereby propose be defeated through opposition by a powerful group who, as is still fresh in our memories, took advantage of the shortcomings of our election rules to create several thousand decisive votes at the last general election of councilors, and should the measure for a tax increase pass over the opposition of all the vitally affected Chinese and Japanese, I must point out that the responsibility for the repercussions must fall on this group and the municipal authorities alone." He ended with a firm, unyielding flare in his eyes.

After he returned to his seat, Tony Keswick went to the stage. "Mr. Chairman." He glanced at Scheel from the podium. Scheel signaled him to go on. "I must object to Mr. Hayashi's unsound suggestion. Bank loans are no longer an option. Our notice of the meeting mailed to you had explained clearly the reasons, and why the tax surcharge is the only solution. Mr. Hayashi's proposed alternative will run us into bankruptcy. By all the forces of command, I ask you to reject this amendment."

The audience's voices amplified. Scheel stretched his arms over his podium. "We'll now put the alternate amendment to a vote."

Keswick took a step back. A draft blew over the stage and he fastened the top button of his coat. In the front row, Hayashi rose from his seat and climbed up the steps to the stage once again. Clark followed him with his eyes. The old fox walked up to Keswick. From his side pocket, he pulled out a pistol.

"Watch out!" Clark jumped to his feet.

Too late. Hayashi aimed the gun point-blank at Keswick and fired two shots into his chest. Keswick's eyes widened as he fell backward onto the stage.

A frenzy broke out among the audience. The men sitting on stage rushed toward Hayashi and seized the gun from his hand. The Japanese ratepayers flung the cushions on their seats into the air and stormed toward the stage. Those in folding chairs followed suit, hurling their chairs into the air without regard to the others sitting around them and charging forward to the track. "Banzai! Banzai!" they roared.

At the sight, Clark rushed onto the track away from the rage.

Calmly, Hayashi stood. A smile curled across his face as he slid his hands into his pockets.

Alarmed, police Commissioner Bourne dashed with his men toward the steps of the stage to block the stampede. Still, a mob of them got through. They lifted Hayashi onto their shoulders. "Banzai! Banzai!"

Bourne and his men ran after them. One of the rioters carrying Hayashi lost his balance and Hayashi tipped to the side. The others holding him up steadied the old fox and let him down.

Immediately, the police chased them off. They cuffed Hayashi's hands and hustled him away. Medics arrived and carried Keswick into the ambulance. All around, flashbulbs popped. News photographers swarmed onto the racetrack as another group of police officers led Scheel and the British and

American Council members to a secure place. Hundreds of non-Japanese voters were still scrambling to get away from the riot and confusion.

A police officer tapped Clark on the arm. "Mr. Yuan, you've got to go. Come with me." He turned to lead the way.

Before they left, Clark looked once more at the ambulance driving away. The wail of the siren ebbed. The glory of Western colonialism was coming to an end.

HOLLOW NAME

AS THE OLD SAYING GOES, his time had not arrived. Keswick did not die from Hayashi's attack. The bullets penetrated his chest, but his heavy winter coat shielded him from certain death.

The amendment to impose a surcharge on land would pass, but at what cost?

The answer was one that Clark wanted to hear from Keswick's own mouth.

He came out of the hospital elevator to the reception desk. The nurse pointed him down the hallway to a single-occupancy room reserved for patients willing to pay the rate.

Only a week had gone by since he was shot, but Keswick already recovered enough. In two days, he would be discharged. His first intended act in response to Hayashi's attempt to kill him when he returned to work? Concede to the Japanese.

Bowing to their pressure once again, Keswick planned to relinquish police control of the entire Western Road to the Japanese. The Western Area Special Police Force, or the WASP, which Hayashi demanded more than a year ago but which the SMC had stalled in creating, would now be formed. It would take charge of the parts of the Badlands previously patrolled by the

Municipal Police, and it would answer only to the puppet city government.

In the patient's room, Clark demanded Keswick give him a forthright answer.

"This agreement is a betrayal of the Chinese residents," Clark said. "Your agreement with them protects the foreign nationals. What about the Chinese? The foreign nationals get to be handled by the foreign affairs branch of the Municipal Police, but all Chinese will be given to the puppet police bureaus and courts? Does the SMC still have any concern for the Chinese living in the International Settlement? What will I say to them?"

Keswick didn't attempt to defend himself. "I'm sorry." He bent his fingers protruding from the sling. "I'm trying to do what's best for everyone. It's the only way to keep the Japanese ratepayers from revolting. We've pushed things a step too far. This way, at least, we'll get the tax money we need to keep crimes under control within the Settlement. That would benefit the Chinese too. As long as they don't go into the Badlands, they'll be fine."

Clark shook his head. He wished the Chinese would stay out of the Badlands too. They might have a chance if the lure of the white drug wasn't so great. The ones who couldn't help themselves were the laborers, the coolies, the homeless, and the downtrodden. The ones who craved the poison enough to risk being caught by the puppet police were the ones most in need of escape and the least able to resist a quick cure for their pain.

Keswick sighed. "This will be my last act as Council chairman. After this, I'll be stepping down. John Liddell will be taking over. Maybe he'll do a better job than I can."

Clark got up. There was no use in pursuing his point. Keswick had already given up.

"You may disagree with me, Clark, but we have no other way to protect ourselves except to maintain the truce."

Clark opened the door. "You take care," he said and left the room.

Maintain the truce?

He strode down the corridor. What Hayashi said to him at the meeting at the racecourse repeated in his head.

We may be obliged to meet violence with violence.

They may be. Dai Li planned on doing that already. Last night, Pearl told him the names of the people Dai Li had on his hit list. Shen Ming, director of the puppet tax bureau for the Zhejiang and Jiangsu provinces. Pan Tse-Tung, head of Wang Jing-Wei's bodyguards. Shen Zhu-Sheng, of the Shanghai puppet tax bureau. Gimitsu Shozo, supervisor of the Japan-China Silk and Cotton Mill. Plus the Japanese soldiers, sailors, and Chinese puppet police.

And those were only Juntong's targets. There would be more. From rogue resistance groups acting on their own, as well as underground Communists, and even more deadly organized bands like the Heaven and Earth Society to which his own sister belonged.

Let the bloodbath of 1941 begin.

More than ever now, Clark knew, he had to decide. Who could he trust, and who must he guard against? Who were neither friend nor foe?

At this point, the SMC for him was dead. If he had any true foreign friends left, they would not be the British and American members of the Council.

On the other hand, when Joseph Whitman called, he would never hesitate to answer. The quiet senior diplomat at the American consulate was among those on whom he could still readily rely.

Whitman's powers were limited. He'd always been honest

about that. But behind the scenes, he would exercise discretion and pull his strings. He had made that clear to Clark.

It didn't surprise Clark then when Whitman invited him to dinner after Keswick signed away the Council's right to police the Badlands to the Japanese. And it turned out, that wasn't all Keswick gave up. He also agreed to increase Japanese representation on the SMC to five. Next time around, they wouldn't have an election. The Council members would simply be appointed. Those were the legacies Keswick left behind before he passed on his seat to his fellow British businessman John Liddell. In silence, all his British compatriots accepted the terms. The American Council members did not challenge him either.

Joseph Whitman was the only one who telephoned Clark to express any kind of regret.

On entering the American Club, Clark checked in with the concierge. In the past, the Club didn't allow Chinese. But now, with so many Americans departed from the city, its rules had become lax.

The attendant at the reception desk took his coat and hat, and pointed him to the elevators past the capacious bar next to the billiard room. Clark thanked him and made his way into the main lobby. This seven-story building, one of László Hudec's masterpieces, with its dark oak panels, high beams, and white door frames, was America's architectural statement to Shanghai that they were here to stay. And why wouldn't one stay? This place was a haven, with its Italian marble double staircase leading upstairs to the card room, the lounge, the library, and even a mahjong room designed by Chinese interior designers, or downstairs to the gym, the bowling alley, and the Turkish bath.

Illusions, Clark thought as the elevator attendant took him up. In 1941, all the symbols of Western power and greatness in the East were nothing more than illusions.

The elevator arrived on the fifth floor and Clark stepped out onto the maple-wood floor of the splendid dining room. Within the polished white walls, where the red and gold velvet curtains hid the blackening reality outside the windows, the sparkling crystal chandelier's rays continued to feed the illusion of grandeur to the poor souls dining below its light.

The host brought him to the table. Joseph Whitman had already arrived.

"Good to see you," Whitman greeted him with the familiar warmth which could only come from a genuine friend.

Over dinner, Whitman gave him the truth of what was happening in Washington. "It is simply not possible to convince the American public to risk their own lives for another country on another continent," he said after the waiter served them their wine. "They didn't do it for France, and they're not going to do it for China. Military aid is out of the question. The American people won't support it."

"I know." Clark held on to the stem of his glass. At least, Whitman was honest.

"It doesn't mean our government is sitting on the side. Roosevelt understands the implications if the Axis countries win. I know it's little consolation to you right now that we're imposing economic sanctions." He paused to let the waiter finish serving them their first course. When the waiter walked away, he continued, "The economic sanctions are not simply moral objections. Japan is a small country. It's desperate for the natural resources to wage an all-Pacific war. That's their Achilles' heel. They depend on us for steel, scrap iron, and copper. Our embargo on metals is crippling their plans. They can't go on, and we now have a bargaining chip. In time, they will cave. I honestly believe that."

"I hope you're right," Clark said. How many lives would be lost though before Japan gave up?

"There are plans in place to give air support to Chiang Kai-Shek and the Chinese Nationalists."

"Yes?"

"What I'm telling you is strictly confidential." Whitman glanced around to make sure no one was listening to them and leaned forward. "Roosevelt signed an executive order last year to allow our army and navy pilots to resign to join a new volunteer air force in Kunming. He issued the executive order after Germany took France. The new air force is called the AVG. They're specifically formed and funded by our administration. He also authorized a shipment of Curtiss Hawks to China. The shipment was slated for the RAF, but it's coming to China instead. The aim is to give the Chinese army air support in Kunming, so they can protect their supply line from the West even if Japan takes over the ports in Shanghai."

Clark finished his dish. "It is a lifeline. Thank you for telling me."

His face full of sympathy, Whitman stared at him. He put down his fork. "I've wanted to ask you this for a while. Would you ever consider working for the United States government?"

Clark raised his wine glass. "What kind of work?"

"Our Office of Strategic Services needs people who know the Chinese culture and who can read and speak Chinese. I know you have your family business here, but if you're interested, I can get you out of Shanghai to America."

The OSS? In America? Clark sat back in his seat. "You want me to spy on my own government?"

"Well . . . there's Mao too and his CCP." Whitman reached out for his water. "Whatever you do, we're on your side. We're behind the KMT." He looked at Clark, his eyes stern. "The more important thing is, you can get out of China. If things get worse here, you can save yourself."

Clark frowned. He swirled his glass. "I have a family here. What about my family?"

"You can bring your wife and child, of course."

"And my mother? My sisters?"

Whitman tucked his chin and didn't answer.

Clark put down his glass. "I appreciate your offer, Joe. But I can't abandon my mother and sisters."

Whitman clasped his hands on the table. "I understand. Just remember. You have allies. I'm not talking about your country, I'm talking about you. Just don't forget that."

LUXURY OF LOVE

THE NOISES from the bathroom brought Eden out of her sleep. Her mind still drowsy, she half raised her eyelids and turned over. Instinctively, she reached out her arm. Empty. Her hand fell onto the wrinkled bed sheets.

She opened her eyes and sat up. The bathroom door was open and she could see Alex shaving at the sink.

What time was it? She brushed back her hair and looked at the clock. Quarter to eight. What was he doing up so early on a Saturday morning?

She got out of bed and poured herself a glass of water from the jug on top of the dresser. Faint beams of winter sunlight gleamed through the slit between the curtains. She walked over to the window and pushed back the drapes to let the sunlight flood in. Outside, the shop doors were still closed. An elderly man strolled down the street. A few bikers swooshed by and soon passed out of sight. This might be the only time during daylight when this weary and beaten city could see a little peace.

"You're up." Alex came out of the bathroom. He proceeded to the closet and took out his clothes.

"Yes." Eden let go of the curtain. "I didn't sleep very well last night."

"Oh, yeah?" He put on his pants.

It wasn't only last night. Insomnia had been plaguing her for a while. "I . . ." She stopped. The words were on the tip of her tongue, but somehow, she couldn't let them out.

What happened to Isaac's parents? He hadn't heard from them for months, and neither had her family. All they knew was, Pétain passed a set of anti-Jewish laws, France's own version of the Nuremberg laws. The citizenship of Jews was revoked. They were prohibited from schools and almost every profession and industry sectors. And now, rampant rumors abounded. The Vichy government was arresting Jews and deporting them to internment camps.

At home, her parents stoically went about their days, keeping a lid on the subject even as it hung like a thunderstorm over their heads. Isaac never complained either. He never complained anymore.

Maybe this was the best way to cope. If it was, it didn't help her. They were all pretending. Pretending to be optimistic and avoiding talking about their worst fear.

She wanted to cry. She wanted to shout. The Weissmans might be in danger. Perhaps danger had already befallen them. She should be able to say this. They all should be able to talk about what the changes in France and the lack of news from Isaac's parents meant.

The Weissmans weren't all that bothered her. What was happening in France was happening everywhere else in Europe. How quickly the French submitted to Hitler to take all rights and freedom away from the Jews. If Hitler won his war with Britain, why would Britain act any differently? And when that happened, the entire Jewish population in Europe would be rounded up and sent to camps. Would they be forever imprisoned and enslaved?

What about the Jews who escaped to China and Southeast Asia? If Japan won, if they controlled all of Asia, would they leave the Jewish people alone? Or would they adopt the anti-Semitic laws in Europe and round up all the Jewish people and put them away in camps too?

Maybe that was why her parents and Isaac kept silent. Talking would bring too much fear and pain. If they didn't talk about it, then what was happening wouldn't feel real.

"I wish. . ." she muttered. By the side of the bed, Alex buttoned his shirt in front of the mirror. When she came over last night, she wanted so much to tell him everything about how she felt. She couldn't for most of the evening. His friends from the radio station and their girlfriends were here. Wines, liquor, fascinating conversations about affairs of the world were always what he enjoyed.

When the company left and they were alone, she still couldn't bring herself to trouble him.

Why couldn't she talk to him? Every time something distressed her, the words would nearly slip from her lips, but a feeling of incongruity always compelled her to hold them back.

Like now.

His mind wasn't even here. His thoughts were entirely somewhere else.

He buckled his belt.

"Are you going out?" she asked.

"Yes." He slipped on his watch. "I have to go meet a source."

"You didn't tell me." She thought they would be spending a lazy Saturday morning together.

"It's early on Saturday. I figured you could sleep late and rest."

She came closer to the bed. In his way, he was being considerate.

So why did it irk her still?

"I'll only be gone for a few hours," he said. Excitement lit up his eyes and he lowered his voice. "This is top secret. I'm chasing a huge story. A trusted advisor of the German ambassador in Japan is here. His name is Richard Sorge. He's highly regarded by the Nazi party. He also lived in Tokyo and worked as the Japan correspondent for the *Frankfurter Zeitung*."

"That's the top newspaper in Germany."

"Yes. So he has a lot of friends in Japan too. Basically, he's a key conduit between Germany and Japan. He even has a Japanese diplomatic pass. But I've got a source who's telling me he's a Soviet spy."

"Are you serious?"

"Very. He's been working for the Comintern for more than twenty-two years. He's built a spy ring that reaches as high up as the Japanese Prime Minister's office. The person I'm going to meet with now has information about him and his visit. I have to go and find out what's going on."

"Yes, of course." She crossed her arms. A German Nazi who was secretly a spy for Stalin would be a stunning, huge scandal.

But deep inside, she wished she didn't have to be by herself. Not this morning.

He came over to her. "Stay here as long as you like. If you're still here when I come back, I'll tell you all about it."

She put on a bright face. "Can't wait."

He stroked her cheek and gave her a kiss on her forehead. Just then, she wanted to tell him how worried she felt. Scared, even. All the words inside her choked her throat, but she dared not let them out.

She couldn't. Alex chased adventures, not burdens. A heap of emotions about things he couldn't control would only be a burden.

What could he do about her worries anyhow?

She smiled at him again. He dropped his hand from her cheek and let it slide gently over her satin nightgown and down her back. "You have my keys. Stay or let yourself out if you like." He crinkled his eyes with a grin and started to leave.

"Alex," she called him back.

"Yes?"

"Do you love me?" The question fell out of her mouth. Why did she ask that? She wasn't even thinking it.

He gazed at her. The look in his eye was not one of intense feelings, although not one of blithe dismissal either.

She held her breath. The question raised a wall between them and she wished she could take it back.

He looked her in the eye. His voice as honest and convicted as she'd ever heard from him. "In times of war, love is a luxury we can't afford."

He lowered his gaze and walked away. As he reached the door, he gave her a soft smile before he left the room.

Alone, Eden looked out the window again. She clutched the lining of the curtain and tried to untangle her thoughts.

Was love a negligible accessory to life when battles were raging, and people were being forced from their homes, stripped of their rights?

She hung her head. Shame, guilt, anger, and fear intertwined in her mind. She couldn't think straight.

What lay in the future when she looked ahead?

A bleak, dark world. A map of continents where Jews were never welcomed nor allowed.

Where would her family fit in?

Where would she fit in?

If Alex returned to America, where would she go? Was their future already clear before her eyes? Was it inevitable their paths would eventually diverge?

She swung around and moved away from the window. Mechanically, she washed up, gathered her clothes, and got dressed. As she picked up her purse to go, the stillness of the room struck her. The bed, the chair, the desk, and the wardrobe.

None of it felt permanent. They were just objects, useful today and easily forgotten tomorrow. If needed, they could be replaced. If discarded or left behind, their losses would be inconsequential. Nothing here exhibited a personal touch.

Quietly, she walked out. Her feelings once again held inside, she closed the door of the apartment and moved on ahead.

BANK WAR

THE MORNING NEWS from the XCDN, the radio arm of the British-operated *North China Daily News*, came on as Clark put on his shirt and tie to go to work.

> *Today is Friday, March 21, 1941. At 3:00 a.m. last night, a gang of eight gunmen dressed in Chinese police uniforms forced their way into the dormitory of the Shanghai Commercial and Savings Bank.*

All at once, terror gripped him. He dropped his hands from his tie. Gao Zhen was the director of that bank.

> *The intruders flipped on the lights and opened fire at the bank clerks who were asleep. Seven were wounded and three were killed. Afterwards, plainclothes police from the Western District Police Bureau arrived with four Japanese military police. They dragged the remaining bank clerks and employees from their beds, a total of a hundred twenty-four people, and took them to the Western District Police Station at 76 Jessfield Road, where they are now incarcerated . . .*

The station at 76 Jessfield Road was where Wang Jing-Wei's

lackeys interrogated, tortured, and executed anti-Japanese suspects.

> *Also, at seven o'clock this morning, a frantic employee called the Shanghai Municipal Police and reported a suspicious package with a ticking sound was left at one of the bank counters. The SMP arrived and discovered a bomb wired for both time and contact explosion. Luckily, the police were able to disable the bomb before it went off. The Central Bank of China was not so lucky. An hour later, a bomb exploded at its Canidrome branch shortly after it opened, killing seven and wounding fifteen . . .*

Clark walked toward the radio. What was happening?
Outside of his room, Wen-Ying knocked and called out, "Ge!"
He stared at the door. "Come in."
Wen-Ying swung the door open. "Did you hear—"
He held up his hand to hush her and turned up the volume.

> *No one has claimed responsibility for the bombings. Regarding the arrests of the employees of the Shanghai Commercial and Savings Bank, Li Shiqun, the Minister of Police, has issued the following statement. He said, "The Chungking terrorists have been mounting increasing attacks against the Reform Nationalist Government. The authorities of the foreign concessions have so far failed to take any action and have allowed Chungking's agents to move about freely to break the law. Therefore, our ministry has no choice but to arrest those who are working for the Chungking-controlled bank, which we have evidence is funding the Chungking-backed terrorist activities*
> *. . .*

"There's no such thing," Clark said to Wen-Ying. Gao-Zhen and his bank were not controlled by Chiang Kai-Shek's regime, nor had his bank been financing any resistance activities. Any money Gao and his bank had given to the Kuomintang was limited to the contributions Clark himself had forced them to give before the war began.

Minister Li's statement continued to say the prisoners would be given
maximum protection and comfort, and will be released as soon as the
Chungking regime expressly pronounces its repentance and promises to
order its agents to cease their reign of terror. He further warned that if his
demands are not met, his ministry will be forced to take similar measures to
punish the entire staff of all of the Chungking-controlled banks and
financial establishments in Shanghai proper . . .

Wen-Ying turned off the radio. "Ge! We have to do something."

"I know."

"This is revenge. Wang Jing-Wei's retaliating for our attack on his puppet China Reserve Bank."

"The attack on the China Reserve Bank . . . that was Tian Di Hui?"

Wen-Ying gasped and clamped shut her mouth, then admitted, "Yes."

Clark slapped his forehead. The China Reserve Bank was the organ that issued the puppet regime's currency. Last week, a group of rogue assassins broke in and attempted to kill the bank's manager. They failed to kill their target, but they damaged the building with homemade bombs and they killed a security guard when they ran away.

This was one of the problems with resistance groups like the Heaven and Earth Society. They didn't answer to anyone. They weren't beholden to either Chungking or Dai Li. These groups would act without the necessary inside information to strategize their attacks.

"Do you blame us?" Wen-Ying asked.

"No." Clark put his hands on his hip and looked down. What was done was done. Anyway, Wang Jing-Wei was just looking for a reason to interfere with the Chinese banks he didn't control. If he had his way, he'd shut them all down and force everyone to use his regime's worthless new currency.

Even if Tian Di Hui hadn't initiated the fight, eventually Wang Jing-Wei and Japan would encroach upon the monetary markets within the International Settlement. They already had the police force. The SMC was almost theirs too. Trampling on the city's financial institutions was the obvious next step. If Japan wasn't willing yet to directly invade the Settlement, it would do so by cutting off the arteries that gave the city life, one by one.

"We won't back down," Wen-Ying said. "Tian Di Hui won't be intimidated. We'll fight fire with fire."

Her words alarmed him. "What do you mean? What about the bank employees being held hostage?"

"Maybe we'll try to rescue them." She turned around. "I have to go."

Rescue them? At Wang Jing-Wei's own chamber of torture at 76 Jessfield Road? That would only put the innocent bank employees at greater risk! He cried out, "Wait! Wen-Ying!"

No use. His sister had already left.

He couldn't rush off and act in haste like she did. He owed Gao Zhen too much, for the way he compelled him to give money to the KMT, and for the torture he suffered at Shen Yi's hand.

He put on his suit jacket. He had to find a way to save Gao Zhen's employees. He had to save his bank from the puppet regime.

Quickly, Clark went downstairs. His mother, Xiu-Qing, and Mei Mei were in the dining room eating breakfast. "Mei Mei," he called for his youngest sister. "Come into the study."

Mei Mei looked up from her bowl of congee. "Now?"

"Yes." He led her into the study and unlocked the top drawer of the desk. "Here's our savings account passbook, the key to our security deposit box, and our family seal." He put the items on the desk, then pointed at the large calligraphy scroll which concealed a safe behind the wall. "There are gold bars in our safe deposit box. Bring them all back and put them in there. Also, withdraw half of the American cash and lock everything in the safe."

"Is something wrong?" Mei Mei asked. Her face had turned pale.

"No." He relaxed his face and tried to reassure her. "Not for us. The news report said there had been several assaults on banks this morning. This is just a safeguard, but I need you to take care of it right away."

She frowned and picked up the items on the desk.

"I'll tell Huang Shifu to drive you. I'll take a taxi to work. Bring two of our Russian guards with you. And dress down. Don't look conspicuous. Handle this quickly and come home."

"All right." She closed her hands around the passbook, keys, and seal.

"Don't tell Ma or Xiu-Qing. No need to scare them."

"I know."

He said goodbye to his sister and left the room. At least this problem could be immediately solved.

On his way out, his mother called out, "Aren't you going to eat breakfast?"

"No," Clark replied. "I'm leaving." He went straight to the door outside. When Huang Shifu opened the car door for him, he instructed him to drive his sister instead and got into the first taxicab that came along.

"Kiangse Road, Foochow Road," he said to the taxi driver.

The taxi driver steered the wheel and headed to the intersection of the building that housed the SMC. The SMC was practically useless, but it would be the place where he could find out what the foreign governments would do and if any negotiations were taking place between them and the KMT.

"What did you expect?" Pearl lit a cigarette. "If those old foreigners were going to safeguard this city, they would have done so already." She blew out a cloud of smoke.

Clark chugged his shot of *maotai*, the Chinese white wine. Three days had passed since Wang Jing-Wei's police abducted the employees of the Shanghai Commercial and Savings Bank. All that had happened was back and forth between Chungking and the American consul-general in Shanghai. The KMT in Chungking pleaded with the U.S. for protection for the banks, and the U.S. Embassy urged the SMC and the Shanghai Municipal Police to give the banks whatever protection they needed. Even a potential shutdown of all the Chinese banks in Shanghai wasn't enough to move them to act in any meaningful way.

"Any word from Dai Li? Does he intend to save the bank employees?" Clark asked.

"He hasn't contacted me. No one else in Shanghai has heard from him either." Pearl poured them both another shot. Clark chugged that one down too. How depressing. Even the KMT would not save them while watching them die.

The bank officials he personally knew told him they had contacted Chungking for help. They, too, got no answer.

"A hundred twenty-four lives." Clark twirled the little cup between his fingers. "All to be ended this way. We're not even counting the seven killed in the later explosions."

"Wang Jing-Wei's people claim Chungking's terrorists caused those explosions." Pearl blew out another trail of smoke from between her lusciously painted red lips.

"Ghosts would believe them." Clark pushed his empty cup toward her.

"You'll get drunk," she said. Nonetheless, she refilled the cup.

Let him get drunk then. He swallowed another shot. Get drunk, and he wouldn't have to think about any of this anymore.

The morning edition of the Chinese newspaper *Shen Pao* brought no good news for the kidnapped bank employees. The puppet government had now issued a new statement. If any of their own China Reserved Bank personnel were assassinated, they would kill the same number of the employees of Gao Zhen's bank.

Clark scowled and tossed the newspaper onto his desk. He picked up the phone and dialed Gao Zhen's office.

The secretary picked up. "Hello?"

"Yes. Is Director Gao there?"

"Who is this?"

Clark hesitated. "Yuan Guo-Hui."

A pause on the other end. "Director Gao is temporarily away. Can I take a message?"

"No." Clark dipped his head. "Thank you." He hung up. He'd called many times already and left messages. He had called Gao at home too. Clearly, Gao didn't wish to speak to him.

He didn't blame Gao. They hadn't spoken in years. Not since Shen Yi kidnapped him and tortured him.

Clark propped his elbows on the desk and dropped his forehead into his hands. A knock came on his door.

"Come in." He looked up.

His secretary entered. "Director Yuan. This Mister Tang wants to see you."

Before Clark could react, Tang Wei entered.

Clark bolted up from his seat. "What did you come here for? I told you never to come again."

His secretary took a startled step back, but Tang Wei sauntered in. "I came to talk to you about the Shanghai Commercial and Savings Bank employees. You don't want to hear what I have to say?"

The bank employees. . . Clark held back. He glanced at his secretary. "Close the door."

The secretary darted her eyes from Clark to Tang Wei, then shut the door and left.

"Really," Tang Wei said and strolled over, "we haven't seen each other in more than two years. This is how you greet me?" He sat down, entirely at ease.

Glaring, Clark squared his shoulders and lowered himself into his seat. "If you have something to say, then say it quickly."

Tang Wei lit a cigarette. "Actually, those employees now being held are innocent. You and I both know that. But the environment is in chaos. We just want to live peacefully too. That's why I've come to you with a proposal. If you will agree, then the higher-ups of the Reorganized Government will also agree to do it this way."

"What way?"

"Our regime wants Chungking to make a public statement and call for all the resistance violence to stop. Chiang Kai-Shek's entourage is stalling. It's frustrating. They're too far away to feel any sense of urgency." Tang Wei looked at Clark and blew out his smoke. "You're here though. You can see how serious this matter is. Perhaps you can make a statement."

"Me? You're joking. I'm not a Nationalist official anymore. You're not either. You're telling me to issue a public statement? To say what? To represent who?"

"Aaay." Tang held up his hand to stop him. "Reality is not so simple. From beginning to end, you were once a KMT agent. You and I are not the same. You haven't joined the Reorganized Government. People still regard you to be on the KMT's side. And now, you're a Shanghai Municipal Council member. What you say will of course have sway."

Clark pressed his lips closed. What kind of ridiculous reasoning was that? These goons couldn't get Chungking to cave to their demand, so they wanted to use him as their mouthpiece to confuse people.

"You think so highly of me, thank you," Clark said sarcastically. "But you're wrong. My words will have no effect."

Tang chuckled. "Whether they will or not, why do you care? I'm offering you a chance to save more than a hundred lives. As long as you can rescue these people, why concern yourself with anything else? You can bring this to an end."

Clark swallowed. A hundred and twenty-four lives. And a way to help Gao Zhen.

But to publicly call for the resistance to stop? Never mind that it would put him at odds with Dai Li and the KMT, it would demoralize everyone colluding with him on plots against Japan and Wang Jing-Wei, and all the others fighting for resistance in groups he didn't know.

Tang tapped the ashes of his cigarette off into the ashtray. "You keep seeing the new Reorganized Government as the enemy. I tell you, Wang Jing-Wei has reasons for choosing peace with Japan. He thinks, rather than continuing the war with Japan and all the bloodshed, negotiating peace with them would spare more Chinese from misery and grief. And look, Japan has formally agreed to turn the government back over to him, hasn't it? We've reclaimed authority and brought our own people back in. That's the first step. And now we can begin to pursue Chinese sovereignty. We can finally get rid of the Western imperialists and focus on getting rid of the rural Communists too. Compared to Chiang Kai-Shek's policy, it's not a worse alternative."

"Sovereignty?" Clark sneered. "Wang Jing-Wei's nothing but a Japanese puppet. All this garbage language you made up about friendly neighbors and mutual support. Japan doesn't even give him reparation money to rebuild after their army destroyed all the land. He's operating a crime syndicate of opium dens and gambling houses to fund his administration. How is that sovereignty?"

"Well, we can debate that." Tang Wei took another drag from his cigarette. "If Chiang Kai-Shek isn't getting into our way, and the country smoothly adapts the Reorganized Government's new currency, a lot of funding problems would be resolved."

"What about 76 Jessfield Road? Is torturing Chinese people something Wang Jing-Wei is doing to spare them misery and grief too?"

"That's not the right way to put it. A lot of the violence originated from the Chungking loyalists themselves. If they would stop their terrorist tactics, there would be no need for the police to exert such stringent force."

"You're using strong words to distort truth."

"Forget it, forget it." Tang waved his hand. "I didn't come today to argue politics with you. Regarding the prisoners from the bank, what do you want to do?"

Clark clenched his teeth. What should he do? Stand his ground? Or save a hundred and twenty-four lives?

A statement from him? Humiliating to him, sure. Chungking would lose face too. That was what the puppet government really wanted, wasn't it? They didn't really expect the resistance fighters would stop only because Clark went out and called for them to do so. They couldn't get Chungking to give in, so they wanted to humiliate them.

But one hundred and twenty-four innocent lives.

No one would be coming to the prisoners' rescue. The Heaven and Earth Society could try. If they did, they would fail. Trying to break into the fortress of 76 Jessfield Road would only bring their members to certain death.

"You only have this one chance," Tang Wei said. "After this, I can't guarantee their personal safety anymore."

His chest trembling with anger, Clark said, "A public statement. What do I have to say?"

Tang Wei reclined back. "See? You and I are still aligned after all." He began to lay out the terms. Everything he said passed through Clark's ears like white noise. After all he had done, he now had to succumb to Tang Wei's demand.

The power of Japan had overcome him and forced him to kneel. And this time, he had no way to fight back.

———————

At Gao Zhen's home, a lane house on Route Doumer, Clark waited outside while their houseboy went to inform the master a guest had come to see him. From the wary look on the houseboy's face, Clark knew the Gaos did not deem him a welcomed guest. He paced in circles before the door. If Gao Zhen absolutely refused to speak to him, he would have no other way but to send a message in writing.

The houseboy returned with Madam Gao. Her eyes looked like they could shoot arrows of fire.

"Yuan Guo-Hui," she yelled at him. "You still have face to come see us?"

"Gao tai tai," Clark pleaded, "I have a very important matter to discuss with Uncle Gao."

"Whatever important matter, we don't want to hear it. We don't want to be connected to anything related to you. Ah Bing, shut the door." She started to turn around.

"This isn't about me," Clark yelled. "It's about Uncle Gao's bank employees. I can save them."

Madam Gao halted her steps. She hesitated for a moment, then reluctantly nodded to the houseboy to let Clark in.

"Go pass the word to Old Master," she said to the houseboy, then turned to Clark. "You better not be speaking empty words." She flung her arm down to make the point. The red silk scarf around her elbow flitted like a warning signal as she walked him into the sitting room.

Steeling himself, he followed her. A maid came in. "Madam, shall I bring the tea?"

"No need," Madam Gao said and sat down on the couch. She tossed her head to tell Clark to take a seat across from her.

Gao Zhen came in and sat down beside his wife. His demeanor looked less harsh than Madam Gao's, but he showed no desire at all to see Clark. Clark noticed he had grown out his hair on the sides of his head to cover up the wound of his lost ear.

A wave of regret swarmed him. "Uncle Gao."

Gao Zhen did not acknowledge his greeting. "What do you want to talk to me about?"

"The Western District Police are willing to release your employees."

"Is that so?" The side of Gao's face twitched. Anger and despair crept into his eyes. "Is this matter related to you? Am I being dragged into your problems again?"

"No! No!" Clark denied. "I have absolutely nothing to do with the abductions, or anything involving the banks. I have no connection with the Chinese police or the Reorganized Government either. Wang Jing-Wei's people approached me."

Gao calmed down a bit. "They approached you? Why? If you have no connection with the banks or the Reorganized Government's side, why did they come to you?"

"They want me to make a statement. They couldn't get the Nationalist Government in Chungking to admit their fault and to promise to stop instigating attacks against their people. They want a way to save face and to compel a denouncement of the resistance attacks. They've chosen me."

Gao creased his forehead. Madam Gao asked, "Why did they choose you?"

"Because I used to work for the KMT, and I'm a Chinese on the Shanghai Municipal Council."

"Are you willing to make a statement then?" Gao asked.

"Yes. I already thought through this clearly. Tomorrow, at four o'clock in the afternoon, there will be a press conference. I will make a public statement according to their terms. And then, they will release the employees."

Madam Gao narrowed her eyes. "You're willing to do this, why? How will this benefit you?"

"If I can save a hundred and twenty-four people's lives, then I don't need any personal benefit to me," Clark said. He hooked and twiddled his fingers. "And maybe, it's a small reparation I can pay to Uncle Gao for what befell him two years ago," he said with all sincerity.

Gao let out a deep sigh. "All right. Then I'll wait for your news tomorrow. I hope what you're saying is true."

Clark loosened his hands. At least, he could finally do something for Gao Zhen for all the troubles he'd brought to the man.

40

MOUTH AGAINST THE HEART

AT THE PODIUM in the ballroom of the Metropole Hotel, Clark gazed out to the audience of reporters and the sea of Chinese faces waiting for him to speak. He suspected most of those here who weren't with the press were imposters paid for by the Japanese. Or else they were forced to be here by the puppet regime. Either way, they didn't matter. The only thing the Japanese and the puppet government wanted was a photo to tell the story of how the Chinese in fact wanted a truce with their oppressors.

He stepped up to the microphone. Behind him, Li Shiqun, the puppet regime's Minister of Police, stood. Li's presence was a show of unity and support to the public eye, and a reminder of the threat to the person about to make the speech. Clark inhaled a deep breath. "Good afternoon, everyone. Four days ago, the Western District Police Bureau conducted a raid at the dormitory of the Shanghai Commercial and Savings Bank. The raid was part of an investigation. . ." He paused. He could hardly recite the next words. In the audience, with his arms crossed, Tang Wei looked directly at him and smiled.

Against all will, Clark went on. "It was part of an investigation following the police's receipt of a tip that the attack at the China Reserve Bank two weeks ago was plotted by a group of people residing in the dormitory." This was an outright lie. He couldn't believe he was officially blaming the innocents to help the puppet government portray themselves as victims.

He clutched the edges of the podium and continued. "With the China Reserve Bank's issuance of a new currency this year, and the expectation that the new currency will become the standard form of exchange throughout China, independent banks in Shanghai are concerned this may harm the strength and future of their institutions. Their employees feel insecure about their jobs and careers. Their fear and self-interest led a group of them to undertake a criminal action." He lowered his eyes. He hated these bogus words coming out of his mouth. How many people out there would believe these lies? Even if none, they would now all think he was in league with the enemy.

"Nonetheless, the Reorganization Government's ultimate interest is peace. After negotiations, the Ministry of Police has agreed to release all one hundred and twenty-four detainees. At five o'clock this afternoon, they will be taken to the headquarters of the Shanghai Commercial and Savings Bank, where they can reunite with their families." The reporters in the crowd buzzed, but he wasn't done. The toughest part for him was still to come.

He gritted his teeth. "With this announcement, I hope we will all begin a new page. This is the first act of the Reorganized Government to end the strife between the different factions among our people. Within our city, deadly attacks by rebels must stop. Their riotous tactics are criminal. They're making this city uninhabitable, and they're interfering with people making a living. As peaceful citizens, we must condemn their actions. Rebels cannot continue to terrorize Shanghai without laws and without morals for their own self-interest. Lay down your weapons. Support Wang Jing-Wei. Support peace." He spat out the last word. "Thank you," he mumbled and left the podium, ignoring the camera flashes and shouted questions from the reporters. A spokesman of the Ministry of Police stepped into his place at the podium. Clark made his way straight to the door, passing Li Shiqun. The puppet Minister nodded his approval. Clark gave him a cold stare and left the room with the bodyguards flanking him on each side.

The Sambuca was still near empty when Clark came and ordered a whiskey straight-up at the bar. His rendezvous with Zhou Ke-Hao couldn't have come at a better time. After that brutal press conference at the Metropole Hotel, he needed a stiff drink. Maybe two. Maybe more.

He waved to Mauricio, who was at the far end of the bar talking to a guest. While the bartender was serving his drink, Zhou Ke-Hao appeared beside him. Clark started to greet him, but Zhou's stern face left him confused.

"I couldn't have guessed you're a coward after all," Zhou said.

"What?"

"I went to your press conference. I heard what you said. So, my band of brothers, they are criminals now? We're terrorists acting without laws and morals for our own self-interest?"

"Of course not!" Clark said. "That was just a phony statement to appease the puppet government. You can't possibly believe a word of it."

"Why do you need to appease them? Aren't you on our side? Or have you been double-crossing us this whole time?"

"No! Of course I'm on your side. I would never double-cross you. That press conference, I had no choice. They demanded I say what they asked to the public or they'd kill all the bank employees they kidnapped."

Zhou wasn't moved. His cold stare kept Clark at arm's length.

"More than a hundred innocent people would die if I didn't do what they said." Clark tried to make him understand. "I did it to save them."

"What about the lives of my band of brothers? Some died already carrying out the plots you told us to execute. You put them up to sacrifice their lives. Why shouldn't the bank workers bear the same burden? My brothers and I don't just take life-threatening risks. We no longer have homes or jobs. We move from one dingy safe house or third-class hotel to another. We're given subsidies that are barely enough to live on. We do this to bring our country back from the traitors and enemies. What have these bank employees done? They have their jobs. They have their salaries. They have their families. They haven't sacrificed a single thing. If we're all striving for the same thing, why can't they bear a share of the sacrifice?"

Clark fell speechless. "This . . ."

"Or maybe I judged you wrong," Zhou said. "Maybe all this time, you're no different from the other rich clans. In the end, when it comes to who you'll protect, it'll be your own kind. Bankers and entrepreneurs. Lowly people like us are just dumb fools you can use to protect your wealth."

"It's not like that," Clark said. "Truly, it's not like that. Zhou, you know I'm not that kind of person."

"Do I?" He lifted his chin, but a sliver of doubt rose, and anger and confusion wrestled on his face. He gave Clark a cold stare and picked up the drink the bartender served to Clark. "We'll see what you do as your next move." He downed the whole glass of whiskey, slammed it down on the bar, and walked away.

Clark slumped back onto the barstool. Mauricio came over and put another glass of whiskey in front of him. Clark picked it up and downed it, then stood up. He took out his wallet and placed a bill on the bar. "Thank you."

Mauricio smiled and waved goodbye.

The street was already dark when Clark stepped outside. He

swept his eyes back and forth and surveyed the scene. This was Blood Alley, not the Badlands, but these days, one had to always be on guard. He had to stay alert, even if guilt was nearly consuming all of him.

He turned left, picking up his pace but not hustling so fast that he'd appear afraid. Fear attracted robbers, bandits, kidnappers, and any scoundrel with wicked intent. The group of half-drunken Marines up ahead was safe. He veered toward them. Any straggler loitering alone, or small groups of two or three ruffians, he tried to avoid.

At the entrance to the alleyway, a hard object—a tube, or a stick—jabbed against his back. "Don't move."

A gun.

Clark's heart somersaulted. He'd gauged every part of his surroundings. Where did this thug come from?

"Turn this way." The unknown man behind him pushed him toward the alley with the barrel. The rowdy Marines passed by, but Clark couldn't cry out for help.

His heart thumping, he walked into the alley as he was told. Was this the end of him?

"Keep going," said the assailant.

Where had he heard this voice before? Clark turned his head slightly and tried to steal a glance. "Who are you?"

"Who am I? Yes. You've long forgotten me. Turn around."

Carefully, Clark did as he said. Under the moon and the faint street lights leaking into the alley, he could make out the person's face. He couldn't believe his eyes. His fear vanished, and a tide of joy and relief swelled. It was his old friend. His right hand who he thought was killed in the train explosion when they went to deliver dynamite to the Kailan Mines.

He reached out his hand. "Xu Hong-Lie!"

"Don't move!" Xu ordered, his gun still pointing at Clark.

Clark frowned. This was Xu Hong-Lie. But his face. A rough, lumpy patch of scars had taken over the lower part of his left cheek and jaw. A similar patch covered the skin of the back of his hand, wrist, and the part of his forearm shown above the cuff of his sleeve. "You—"

"Yuan Guo-Hui, you despicable knave. Such a waste I trusted you."

"Hong-Lie, whatever's the matter, let's slowly talk it over."

"You and I have nothing to talk about. I came to find you today only to clean up a rotten element like you."

Utterly confused, Clark quickly assessed the threat. He was taller and bigger than Xu, and Xu seemed frailer than he used to be. Could he subdue or disarm him? Was there any way to persuade him to talk before he shot?

"If I hadn't seen it with my own eyes, I wouldn't even believe it," Xu said. "Through a thousand tons of toil and ten thousand drops of anguish I came back. Full of hope, I return to find you. So it turns out, today, you're a puppet for Japan too."

"It's not what it looks like," Clark said. "That's a misunderstanding."

"A misunderstanding? You are taking me for a fool?"

"No! I can explain. Hear me out." Clark glanced at the gun, then Xu's face. A thought popped into his head. "What about Xiu-Qing? Don't you want to know how she is? Even if you don't want to hear what I have to say, don't you want to hear about her?"

"Don't talk to me about Xiu-Qing!" Xu raised his gun and pointed it at Clark's head. His face twisted in agony. "A *junzi* wouldn't steal the love of another. You thought I was dead, and you took advantage and made your move in. You're truly despicable!" He curled his finger around the trigger.

"Wait!" Clark shouted. "You've misunderstood entirely. I have no relationship with Xiu-Qing. She gave birth to your son. Your son!"

Xu wrenched his face. In the split second as Xu tried to process what he heard, Clark grabbed his wrist. He twisted his arm around and pushed him up against the wall while he squeezed his wrist as hard as he could to make him drop the gun.

"Aaou!" Xu cried. "You . . . You . . ."

"You listen to me!" Clark told him. "I never touched Xiu-Qing. We thought you died. She came to find me and told me she was pregnant. She almost killed herself. I offered to marry her, so she and your son could live on in quiet peace. I never touched her once."

Xu grunted. He squirmed and writhed, trying to wriggle himself free. "You're lying. I came back and found out she got married. I heard she married you. I couldn't believe it. Then I saw you and her with my own eyes, with the kid."

"The kid is your son!" Clark pressed him against the wall again. "Even if you don't believe me, you can give her a chance to explain it to you herself. If you still don't believe me then, fine. You can kill me." Clark released him and picked the gun up from the ground. He held it out to Xu. "Your child's name is Fu. For *Fu guo*. To revive the country. He looks very much like you."

Xu stared at him, then at the gun. Slowly, he took the gun, but pointed its barrel down. A tear dropped from the corner of his eye.

"Come," Clark said. "Let's find a quiet place where I can explain everything to you."

Slouching, Xu put his gun back into his hidden holster. His rage was gone. All that was left was a lost, deflated shadow of a man Clark used to know.

"Let's leave," Clark said and led Xu out of the alley. Whatever happened to Xu, it must have been tough, or else he wouldn't have been gone for almost three years.

But his friend was back now. No matter what, he must now do everything he could to help him restore his life.

41

CLUTCH OF THE AXIS

"THIS POOL IS the best swimming pool in all of Shanghai," Ye Ting, the actress, declared. In her new bathing suit under a long flowing white blouse, she bounced over to a chaise lounge chair. The gentle May wind breezed through her hair as she took off her straw hat and dropped her bag to the ground.

Eden joined her and sat down on another lounge chair beside her. Dear Ava could not have guessed what a great gift she'd offered when she gave Eden the keys to her apartment. Not only did her apartment give Eden a place of refuge, it gave her access to the complex's pool, which was one of the few luxuries Eden could offer to Ye Ting in return.

What Ye Ting wanted most though wasn't the swimming or a soak in the sun. In fact, she did everything she could to cover up her snow-white skin. She said if she looked dark, her fans would think she was ugly.

Privacy was the reason why the actress liked this place. Here, the Western foreigners who made up most of the building's residents didn't recognize her. The building management's rules prohibited the Chinese staff from intruding upon her. She could shed her movie star persona and relax to please herself without constantly making an effort to charm the men holding her reins.

On the lounge chair, Ye Ting lay down under the big umbrella and threw a beach towel over her legs to shield herself from the sun. She adjusted her straw hat and sunglasses while Eden handed her a bottle of watermelon juice.

"Thank you." Ye Ting took the juice. She opened the cap and spilled a few drops on herself. "Shit!"

Eden winced. Ye Ting's foul mouth still grated on her ear, although she'd learned not to fault her for it. She opened a bottle of Ewo beer for herself.

Ye Ting pulled out a paper fan and lay back down. "I tell you, Eden, if I didn't have you to bring me here, I would never have any peace in my life. Everywhere you go now, it's dangerous!"

"I know." Eden sighed. Whatever Shanghai once was, the opulent glamour was gone. Today, it was a tawdry, poverty-stricken war zone. The illusion of grandeur and safety existed only within these walls, and other commercial fortresses like it.

"It's bad enough with all the shootings and bombings," Ye Ting said, "but now those Nips won't even let people eat."

"What do you mean?"

"Haven't you seen all the riots at rice shops?"

"Yes," Eden said. These riots were now a common sight. The price of rice had risen to such an extraordinary height, angry mobs of hungry people had taken to looting and smashing up shops every day. Inflation further exacerbated the problem. After the slate of blatant attacks on the banks, the conversion rate of Chinese dollars to U.S. dollars had shot up to 1,875 to one. Back before the Japanese invaded the city, it was three to one.

"The Japanese are taking all the rice for themselves, that's why," Ye Ting said. "They control Indochina now. They ship all the rice grown from there to Japan. And then, they seized all the rice they can in China. They feed our rice to their soldiers.

They're keeping rice from coming into Shanghai on purpose to starve people."

"Is that true?" Eden sat up. "How do you know for sure?"

"The owner of Six Fortunes Enterprises told me. His name is Miao Han. His company trades and ships rice. He's chasing me right now." Ye Ting giggled.

"Do you have any way to get proof of this?" Eden asked. This would make another good piece for her to write about.

"Probably." Ye Ting smiled confidently with a seductive raise of her eyebrow. "Miao's head over heels in love with me! I can ask him where the Japs tell him to ship his rice, but you have to promise not to name him or me."

"Never," Eden said. "When have I ever implicated you? I haven't broken my promise to you so far, have I?"

"No." Ye Ting raised her bottle of watermelon juice and took a sip. "Honestly, Eden, I'm very worried. I don't even care if I make it to Hollywood anymore. I don't even care if I'm a big movie star or not. The world is so unstable. I think my best option is to get married. The problem is, I don't know which man to place my bet on. Miao Han asked me to marry him three times already. But he's only rich because he does business with Wang Jing-Wei. No one recognizes Wang Jing-Wei as the real government. What if they get overthrown? What would happen to me then? Besides, his face looks like a toad."

Eden laughed. Ye Ting's lips too lifted to a smile, but then she sighed. "I still have contact with some of my old lovers in the foreign concessions. I think they'll like it if I go back to them, but who would risk counting on them? When the Japs take over all of Shanghai, they'll probably chop their heads off." She dropped the corners of her mouth and made a gesture of cutting her finger across her neck.

Eden raised her beer to her mouth and ducked her head.

"Maybe the safest thing to do is to hitch onto a Japanese," Ye Ting blabbered on. "There's a Japanese commander who told me he wants to marry me, but I don't trust him. He tells me he loves me but I know it's all hooey. After all the terrible things they did to the Chinese, I wouldn't trust any of them to treat me well if I married one of them. Besides, Japanese men are so horny. They're always touching my arms and my legs when I have to entertain them or have dinner with them. Ugh." She rolled her eyes behind her sunglasses.

"That's terrible." Eden offered a sympathetic glance. She could imagine the lechery Ye Ting had to endure. After all, Ye Ting was only a woman fending for herself alone, even with all the camera lights and glitter shining on her on stage.

"All men are terrible," Ye Ting concluded. "Chinese men are bad too. They're always trying to eat my tofu."

"Eat your tofu?"

"Yes. It means they try to touch me like perverts, or take advantage of me."

Eden shared a helpless smile. At least, Ye Ting was taking her lot in stride.

"I could marry an American Marine," Ye Ting said. "There is one who I met when I was still a taxi dancer. His name's Tom. He likes to take me to fancy American restaurants and show off Western things to me. Last week, he took me to the Doumer to see *Dangerous*. Chinese men I know don't watch American movies. They can't speak English. Anyway, Tom and I went to the movies. I let him treat me to dinner. If I want, I could probably seduce him and make him fall in love with me. If I marry him, I can follow him to America."

"Oh?" Eden took a gulp of her beer. "Then why don't you?"

Ye Ting pulled down her sunglasses and gave her an obvious glance. "American Marines make no money. Tom isn't wealthy at home either. His father is a postman. Can you imagine that? I don't want to live like a pauper. I'm not going to marry him."

Eden smiled and reclined on her lounge chair.

"What about you, Eden?" Ye Ting sat up. She took off her sunglasses. "Do you have anyone you want to marry?"

Eden tightened her grip on her beer. Immediately, she thought of Alex, and it annoyed her she would think of him. Marriage wasn't something she and Alex ever talked about. Customs and traditions weren't important to him. If she ever brought it up, it'd only make him feel bound, and it would drive a wedge between them.

She put on a smile. "No. No one right now. Maybe someday."

Ye Ting lay back down. She flipped over onto her stomach. Eden put down her beer bottle and let her mind wander. How long did she plan to remain this way? Would she never want to marry either? What did she want for a life in the future?

Could she even indulge in the luxury of thinking about love and marriage at a time like this?

"Eden?" Ye Ting gazed at her. "I heard something I don't know if I should tell you. I'm afraid to scare you."

"Why would I be scared? You can tell me."

"At a banquet I went to two nights ago, I sat at a table with that Japanese commander and a German colonel. His name is Josef Meisinger. He's the new chief representative of the SS for Asia and he came to Shanghai in June. He's very ugly. He's bald, and big like a gorilla. He has coarse skin like a snake. He said some crazy things."

"What kind of crazy things?" Eden asked. She tried to keep her voice detached.

"He kept telling the Japanese commander he should kill all the German and Austrian Jews in Shanghai. He said Jews were vermin. He thought Japan should set up a concentration camp on Chongming Island by the Yangtze River, or better yet, send them off on freighters away on the sea and let them starve to death."

Eden froze. "And what did the Japanese commander say?"

"The Nip thought he was crazy! Even the Japanese big foot couldn't believe he was serious. He laughed along and got bored, so he started talking about Japan having the most superior airplanes in Asia, and how they measure up to American planes and British planes, which in turn bored me." She switched to her side. "Eden, would the Germans really do such horrible things to Jews? Or are they just talking shit?"

Eden stared at her lap. "They would. I believe they would."

A terrified look of shock crossed Ye Ting's face. She reached out and put her hand over Eden's. "You know, Eden, I don't want anything to happen to you. You're my best friend. My only real friend."

Her confession caught Eden by surprise. "I am?"

"Yes. None of the men I know are true friends. They all want something from me. I don't have any girlfriends either. All the other women I know are jealous of me. Except you."

"But I benefit from you too. I get inside stories from you."

"Yes, but I think you'd treat me well anyway even if I had no secrets to tell you."

Looking at Ye Ting's genuine eyes, Eden's heart softened. She stared at Ye Ting's hand on her own, then looked up. "You're my best friend too," she said and smiled back.

"Really?"

"Yes," she said. And it was true. Her old friends like Marion and Ava were gone. Men she loved or thought she loved—Neil, Clark—they were no longer part of her life. And Alex. What was Alex? A lover? A partner on a mission? If she really needed him one day, would he be there for her? Or would he have to run off to chase the next big story?

With a bittersweet smile, she glanced back at Ye Ting. Yes. She could honestly say, Ye Ting was her best friend too.

4 2

BACK FROM THE DEAD

"WHERE ARE WE GOING?" Xiu-Qing asked as Clark led her and Little Fu down the path in the Public Garden.

"Just a little further ahead," Clark said. He didn't want to spoil the surprise.

"Ma Ma! Ma Ma! I want to go to that side." Little Fu tried to run toward the grass. Xiu-Qing, who was holding his hand, pulled him back. "Wait a little longer before we go." She led him behind Clark. "Ba Ba wants to go to the place up ahead first."

Clark chuckled and led them to the bench by the flowerbed. From afar, Xu Hong-Lie rose to his feet.

As they came closer, Xiu-Qing stopped. Shock overtook her face and her eyes widened.

"Xiu-Qing." Xu Hong-Lie came forward.

"Hong-Lie?" Her voice shook. "Hong-Lie? Is it really you?"

"Yes," he answered, his eyes brimming with tears.

"Hong-Lie." She dropped Little Fu's hand. Xu Hong-Lie walked up to her and she gingerly touched his cheek.

Clark picked up Little Fu and held him as he watched.

"Where have you been? What happened to you?" Xiu-Qing brushed her fingertips over his scar. Her body visibly trembled.

"A long story if I start telling you." He grabbed her hand and pressed it against his face.

"Let's sit down, then we can talk," Clark suggested and tossed his head at the bench. "Hong-Lie, this is Little Fu, your son."

Xu Hong-Lie turned his eyes to the boy. Little Fu looked back at him, his young mind not yet able to comprehend the importance of the man standing before him.

"He looks a lot like you, doesn't he?" Clark asked.

Xu nodded. He broke into a smile. "Can I hold him?"

Clark handed him the child. Xu embraced the boy and sobbed. Xiu-Qing was now crying too. Seeing them cry, Little Fu started to wail.

"You two, don't cry anymore. You're scaring your son. Here, let me hold him. Let's go over there and talk." Clark offered his arms and Xu handed back the boy.

Little Fu calmed down. They sat down on the bench and Xu began to tell his story.

"I was sitting in the car. The train had only left the Hai River Station moments ago. It was a local train, so it wasn't moving very fast. The fields outside weren't entirely dark yet and I could still see the scenery. I spotted several motorcycles coming up. All the riders were wearing masks. Immediately, I thought, bandits! Two of them came quite close to where I was sitting. I jumped up from my seat, and I saw one of them flinging up his arm like he was about to hurl something at the train. My instinct took over then. I shouted, "Attackers!" and I ran toward the front of the train. I was in between two cars when the first grenade exploded. It hit the car I had just run out of and ripped its side apart. The blast hit my face, my left shoulder, chest, and arm. The explosion made the train rock and I felt the car falling to the side. It must've come off the tracks. I thought to jump away, but then the train rocked again and I was thrown into the air. I didn't know if I would get clear or be crushed under the falling train. Then my body slammed onto the ground."

"Oh!" Xiu-Qing involuntarily whimpered. She reached for Xu's hand on his knee and held it. Clark shifted his eyes quickly to Little Fu waddling back and forth on the grass to make sure he was okay.

"I should've died then," Xu said, "but it turned out getting thrown off the train saved my life. No one else knew there were cargoes of dynamite on the train. When another grenade struck the freight car, the entire train exploded. I think everyone died. I'm not sure. I was lying on the ground on my back. I'd never felt so much pain. Very soon, I fainted. I was sure I'd be dead then."

Xiu-Qing covered her mouth. Tears streamed from her eyes as Xu Hong-Lie rounded his shoulders and continued. "When I woke up next, I was in a farmhouse. My face and parts of my body were badly burned. I found out, the attackers were Communists. They wanted to sabotage the train to the Kailan Mines. They heard the train carried a Japanese official. After the incident, they found me on the ground and brought me back. From the way I was dressed, I looked like I might be affiliated with their target or the mines' management, and they wanted to know if I had any confidential information. Even in my dire state, I knew I couldn't tell them who I was, so I made up a story. I told them I was an insurance adjuster for the Shanghai Public Utilities Company, and I'd come to the mines for an assessment. They didn't believe me much, and they kept questioning me. I stuck to my words and wouldn't change what I said. Some of them began to believe I was telling the truth. However, that meant I had no value to them, and they were afraid I could divulge who they are. They wanted to kill me."

Clark stared at the ground. This was the second time he'd heard this story, and the thought of people wanting to kill his friend still haunted him.

Xu patted Xiu-Qing's hand. "Nonetheless, maybe Heaven above felt my life shouldn't end yet. During the period of time they were questioning me, a twin brother and sister took care of me. They were seventeen years old. Where that Communist group kept me was their father's house. I lied to them. I told them that when Japan invaded Shanghai, my whole family was killed. I convinced them I hated the Japanese and I wanted revenge. Over time, they became sympathetic toward me. When the Communists debated if they should kill me, the twins begged their father to save me. I also promised them I would join the Communist fight with them against the Japanese when I recovered." He turned to Xiu-Qing. "I did that because I wanted very, very much to live and to come back and see you." He put his arm around Xiu-Qing and she fell into his embrace.

"What happened then? Why did you stay there so long and how were you able to come back?" she asked.

Xu turned his forearm, which showed a large patch of lumpy scars. "I was severely injured. It took me nearly a year to fully recover. I was very lucky the twins' father had a compassionate heart. He allowed me to stay with them to slowly nurse my body back to health." He looked at Xiu-Qing. "Truthfully, I was in so much pain. If it weren't for you, I would've given up early on. But I held on to the thought of coming back to see you. No matter what, I wanted to live and come back to see you."

Xiu-Qing nodded again and again. "All along, I still kept thinking of you too."

"When I finally regained my health, I had no money. I took on odd jobs working for the farms nearby. I became a member of the Communist group, even though I privately didn't want to follow Mao Ze Dong. Often, when they attacked the Japanese, I would join in. For survival, I had to do it to gain their trust." He flashed Clark a hesitant look.

"The most important thing is you're still alive," Clark said.

Xu looked down with a subdued smile. "For the next year, I did my best to save money. Even if I had to go hungry some nights, it didn't matter. When I eventually saved enough, I began plotting the way to come back. I secretly obtained falsified documents to pass Japanese checkpoints. When I left, I didn't tell anyone. If they knew I wanted to desert them, they would've killed me. To the twins and their father, I do feel much regret, but my only goal was to return and find you." He tightened his arm around Xiu-Qing.

Clark looked away to give them a moment to relish being in each other's presence. Little Fu tottered back. "Ma Ma, let's go play."

At his childish request, they all laughed. Clark pushed the boy lightly toward Xu. "Little Fu will have to change the way he talks and call you Ba."

Xu's eyes lit up with a wide grin. He put his hand on the boy's small shoulder.

"What do you plan to do next?" Clark asked him. "Do you want to come back to our company?"

"About that . . ." Xu frowned. "Of course I'm grateful for your offer. However, I can't stay here. To the Communists, I'm a traitor. In Shanghai, many people know me. If someone wants to find me, my scars would make it very easy to identify me. Together with me, Xiu-Qing and Little Fu would be at risk too. To be safe, I can only go far away to a place where no one knows me and adopt a false name." He held up Xiu-Qing's hand. "When I was saving money, I didn't only plan to come back here. I plotted for us to leave. I have enough to take us to Hong Kong and start over. Will you come with me?"

Xiu-Qing's eyes welled up again. "Why would I not come with you? Right now, it's like you've been revived from death. From now on, I never want to be separated from you again."

Watching them, Clark felt elated. These last two years, Xiu-Qing had to carry her grief alone and live a life of lies. Now, she and Xu Hong-Lie were reunited. Xu, too, had made it through all his hardships, and Little Fu could grow up with his real father.

For once, something he'd done was bringing forth a happy ending.

STORMS OF BETRAYALS

AT THE PORT where passengers were boarding a small ship to set sail to Hong Kong, Clark gave Xu Hong-Lie back his canvas bag. Xu, who was already carrying a suitcase, slung the bag onto his shoulder. Altogether, they didn't bring many pieces of luggage with them. Most of what they were carrying now were necessities hastily bought and kept by Xu at his hotel in the last few days. Xiu-Qing had to leave almost everything belonging to her and her son at the Yuan residence so as not to raise any suspicion they were leaving.

Xiu-Qing picked up Little Fu and said to Clark, "Little Fu, Little Fu, say goodbye to your gan father. Say goodbye."

Little Fu wiggled in her arms and said to Clark, "Ba Ba!"

Clark laughed, as did Xu. Xiu-Qing apologetically raised her eyes.

"Let him take his time." Clark stroked the boy's hair. "Slowly, he'll learn to change how he speaks."

"Yuan Xiong," Xu said to Clark, addressing him now as an older brother, "thank you for taking care of Xiu-Qing and my son all along. I'm very grateful."

"Me too," said Xiu-Qing. "Guo-Hui Ge, I don't know how we could ever repay you."

"Don't mention it," Clark said. "From now on, live well."

"Regarding Popo, I really did her wrong. I know she'll never forgive me. Now, you'll have to do all the explaining. I really can't get over how sorry I am."

"My mother's side, let me handle it. You take good care of Hong-Lie and Little Fu. By the way, this is a little gift." He took out an envelope of cash. "Take good care from now on." He stuffed it into Xu's hand.

"No." Xu pushed back his hand. "We can't accept this. You've done too much for us already."

"Take it," Clark insisted. "In the future, we don't even know when we'll see each other again. Consider this my gift to my gan child." He smiled at Little Fu.

"Then . . ."

"All right. You all better board the ship. When you reach Hong Kong, contact me."

Xu nodded. They gave him one last grateful look and left to join the other passengers.

Clark watched them step onto the plank. Little Fu. These two years, he'd grown to think of the boy as his own son. He'd miss the little fellow for sure.

And now, he'd have to go home and face the wrath of his mother.

"Ludicrous!" Madam Yuan slapped Clark hard on his face. The sting burned his cheek but he accepted her anger without refuting her.

"You fooled me like this? Why do I have a son like you? You take this family as one big joke?" She pointed at him, her body shaking with anger.

At the living room's side door, Wen-Ying and Mei Mei peeked in. Neither dared to come inside.

"I'm sorry." Clark kept his head down. This scene could not be avoided. He knew his mother would be enraged.

"And that woman! She had the gall to tell such a big lie! Pretending she gave birth to my grandson, letting me indulge her bastard child so extravagantly, taking advantage of our Yuan family's name and money. How could she do something so shameful? That immoral whore."

"It's not her fault," Clark said. He could take any reprimand and insults himself, but he couldn't bear hearing insults against Xiu-Qing and Little Fu. "I told her to do this."

"You've gone crazy, you!" Madam Yuan shook her finger at him. "You irreverent son! Do you want to infuriate me to death?"

Clark grimaced. It wasn't his wish to upset his mother so horribly either.

Wen-Ying shook her head and entered. "Ma." She stroked her mother on the back. "Whatever is the matter, we can slowly talk about it. Don't be so angry anymore. You'll damage your health."

"My health? Your brother wouldn't care if I died. What do I need my health for anymore?" Madam Yuan began to cry.

Mei Mei, who followed her sister in, gave their mother a handkerchief to wipe her tears.

"Ma, I'm very sorry." Clark tried to apologize again.

It only aggrieved her even more. His mother began to bawl. "What did I do wrong in my past life? Why do I have such a son? I already lost my husband, and my son tricked me with a fake wife. They even brought a fake child. What god did I offend? Why am I being punished like this?" She sobbed uncontrollably. Wen-Ying eyed Clark and signaled him to go away. Clark hesitated, but she urged him again with a glare.

Helpless, Clark said, "Ma, everything's my fault. I have no face to look at you anymore." He kept his head down and left the room.

In the hallway, a houseboy timidly approached him. "Young Master."

"Yes?" Clark muttered.

"You have a phone call in the study. The caller speaks English."

Much as he didn't want to talk to anyone right now, Clark went into the study and picked up the phone. It was John Liddell, the SMC chairman who took over from Tony Keswick.

"Would you be able to come to our special meeting tomorrow?" Liddell asked. "My secretary said she hasn't received a response from you yet. We need to talk about what to do about Germany's invasion of Russia. Also, Kenneth Bourne's going on leave in August back to England. His deputy, Henry Malcolm Smyth, will be taking over while he's gone. We need to talk about how to make sure everyone on the Municipal Police force will submit and answer to Smyth, including the Japanese and Chinese police recruits."

Clark tapped his fingers on the desk. He'd missed the last two SMC meetings already. In truth, he didn't care anymore. Japan had already infiltrated the Settlement police and government so deeply, it was a waste of his time to bother and take it seriously. His continual participation was only to give himself a front to divert suspicious eyes away from his resistance activities. "Sure, I'll be there," he said airily and turned the top page of an old document next to the abacus.

"Good. I'll see you then." Liddell hung up the phone.

The houseboy knocked on the door. "Young Master?" he asked, hunching his shoulders and turtling his head.

"Yes?" Clark asked. "What now?"

"There's someone here to see you? His name is Zhou Ke-Hao."

Zhou? Why would he come here? Aside from the one time he visited to secretly ask for support for his renegade resistance group the Whangpoo Brigade, Zhou had never come to his home to look for him. With their covert activities now, they had agreed to avoid any situation where someone could make a connection between them.

"Invite him in, please," Clark told the houseboy. "Bring him here." It would be better to keep their conversations secret in the study.

The houseboy left and brought Zhou in. The antagonistic look on Zhou's face surprised Clark. Even if Zhou was still displeased with the phony speech he made to denounce the resistance, it shouldn't have brought him here with such hostility.

The houseboy shifted his eyes from Clark to Zhou, then left and closed the door.

"Xiao Zhou—" Clark started to say.

Zhou cut him off. "Do you know what happened?"

"No. What happened?"

"The Western District Police arrested my brigade brother Ren Tian-Ming."

"What?" Clark snapped into attention. Ren was part of the Whangpoo Brigade before they joined forces with Juntong. "Why?"

"Ask Dai Li why."

Clark frowned. "Ask Dai Li? I don't understand."

"Somebody ratted him out. Someone gave Wang Jing-Wei's thug police Ren's name and address and told them Ren was Chen Lu's assassin. They showed his picture to Chen's bodyguard the night of the murder and the bodyguard identified him."

"How is that possible?" Clark asked. His whole body sank. Chen Lu was the puppet foreign minister who Zhou, Ren, and the rest of their group killed at Dai Li's behest. Clark himself gave them instructions on how to execute the plot.

In utter disbelief, Clark asked again, "Who could've done this?"

"Are you pretending? Or can you really not see?" Zhou asked. "Dai Li fed them his name. Dai Li's people gave him up to the

Chinese police. Besides my brigade, only he, Juntong, and you know Ren Tian-Ming was involved. No one besides you all knows where Ren lived. Juntong arranged that secret hideout."

"Are you sure? What reason would Dai Li have to do this?"

"Because Ren's a Communist. Good thing our brigade has a mole in the Western District Bureau. Dai Li uses us to take down Wang Jing-Wei's people and the Japanese, fine. We made a deal by our own choice. But behind our backs, he's colluding with Wang's side at the same time to eliminate Communists. This kind of behavior, it's too vile and despicable."

What Zhou said hit Clark like a thunderclap. He knew Dai Li could not be completely trusted. Even so, he could not imagine that cold-blooded animal giving up a man who had risked his own life for their cause. Not even if the man was a Communist. And giving him up to such a horrible fate too! The Chinese police at 76 Jessfield Road wouldn't let Ren off easy. They'd torture him.

"Xiao Zhou," Clark said in a shaken voice, "if this is true, I take personal responsibility for it. I will personally demand Dai Li to account for this. Maybe we can still save him."

"Save him?" Zhou laughed. "You think Dai Li will answer to you? You think there's any chance Ren could get out of prison alive?" He pounded his fist on the desk. "It's impossible to save him. Our mole did the only thing he could. He slipped Ren a cyanide pill. Rather than suffering pain, and risking exposing any of us, we gave him a quick death."

Clark fell back against his desk. How horrible. This was terrible.

Zhou straightened his stance. His face hardened. "From now on, we will each go our separate ways." He knocked over the pens and the penholder on Clark's desk. With one last furious look, he went to the door and swung it open.

"Zhou!" Clark called out after him. Zhou ignored him and stomped out. Clark fell back again, trying to make sense of everything. The more he thought, the angrier he felt.

He strode out of the room and left his home. He had to get to the bottom of this. He had no expectation of Dai Li deigning to account to him for what had happened. Still, he wanted answers.

On the street, he hailed a taxi to the Chamber of Golden Clouds.

"I don't know if Dai Li did or did not give Ren Tian-Ming up to the Chinese police," Pearl said after Clark barged in on her and she shoved him into a smaller, empty dining room away from prying ears.

At the Chamber of the Gold Clouds, another night of pleasure had just begun. In a large private banquet room, Pearl and her girls were entertaining a group of men, offering them a feast of delicacies and lust, all in exchange for a mound of cash. Or, a reaping of state or military secrets if the wine, drugs, and lascivious beauty would melt their guards.

At the moment, Clark's sudden appearance was most definitely not welcomed. But hell would turn over before he would leave her alone unless he got an answer.

"A jealous admirer," Pearl explained to her guests and rushed him away.

"Have you come to spoil my rice bowl?" She stuck her hands on her waist. "I'm in the middle of conducting business!"

"I don't care. Tell me if it's true. Tell me if Dai Li sold out one of Zhou's friends," Clark demanded.

Pearl threw up her hands and shook her head. "I really don't know anything about Ren Tian-Ming. If you want, I'll ask Dai Li for you. But I believe you already know he won't give Zhou and his unit any redress even if he did give up Ren. From the beginning, you should've known what kind of ruthless person Dai Li is."

Clark shoved the chair beside him, his chest still heaving and his body still shaking with fury.

Calmly, Pearl lit a cigarette from a fresh pack on the table. "What I can tell you is, Dai Li does collude with Wang Jing-Wei's secret services sometimes. You know all the Chinese people the Japanese publicly execute at five o'clock every day? They're all Mao's bandits. They were captured with Dai Li's help."

"Why? Why would he do this? Chiang Kai-Shek and Mao Ze Dong have agreed to work together. We're trying to take down Wang Jing-Wei's regime."

"Because Chiang Kai-Shek ordered him to."

"What?"

"To Chiang Kai-Shek, Mao Ze Dong and the Communist Party are still his biggest enemy. Dai Li is in secret contact with Wang Jing-Wei's deputy, Zhou Fo-Hai. They collaborate together to take down anyone they know who is with the CPC. Chiang Kai-Shek has the same kind of setup in Nanking to strike down the Communists there too." She paused and looked directly at him. "I've also passed on instructions to Juntong agents in collaborative plots to eliminate Communist bandits."

"You too?" Clark pointed at her in utter disbelief.

"Of course. You understand I can't defy Dai Li's orders. Even if I have a choice, I would comply. Think about it. What the Communists are advocating for won't benefit me. They'll only harm me. My world is a world of blossoms. A world of wanton leisure. It always will be. If the Communists hold the power, I will be finished. Therefore, I have no regret stamping them out first."

"Even if you'd have to collude with traitors?"

"Yes."

This was too much. This crossroad was not one Clark expected to reach.

Who was the enemy? And who were the allies? Was there no

one who could stand up for a baseline of justice in this fallen land of calamity?

"Young Master Yuan, I think you need a good night's rest. Our work is not done. There are still many things that need your support." She stubbed out her cigarette. "I have to get back to my clients. If you want, I can send a girl to keep you company."

"Rubbish."

"As you wish then." Pearl opened the door. She called the servant girl standing out in the hallway. "See our guest off."

The servant girl came. Pearl gave Clark a sweet smile and left.

His mind in turmoil, Clark followed the servant girl to the entrance and walked out.

On the dark streets, gangs of hoodlums roamed. Addicts debilitated in mind and body crawled on the ground. Malnourished faces of prostitutes haunted everyone while dealers stalked the passersby.

Clark walked up to the closest rickshaw and climbed in. The coolie pulled him away and he kept his eyes down from the sights around him. A sense of hopelessness set in. If the Japanese could ever be driven out, there would be nothing left to save. The soul of the country was broken. Irreversibly broken.

A CITY ABANDONED

THE TRUMPETS and drums pounded out the melodies and beats of "The Stars and Stripes Forever" as the seven hundred and fifty members of the U.S. Fourth Marine regiment marched down the Bund one last time before they evacuated for Manila. Standing together with the members of the SMC, along with foreign consuls, diplomats, commanding officers of military units of different countries, and local business and civic leaders, Clark watched the cheering crowd wave American and Chinese flags as they watched the last American military unit in Shanghai depart. The exuberant mood was warranted perhaps, as this was the community's final farewell to a corp of servicemen who for so long had been a part of the fabric of this society. This was a moment for showing their appreciation, hence Clark's own presence here along with the other important figures standing beside him.

But what a big joke. And who was the joke on? As he watched the Marines embark on the *President Harrison*, he couldn't help but think. Were the cheers and upbeat music a celebration of the International Settlement losing the final shade of mirage that it was under any military protection? Were they a hail to American and Western weaknesses in the face of Japan's emerging military might?

True, the United States was tightening its squeeze on Japan. Two days ago, on November 26, U.S. Secretary of State Cordell Hull gave Emperor Hirohito a demand for Japan to remove all troops from China and Indochina and to end its alliance in the Tripartite. Earlier in July, Roosevelt finally embargoed all sale of resources to Japan, including oil. Further, he froze all the U.S. bank accounts of all Japanese citizens, companies, and entities, effectively stopping any Japanese from accessing their personal or government assets held by the United States.

Why withdraw the Marines then? Clark could only come to one conclusion. If the United States meant to enter into war with Japan, it did not intend to make China a battleground.

Shanghai was on its own.

The *President Harrison* blew its horn and steered away from the harbor down the Whangpoo River. The loud cheers died down and the masses of people dispersed. Clark slipped his hands into his trench coat and walk away. He expected this. Nearly everyone in Shanghai expected this, except for the delusional few who were still convinced of their Western invincibility. The yellows would never touch someone white, no matter how international politics played out. Or so they believed anyway.

Maybe they were right. Clark didn't know. Nor did it matter. What mattered was his family was Chinese. Down the road, when the Japanese decide to drop all pretense that it didn't own the International Settlement, their wrath would catch his own family in the flood.

He knew this. It was why he wanted to move his family away. Since he found out Dai Li was colluding with Wang Jing-Wei's regime, he'd been planning and looking for their way out. No place was truly safe, but they could be more out of reach from the worst. Hong Kong, Macau, Singapore, the Philippines, even inland China.

The problem was his family. Wen-Ying wouldn't leave. She was committed to the Heaven and Earth Society, and she swore she would not leave her Society brothers and sisters behind. His mother still refused to forgive him. When he suggested she move and go elsewhere for her safety, she accused him of trying to cast her away, that he no longer wanted his own mother. In her blind fury about his fake marriage, she couldn't see that disaster was within an inch from her eyes, and danger emerging slowly had a way of blindsiding those who'd adapted to threat until it hit.

Even Mei Mei wouldn't go. She said she wouldn't go alone. Somehow, he suspected she had other reasons, but after expending so many words trying to persuade them, he was exhausted.

He couldn't run away alone and leave them behind.

His heart heavy, he came to the steps of the monument of the Angel of Peace. "Eden?"

The woman looking out from beneath the statue turned around. It was her. He would never forget that face.

"Clark?"

"What are you doing here?"

She almost choked up, but managed to show him a bright smile. "Probably the same thing as you. I came to watch the U.S. Marines' farewell march."

Neither of them needed to explain to each other what the Marines' departure meant. They walked toward the balustrade. "It's good to see you." He tried to keep a friendly, casual voice.

She smiled again, like she had a thousand words to say but couldn't let them out. "So, you think the SVC can hold the fort if the Japanese attack us?"

He chuckled. She was being facetious, of course. The two thousand strong of the Shanghai Volunteer Corps could hardly stand a chance against the Kenpeitai, let alone the army of Imperial Japan. He gazed out to two military vessels docked on the river. "There's still the USS *Wake*, and the HMS *Peterel*."

This time, it was her turn to laugh. The American USS *Wake* and the Royal British HMS *Peterel* were once the symbols of colonial dominance in Shanghai. Right now, they remained here, for what? Communications? Espionage? Nostalgia?

"Remember the first time we came here together to the Bund?" Clark asked.

"Yes."

"I told you then that this city would be your home, and no one would harm you here. I'm sorry I gave you my word too soon."

She gazed back at him. "And I told you this is my home. Whatever happens from here on, I'm ready to face it like the rest of you. China's still the only place that would take me, so I'll stand with her."

Her firm response puzzled him. "Can't you get out?" he asked. He didn't want to intrude, so he didn't say out loud what he meant. But surely, Alex Mitchell could marry her and take her to America with him.

"Get out?" She looked away from him, her face wrestling with emotions he couldn't read. "Not unless other countries accept people like me."

Clark creased his brows, but let the subject slide.

She turned to face him again. "How's your wife?"

"My wife?" He laughed. "She left me."

"She left you? Why?"

"You want to know the truth?" He folded his arms over the bar of the balustrade. Suddenly, he felt free. Everything he'd done in the last five years had led to nothing. He'd made every effort, exerted every ounce of strength, and made every sacrifice demanded of him. In the end, he could not save his beloved home or the city. He could not protect his country. Soon, when the occupation spread into the International Settlement, the little power he had left to support the resistance would be gone too. What else was there to hold him back now? He only wanted to be free. Before Japan came and clamped down on everything he cherished, he wanted to seize his freedom and fly free. He could tell her everything.

"My marriage was a sham," he said. An easy smile came to his face. "The woman I married was the girlfriend of someone who worked for me. His name is Xu. He and I were on a mission to Peking to bomb the Kailan Mines. The mission failed and we thought he died in a train explosion. They didn't know it at the time, but she was pregnant with his child. When Shen Yi demanded we separate, she said she wouldn't end her threat until you got married. It was a ridiculous demand, but she's ridiculous. She wanted proof we were really separated. In the end, I offered to get married myself. Without you, I didn't care anymore one way or another if I'd ever found someone to marry. So I faked a marriage with the girl who was pregnant to give her and her son a name and to save her from being shamed."

"Clark!" Eden's mouth fell agape. "I had no idea."

"Five months ago, Xu came back. It turns out, he survived. It took him more than two years to recover from his burns and make his way back. They all reunited and left for Hong Kong. That was how my 'wife' left me."

Realization dawned on Eden and she raised her hand to her cheek. "I don't know what to say. I didn't know . . ."

Clark laughed, a bittersweet response to all that had happened beyond his control. "I did something good there, didn't I? Shen Yi agreed to drop the whole matter once and for all after that. Gao? I saved his life, even if he blames me forever and he lost his ear. Xu and his girlfriend and their son are back together as a family. My mother's furious at me, but that's all right. I'll just have to bear the plaque of a sinner before her for the rest of my life."

Her fingers dropped and slid to her chin. "Clark . . ."

"You know what though? For all that happened, the only real loss I felt was losing you. What Shen Yi wanted was for you and me to both suffer. She got her wish." He held on to the balustrade and rocked back with his eyes cast down. "Maybe she didn't get her wish after all. At least, you didn't suffer. Or not as much as she wanted you to anyway." He looked up and flashed her a smile. "I'm glad you're happy."

"I'm happy?" she asked, meekly as though she was confused.

"You are happy, aren't you? With Alex?"

She gazed back out to the river.

"You love him, don't you?" Clark asked. Perhaps he shouldn't have, but he wanted to know.

A Japanese cruiser sailed past the USS *Wake* up the river toward Soochow Creek. Eden tightened her shoulders and looked into his eyes. "In times of war, love is a luxury we can't afford."

Clark straightened his stance. She let out a quivering breath, then turned around and walked away.

He watched her back as she merged into the crowd.

. . . a luxury we can't afford . . .

He stood for a long while with a blank face. Was that a warning? An admonition that he should refrain from speaking to her about the matter of love?

Let it be then. What he felt, and the dreams he couldn't achieve, let them be buried within him or else vanish in the wind with the dust.

Trembling, Eden swerved into the array of people dispersing from their farewell to the American Marines. As she walked, she looked ahead, stifling her anguish and pain. Behind her, the statue of the Angel of Peace held open her arms, as though she was offering the souls of the powerless to the wildfire spreading across the city, rather than bringing them into her protective embrace.

Cruel. How cruel was fate to keep toying with them in her hand?

A pair of Japanese soldiers passed. Immediately, the pedestrians stopped, keeping their distance and bowing their heads. The Japanese hadn't even moved in yet, but already, everyone was behaving as they would in the occupied districts.

Eden did the same. When the soldiers were gone, she continued down the road.

Memories rushed to her mind. She remembered the first time Clark brought her here, when they looked at the flags of the nations flying in the wind. Once, they had hope. They shared the same dreams. For a time, however short, they were happy together. If Shen Yi hadn't forced them apart, they would still be in love.

Even now, she could feel his love. In his presence, she always felt it, no matter how hard he tried to hide it.

Just now, the way he looked at her. The way he talked to her. She had no more doubt. Soulmates. They were soulmates.

What use was it? She gave him up. For his own good, she willed him to move on. She had moved on herself too.

Was she happy?

What was happiness when Hitler and his Nazis were overrunning a continent and persecuting her own people? What was happiness when the Mikado and his army were enslaving and brutalizing those in the nations they conquered? And if they fell in line with their ally Germany, the safety of her own people here could not be guaranteed.

In times like this, she did not aspire to something as nebulous as happiness.

Security, peace, shelter, food for all the people swept up by the tide of evil. Alex was right. In times of war, love was a luxury they couldn't afford.

Did she love Alex?

Yes. She loved him. Maybe more than he loved her. He had the wisdom to prioritize what was important within their sight.

It didn't matter anymore. A war of the worlds was coming. There was no more time for anything else.

PEARL HARBOR

A LOUD POP outside brought Clark out of his dreams. Several more followed. Who was setting off firecrackers in the middle of the night?

Boom!

Ba Boom!

These weren't firecrackers. Something exploded. What was going on?

From a distance, he heard the phone ring. The ringing stopped, followed by the pounding of footsteps coming to his room. A houseboy knocked. "Young Master? Young Master?"

Clark got out of his bed. He opened the door. "Yes?"

"You got a phone call. The caller speaks English and he said it's urgent."

Phone call? He switched on the light. "What time is it?"

"Four in the morning."

Clark nodded. Whatever was happening, a phone call in the middle of the night could never be good. He followed the houseboy downstairs. The pops and booms continued and his sisters too had woken up.

"What's happening?" Wen-Ying asked from her bedroom doorway.

"I don't know," Clark said as he walked by, leaving her and Mei Mei looking at each other, confused.

In the study, he picked up the phone. "Hello?"

"Clark? This is John Liddell. Japan just attacked Hawaii."

"They attacked the United States?" Clark jolted awake. Unbelievable! Of all things, he did not expect Japan to attack the United States.

"I'm calling you to let you know Japan and the United States are officially at war. Just now, the IJN attacked the HMS *Peterel*. The USS *Wake* surrendered."

So that was where the explosive sounds came from. A battle was taking place on the Whangpoo River as they spoke.

"There'll be a meeting between the SMC and the Japanese at 6:00 a.m. at the Council chamber. I'll see you there." Liddell hung up.

Clark put the receiver back on the phone.

Wen-Ying and Mei Mei came in. "Ge?" Wen-Ying asked. "What's happening?"

"Japan's war is here."

His sisters look at him in alarm.

Yes. The end of the International Settlement had finally come.

The incessant screech of the ringing phone woke up everybody in her home. Eden threw her blanket off and got up. "I got it!" she shouted as she went to answer the call. The thunder of explosions came through the living room windows as she tightened the tie around her robe. When she picked up the phone, it was Dottie Lambert, *China Press's* secretary, on the line.

Dottie wasted no time with formalities. "The Japanese attacked Pearl Harbor in Hawaii," she said. "Come to the *China*

Press office at once. We're having an emergency staff meeting, and then we're shutting down."

Goosebumps crawled over Eden's entire back and arms. "What? What do you mean—"

"Come now!" Dottie cut her off. "I don't have time to explain. I have to call all the others on the staff." She hung up.

Her parents and Joshua came out of their rooms. Her father turned on the lights. "Who was that?"

"It was Dottie." Eden held the phone against her chest. "Japan just attacked the United States."

On her bike, Eden peddled as fast as she could. The sun hadn't yet risen, but people were slowly awakening to the city's looming change of guards. Pockets of homeless beggars scrambled from one street to another, looking for an escape. She glanced at the others riding on bikes beside her. One of them, she recognized as John Barclay, an outspoken British reporter for the *Oriental Affairs*.

"Barclay?" she yelled out.

"Eden Levine!" He looked over from his bike. "Where are you going?"

"To my office. You?"

"I'm going to the Bund to see what's going on."

She turned her eyes toward the Bund. A large, orange fire burning on the river spread its incandescent glow over the dark sky. Her reporter's instinct seized her and urged her to go and see what was happening too. If only Dottie hadn't sounded so urgent and said their newspaper was closing down.

Above her, IJN warplanes roared.

Up ahead, three Japanese sailors stood across the road. They pointed their rifles with bayonets at those heading toward them. Eden exchanged a glance with Barclay and they turned to take another street.

No use. Armed Japanese soldiers were there too, marching closer, blocking every road leading to the Bund. Barclay raised his head up to the top of a building on their block. "If we go up to the roof, we can see everything."

Eden looked at the building, then back to the streets. "No. You go ahead." The Bund wasn't her destination. She could circle around and take a different route. The detour would take her longer, but she could still get to her office.

"Suit yourself." Barclay took off. Eden inhaled a deep breath and continued on.

At the *China Press* headquarters, the staff huddled in groups. Everyone wore a worried face. Eden stood at her desk, watching as some of the reporters read out loud the incoming newswires while others bombarded them with questions. A whole American fleet, it seemed, had been destroyed.

Charlie came out of his office and everyone hushed.

He came and stood before the staff. "As you all must have heard by now, Japan launched an attack on Pearl Harbor at 5:55 UT." He folded his hands in front of him and took a look around the room. "While we've never anticipated a Japanese attack on the United States, we've all been expecting Japan to take over the International Settlement the first chance they could. Earlier, I've been advised by the American Consulate there will be no military protection coming to Shanghai despite the fact that the two countries are now at war."

A buzz of alarm rose from the staff. Charlie continued to speak. "I know this is not what you want to hear, but this outcome is not unforeseen. On my part, I've decided to close down the *China Press* for your own safety."

The room turned dead somber. Eden hugged her arms close to her chest and bit her lip. Yes, they'd been expecting an eventual Japanese takeover, but she did not realize the phone call that woke her up today would mark the end of the one thing she had done well for the last five years to fight back.

"Speaking of safety, many of you had spoken out for your beliefs about what was right. In these dark hours, you served as the voice of justice and the voice for the oppressed. For that, you should always be proud." He paused and tightened his face. "However, I won't lie to you. For your courage in speaking out, you're also now in danger. Especially those of you who have spoken out against Japan. I regret that I can't protect you anymore. I also know that we all did what we did with our eyes open. All I can advise you now is to do what you can to save yourself and your loved ones. On each of your desks is an envelope. Dottie and I have been preparing for this day. We've set aside a sum of cash for each of you. I know it's not enough to compensate you for everything you've done, but we tried. If you can find a way out of this country, I suggest you do so immediately. If you can't, I wish you Godspeed. In two hours, my family and I will be taking the last ship departing for Sydney. When I return home, I will continue to do everything I can to urge my country and the world to come to your rescue." He bowed his head, holding back his tears. "It's been an incredible honor working with all of you."

The staff held silent for a moment. Emmet Lai stepped up to Charlie and offered him a handshake. Other followed. Charlie gratefully shook hands with them, but soon told them to stop. He spoke to everyone again. "We're all running out of time. The Japanese army could be entering this building very soon. You should gather your personal belongings as quickly as possible. If there's anything that might be used against you, take it and destroy it. And hurry!"

Immediately, everyone went to their desks to clear out. Eden picked up the envelope of cash on her desk. The newswires were still coming in and the curious few who went to check told everyone Japan was attacking Malaya, Singapore, and Hong Kong too.

Resigned, Eden put the cash into her purse. Her desk had

nothing except notes and articles relating to local entertainment news. Alex had warned her never to leave anything written by Apollo Eirene traceable to herself.

She caught Charlie before he left. Holding back her tears, she said to him, "Safe journey."

"Thank you." Charlie nodded. "You've done excellent work here. Maybe one day, you can do it again."

He put on his hat and took off. In a mix of sadness and confusion, the rest of the staff started to leave. There would be time for goodbyes later, maybe. For now, it was best they cleared out like Charlie said.

The elevator could not accommodate everyone leaving at the same time. Some decided to take the stairs and Eden followed them. In the stairwell, Eden gazed up.

If she went to the roof, she could see what was happening on the Bund.

Against the flow of exiting people, she ascended the steps. When she pushed open the door to the rooftop of the building, the blazing red ball of fire on the river was still burning. Half of the British warship HMS *Peterel* had sunk into the water. Two smaller fires floated between the sinking ship and the USS *Wake*, which now flew a white flag on its masthead. On the waterfront, the shadows of Japanese military fleets emerged with the twilight of the morning.

And then, everything went quiet. The last trace of the HMS *Peterel* disappeared under the water and the gunfire stopped.

Bracing herself, Eden walked back into the stairwell and onto the streets.

THE NEW MASTERS

"To the U.S. Consulate," Clark ordered Huang Shifu. The SMC meeting wouldn't start untill 6:00 a.m. If he had to guess, the Japanese were coming to takeover the control of the International Settlement, and he had no time to lose.

Near the Bund, troops of Japanese soldiers were already marching down from Soochow Creek. If he didn't have a car, he would've been too late.

In front of the American Consulate building, Huang Shifu pulled to a stop. Clark raced out of the car and rushed inside. The security guards who normally stood at the entrance were nowhere to be seen. Only people dressed in civilian clothing hustled about. The elevator operator hadn't shown up yet at this hour, and likely wouldn't be coming for the rest of the day either.

Quickly, Clark took the stairs and ran up to the fourth floor to Joseph Whitman's office. When he opened the door to the reception area, the consul's staff froze. They stared at him wide-eyed.

"Joe Whitman?" Clark asked. "Is here he?"

Relief washed over their faces when they realized he was not the Kenpeitai or the Japanese army. One of them recognized him from the days when he was an agent for the Nationalist Government and pointed him to a conference room where smoke was coming out. Clark thanked him and made his way straight to see his friend.

In the conference room, black smoke trailed from a tin box where Joe and his assistants were burning a stack of papers and notebooks. The morning wind blew in from the windows and the smell of destruction carried across like an omen of death.

"Joseph!" Clark called him at the door.

Whitman looked up. Beads of sweat dripped from his forehead.

Clark came into the room. "Joseph. They said Japan attacked the United States."

The assistant stared at Whitman. He waved to signal them to continue and stepped toward Clark. "Yes. There's been a disastrous attack on our naval fleet at Pearl Harbor today. After that, Japan launched a series of coordinated attacks on Malaya, Singapore, Hong Kong, and here too."

Clark put his hand on the back of a chair. "Will the U.S. fight back?"

"They will, I'm sure, but not here. Not in Shanghai," Whitman said. He tossed the codebook in his hand into the tin of fire.

Clark steadied himself. The American military would not be coming. Not even with a direct attack by Japan on their land. "What will you all do now?"

"The USS *Wake* was supposed to evacuate us if Japan moved into the International Settlement. It didn't work out that way. The Japanese Marines stormed the *Wake* an hour ago. Commander Smith surrendered. The *Peterel* put up a fight though. Lieutenant Polkinghorn decided to scuttle his ship rather than to let it fall to Japanese hands." He glanced at the secret documents they were burning. "We're trying to salvage the damage from losing the *Wake*."

"Joe!" A familiar voice interrupted the room. It was Greg Dawson, the American pilot.

"Greg?" Clark asked, thoroughly surprised to see him.

"Clark! What are you doing here?"

Clark lifted his hand. Where would he begin to explain? He wanted to know what was really happening before going to the SMC meeting.

"Clark." Greg slapped his back. "I wish I could stay and chat, but I've got to leave. I'm on a mission." He glanced at Whitman. "You ready to go?"

"Yes," Whitman said. He picked up a briefcase on the conference table. "Clark, I hate for this to be the way we say goodbye. It's been decided that I depart Shanghai now with Captain Dawson. He's flying me out to Kunming before total war breaks out here and the Japanese take over. I'm bringing back to the U.S. all the intelligence information we have on Japan."

Clark nodded. "At least I got a chance to say goodbye." He looked at the two consulate staffers still burning documents. "What about them? And the rest of the people in your office?"

"Consul General Stanton will remain here with them. We can't get everyone out, but I think they'll be okay. The Japanese will use them to negotiate for a release of the Japanese Embassy and Consulate personnel in the United States, and our government will want to do the same." He gripped Clark by the arm. "If you ever need me for anything, get in touch with me. The Swiss Embassy can send a message. I can't guarantee anything, but I'll help if I can find a way. Remember, the link that makes up the chain."

"Thank you," Clark said. How sorry he was to see his friend go.

Whitman grabbed his coat. At the door, Greg said, "Clark, tell your sister to be careful. Tell her to check her radio for my signals. I'll try to contact her soon."

"Sure." Clark put his hands in his coat.

"You take care too." Greg waved goodbye and hurriedly led Whitman out.

Clark slowly returned to the entrance to the stairway. Realization sunk in. He was completely on his own.

In the Municipal Council chamber, the British and American members joined John Liddell, along with SMP Deputy Commissioner Smyth, who was standing in for Commissioner Bourne while Bourne was on leave back in London. Not all the members were present. Tony Keswick had flown to Singapore a while back and was actually en route home to England to report to Winston Churchill. Two other British members, as well as American Norwood Allman, were away on business too. Chances were, none of them were ever coming back.

The Chinese members were present, as were the Japanese members Okamoto Izamu and a new person who replaced Hayashi Yukichi.

Also present were Japanese Consul-General Horiuchi Teteki, and officers of the Japanese navy, army, and gendarmerie.

Horiuchi had not come to negotiate. "Our Imperial forces are now in the process of occupying the International Settlement," he said. "We have spoken with the British and American consuls, and we hope to proceed forward peacefully without any cause for further armed incidents. We request now that those of you who are non-Japanese foreign nationals to please resign from the Council immediately." He sat back. His assistant put in front of each of the British and American members a single resignation notice.

Liddell stared at the paper, his face darkened with indignation.

His fellow countryman Godfrey Philips scowled and crossed his arms. Cornell Franklin, like the lawyer he was, held up the sheet and scrutinized the terms. Clark watched and waited to see what they would do.

Eugene Townsend, the American who owned the Asia Glass Company, picked up the pen. "Consul Horiuchi, our governments are far away. Those of us who are here of course understand things differently. In the general interest of the Settlement, I agree it's best for us to continue forward based on mutual understanding and goodwill." He pulled the resignation notice toward himself to sign his name.

"Hold on." Liddell shot Townsend an irritated look. "Consul, your country attacked Hawaii. In response, America declared war on Japan. As far as I understand, Japan and Britain are not at war. Is it really necessary to remove all British representation for the Settlement's governing body? Our presence on the SMC has been a tradition since the 1800s. We can offer you assistance, even legitimacy, I dare say, if we remain on board."

"Thank you for your offer to help, Mr. Liddell." Horiuchi said with firm eyes. "Your assistance or offer of legitimacy won't be necessary. As far as war is concerned, you might want to consider whether it would be better if you amicably resign now at your own choice and discretion, or to lose face when your removal would be compelled when Winston Churchill decides to join forces with his American friends."

Liddell stiffened his lips. Townsend brushed his pen across the bottom of his resignation notice and pushed it toward the Japanese on the other side of the table. Cornell Franklin glanced at him and did the same. Reluctantly, Liddell and Philipps followed suit.

"Consul." Clark raised his hand. "I would like to voluntarily resign as well."

"Mr. Yuan?" Horiuchi lifted his brows. "Would you not want to work together with us going forward?"

A dangerous question. Clark lowered his eyes and chose his words carefully. "Out of respect, Consul. I'm part of the old guard. Please consider my resignation a salute to a new beginning."

Horiuchi smiled. "Very well."

Clark kept his eyes low. A new beginning did not mean a beginning for Japan. He meant a new beginning for the day when China would reclaim its land, however tangential that goal might be now.

Director Dong spoke up. "I would like to resign too."

Horiuchi barely gave him a glance. Then again, the Japanese would have little use for someone as advanced in age as Dong. "I'll have my assistant draw up a resignation notice for both of you right now." He waved for one of his aides standing behind him and whispered his instructions. The aide immediately left the room to type up two more notices.

Horiuchi returned his attention to the men at the table. "In the next coming days, our military will assume control of all major banks and businesses within the International Settlement. I'd like you to continue to operate in this office to notify your compatriots to cooperate with the transfer of management." He turned to Clark and Townsend. "All factories and enterprises should continue to operate. While our authorities will oversee all businesses from now on, we have no wish for the power transfer to disrupt commerce." He looked at Townsend. "For those who understand the value of mutual understanding and goodwill, like Mr. Townsend, there will be ways for them to work with us. Perhaps even rewards."

"Sure, sure," Townsend eagerly agreed. "Absolutely."

In his seat, Clark kept his reaction cordial. Of course the Japanese wouldn't want to disrupt commerce. They could now loot all the industrial production in the Settlement to feed their war engine.

The aide returned and handed Clark and Director Dong each a

resignation notice. Clark picked up the pen and signed his name. He'd give up his seat, but Heaven could finish him first before he let his family's company be used by Japan to oppress his own people.

Horiuchi turned to Deputy Commissioner Smyth. "Starting today, all SVC training will be suspended until further notice. Our military will be collecting all their guns and equipment. The SMP will continue to serve, but it will be incorporated into the police bureau of the Chinese Reorganized Government."

Smyth glanced over at Liddell. Powerless, Liddell dropped his eyes. Smyth hunched his shoulders. "Yes."

"Lastly," Horiuchi said to the British and American Council members, "beginning tomorrow, all British and American citizens, as well as Filipinos and Indians, will be required to register with the Japanese Gendarmerie. There will be a room set up for that purpose at the Hamilton House across from the Metropole Hotel. The requirement will be announced in the *Shanghai Times*. It would be helpful if you all would spread the word to your countrymen and expedite the process."

Clark lowered his eyes again. The *Shanghai Times*. That publication was one of the few pro-Japan foreign papers. Its owner and editor, E.A. Nottingham, was considered as nothing less than a traitor by his fellow Englishmen.

"That will be all." Horiuchi stood up. His entourage followed. "We appreciate your cooperation, gentlemen." He twitched his lips into a sneering smile and marched out of the door without looking back.

───────

When Clark arrived home, Wen-Ying and Mei Mei were anxiously waiting in the living room. Not only them. The entire household, from the security guards to the drivers, to the houseboys and the maids. They were all waiting for him, looking to him to bring them not just news, but answers and directions for what they should do next.

He wished he knew the answers too.

He loosened his tie and walked in. "Where's Ma?"

"In her bedroom," Mei Mei said. "She's terrified. She's packing up all her valuables in case we have to flee the disaster."

"What news have you heard?" Wen-Ying asked.

Clark glanced at the doorways. Their servants were listening. "Let's go into the study."

They followed him into the study and he shut the door.

Wen-Ying was the first to speak. "We've been listening to the radio all day. Japanese troops are everywhere on the streets. No one dares to go outside."

"I know." Clark walked to the desk. It had taken him hours to get back. Japanese tanks and their Bluejackets were blocking all the roads, and people were either hiding in their homes or swarming to flee.

"It's not safe here anymore, right? I didn't go in to work. A coworker of mine, a Chinese clerk at the British Consulate called me. He said the Japanese detained Findlay and all the Britons." Findlay was Wen-Ying's boss, whom she much despised.

"They likely detained the American Consulate officials too. I was at their office this morning." Clark looked up. "No. It's not safe here. We need to find a way to leave Shanghai as soon as possible before the Japanese close off the whole city."

Mei Mei's face fell. "What about the servants? And our workers? What would happen to them if we leave?"

Clark grimaced. This was the toughest part. "We can't help them anymore. We can't take the servants with us."

"Not even Huang Shifu? And Xiaochun."

"No." Clark shook his head. "Not even them."

Mei Mei's lips curled down as though she was about to cry. His own heart ached too for all the loyal people they would have to leave behind. But right now, his first responsibility was to save his mother and sisters.

"We can't tell anyone we're trying to escape," he said. "The Japanese high officials expressly told me to keep the factory and business operating. I will go back to the office and the factory tomorrow. If anyone shows up, I'll give them the choice to voluntarily resign with a bonus, if that's what they want. For those who want to keep working, they can do so until the Japanese take over management."

"Take over management!" Wen-Ying glared. "Ge! You're not going to let them, are you?"

"It's not up to me anymore," Clark said.

Wen-Ying dropped her face. "What do you plan to do?"

"I don't know yet." And he didn't. But no matter what, he would not let those demons take his ancestors' hearts and sweat.

He eyed his sister. He could tell Wen-Ying was scheming something. "Mei Mei, go help Ma pack. Try to calm her and help her not to worry. Pack for yourself too. As soon as I find us a way out, we're leaving."

"Yes." Mei Mei lowered her head and walked out.

After she left, Wen-Ying walked to the scroll which concealed their safe. "How lucky you thought ahead and took all our gold and cash out of the bank. It should be enough for you to take Ma and Mei Mei somewhere and start over."

Clark came closer to her. "I don't intend to leave you behind."

"I can't leave."

"I've heard enough. You're thinking about your brothers and sisters in Tian Di Hui." He stood in front of her face. "I'm your real brother. Do I not count for anything? How do you expect me to leave you behind?"

"Ge—"

"If we can find a way to leave, we're all leaving." He closed the conversation and went to the door. Before he walked out, he looked back at her. "We all have to leave someone behind."

He swung the door open. Did she think she was the only one who had to accept the pain of letting go? Eden might not love him anymore, but it pained him nonetheless to know he would have to leave and never see her again, and to never know what would happen to her.

THE DAY AFTER

HOW DIFFERENT THE city looked in only two days' time. Yesterday, Japan had bombed an entire American fleet at Pearl Harbor. Following that, they began a war to take over all of Asia.

As for Shanghai, the home Eden had come to know, the city that people had once called the jewel of the Orient, she could not recognize it anymore.

This morning when she came to the Embankment House to check on the situation with the Jewish refugees, she'd passed by troop after troop of Japanese soldiers patrolling on foot. They toted their Arisaka rifles fitted with bayonets. They proudly showed off their white armbands bearing the red rising sun.

Replace that sun with the swastika, and there would be no difference between them and the Nazis in Europe. The people who wore their fanaticism on their sleeves were taking over the world.

What happened to the human race? They'd arrived at the cutting edge of advancement of the twentieth century. Thousands of years of discoveries, knowledge, and scientific progress should've brought them to a more enlightened world. Instead, all their developments were culminating in the highest form of terror mankind would ever know.

And they would pass on the terror from this generation to the next. Above the Kaiser Wilhelm Elementary School, the Nazi flag sporting the black swastika flew. Evil was flouting its triumph.

On the Bund, all British, American, and Chinese Nationalist flags had been taken down. Roosevelt declared war with Japan yesterday, and Churchill did the same today. So now, the Britons and Americans in Shanghai were marked by a different symbol. The Dutch and the Belgians too. This morning, the *Shanghai Times* announced that all citizens of belligerent states must register with the Japanese Gendarmerie. After registration, Shanghailanders would have to wear a bright red armband stamped with A for Americans, B for Britons, or N for citizens of the Netherlands. Further, those who wore these armbands must not enter certain stores and public places.

Yes. Fanatics fueled by ultra-nationalism and the desire to subjugate the world to totalitarian rule liked to force those they called enemies to mark themselves. The armbands of shame these Shanghailanders wore now were no different than the yellow badge of the Star of David. Once worn, those who were most vulnerable would have no way to hide.

She'd seen it all before.

These poor people. How long would it be before they, too, would be shipped off to internment camps?

And the Jewish refugees. They were still coming here. A thousand had arrived not too long ago from Poland. Could they still come here? Would they want to anymore? How could she or any of the local Jews help them now? They depended so much on American Jews to fund all the donated food and supplies. How would the Americans send them money anymore?

When the refugees at the Embankment House asked her what the Japanese takeover meant, she did not know what to tell them.

Even Sir Victor Sassoon would not be able to help them if he were here. The Japanese froze all the British taipans' accounts. They took over all the British and American properties. Banks, insurance companies, private clubs, hotels. Notices were posted on the doors and gates of the most prestigious premises, proclaiming they were now under Japanese military control. The Hong Kong and Shanghai Bank, the Cathay Hotel and the Park Hotel, the Shanghai Club and the American Club. They took over the racecourse too.

Actually, the one thing she was thankful for was that Sir Victor was not here. By mere chance of luck, he'd gone off on a trip to Bombay. He was a good man. A brilliant, generous man. She was glad he got out. Who knew what the Japanese would have done to him if he hadn't left?

As for her own family, they were safe. At least, it seemed to be the case. What a stroke of luck they'd chosen to live in Frenchtown. For now, at least, Frenchtown was still recognized as an independent jurisdiction, and the Japanese hadn't made a move in there yet. They'd be safe until the Germans or the Japanese decided Frenchtown should be theirs.

A convoy of camouflaged tanks and armored trucks trundled down the intersection up ahead. Their sputters and vrooms sounded even more threatening now that there were no other noises on the streets to drown them out. All buses, trolleys, trams, and taxis had stopped running. Even private motor cars were few and far between. Traffic lights everywhere ceased to operate. On hearing the noises, the rickshaws and bicycles in front of the convoy scattered to the side to make way.

Eden halted her bike. After the convoy passed, another army truck rolled down behind it. The soldiers on the moving truck threw pages and pages of flyers and leaflets out onto the road. When they were gone, Eden rode forward again. At the intersection, leaflets showing caricatures of Churchill and Roosevelt clinging to each other in terror were strewn all over the ground. Commingled with the leaflets were flyers with the large, bold warning:

Gendarmerie in Western Sector forbids rumors.

Offenders will be severely punished.

Rumors. There were no rumors. Only truth. But in occupied Shanghai, truth was no longer allowed. All free foreign and Chinese newspapers had been shut down.

She looked down the street where the convoy had gone. One of the armored trucks had stopped. The troops were storming into a bookstore.

So it wasn't only newspapers and journals. They meant to censor books too.

Eden watched as the soldiers carried out stacks of books and lit them on fire.

Yes. She had seen it all before.

She stepped back on the pedals and rode on back home. In her heart, she felt fear. Where was Alex? Why hadn't she heard from him since last night?

Outside, Clark circled his factory building. This battery production plant had fed prosperity to his family since before he was born. The Yuan Enterprises had its hand in many other businesses with their dealings in trade, but battery manufacturing was what kept them ahead, thanks to his father's foresight into the value of industrial resources.

He gazed up from the ground to the roof to the Heaven above.

Were his ancestors looking down now, watching him? His family properties had always passed from one generation to the next. Now that they were passed on to him, what he would do would be to destroy them. Completely.

The ancestors would understand, wouldn't they? They would be proud, yes. They wouldn't want everything they'd worked for to end up in the Japanese's hands either.

And he would not give over something that would provide Japan what it needed most. Energy.

What would be the best way to obliterate everything? He could set the factory on fire, but that would require a lot of fuel, and there was no way to get a big enough supply of oil before his family's attempt to escape. The Japanese military had locked down all petrol stations anyhow.

He could blow up the plant and all the machinery inside. He still had a load of grenades and dynamite he was supposed to transport for Dai Li. With the IJN setting up checkpoints on every road leading out of Shanghai, he wouldn't be fulfilling this transport job anyway. And by tomorrow, if all went as planned, he'd be gone.

He doubted Dai Li would lose sleep over his departure. For Dai Li, he was of no value anymore.

The question was, could he set all the dynamite off by himself without the Japanese army hearing the sounds of explosions and coming onto the site before the plant could be completely destroyed?

A sequence of explosions went off from somewhere nearby. Clark listened and smiled. Resistance fighters of all kinds were coming out in full force. The chaos hadn't ended since the attack on Whangpoo River began yesterday. For the Japanese, the transfer of power from the Western overlords was the easy part. The Chinese? That was a different story. For the resistance, there was nothing more to lose now.

This must be maddening to Wang Jing-Wei and his people.

Japan decided to wage a world war right in the heart of Shanghai, and his running dogs were the ones who had to bear the deadly consequences.

Clark checked his watch. None of that concerned him now. The most pressing matter on his mind at this hour was a phone call that would save his family. The call should come in five minutes.

He went back into the plant. Surprisingly, many of the workers had shown up to work. They had nowhere to go, and they had no way to get out. In the midst of uncertainty about what would happen next, they decided to continue doing what they would normally do. It was a way to cope, he guessed. It was a way to find some normalcy when nothing in the world was normal anymore.

When he came in this morning, he told them what Horiuchi wanted him to say to the workers. Keep on working. The factory would come under Japanese management soon, but they would all still have their jobs, and they would be paid.

It was a flat-out lie. Soon, they wouldn't have their jobs anymore, since he was planning to destroy this plant. Then again, why should he trust the Japanese to treat his workers well? Working for the Japanese could be tantamount to slavery, or worse.

He went into the factory office and locked the door. Right on time, the phone rang. "Hello?"

"Clark? Mauricio."

"Yes." Clark turned his back toward the door. Mauricio, the owner of the Sambuca Lounge on Blood Alley, still had many tricks up his sleeve.

"It's all arranged. Tomorrow morning, 5:00 a.m., there'll be a sampan waiting at the dock on Whangpoo River where we talked about. It'll take you and your family downstream to a bigger motorized boat in the open water. The boat will take you to Macau."

"Understood," Clark said. 5:00 a.m. should give him enough time to bring down the factory in the middle of the night. All he had to do now was to go home and tell his family to pack and get ready.

"One more thing."

"Yes?"

"I tried to call Eden Levine. I haven't been able to reach her. I'm blowing out of here myself now and I don't feel right leaving this news to her family. I don't know them. If you can somehow reach her before you leave town, can you pass this news to her?"

Eden? Clark frowned. "What is it?"

"The Japs arrested Alex Mitchell."

"What?"

"They rounded up all the reporters they could find on their blacklist this morning. Alex Mitchell's one of them."

Clark gulped. "Dear God."

"You don't have to tell me. They're going after anyone who they consider anti-Japan. My source told me they took all of them to the Bridge House. That place isn't just a prison. From what I've heard, it makes 76 Jessfield Road look like a resort."

Clark tightened his grip on the receiver.

"One more thing," Mauricio said. "Her friend Isaac Weissman was arrested too."

"Isaac? Why?" Clark asked.

"He was with Alex Mitchell when they took him. They were at Alex's flat. That's all I know."

Clark bit his lip.

"Listen," Mauricio said, "I got to scram. I'll see you in Macau?"

"Yes," Clark said, his mind trying to figure out how to break the news to Eden. "Safe trip."

"Good luck to you too." Mauricio hung up.

Clark sucked in a deep breath. Why hadn't Alex left Shanghai already?

If he were Alex, he would've left months ago and taken Eden with him.

He left the office, got into his car, and directed Huang Shifu to head to Frenchtown. This was not news he could deliver to Eden over the phone.

This was not the parting gift he wanted to leave for the woman he loved.

———

"Hello," Eden greeted her parents and Joshua when she arrived home. She took off her boots and put on her slippers. "Did anyone call?"

"You mean Alex?" Joshua looked up from his book. "No. Sorry."

Eden hung up her coat. "No school today?"

"No. We called the school office and they said it'll reopen tomorrow."

Her mother put down her knitting. "How are the people at the refugee center?"

"They're getting by, for now." Eden sat down with them. "Laura Margolis said she'll meet with Captain Koreshige Inuzuka. He's the man the Japanese are putting in charge of Jewish affairs. She said they're on good terms. He lives in the penthouse of her hotel. She's going to ask him to release the account holding the funds from the JDC." The JDC was the Jewish Joint Distribution Committee in America that had been sending large donations of money to help the refugees.

She flashed a quick smile, trying to keep up hope for her family, and perhaps for herself as well. But if Inuzuka refused, they would be completely out of money to feed the refugees. And there was a good chance he would refuse since those funds were held in a bank account registered to Americans.

Her father took a slow drag from his pipe and returned to

reading the latest issue of the *Shanghai Jewish Chronicle*. Eden sighed and looked on. This would likely be the last issue he'd get to read.

"What do you think will happen to us?" Joshua asked. It was a question none of them wanted to raise since yesterday morning.

Eden glanced at her mother, then her father. She took a good look at her brother. He'd grown so much. Seventeen years old. This should be the beginning of his life. He should be thinking about what he would do when he finished secondary school. Instead, he was starting his adulthood under a cloud of fear and despair.

"Will they let the Nazis come and put us in camps?" He clutched his book. "That's what the Nazi leaflets said. They were telling people this should be done when they held their rally."

"What rally?" Dr. Levine asked.

"Their rally at the racecourse." Joshua hunched his back. "Sorry, I know I wasn't supposed to go to the racetrack. David's older brother took us there last month. I didn't go to place bets, I swear! David and I just wanted to watch the race."

Dr. Levine ignored his explanation. "Tell me about the rally. What did you see?"

"We were sitting in the stands. Suddenly, there were leaflets flying all over. The Nazis were throwing these out from the top floor of the Park Hotel. The flyers were in English and in Chinese. They were telling people why Jews are degenerates and should never be trusted. They said all Jews should be put in camps and eliminated. A group of them were outside the racecourse when we left. They were holding posters and shouting slurs. David's brother said that was the first time a Nazi rally ever took place in Shanghai."

Dr. Levine took a deep drag of his pipe. Eden sat with her hands closed. What could they say to Joshua, when they didn't know the answer themselves?

The phone rang and saved them from having to tell him the

truth. Mrs. Levine answered. "Yes . . . please send him up." She hung up. "That was the concierge. Clark's here."

Eden sat up. "Clark?"

"Yes." Mrs. Levine went back to her seat. "Maybe he came to check up on us. He's such a nice young man." She started knitting again.

The doorbell rang and Eden got up to invite Clark in. She was still torn as to how to greet him, but the grave, urgent look on his face chased off all her feelings of unease. "Eden." He took off his hat.

"Hello," she greeted him.

He came inside. "Dr. Levine, Mrs. Levine. Joshua."

"Clark!" Mrs. Levine stood up. "Come on in. Please, have a seat. What brought you here? Would you like some tea?"

"No, thank you." He wetted his lips. "I have some urgent news to tell you." He frowned and looked at all of them. "Alex Mitchell and Isaac were arrested by the Japanese this morning."

Eden's heart dropped. Her whole center collapsed and she felt like she had fallen into a deep void. "No!"

"Both of them?" Dr. Levine's eyes widened. The newspaper he was holding fell to his lap.

"Yes. Both of them."

"Isaac too?" Mrs. Levine asked. "Why Isaac?"

"Apparently, he was with Alex when Alex was arrested."

"Why?" Eden asked. "Why was Isaac with Alex? The two of them aren't even friends."

"I don't know," Clark said. "All I know is they were both arrested. Mauricio told me. He tried to call you but couldn't reach you."

"I was at the Embankment House," she said. Fear seized her entire body. "Can he do anything to help?"

Clark shook his head. "He's gone. He left Shanghai."

"He left Shanghai?"

"Yes. He's not coming back."

Eden fell back a step. This was what she was afraid of. The Japanese would never let Alex go alive.

And Isaac. What would happen to Isaac? She couldn't breathe.

"They're not the only ones," Clark said. "Mauricio said they arrested everyone they could find on the blacklist. They're arresting anyone they consider anti-Japan."

Anyone anti-Japan. Eden tried to breathe. Her legs and knees shook. If the Japanese knew she was Apollo Eirene, they would surely come after her too.

Clark grabbed her arm and steadied her. In terror, she gazed back.

Charlie might have saved her life. These last three years, everyone thought she'd given up writing hard news and become a frivolous entertainment reporter.

She stifled her fears and asked, "Is there anything we can do? Is there anything anyone can do to save them?"

With frightened eyes, her parents and Joshua looked hopefully at Clark.

Clark's frown deepened. She almost lost hope, but he raised his eyes. "Maybe. I have one last debt to collect from someone who owes me. Let me see if he can help."

48

DEADLY LOVE

Kenji Konoe.

The Japanese aristocrat who owed Clark his life. When Japan invaded Shanghai four years ago, Clark saved him from a Heaven and Earth Society assassin's fatal shot.

Japan was now the enemy of the free world. From here on, they would always be enemies. It was time to settle their debt once and for all.

Konoe must be sensing the same reckoning too. At his home in his private dojo, the tranquilly designed room where he was practicing the way of the sword, Kenji Konoe quietly wielded his bamboo *shinai* backward. Then, in a flash quicker than a blink of the eye, he swung it high up with a powerful shout and brought it down level at the middle of his chest. Under his *shitagi* shirt and wide *hakama* trousers, the outline of his body stood in perfect form.

He eased up and lowered his sword, and walked toward Clark.

"I'm sorry to interrupt you," Clark said.

"Not at all." Konoe smiled. "My practice hour's nearly over anyway." He raised his *shinai* and gazed at the handle. "Are you familiar with *kendo*?"

"No."

"It is not just any form of sword fight. *Kendo* is a coalescence of spirit, sword, and body. The sword cannot merely injure and hurt. You must cut the opponent the correct way, and only with the correct part of the sword. You cannot attack too deep or too shallow. Your body, posture, and hands must be in the right positions. Everything must be in balance."

"Balance?" Clark shifted his eyes to the floor and pondered the notion.

"Yes. Also, your spirit must be clear and alert. There cannot be any break in your focus. You must never let extraneous emotions such as joy or defeat affect you. Finally, you must honor and respect your opponent. If you disrespect your opponent, you could lose your match." He lowered his *shinai*. "Since I came to China, I have yet to find a worthy opponent." He went to the side of the dojo and placed the *shinai* upright against the wall.

"You know," he continued, "the way of the sword is not merely a sport. We Japanese no longer fight with swords. This ancient method of fighting is outmoded. Swords are no match for guns, airplanes, and machines. Nonetheless, our ancient practice of combining the spirit and body in the methods we use to fight taught us how to strike. It makes us superior. It is what enables us to win even when the odds say a victory is impossible. We stay focused, and we strike at the right place. It was how we knocked the United States off balance. It was how we destroyed their entire fleet at Pearl Harbor."

"You knocked the United States off balance?" Clark asked. "I thought they knocked you off yours when Roosevelt cut off all your supplies of oil, rubber, and metals."

Konoe pressed his lips together, but quickly recovered. "It was true. Roosevelt caused us some setbacks. But none of that matters now. Very soon, Japan will command all of Asia. We will have access to natural resources from China, Malaya, Singapore, Indochina, not to mention Korea and Formosa, which we already rule." He smiled. An irrepressible, exhilarated glow shone in his eyes. "Our work is about to begin. A greater Asia, led by Japan." He looked excitedly at Clark. "The Emperor asked me to join a select group of men. Our job will be to implement the New Order throughout our colonies. From now on, I will commit myself fully to ensuring Japan will exceed all the Western nations. No Western power will ever compare. We will be the helm of the entire Asian sphere, while they remain divided, and none of them can claim to be the leader of the Western world. Not even Hitler. Japan will be invincible."

"But you are not invincible," Clark said. "Everything you're about to do, you'll be able to do it only because I once saved your life. You can defeat my country. You can even kill me, but you'll still owe me." He stepped forward. "I know you, Kenji Konoe. You don't want just victory, or power, or money. Those are for men beneath you." He went to the side of the room and picked up the *shinai*. "You want to be transcendent. You want to have a clarity of mind and purity of existence above everyone else. You can't be that now, because you owe me." He swung out his arm and pointed the *shinai* at Konoe, and looked him in the eye. "You're not in balance."

Konoe glared. He raised his chest and tightened his face.

"Of course, you can carry on," Clark said. He slowly stepped away past Konoe and bounced his hand holding the *shinai*. "You can ignore this inconvenient fact and carry on until you have all of Asia bending their knees before you. Your country's military strength can deliver you that. But if you don't acknowledge that the great Kenji Konoe owed his life to a Chinese, well, that would be disrespectful, wouldn't it? If you disrespect your opponent, then maybe you never won the match."

Konoe swung his head over his shoulder. "Is that why you came? To harangue me? To hold this against me?"

"No," Clark said. "I came to help you restore your balance. I came to ask for a favor. If you help me, we will consider ourselves even."

Konoe straightened his stance. "What do you want?"

"The Japanese military arrested two men, Alex Mitchell and Isaac Weissman. Can you get them released?"

"Alex Mitchell? You want me to release Alex Mitchell?"

"Yes."

"I can't do that."

"You can't?" Clark strolled back to the wall. "Looks like Kenji Konoe is not omnipotent either." He put down the *shinai* back down on the floor.

"Wait." Konoe raised his hand. He clenched his fist, but exhaled and released his hand. "I will look for them. When I find them, I will secure their release. On one condition. You have to guarantee Alex Mitchell will never say another word against Japan," Konoe said with a firm face. "I ask this for his own good. If he's released and he goes back to attacking my country, I won't be helping him again."

Clark nodded. "I understand." He walked toward the door. "Thank you." He glanced at Konoe one more time and started to leave.

"Clark," Konoe called out.

Clark turned his head.

"You're a worthy opponent."

Clark smiled. He gazed ahead and continued walking down the corridor.

By the time Clark arrived home, it was already seven o'clock. The visit to Eden's home and Kenji Konoe's residence caused him much delay. He now had to dismiss all the servants early for the night and tell his mother and sisters to pack for their escape before dawn tomorrow morning. He had to pack for himself too, as well as destroy their battery plant.

Could he leave? He agonized over this question the entire way home from Konoe's. Until Alex Mitchell and Isaac were safely released, could he leave Eden behind in this horrendous situation?

Konoe would not back out of his word. However treacherous and nefarious the other Japanese might be, Kenji Konoe would not break his promise to him.

Still, his heart could not rest at ease.

His mind told him otherwise. His first responsibility was his family. He had to get them to safety.

He could get himself somewhere safe first. Once he landed, he could work with Mauricio to bring Eden and her family to Macau too, if that was what they wanted. They would be illegal refugees, but it would be safer.

He took off his coat and gave it to the maid. "Where's Tai Tai and the Misses?"

"Tai Tai and Daxiaojie are in their rooms. We're about to start dinner. Erxiaojie is out."

Mei Mei was out? "Out where?"

"I don't know. She didn't say."

Clark frowned. Why did she go out today at all? At this hour too? The Japanese troops were overrunning the place.

He went to Wen-Ying's room. "Do you know where Mei Mei went?"

Wen Ying paused. She was writing a letter at her desk. "She went out?"

"That's what the maid told me."

A houseboy came to him. "Young Master, phone call."

Clark exchanged a glance with Wen-Ying, then went into the study. He half sat down on the edge of his desk and signaled the houseboy to close the door. "Hello?"

"Yuan Guo-Hui, this is Zhou Ke-Hao."

"Xiao Zhou?" Clark stood up. They hadn't spoken to each other since Dai Li betrayed Zhou's sworn brother to the puppet police. "Where are you?"

"Where I am is irrelevant. I really don't know if I'm doing the right thing calling you. My sworn brothers and I have joined the Communists."

"Zhou." Clark sank back against the desk. "What good would it be for you to do that?"

"What good would it be? At least Mao Ze Dong won't betray us. Anyhow, I'm not calling you to discuss that. I'm calling about your sister, Yuan Wen-Li."

"Wen-Li?" Mei Mei. "What about her?'

"I'm not involved in any way. It's only what I heard. A group of student Communists is plotting to kill a high-level Reorganized Government official tonight. His name is Tang Wei."

Tang Wei. Clark's pulse started racing. What was this all about?

"Your sister appears to know him. From what I understand, they plan to use her as a bait to lure Tang Wei out. She's telling Tang Wei you want to meet with him to discuss collaborating with Japan. When Tang Wei arrives, they will ambush him."

Clark's heart began to pound. "Wen-Li . . . is she one of you?"

"You mean is she a member of the Communist Party? No. Does she have a boyfriend named Liu Zi-Hong?"

Liu Zi-Hong? Liu Zi-Hong! "Yes. Did he tell her to do this?"

"I don't know. I don't have all the details. Her connection with the group seems to be through him."

Clark stood up. That little twit. What had he gotten Mei Mei into?

"I'm telling you everything I know," Zhou said. "Unlike your ruthless, disloyal cohorts in Juntong, I wouldn't betray someone and harm their sibling. I want to warn you your sister is in danger. She invited Tang Wei to meet her at the Celestial Palace restaurant in the French Concession at eight o'clock."

Eight o'clock. Clark checked his watch. He needed to get there. He needed to get her out of there before any incident erupted.

"Thank you," he said to Zhou. At once, he hung up the phone and raced out of the house.

The car screeched to a halt in front of the Celestial Palace's opulent facade. Clark thrust open the door and got out. At the restaurant's entrance, people were pouring out, screaming. A string of gunshots fired off inside.

He ran into the crowd and pushed his way in through the fleeing guests. The main dining room was now empty with abandoned tables of dishes and drinks. Broken glasses and fallen chairs spilled all over the floor. He rushed back to the corridor leading to the private dining rooms. At the end, two bloodied bodies lay still on the floor. Both were men. A lone waitress stood crying, with her back against the wall.

With shortened breaths, he took his gun out of his holster and trod forward. As he passed by the corpses, the terrified waitress stared at him, too frightened to move. He took a quick glance at the faces of the two bodies. He didn't recognize either of them.

He went into the last dining room. Another waitress was lifting someone up from the floor behind the banquet table. She cried out to a stunned waiter crouching down, "Call the ambulance! Call the ambulance!"

Warily, Clark walked up to them. When he saw who the waitress was holding on her lap, his heart dove. On the floor, Mei Mei moaned. Blood was soaking the abdomen of her dress. The waitress who was trying to help her was still crying out, "Call the ambulance! Call the ambulance!"

He shoved the gun back into his holster. "Mei Mei!" He knelt down and grabbed his sister's shoulders. "Mei Mei!"

"Ge . . ." Mei Mei opened her eyes. She kept her hand on her wound.

"What happened?" He put his hand over hers.

"I . . ."

"Never mind. I'll take you to the hospital."

The waitress and waiter moved back and let him pick her up. He carried his sister in his arms and told her, "Hold on. Hold on just a moment. The car is right outside." He hurried out of the dining room and down the hallway.

"Ge . . ." She started to cry.

The waitress who was helping her ran after them. "She and her friend, a man, were waiting for another guest. I was still serving their drinks. Suddenly, a group came. Two of them pulled out guns and tried to shoot her friend. They missed and a bullet hit her. When they saw they shot her, they ran away. But her friend had a gun too. He chased after them and killed those two back there. When the restaurant guests heard the gunshots, they all fled. Her friend and the other attackers ran away too."

Attackers. That bunch of rice buckets. They didn't get Tang Wei, but they shot Mei Mei. Then they ran away and left Mei Mei to die.

Liu Zi-Hong. That worthless lowly animal. If anything happened to Mei Mei, he would castigate him until he destroyed him.

He hugged his sister closer against him and raced outside to his car. The waitress stopped at the entrance of the restaurant. Huang Shifu saw him running out and sprung out of the car to open the door to the backseat.

"To the hospital!" Clark yelled.

Huang Shifu sprinted back into the driver's seat. He slammed on the gas pedal and started the car down the road. In the backseat, Clark held on to his sister on his lap. "We'll be there soon. Hold on longer. We're almost at the hospital," he told her over and over.

Her bleeding didn't stop. Her face and lips turned pale and her body shook. The car sped ahead. When they reached the hospital, Clark ran inside and shouted for help.

A team of medics came and put Mei Mei on a stretcher and wheeled her inside. By now, she'd nearly passed out.

"You'll be fine now." Clark ran alongside the stretcher. "It'll all be fine now." He touched her arm before they took her away.

In the hallway, he raked his fingers through his hair and grasped his scalp. Why? Why did this have to happen?

He turned back around and looked at the closed door of the emergency room.

Please. He squeezed his hands. Please don't let her die.

Don't let her die.

In the hospital's waiting area, Clark sat with Wen-Ying and his mother, struggling to stay awake. His mother and Wen-Ying were tired and worn too, but how could they sleep? Mei Mei had been in surgery for hours.

He looked over his shoulder and shifted in his seat. His poor mother. She looked older than he'd ever seen her. Of the three children, Mei Mei was the closest to her. How could she handle a trauma like this?

Wen-Ying stroked her mother on the back. This agonizing wait.

A figure burst down the hallway toward them. As soon as Clark saw his face, fury besieged him.

"Wen-Li!" Liu Zi-Hong ran toward them, flailing his arms. "Wen-Li! How's Wen-Li?"

"You son of a bitch!" Clark grabbed him by the collar. "What did you let my sister do?" He punched Zi-Hong in the face. Once. Twice. And again. He could contain his fury no more.

Wen-Ying screamed, "Stop!" She tried to pull him back, but

he swung his arm and she couldn't hold him. He continued to punch the bastard.

"Ge!" Wen-Ying shouted again. "Ge! Stop!"

The hospital staff rushed over and pulled the two of them apart. "Sir!" one of them shouted at him and Zi-Hong. "You're not allowed to fight in the hospital. If you keep fighting, we'll make you both leave." He stood between them and stretched out his arms to keep them apart.

Catching his breath, Clark glared at the creep. A nurse tried to examine Zi-Hong's face and asked him if he was okay, but he brushed her hand away and told her he didn't need her help.

"No more brawling," the hospital attendant warned, and they walked away.

Clark spat out his words, "You despicable animal."

"It wasn't me." Zi-Hong shook his head. His eyes welled. "It wasn't me. I would never let Wen-Li take part in something dangerous. I've always kept her out of what I do. It was the others. They convinced her behind my back. They covered me inside a drum. They didn't even have the nerve to tell me what happened. I only found out just now. If I'd known, I would have never let it happen. Believe me. Please believe me."

The useless twerp. Clark pointed at him. "No matter what, this whole thing arose because of you. If you bastard never existed, Mei Mei wouldn't have been injured."

"I'm sorry," Zi-Hong cried. "I'm sorry. I love her. I really love her. I don't want her to die either. Please let me wait here too. I just want to know she'll wake up. Please."

Clark bared his teeth. He couldn't forgive this imbecile. He couldn't. "Get out." He pointed at the exit. "You get out. We never want to see you again. Wen-Li never wants to see you again."

"I . . ." Zi-Hong sniffed. He bawled and took a step closer. "Please . . ."

Wen-Ying came up to him. "Leave. Don't come back anymore."

Zi-Hong looked from Wen-Ying to Clark, then to Madam Yuan. Madam Yuan turned her face and eyes away. He looked back at Wen-Ying, then dropped his head. "All right." He laughed. A bitter, hopeless laugh. "All right. In case Wen-Li doesn't make it, then I, Liu Zi-Hong, will bear the name of criminal for the rest of my life." He scrunched his face in despair and left. His figure disappeared out of the exit and Clark sagged back down into his seat.

A due owed to enmity from a past life. He didn't know in which lifetime Mei Mei invited upon herself this cursed tie to Liu Zi-Hong.

He tossed back his head and closed his eyes. His mother began to sob. She'd cried so many tears already tonight, but she was sobbing again. If he could, he would say to her a few magical words of comfort, but he had no more energy left.

49

FRAIL LIFE OF A BEAUTY

THE DOCTOR STARTLED him when he nudged Clark awake. Clark opened his eyes and looked around. When did he fall asleep?

"Mr. Yuan?" the doctor asked.

"Yes," Clark answered. A nurse was waking up Wen-Ying and his mother.

"The operation is over," the doctor said.

Clark jumped to his feet. "How is she?" he asked. "How's my sister?"

"She's stable for now." The doctor nodded at his sister and mother, who had come closer to hear the update. "Her injuries are quite severe. She lost a lot of blood. The bullet penetrated her liver and she has massive tissue damage. We'll have to wait and continue to observe her."

Madam Yuan lost her balance. Wen-Ying wrapped her arm around her mother to help her stay on her feet.

"We've taken her to Room 206," the doctor said. "She's very weak but awake. You can go see her, but stay no more than ten minutes. She needs to rest."

"Thank you." Clark nodded. His heart felt relieved. His sister was alive.

"Come with me." The nurse invited them to join her. "I'll take you all there."

Wearily, they followed the nurse. His mind still recovering from the haze of fatigue and sleep, Clark's eyes wandered to the reception desk in front of the lift. On the wall, the hour hand of the clock pointed at six. They'd missed the sampan he'd arranged to take them to the ship to Macau.

Later, he told himself. He couldn't worry about that now. He'd try to find another snakehead later if the Japanese hadn't shut down all avenues of escape.

In the patient's room, they found Mei Mei on the bed with her arm hooked to an IV drip. Mei Mei glanced meekly in their direction.

"Mei Mei! Mei Mei!" Madam Yuan ran over to her daughter. "Why did you do something so foolish? Why did you sacrifice yourself for those beasts? Those beasts! They hurt you like this!"

"Ma . . ." Mei Mei tried to answer her.

Wen-Ying came to her mother's side. "Ma, don't agitate her. Let her rest."

Madam Yuan tried, but nonetheless broke down. Wen-Ying patted her on the back and pulled her back so to not disturb her sister.

Mei Mei glanced over at Clark and he came to her other side.

"Ge." She tried to smile.

"You just had surgery. Don't talk so much. Get a little rest."

"I must look terrible right now."

"No, you don't." He stroked her hair. "You'll forever be the most beautiful girl in Shanghai."

She grimaced, as though in pain. "Ge." She strained to pull her arm out from under the blanket. Clark grabbed her hand and bent closer. "What do you need?"

"I just want to tell you I'm sorry. I'm sorry I caused you all this trouble."

"Don't say it anymore."

"I know you disliked Zi-Hong all along. But I love him. I really love him. All this time, you didn't want me to see him. He got so immersed in his political activities too. I feel like the distance between us kept growing wider and wider."

"Wen-Li." Clark squeezed her hand. If he could go back and redo everything, he'd do anything to make her whole again.

A tear fell from her eye. "And then, seeing Japan encroaching on us, and our whole country falling apart, I felt so useless. I thought, Zi-Hong was right. We have to fight back. We can't let all the traitors hand our country to Japan." Her breathing became labored, but she continued to speak. "The more involved he became with politics, the further he pulled away from me. When our friends suggested I lure Tang Wei out, I felt it was something I had to do. They told me Zi-Hong would be proud of me. I wanted Zi-Hong to know I support him. I just want him to know I stand on his side."

"Never mind." Clark tried to console her. "Never mind all this. The most important thing now is your recovery."

"Actually, I . . ." Her head fell to the side of the pillow. She closed her eyes and stopped talking.

"Mei Mei?" Clark shook her lightly. She didn't respond. He shook her again with slightly more force. Still no response. Fear engulfed his heart. "Mei Mei!"

Madam Yuan and Wen-Ying shouted at the same time, "Mei Mei!" They both reached their arms out to her body. Trembling, Clark raised his finger under her nose. No breath.

"Doctor!" he shouted. "Doctor!" He ran to the door and shouted down the hall. "Call the doctor!" He looked down the hallway to the left, and to the right. "Call the doctor!"

The nurses came running toward him. A doctor followed. They ran into the room and got to work at once to resuscitate the patient. Time passed as Clark watched helplessly from the side of the room. When the doctor turned around and shook his head, Clark's own mind went blank. Reality seemed to have fallen away.

Beside him, his mother wailed. She hurled herself onto her daughter's body while the nurses tried to calm her down. Even Wen-Ying broke out in uncontrollable tears.

The sun of a new day had already risen when Clark walked his mother out of the hospital with Wen-Ying. His mother fell into a complete daze. How could he pick up all the pieces and fix this now?

At the entrance, Huang Shifu opened the car door with a dour look on his face. Their car, though, wasn't the only vehicle waiting. About twenty feet behind their Cadillac in the driveway sat another black sedan. The person seated in the back passenger seat rolled down the window. From inside the car, Tang Wei gazed at Clark and smiled, then waved his hand.

For all his reluctance to see this treacherous thief now, he said to Wen-Ying, "You take Ma home first."

She frowned, then took note of Tang Wei in the other car. Immediately, she turned her face blank. "Be careful," she whispered to Clark and brought her mother away to their car.

After they drove away, Clark walked over to Tang. Tang's driver had gotten out and he opened the door of the backseat. There, Tang Wei invited him to take a seat beside him. Clark took a deep breath and climbed in.

The driver returned to his seat and drove them onto the street. Tang Wei took out a pack of cigarettes. He offered it to Clark and Clark shook his head. He took one out and lit it for himself, and inhaled a deep drag. "I'm very fond of little Wen-Li too. Her passing away makes me very sad."

Clark didn't answer. So Tang Wei already heard the news. He must've had insider sources within the hospital.

"You should all try your best to curb your grief and adapt to changes."

"Thank you for your concern," Clark replied. He doubted this snake felt any real sympathy. This betrayer of conscience didn't wait at the hospital and invite him into the car to give condolences, did he?

"Sorrow for losses is one thing. Nonetheless, I must ask you. When Wen-Li contacted me to meet her, she told me you had a change of heart. She said you would like to collaborate with the new Chinese regime. Is that true?"

Clark curled his fingers on his lap. No. Of course, that was a lie. But Mei Mei was dead, and the last thing he would do was to implicate her and soil her name.

"Yes," he said. "It's true."

Tang raised his brows. "I still have doubt." He took a drag of his cigarette. "You've been staunchly against joining the new regime. Why would you change your mind now?"

"It's obvious, isn't it?" Clark shrugged. "Japan is already taking over the entire city. What use is it for me to continue to resist?" He put on a helpless face. "The Japanese are about to take over my family's business. Money is secondary. I still want to preserve my family's legacy. My hope is, if I can work with the Wang Jing-Wei's regime, the Japanese army will let me stay on and continue as the manager of my company, even if it's in title only."

"You're really giving up?" Tang gave him a side eye. "You and she really weren't working with those Mao bandits to try to kill me?"

"Mao bandits!" Clark laughed. "Even if you doubt me, you have no reason to doubt Wen-Li. First, I would never bring her into any risky political plot. You should know that. Moreover, you know what kind of person she was too. There's no way she'd know how to tell you such a lie. Think about it yourself. An attempt to murder. Would she have the ability to carry it out?"

Tang Wei frowned and gazed down. His earlier suspicions seemed to waver. "How did those Mao bandits know where I would be then?"

"You ask me? Who should I ask?"

Tang blew out his smoke. His brows still furrowed with doubt.

"Working with Mao bandits," Clark sneered. "What do you take me for? Is my Yuan family's name so cheap? Why would I give up my family's name and status to join that bunch of uneducated peasants?" He glanced sideways at Tang to see if he bought his act.

Tang laughed. "A capitalist to the heart." He sat back at ease. "Yuan Guo-Hui, no wonder you're blessed with fortune."

Clark ran his eyes over the interior of the car and the driver. "You're not doing too bad yourself. You got your own car and driver now."

"Better than when I worked for Chiang Kai-Shek. Very soon, this will become a true luxury. The Chinese government will be issuing an order to restrict the use of motor cars after next week. Only essential vehicles will be allowed. Petrol is in short supply, you know."

Clark noted the haughtiness in his voice. The Chinese government. Tang meant the puppet government, of course.

"Don't worry," Tang added. "If you join us, you and your family will be able to continue to ride your Cadillac around." He widened his grin. "Let me ask you. If you do join our side, what can you do for us?"

Clark hadn't thought about that. He had to think of something, quick. "I'm still in good standing with the people in Chungking. After the Pearl Harbor attack, I contacted Chungking. I offered to be their eyes and ears on what's going on in Shanghai."

"You're offering to double-cross them and gather information from their side for us instead?"

"Yes."

"Hm." Tang cocked his head, musing on the idea.

"They're completely cut off from Shanghai now. They'd be eager to have a source."

"Good." Tang stubbed out his cigarette in the ashtray on the door on his side. "This option is feasible. We can give it a try. Poor Wen-Li lost her life for this. For Wen-Li, we can give you a chance to prove yourself." He slapped Clark on the back. "Yuan Guo-Hui, you should've switched side long ago. You and I were friends at one time. I've always regretted losing a friend like you."

"Me too," Clark said. It took everything within him to put a sincere smile on his face.

"All right. You've got to be tired. I'll take you home. Rest well. When you're done taking care of Wen-Li's last rites, we'll talk again."

"Yes," Clark said. He looked out the window and wondered how he had ended up in this hell. He'd become a collaborator, and his little sister was dead.

He needed to go home. Reality, it had to be somewhere. He needed to find his way back.

50

THE BRIDGE HOUSE

RETURNING HOME FROM THE FUNERAL, Wen-Ying gently walked Madam Yuan back to her bedroom. Since Mei Mei's death a week ago, their mother had turned into a catatonic shell of herself. Nothing anyone did could bring her spirit back.

Clark didn't blame her. He almost couldn't hold everything together himself. Only four years ago, they held their father's funeral. He had not foreseen such a thing would repeat in his family again so soon.

The funeral this time was much smaller. His family, without discussing it at length, had gone ahead and made arrangements for a quiet burial. Somehow, he felt this would be what his little sister wanted.

His mother didn't participate much. Every morning, she washed her face with tears. For hours on end, she sat in Mei Mei's room, looking over all the magazines, clothes, decorative figurines, and keepsakes her deceased daughter had left behind. Whenever she found something she thought Mei Mei cherished, she would tell Clark or Wen-Ying, "This goes with her." She'd give these mementos to them to be buried with the body.

Wen-Ying, never one to care for impractical things, followed along with whatever Clark decided. In truth, Clark himself didn't do much. Good old Huang Shifu and their maid Xiaochun. They stepped in to work out all the logistics with the funeral home. This wasn't part of their jobs, but they lent their hands when he needed them most. All he had to do was to give his yes or no. Where would he find such loyal help again?

He went into Mei Mei's bedroom. On her desk, a pair of small porcelain puppies continued to smile. They smiled because they didn't know their owner was never coming back.

Did Mei Mei ever want to own a real puppy? Had she ever talked about it?

Clark couldn't remember. Since he returned to Shanghai from overseas, he'd been riding so many storms. He had his hands full handling what he thought were matters impacting the world. Mei Mei's juvenile pursuits, her trivial hobbies, her childish romance —he never took them seriously and nothing about them warranted his close attention. His job was to keep her safe and provide her a good home until she fully grew up. Or so he thought.

But he didn't keep her safe. And she did grow up. Right before his eyes and he didn't even know it because he was so preoccupied with everything he was doing himself. She'd grown up enough for her little romance to be caught in a maelstrom of political strife.

Could he have done anything differently to avoid her death? If he had paid closer attention, would he have seen what was coming and put a stop to all the outside influences that never had her best interests at heart?

He put one hand on his hip and rubbed his forehead with the other.

A houseboy appeared at the door. "Young Master?"

"Yes. What is it?"

"A messenger came by. He delivered this." The houseboy showed him an envelope. It was addressed to him with no information to identify the sender.

"Thank you." He took the letter. The houseboy bowed and left the room.

Puzzled, Clark unsealed the letter. Inside, he found a short, unsigned message.

Pick up the package outside the Bridge House tomorrow.
10:00 a.m.

Clark folded the message. Kenji Konoe. The message came from him.

He did it. The Japanese aristocrat delivered on his promise.

At least, there would be good news for Eden and the Levines. Tomorrow, he would go and fetch Alex Mitchell and Isaac Weissman, and bring them back.

Live people should not go near.

So went the whispers of warning the Chinese gave to each other when it came to the Bridge House. This art deco building, named for the bridge which spanned the Soochow Creek two blocks away, was originally built in 1935 as an apartment complex to house Westerners. Today, it served as the headquarters of the dreaded Kenpeitai, the Japanese military police.

In his car across from this house of terror on North Szechuan Street, Clark waited for the building's door to open for the release of Alex Mitchell and Isaac Weissman as Kenji Konoe promised. He arrived almost right on the dot at ten. It wasn't a reflection of his punctuality, but more a heed to the warning to stay away. He didn't want to be near this place a minute longer than he had to. This building was where the Kenpeitai tortured and killed those they arrested for any reason or no reason at all.

Huang Shifu apparently felt the same way. When Clark instructed him to drive here, the poor driver stiffened up. "Are you joking?" he asked Clark. He drove with caution as Clark had never seen before, and he slowed to a crawl when they approached their destination. As they sat here now, Huang Shifu kept his eyes down or straight ahead, avoiding at all costs to catch the sight of the building no living person would want to go near.

At a minute past ten, the front door opened. Two men in Kenpeitai uniforms brought out a staggering white man. Clark's heart jumped a beat. A chill shot up his spine and spread to the skin of his arms. Yes, this place scared him too, but he gathered his nerves and opened the car door and got out.

In his trench coat and fedora hat, he walked across the street. The white man gazed up. Isaac! What did they do to him? A giant bruise covered his right eye, which couldn't open and remained a slit. His lips were visibly swollen too even under his facial hair. His clothes were stained yellow, brown, black, gray, and red, caked with blood and dirt and God only knew what else. He was barely recognizable as the man Clark knew as Isaac Weissman.

The two Kenpeitai pushed Isaac away without saying a word. Isaac stumbled and fell forward to the ground. The Japanese policemen then turned around and retreated inside. Their faces showed not an ounce of emotion as they closed the door.

"Isaac!" Clark ran to help him up. A foul smell assaulted his nose. Isaac reeked!

Isaac groaned. He could barely speak.

Clark looked back at the Bridge House's entrance. "Where's Alex?"

"Alex is dead," Isaac managed to mumble.

"What?"

"He died yesterday."

Yesterday? What? How?

Never mind. He'd have to sort that out later. He pulled back his gaze and said to Isaac, "Let's get you to a hospital." He lifted Isaac's arm and helped him to his feet. Huang Shifu, too, hurried out of the car to help bring him away.

In the backseat of the car, Isaac slumped against the car door and moaned. Clark tried to think. Alex Mitchell was dead? Did Konoe play him? Did he let Alex die on purpose, so he wouldn't have to release him as he promised? Did he order Alex to be killed?

Clark shook his head and pushed away the thought. He didn't believe that. Konoe had too much pride to taint his hands with any individual case of cruelty. Such dirty work was for minions. He liked to keep himself pristine. Besides, if he failed to deliver his promise, then he would still be in Clark's debt. In that case, there was no reason to release Isaac either.

But why didn't they release Alex earlier?

And how would he break the news to Eden?

He did not look forward to that at all.

"Isaac!" Eden called out his name as she entered the patient's room. Her parents and Joshua walked in right behind her.

In the room, Clark quickly stood up. She glanced at him and rushed with her family to Isaac's side, where he was sitting up on the bed with a bandage wrapped around his head. Behind them, Clark quietly closed the door.

"Isaac, are you all right?" Joshua asked him.

"I'm fine," Isaac said. "I'm much better now."

Mrs. Levine frowned and exchanged a look with her husband. Dr. Levine bent over Isaac and lightly held his chin. "Let me see."

He examined Isaac's black and blue eye and lips. Red welts crisscrossed the parts of his forearms that weren't covered by his sleeves. In a grim voice, Dr. Levine asked, "What did they do to you?"

Isaac sat still, but Clark answered. "They tortured him. They beat him up and they whipped him with bamboo rods. See those welts on his arms? They're all over his body. They whipped him on the head too. There's a gash on the back of his head. That's why the nurses wrapped his head in bandages."

"Oh . . ." Mrs. Levine whimpered and covered her mouth. She put her hand on Isaac's shoulder. "You look so thin. How could you lose so much weight in a week?"

Isaac tried to chuckle. "Yeah. The food could be better in prison."

Mrs. Levine pressed her hand over her chest. "Thank you for bringing him back," she said to Clark.

"Yes." Eden gave him a grateful smile. Her heart chilled with fear, she asked, "Where's Alex?"

Clark froze. He blinked his eyes to the side and looked away from her.

"Alex is dead," Isaac mumbled through his bruised mouth. "He died yesterday."

Eden gasped. "How? What happened?"

"It's better you don't know." Isaac stared at his hands.

"No!" She grabbed his forearm. He flinched and hissed.

"I'm sorry." She let go. She pushed his sleeve higher and found a bandage over the spot on his arm where she had grabbed him. "What happened to your arm?"

Isaac turned his face away. Clark answered for him. "Cigarette burn. The burns are all over his body too."

Eden's face crumpled. "What happened?" she asked Isaac again. "What were you two doing? Why were you arrested? Please! Tell me!"

Isaac raised his eyes. "I went to Alex's apartment. I went to tell him he needed to get out of Shanghai. It would be best for his own safety, of course, but the reason I went there was to tell him he needed to marry you and get you out of this place." His voice grew firm and he sat motionless on his bed. "Of all of us, you were the only one with a chance to get out. Even if one of us could survive this, it would be something! All he had to do was marry you. The Japanese are taking over. What was he still doing here, stalling?"

Eden raised her hand to her mouth. This question plagued her too. She'd tried not to think about it for so long. She admitted now, she always wanted to know. She asked in a shaky voice, "What did he say?"

"He said he couldn't leave. He was worried the Japanese would take revenge on his Chinese assistants at the radio station if he ran away. He said he'd stay here and face all the consequences with them. And he wanted to set up an underground radio station to continue broadcasting under the Japanese's noses."

"No!" Eden cried. A sea of conflicts roiled within her. Alex. Yes, it wasn't fair he never made any promises to her about them or their future. No, she didn't and wouldn't blame him for being loyal to his Chinese staff. Yes, it hurt her she wasn't the most important thing to him. No, she would not fault him for wanting to stay and continue to tell the world what was happening here. He was brave! He was so brave to risk his own life for what he believed.

She tried to hold back her tears, but she couldn't anymore.

"What happened then?" Dr. Levine asked. "How did you get arrested? Why did the Japanese take you?"

Isaac dropped his shoulders. "Alex and I started arguing. Suddenly, four gunmen showed up. I found out later they were Japanese plainclothes gendarmerie. No one realized who they were when they entered his building." He paused and clasped his hands. "They thought I was related to Alex or colluding with him somehow because I was at his home. Alex tried to tell them I had nothing to do with his work but they didn't care. They took us to the Bridge house. There, the Kenpeitai confiscated our wallets, our watches, and my collar and tie. A guard then took us to a cell. It was more like a cage, with wooden bars for the door. He ordered us to take off our shoes and go inside. As soon as I climbed in . . ." He wrinkled his nose in disgust. "The stench. I've never smelled anything so pungent in my life."

Eden wiped the tears off her face. She wanted to hear this. She wanted to know what they did to Alex.

"And that wasn't the worst," Isaac said. "The cell was so dark. There was only one dim lightbulb. I had to let my eyes adjust. I saw twenty-five prisoners cramped in there. Almost all of them were Chinese, except for a couple of Russians. I couldn't believe what I was seeing. Several of them were women."

"Women too?" Mrs. Levine exclaimed and shook her head.

"Most of the prisoners looked like they'd been there for weeks. Their faces were emaciated. Their clothes were filthy. They shifted to make room when they saw us, but it was so cramped, they really had no place to move. And then, I saw where the stench came from. There was a wooden bucket. It was what they gave the prisoners to use for a toilet. They only disposed of the waste once every day."

"Ugh," Joshua grunted.

"Later on, they brought in another American and two Britons. One was a banker. They accused him of being a spy, but I don't know if that's true. The other two were journalists. In the prison, they made us sit cross-legged or kneel from six in the morning to nine at night. We weren't allowed to talk. If we tried to lean against the wall or stretch our legs, the guards would beat us."

Eden listened in shock. She'd heard Chinese prison conditions were horrible. This sounded a thousand times worse.

"The conditions were brutal," Isaac said. "The cell wasn't big enough for this many people, so no one could ever lie down. Lice and cockroaches were crawling all over us. Rats and vermin I'd never seen before climbed on us. The place had no heat either and at night, we got very cold. My socks were always damp so if I left them on, my feet would sting, and if I took them off, they'd freeze. And food? Forget it. They gave us a bowl of watery boiled rice three times a day and that was all we got. All the prisoners were ill. They had boils and infected wounds on their skin and necks. No one ever got any medical help. We were all left to die."

Mrs. Levine held his hand. "I'm so sorry you had to go through that. That's inhuman."

Isaac dropped his head. "Yes. But none of it compared to what they did to Alex. They wanted revenge, and they got exactly what they wanted." He looked at Eden. "I'll spare you the details, but they tortured him."

"Don't," Eden said. "Please. Don't try to spare me."

Isaac hesitated. "I . . ."

"I need to know." Eden grabbed the metal bar at the side of his bed. "Alex would want me to know. He'd want the whole world to know!"

Isaac grimaced and looked at his lap. "Of course, he was beaten badly. Every day, the guards would come and take him to the torture chamber. I don't know what floor above us the chamber was on, but I could hear him shriek every time. It would go on for hours. The first day, they tortured him all night. I don't know for how long, but I know they took him some time after nine at night. That's the imposed bedtime. When they brought him back, he barely got any sleep before they woke us all up the next morning at six." He hesitated again and glanced at her. She returned a firm stare and he went on. "We weren't supposed to talk, but at night, when the guards weren't around, he was able to tell me some of the things they did to him. They electrocuted him. They poured water into his mouth and up his nostrils. They interrogated him and accused him of being an American spy."

Eden shuddered. She tightened her grip on the metal bar of the bed and tried to swallow away the constriction in her throat.

"The next day, they took him again. When they brought him back, his legs were twisted. They beat him with a bamboo cane. Every day, he would come back with more injuries. They tied him up and the ropes scraped open his ankles and wrists. His wounds got infected too. I pleaded for them to let him see a doctor, but they ignored me. Later on, they would beat me when I asked for help. It was useless. The water torture got worse. They rammed a hose down his throat, pumped him with water to the point of vomit, and jumped on his stomach. They burned him with iron rods. They hammered slivers of metal under his fingernails."

"No," Eden cried. She wanted to faint. Clark came over and held her back so she could stay upright on her feet.

Isaac glanced at her again, then at everyone else. "It wasn't only his body. He was losing his mind. The first day they brought him back from torture, he tried not to give in. But when they brought him back the next night, he groaned for hours. He must've been in so much pain. I wanted to help him but there was nothing I could do."

"Don't blame yourself," Dr. Levine said.

Still, Isaac's lips curled down. Fear returned and haunted his eyes. "The torture got worse when they started interrogating him about the people he worked with. They wanted to know who his sources were, and they wanted him to tell them what he knew about other journalists they said were anti-Japanese. I know he did everything he could not to give them anything, but I didn't know how long he could hold on. At night, he would say over and over again, 'They're going to kill me.' I tried to comfort him. I did." Isaac began to sob. He paused to take a breath and calm himself. "I didn't think he'd make it. When they started pressing him to tell them who was Apollo Eirene, I did the only thing I could. I told the Kenpeitai it was me. I told them it was me so they wouldn't torture him about it anymore."

"No!" Eden threw her hands up and covered her face. "No, no. I . . . no!"

"I had to," Isaac said. "Alex . . . he was delirious. I was afraid he might give in if he couldn't bear the pain anymore."

"Isaac!" Eden cried. "What'd you do that for? They would've done the same thing to you! They could've killed you!"

"I wouldn't give you up!" He raised his head and looked at her. "I would never give you up. I would bite my own tongue off before I give you up. I'd rather die."

His answer stunned her. Isaac . . . would die for her?

Die . . . Alex was dead. They killed Alex. They tortured him and killed him.

"Eden! Eden!" Clark caught her before her legs gave out. He pulled her over to a chair and let her sit down.

Her mother came to her. "Do you need some water?"

She couldn't answer. She felt lost. Why? Why were all these bad things happening to them? And Alex. How horrible, horrible it was he had suffered like this. And Isaac. How they tortured him too.

She turned her gaze back to Isaac. "Did they hurt you because you told them you were Apollo Eirene?"

"Yes," Isaac admitted. "I don't think they believed me though. They gave me a good beating. After that, they asked me a lot of questions. When I couldn't answer, they'd beat me again, or burn me with a cigarette. I started to understand what Alex was going through. Lucky for me, they released me before it got worse. And I did get them to stop questioning Alex about it so Alex never gave you away before he died. He died right beside me. We'd been kneeling in rows facing the cell's door for hours. He finally collapsed. The guard came to check on him and he was dead."

Eden frantically shook her head. It wasn't supposed to be like this. Apollo Eirene was supposed to help bring justice. It was supposed to help make things right. Why couldn't justice prevail? Why was evil winning at every turn?

Maybe this was the end. Maybe this was how the world would be from now on. She was nothing but an insignificant individual, one who the world did not even welcome at that. She could do nothing. All she could do was sit by and watch as the world was reborn into a darker place. A place ruled by terror, oppression, and death.

A DEBT REPAID

BEASTS.

Clark thought on his way back home. The Kenpeitai were even lower than beasts.

What kind of inhuman punishments were they inflicting on people right here in his own city?

He should've known. The Japanese army was capable of anything. He'd heard the news and rumors about Japanese brutalities coming out of the countryside in places where battles were being fought. What Isaac said about the tortures happening in the Bridge House only confirmed what Clark already knew.

Collaborate with these demons? Never!

He had to find a way out.

Could he still get out? Could Mauricio still find a boat? Could he still get his family out? Maybe even Eden and her family? What about the servants? He couldn't take everyone, but could he take the most loyal ones who had worked for the longest for his family? Could he take Huang Shifu? What about Xiaochun, and her son? But what about the other amahs and houseboys who also had children? How could he save everybody?

He couldn't even be sure he could find a boat for his family anymore, let alone all these others. All commercial and international ships had left the Whangpoo River. Only IJN cruisers docked at the waterfront's ports now, and small fishing boats and junks carrying lumber, hay, and coal still plied to and fro.

The car entered his driveway and he still couldn't figure out the answer.

When the houseboy opened the door, he stood back with his back hunched. He couldn't look Clark in the eye.

Clark handed him his coat. "What's the matter?"

With a pained and sorrowful face, the houseboy looked over to the living room where Wen-Ying was sitting alone.

Clark walked toward his sister. He'd never seen her like this. She sat motionless, staring into space. When he came closer, he saw she was crying. Silently crying.

"Wen-Ying?" Clark sat down next to her. "Are you all right?"

She didn't look at him. She remained still. "Ma's dead."

What did she say? Their mother was dead? "What are you talking about?"

"Ma killed herself. When we left her alone in her room, she took morphia and killed herself."

"That's impossible." Clark shook his head. "That's impossible."

"Her body's in her room. You can go see it."

He jumped off the sofa and ran to his mother's room. On the bed, his mother's frail body lay. Her already pale face had taken on a blueish hue. Her lips had turned purple.

"Ma!" He ran to her bed and shook her. "Ma!"

She didn't wake up. He found himself crying now too. He picked up her body. "Ma." He hugged her body and sobbed.

"She left a note," Wen-Ying said from the door. She came in and picked up a note from the vanity table. Clark pulled himself up and took the note.

Gun-Hui, Wen-Ying,

You two take good care of yourselves from now on. Ma can't be here to watch over you anymore. But you two never needed anyone to watch over you. No matter how much the world changes, you two always know how to face everything, unlike me. The ones who needed me were your Ba and Mei Mei. Now, they're both gone. When your Ba died, my own soul and spirit almost left with him. But later on, I thought I had a grandchild, and I was happy to become a grandmother. After Little Fu left, Mei Mei always stayed by my side. I wanted to die then, but I couldn't bear to part with my daughter. I still had my daughter. I couldn't stop worrying about what would become of her if I left her behind.

Guo-Hui, I forgive you for all the mistakes you had made in the past. From now on, whatever you do, remember not to act without considering the consequences.

As for Shanghai, it no longer feels like a place where I belong. The Japanese army has battled their way here. If you two young people can run away, then run away. Run away as fast as you can. If you lug around an old person like me, it would only add to your baggage.

Now, I'm going to the underworld to find your father and your sister. The two of them never know how to take care of themselves. Especially your Ba. He always neglects his health. When I find them, I will take good care of them.

Goodbye, my good son and good daughter,

Mother, Yuan She Su-Lian's words

"Ma." Clark dropped his hands. He was too late. He couldn't even save his own mother.

Wen-Ying gazed at the note in his hands. She said through her tears. "People say beautiful girls have frail lives. They always either die young, or they suffer misfortunes in life. Wen-Li was so beautiful. Maybe it was predestined she would not live long. But I can't stop thinking, if Japan hadn't attacked us, then we wouldn't have known a Tang Wei who betrayed our country. If Tang Wei didn't betray our country, Mei Mei wouldn't have been caught in a scheme where people wanted to have him killed. Then she wouldn't have died. If she hadn't died, Ma wouldn't have killed herself. So in the end, everything was Japan's fault. The Japanese demons, Tang Wei, the Communists. I won't forgive them. As for Tang Wei, I swear, I will finish what Mei Mei didn't finish. I will avenge her. And then, maybe Ma and Mei Mei will rest in peace."

Clark dried his tears. He wanted to console Wen-Ying, but he couldn't think of any words. Perhaps it was best to let her vent. Let her vent her anger, bitterness, and grief for all the misfortunes and darkness they could not control.

He folded his mother's note and put it in his pocket. "I'll go tell Huang Shifu to arrange for the last rites."

Wen-Ying stood still. Quietly, she shed her tears. Clark dropped his head and left the room. In the hallway, their houseboy came looking for him. "Young Master."

"Yes?" Clark answered.

"Sorry to bother you. A messenger came. He delivered this for you." The houseboy gave him an envelope, then quickly backed away.

Clark tore open the envelope. Another message from Konoe. This time, Konoe wanted him to come to his home.

He stuffed the message back into the envelope.

Alex Mitchell was dead too. Let Konoe answer for his death.

———

In the tatami room in his house, Kenji Konoe kneeled with his legs apart across from Clark. He kept his back straight and his hands on his lap. When he said he did all he could to save Alex, he did not exhibit any hint of deceit on his face.

"It took me a while to find out who arrested him and locate where they took him. Even after I learned where they took him, I still had to go through the proper channels to secure his release," Konoe said. He looked as frustrated as Clark felt. "Believe me, it wasn't a simple task convincing the high authorities to give up

Alex Mitchell. They were never going to let him out alive." He bowed his head. "I got to him too late."

On the tatami floor, Clark sat with his legs crossed. What more could he demand? Alex was dead. Even Konoe couldn't bring him back to life. "We have nothing more to talk about then." He started to get up to leave.

"Wait." Konoe looked up. "The problem remains. I still owe you. I promised I would get you Alex Mitchell and Isaac Weissman. I failed. The line between us is still uneven."

Clark's fingers twitched. Lines, balance. What did he care? None of this meant anything to him. They were simply the musings of a megalomaniac.

With great reservation, Konoe uttered, "I can get you out of China."

"What?"

"There'll be an exchange in three days. Six Americans are being sent back to the United States in exchange for six Japanese who are now in New York. These are lower-level government employees. An olive branch to smooth the way for negotiations and release of more important officials," Konoe said without raising his eyes. "I can arrange to attach a condition for the Americans to take you too and grant you a visa to stay there."

New York? Clark tried to comprehend what he was saying. "Are you serious?"

"Yes. The Americans might find it an odd request, but the condition won't cause them any disadvantage. You lived and went to school in the United States. You worked for the KMT, liaising with their consulate. You must still have friends in America. If you can call in any favors to convince the U.S. government you're not a spy, I will get you out of Shanghai to the United States." Konoe looked Clark in the eye. "And then, we can call it even."

Clark's mind surged to alert. "You'll let me go?" He studied Konoe's face. "You must have heard I made an offer to Wang Jing-

Wei's people to work with them. All this time, you've been trying to persuade me to join you. Why would you let me go now?"

Konoe responded with a half-smile. "Wang Jing-Wei is an also-ran. His name's not even worthy of being spoken by my tongue. I don't think joining his regime is what you want to do at heart."

"No." It wasn't. How extraordinary. Konoe knew him better than he thought after all.

"I know your country and mine are at war," Konoe said. "You don't approve of what my people are doing, but I've never treated you as less than a friend and an equal. I've always regarded you as someone of substance who could do something more, something bigger. Your agreement to collaborate with Wang Jing-Wei was made out of force. If you become what you despise because you have no choice, then, you'll be broken. You'll become nothing but a person tainted by the mundane struggles of life of the here and now, and I will lose a kindred spirit, or at least someone who understands the kind of greatness I'm trying to pursue." He relaxed his posture. "If I release you, maybe you'll take the chance to pursue a spectacular greatness of your own."

Clark's heart raced. This was his chance. He could leave all these miseries behind. "Can I take my sister?" He raised his eyes in hope. "She's the only family I've got now. Can I take her with me?"

"You sister, Yuan Wen-Ying?"

"Yes," Clark said. His heartbeat quickened, and he closed his fists.

"I'm afraid not. She's someone my government is watching."

Clark uncurled his fists. "Why? Why would your government be watching my sister?"

"We suspect she's connected to certain anti-Japan terrorist activities."

Clark's heart raced again, this time out of fear. "That's ridiculous. My sister's a woman. A proper young lady from a well-to-do family. How could she be involved with terrorist activities? That's nonsense!"

"Maybe she is, and you just don't know."

"I know my own sister!" Clark said. He had to lie. He had to deny what Konoe said and protect Wen-Ying. "She is not related in any way to anything like that. I guarantee it!"

"Sorry, I can't just take your word for it. I'll help you leave Shanghai if you want. But your sister stays."

Clark sank. No. He couldn't run to save his own life and leave his sister behind. "In that case, I'll have to decline your offer. I'm telling you again, my sister is not a terrorist, and I won't leave her here by herself."

"Then we're at an impasse," Konoe said. "How do we solve our problem?"

Their problem? Yes. The debt. Konoe was stuck feeling imbalanced until he could pay him back for saving his life. Clark's mind turned. He asked Konoe, "Instead of sending me off to America, could you send Isaac Weissman and the family that came with him to New York?"

"You want me to send Isaac Weissman and the people who came here with him to America? Why?"

"An act of mercy?" Clark raised his brow. "Your military police put him through a wringer at the Bridge House. I saw his wounds. He wasn't even guilty of anything. He got arrested only because he was at the wrong place at the wrong time. Giving him a chance to go to a country where he'd be safe would be a good way to pay him reparations for all the maltreatment he endured. As for the family he came with, Isaac Weissman won't leave unless they go too. So it's best you let them all go together. Besides, you know too what Hitler's doing to the Jews in Europe. The war between your people and mine might go on, but between us, maybe we can perform one little act of mercy. Also, you'll be demanding for the Americans to take in a family of Jewish refugees. Consider it a symbolic reminder to them, they're no angels in this war either."

Konoe tilted his head. His lips curled up as he pondered the thought. "Are you sure that's what you want?"

"Yes."

"I'll make the arrangements then. Do you think you can convince the Americans enough to assure them we're not sending people to spy on them? You only have three days."

"I know. I'll work on it," Clark said. Eden. Isaac. They would all be safe. The Americans wouldn't turn them away. He knew a chain with a thousand links that would lead them on the way.

"So what will you do now?" Konoe asked.

Clark looked down and smiled. As a matter of fact, when he came here, he didn't know what he wanted to do. It was Konoe who gave him the idea. When Konoe told him he should pursue a spectacular greatness of his own, it all became so clear what he must do. "I will follow through with my offer to collaborate with Wang Jing-Wei's regime. But now, it won't be because of force. It'll be my own choice. Thank you for enlightening me. You're absolutely right. There is a value to committing oneself to something greater. Something extraordinary. I will use this chance to do something extraordinary and to reach the transcendent plane of no self."

"The Greater Asia Co-Prosperity Sphere?" Konoe looked at him, hopeful and curious.

"The Greater Asia Co-Prosperity Sphere," Clark said. A lie. But what was a lie made in the insignificant realm of the here and now?

52

FAREWELL, SHANGHAI

AT HOME, Eden listened with her family as Clark explained the route which the Italian ocean liner SS *Conte Verde* would take to bring them to New York.

"You will spend the prior evening at the Park Hotel," Clark said. "Behave like you're normal guests. Be aware there'll be plainclothes security guards watching you during your stay. You'll check out at 1:00 p.m. the next day. A Japanese representative will meet you at the hotel lobby and accompany you to the port to board the ship. Once you're on board, there will be security detail who'll look out for you until the exchange takes place at Mozambique." He paused. When none of them raised any questions, he continued. "The ship will depart from Whangpoo River to Lourenço Marques. That's a Portuguese colony in Mozambique. From there, the Americans will transport you to New York."

Dr. Levine and Mrs. Levine exchanged a glance. A look of wild wonder shone in their eyes. Joshua got up and opened a map. "New York! I never thought I'd have a chance to go to New York."

Neither did she, Eden thought. Her heart swarmed with

emotions. Her father, mother, Joshua, Isaac, and herself. They could all escape. They would be out of Hitler's clutches, forever!

But what about all that she would leave behind? What about her old love that was cut short, and love that hadn't died but would quietly extinguish once she departed?

"Do not tell anyone you'll be leaving," Clark warned. "I'll arrange for new suitcases for your journey to be delivered to your hotel. Take only the essentials you need to bring with you. I'll send a car here tomorrow to pick those up. Pack them up like you're giving away things for donations. I'll have them delivered to the hotel. You can repack them in your new suitcases. It is imperative that you do not let anyone know what's happening and where you're going."

Dr. Levine pushed his glasses back into place. "Clark. I'm speechless. I don't know how to ever thank you."

Clark nodded. "I had a telephone call at the Swiss Embassy this morning with Joseph Whitman. He confirmed with me, when you get to New York, someone from the U.S. State Department will be there to receive you and help you settle."

"You thought of everything," Mrs. Levine said. "We would be fine without making all these troubles for everyone. We're just glad we have this chance to go somewhere safe."

"Yes," Dr. Levine agreed. "We made it here in Shanghai. When we came here, we didn't know anything about China. I still can't speak Chinese. I can't imagine it'll be any tougher in New York."

"You'll do fine." Clark smiled. "They might keep you at a temporary location for observation for a while to make sure you're not working for the Japanese. But I think Eden's connection with Alex Mitchell was enough of an assurance for them already. They warned Alex to come home the week before the Pearl Harbor attack. He had a lot of friends in Washington, D.C.," Clark said and looked away. When talking about Alex, he looked slightly hurt. He covered it well to everyone else, but his heartache didn't escape Eden.

"What about you?" she asked. "You won't be safe here either. Can't you come to America too?"

He gazed at her. Her question wasn't merely one regarding safety. From the yearning look in his eyes, she knew he understood. Her heart still mourned for Alex, but Alex was dead. In a different place, without people and circumstances constantly arising to break them apart, could she and Clark have another chance?

The yearning in his eyes tapered, replaced by a sorrow she couldn't grasp.

"There are things I need to do here." He looked away. His refusal pained her to the point she could not rejoice at the gift he was offering to her and her family. He was giving them the gift of a new life. A new beginning and a fresh start. Only her heart was dead.

"Once you're there, you can contact the American Jewish Joint Distribution Committee," Clark said to her parents. "It's a shame they can no longer help the Jewish refugees here. I'm sure they'll be more than glad to help you."

"Yes." Mrs. Levine sighed. "I'm worried for all the people who are here. I feel so awful. What do you think will happen to them?"

"I don't know." Clark clasped his hands. "I don't know."

Eden lowered her eyes to the floor. She imagined the faces of all the thousands of refugees who had disembarked their ships at Whangpoo River. How would they move forward? How could she carry on their hopes so that their lives and memories would not be forgotten?

In the Chamber of Golden Clouds, Pearl poured Clark another cup of wine. "I think you'll be more useful if you continue on in your role with Wang Jing-Wei's people. You'd be more useful to us that way." She paused and looked at him. "I don't understand. If you do this, the Japanese army will know you've sold them out. When that happens, they'll die before they let you escape."

"That's my own business," Clark said. "You just get the word to Dai Li. Before the Japanese troops arrive, Juntong must be ready to counterattack by stealth. The Japanese troops will think they're launching a surprise attack on a Communist depot, but our resistance will be waiting." He took a satisfying sip of his wine, a celebratory toast to himself.

"And then what?" Pearl filled her cup. "It won't obliterate the Japanese army. Even if that whole troop of Japanese die, you won't even make a dent to their army. If you do this, it's the same as you giving a gift of your own death. What a waste."

A waste? Not at all. Not to him. Knowing now what kind of two-faced snake Dai Li was, and how treacherous the KMT could be against Chinese people too, he no longer cared to exert any more effort for them. This plot which he schemed up was one entirely for himself.

Over a twelve-course dinner with Tang Wei and the Japanese commander Kimura, he told them he had good information the Communists were setting up a new resistance depot on the outskirt of Kunshan, a province bordering Shanghai about fifty kilometers away. A few bottles of *shoju* later, Kimura was talking about exterminating all those Communist vermin.

If he so wished, Clark would gladly be of service to help. Those Mao thieves, he lamented with them. They killed his dear sister!

"Even if you love the country, there's still no reason to sacrifice yourself without meaning," Pearl said. "Dai Li shouldn't have agreed to your proposal. How could he let you do this?"

How could he? Clark finished his wine. Of course he could. Dai Li had sacrificed many more people before him, and he'd sacrifice many more after him. Before, Clark had different cards he could play.

Those cards had worth to Dai Li and the KMT. Now? What value did a washed-up heir of a fallen family have to him? At most, Clark could become an informant. A double-agent. But Dai Li already had plenty of those people who were better trained than him for that.

A blow to the Japanese army on the other hand? That would be a boost for resistance morale.

Pearl took a gulp of her wine and pouted. "When you're dead, how will I work with you again?"

"Pearl!" Clark raised an eyebrow and laughed. "Are you saying you'll miss me?"

She threw him a reprimanding glare, then turned up her luscious red lips into a seductive smile. She feigned a look of despair and heartache. "Yuan *gonzi*, you'll never come again? My heart will hurt so much, I'd wish I was dead."

"Well! Very well!" Clark laughed and clapped his hands. Pearl. She sure knew how to put on a good show. "No wonder the whole puppet government and those fools of Japanese officials are entranced by you. Here, let's have another drink." He poured himself more wine and raised his cup.

Pearl held up hers. "Seriously, if I don't see you again, I indeed will always be thinking of you."

Clark smiled and drank. "What about you? What are your plans? This city is Japan's world now. Are you afraid?"

"Me? Afraid?" She smiled and slowly finished her wine.

Shouldn't she be? Now that the city's normal transportation had come to a halt, and all commercial ships not confiscated by the Japanese had left, even haunts like Farren's and Ciro's could no longer maintain their gaiety and glamour.

"What do I have to be afraid of?" Pearl put down her cup. "As you know, my clientele are very thoughtfully selected. All those who come here are either Reorganized Government and Japanese high officials, or wealthy industrialists. Besides, I have so many fewer competitors now. My business will flourish. Now is the time for me to use the Chamber of Golden Clouds to expand my grand magnificent plans."

Of course, Clark looked at her with a warm smile. For Dai Li and the KMT, Pearl and her brothel here were now more crucial than ever. And Pearl? She'd do just fine. The underworld was where she belonged, and where her luminescence would shine brightest.

———

At the harbor, Clark shook hands with Dr. Levine, Isaac, and Joshua. Mrs. Levine dropped her luggage and gave him a hug. Clark gave them all his well wishes. It was hard to believe. He would never see them again. For sure, he would miss them.

Most of all, he would miss Eden.

In the presence of so many people, and especially her family, they couldn't even talk at length before she boarded the ship.

"I hate to say goodbye," she told him.

"Me too." He restrained himself and offered only a courteous nod of sorrow. For the sake of propriety, and the wish to not upset her any more than it would otherwise.

"I'm worried about you."

"I'll be fine," he assured her. It didn't matter if it was true or not. All that mattered was that she would go forth with her mind at ease and start her new life. This time, hopefully, she could do so in a place where she would never have to worry about being safe again. "Take good care of yourself."

"You too." She tucked in her chin. Her eyes welled up and he reached out his hand, wanting to stroke her cheek. But he caught himself in time and pulled back.

"It's almost time," the Japanese security detail said to them. "We should start boarding."

Eden backed away. She joined Isaac and her family and said goodbye again, and they started walking to the platform. Alone,

Clark watched them leave. He wanted the last memory of the woman he loved to be forever seared in his mind.

Halfway up the platform, Eden looked back. Instead of moving ahead, she turned around and ran back toward him, pushing through the other passengers who were also boarding.

"Clark!" She ran toward him. Her family and Isaac watched, stunned by her sudden divergence from their plans. The Japanese representative started to run after her, but Mrs. Levine tugged him on the arm and gestured for him to wait.

"Clark!" She shouted his name again and again as she ran. Unsure what she wanted, Clark ran to meet her halfway. When she came to him again, she threw her arms around his neck and planted a passionate kiss on his lips.

All at once, his guard fell. He wrapped his arms tightly around her and kissed her back. How he wished he could hold on to this moment. How he wished he'd never have to let her go.

"I love you," she said through her tears. "I never stopped loving you."

"Me neither." He brushed her hair from her face.

"I have so much I want to say to you."

"I know. Me too."

She took his hand and pressed it against her heart.

"Be well." He kissed her again. "When you get to America, make all your dreams come true."

Her tears running down from her eyes, she brought his hand up to her cheek and caressed the back of his fingers against her face.

Finally, she let him go. "I'll always love you." She gazed at him, the way she did when they first declared their love for each other under the statue of the Angel of Peace.

Slowly, she walked away, carrying a bittersweet smile as she embarked for a life away from him.

Goodbye, Eden Levine.

He stood at the harbor and watched as she disappeared onto

the ship, remembering the time when they first met and all the times when they'd come here to look at the flags and search for their dreams.

The SS *Conte Verde* pulled away from the dock, out into the harbor, and steered toward the sea.

Maybe one day, a world would really come when all the nations' flags would fly in the unity of peace, and no law or human divide would stop two people from falling in love.

———

The SS *Conte Verde* had set sail two hours ago. From the deck, the city of Shanghai was no longer visible. Still, Eden stood by the railing. It was as close as she could be to the person she loved, the man she did not want to leave behind.

The ocean liner had no mercy on her feelings. It moved farther and farther south, taking her away from the one thing in the world she wanted above everything else.

So many times, she thought she'd left that love behind. Each time, she thought she'd found a new anchor. She realized now. In Shanghai, she had only one true destiny. All the people and places who came in between were only interludes. Even when the interlude was as irresistible and remarkable as Alex. In Shanghai, there was only one place where she belonged, in the arms of the man she truly loved, and who loved her just as much in return.

Why couldn't fate give them a chance? A real chance? How could fate be so cruel to take away all that was compassionate and beautiful in life, and inflict upon the world such immeasurable horror, misery, and pain? After all that she'd seen, and all that she knew, how could she pick up all the pieces of her soul and start life anew?

The sea wind blew, but it could not dry her tears.

"Eden?"

She looked to her right. Isaac, still weak from the gruesome ordeal he endured, walked up next to her. "You'll catch a cold out here if you don't come back in."

A cold? She gazed back out to the sea. So what? Her soul was already cold and dead. Her heart had broken into a million pieces. Streams of tears fell from her eyes and she couldn't stop crying.

"Eden." Isaac put his hand over hers on the railing. "I know you never loved me the way you loved Alex, or Clark, or even Neil. But I always wished you would. And maybe you were right not to love me that way. Compared to them, I never had much to offer you. And honestly, for a long time, I was such a prick."

She turned and looked at him. His self-deprecating joke couldn't chase her pain away and make her laugh.

"I didn't even have the gumption to tell you to your face how I've always felt about you. No wonder you chose everyone else but me." He squeezed her hand with a gentle smile. "I don't dare to hope for you to love me, not when you had the love of all these other men who deserved you more than me. But I also know I'll never want to be with anyone else. I don't think I'll ever find anyone who can understand everything we've been through."

No. Eden swallowed back the sourness in her throat. How could anyone? In America, where people were so far away from all the atrocities they had seen, how could anyone ever understand their loves, losses, and broken dreams? How could they go on and live life as though it was normal again?

"Eden," Isaac said and looked her in the eye. "I still don't have much I could offer you, but I know one thing. If it is up to me, I'll always be by your side. When you feel alone, my arms will always be open for you because in this world, I'm alone just like you. I keep my hope that my parents will stay alive, and one day I'll see them again, but I doubt that will be true. I know the fears that bound you when you're awake, and the nightmares that haunt you when you're asleep. If you give me a chance, I promise, I'll be a good husband. In America, we can build a new life together. Whatever strength we have left, we can give it to our children. In that way, even if we can never mend our own lives, there'll be a reason for us to carry on. We'll make a new life for them, the kind of life we dream of but we ourselves will never have."

Hearing his words, she broke down. Isaac was right. She felt alone. Even when she reached the safe soil of America, she could never truly feel safe again. This world had taught her that nothing at all was constant. Evil could rise. Lies could overtake reality. Violence of unimaginable magnitude could be the norm, and even the strongest of love could be torn apart.

She took Isaac's hand and held it as he pulled her into his arms. The comfort of his embrace gave her the relief she so desperately needed. In the wind, she held on to him. If he would be her last anchor, then so be it. Her soul was adrift at sea, and all she wanted was someone she could hold on to who would understand.

53

SWAN SONG

THE FRAGRANCE of the incense flowed through the air as Clark bowed before the portraits of his parents at the family altar to pay his respects for the last time. He was such an irreverent son. Every parent who had passed away deserved to have their son pay regular respects to their spirits long after their deaths. He would not be able to do that for his father and mother.

Silently, he prayed, "Ba, Ma, your child isn't pious and obedient to you. Please forgive me."

He straightened his back. The portraits of his parents gazed back. Their smiles reflected the days of Shanghai in its prime.

At least, they lived out most of their lives when all they saw were a bright future and prosperity. That gave him a slight bit of comfort.

He took one last look at his parents' portraits and went into the study. At the desk, he sat down and pulled out a map. When he was a child, his parents had taken him to the Jing Xin Temple on the outskirt of Kunshan. Jun Xin, Quiet Heart. The Quiet Heart Buddhist Temple's main hall was situated in front of a small hill, where monks would climb sometimes for their morning exercises. When the Japanese invaded the region four years ago, their troops overran this place and most of the monks were killed. Since then, the few monks who escaped and survived had returned. The area, thin of population even before the invasion and with little economic and strategic value, had recovered when the battalions had moved on.

"Ge?" Wen-Ying called him at the door. "You looking for me?"

Clark stood up. "You're back. Come in." He went and closed the door. "I have something to discuss with you." He led her back to the desk.

"What is it?"

"You need to leave, today."

"Leave? Leave to go where?"

"Wherever you can find safe shelter and hide until you can get away. I trust your brothers and sisters at Tian Di Hui can help you." He wrote down a name and phone number on a piece of paper and put it in her hand. "This is a friend of mine, Mauricio Perez. He's now in Macau. My wish is for you to contact him. For the right sum, he might be able to find you a boat to take you there. Then, you can escape."

"Escape? What are you talking about? I don't understand."

"I have a secret plan to take down a Japanese troop. When they find out what I've done, they'll arrest me, if I'm not already dead."

"Ge." Wen-Ying's voice started shaking. "What are you doing?"

"After Mei Mei's death, I told Tang Wei I indeed asked Mei Mei to invite him to have dinner with me. I told him I wanted to join his side. I told him I've made contact with key officials in Chungking, and I offered to become an informant for the Reorganized Government." He moved the map on the desk closer to him. "I told them the KMT sent me word that the Communist resistance is using the Jing Xin Temple as a covert weapons depot. Tomorrow at dawn, the Japanese troop will storm the temple to take it down. When they do, a group of Juntong resistance fighters will be there to ambush them."

Wen-Ying pulled his arm. "Why are you doing this?"

"Because I want at least one win against Japan."

"One win?" Wen-Ying squeezed the paper he gave her. "You're sending yourself off to the equivalent of death for one win? A win like that won't even strike a fatal blow. For you to make such a sacrifice, is it worth it?" She loosened her fist. "Why don't you join Tian Di Hui? If you want to fight and resist Japan, you can become one of us. We'll revolt against them together. With us, you'll defeat them."

"No." Clark moved away. "I already gave it my all fighting against them. To be honest, even if we win the war, I won't even know who I would've fought for. For Chiang Kai-Shek? For Mao Ze Dong? Or anyone else who would always put his own will before that of the people?" He ran his fingers over the map with a smile of defeat. "It's enough. I don't want to be their tool anymore. The only thing I want is to spectacularly win one for myself."

"Ge." Wen-Ying's eyes welled up. "You can't do this."

"You can't stop me." He smiled at her. "You've always been headstrong yourself. If it was you, you wouldn't change your mind either."

"Don't do this."

He ignored her pleading. "When the time comes, I plan to be on the field to watch the ambush myself. Here." He pointed at a spot on top of the hill. "I remember there's a pagoda here. From this angle, I'll have a perfect view. When I can see the Japanese soldiers march into their deaths, then I can close my eyes too if I die."

Wen-Ying stared at him. "No!"

He leaned back against the desk and stared ahead. "In Shanghai, I don't have any position anymore. I can betray my conscience and become a running dog for Wang Jing-Wei to keep what I have, or I can become weak and powerless like everyone else. Our family business will be confiscated. This house will be taken over." He ran his eyes up the wall and from one side of the ceiling to another. "Maybe I can try to escape. But if I did escape, then what? Did I, Yuan Guo-Hui, come to this world only to live one meaningless day after the next? How would I know Japan eventually won't take over wherever I escape to? If that's the case, where will I go? If Japan wins, I'll be a subject to oppression anyway in the end. If they catch me, I'll be dead. If the KMT or the CCP wins, they'll just plunder everything. They would give up the lives of those who fought for them if it served their own ends."

"How can you think like that?" Wen-Ying asked. "Please! Don't think like that."

"Tonight," Clark said, "I'm going to stay at the factory. Before I leave, I'll plant time bombs inside to set off a fire."

"You want to bomb our factory?" Wen-Ying widened her eyes.

"If I don't do this, our business will fall into Japanese hands. I won't let them use our properties to manufacture weapons against our own people." He walked over to the wall, took down the scroll, and opened the safe. "Take these American dollars and gold bars with you when you go. If you can, find a way to send some to our household staff. When they come for work tomorrow morning, they'll see this villa will be swarming with police."

"No!" Wen-Ying grabbed his arm. "You can't do this! You can't do this!"

Clark put his hand over hers and gently removed it from his arm. "Give all the servants the night off. Get out of this place quickly. Take good care of yourself." He walked out of the room to go to the factory.

"Ge!" she cried out from behind him. But he'd made up his mind. He wouldn't look back.

Tonight, he would execute a spectacular greatness of his own.

He could do this because he fully understood now what Kenji Konoe had been trying to achieve for so long.

No self.

———

At last, the dynamite sticks were all in place, the blasting caps were inserted, and the fuses strung along in a line leading back to the door Clark planned to leave from tonight.

Crouching, he shone the flashlight on each bundle of explosives lined against the walls. In the stillness of the dark, he'd worked through the night to bring his family's battery plant to a glorious, fiery end.

When he was satisfied, he stood up. He walked over to the time bomb and set the timer. Once the bomb went off, it would light the fuses he had set leading from one bundle of dynamite to the next. Soon, the factory would blow up. The whole place would be on fire.

He shone his flashlight at his wristwatch. 2:35 a.m. It was time to go. The bomb would go off in two hours, and he needed to get to the temple before Kimura's troop arrived at the temple in Kunshan.

Quickly, he went into the office and changed into the uniform of a chauffeur. When he was all dressed, he picked up a satchel with his next outfit inside. He put on a wool cap and left the room.

Outside, he locked the chain on the door. A bitter pain rose in his chest. This great place his father had created, and all the achievements his family had made. They would soon all turn to ashes.

He hardened his heart and went to his car. In the driver's seat, he turned on the ignition and steered it away down the empty streets. Back in the factory, the timer was ticking. He had to get out of the city proper before the bomb went off and the Japanese army and police began closing the roads.

At each checkpoint, he showed the guards a passbook indicating he worked for a puppet high official.

The almighty Pearl. He couldn't have gotten this passbook without her.

At the western-most guard post, lined with sandbags and barbwire barricading Shanghai from the suburbs and the rural farming regions, Clark rolled down the window. A boyish looking IJA private flashed the light on his face. Clark took out his passbook again and handed it to him. The private checked the information inside, then waved a Chinese policeman over.

"Where are you going?" the Chinese policeman demanded.

"To Deputy Finance Minister Lu's villa in Jia Ding."

"At this hour? What for?"

Clark glanced at him with a wry face. "You ask so many questions, be careful what you say." He leaned closer to the window and lowered his voice. "You think I want to be driving around at this hour? His mistress is ill. He called me to come and take her to the hospital." He took out a wad of bills and handed it to him. "Don't make any false statements."

The policeman darted his eyes from Clark's face to the cash. He muttered to the Japanese soldier. In the driver's seat, Clark watched as they walked a few feet away from his car. His heart pumped watching the two of them talk. The bomb at the factory wouldn't go off for another hour, but he'd still rather get as far away as he could before it went off. He meant to reach Kunshan. He didn't want any soldier or police to suspect he might be the one who blew up the factory and come after him.

The soldier twisted his mouth and scratched his forehead. The policeman took the cash, then sneaked half of it into the soldier's hand. He stuffed the other half into his own pocket, then gave the passbook back to Clark and waved for him to go.

Clark rolled back up his window. A sheen of sweat dampened

his back. Calmly, he stepped on the gas and drove out of the city proper. Instead of going to the area where the wealthy had their mansions and villas, he went a different direction and came to an old warehouse. The warehouse looked like it hadn't been used in months. A lucky British merchant had closed it down and went back home before he became a citizen of belligerent nations to the Japanese.

Behind the warehouse, a small delivery truck sat waiting. Pearl had come through with her second parting gift.

He took out from the satchel a simple work shirt, a rough pair of pants, boots, and a work jacket. After changing his clothing, he put his wool cap back on and went to the truck. Inside, he found the car keys in the ignition and began driving to Kunshan. If he ran into any Japanese patrols, he'd tell them he was on the way to pick up a delivery. It might work. It might not.

Heaven help him. He hoped he could make it there without running into anyone.

———

At the bottom of the hill behind the Jin Xin Temple, Clark turned off the truck and got out. On the other side of the hill, Juntong fighters should be hidden on the temple's grounds, waiting.

He let his eyes adapt to the dark. Relying on moonlight above, he climbed to the top of the hill. Winter had set in and not a sound of cricket or cicada could be heard. At the pagoda, he sat down on the cold ground and gazed out to the view beneath.

This was it. His last act of defiance before his curtains closed.

When he left the truck, it was 4:43 a.m. The factory should've exploded by now.

He leaned against the base of the pagoda and thought back to the day when he first returned to China from America. How naive he had been, so full of youthful idealism. He really thought he could give something to his country.

Glimpses of old memories glided through his mind. Every calling that had come to him, he'd answered, sacrificing a little more of his soul along the way, not to mention the love he had to give up.

Yes. He'd borne his share. He owed nothing to anyone. Tonight, he would strike one for himself. He would destroy a Japanese patrol. He would bask in the glory of a win before he left the stage.

What would he do afterward? He laughed to himself. He had nowhere to hide. When the Japanese army realized he'd sent the Japanese soldiers here to be slaughtered, they'd want to murder him. In their occupied territories, he had no chance of running away alive.

He took his handgun out of the work jacket's inner pocket and a flask of whiskey from the pocket on the right side. It'd be better to kill himself in one shot than to be tortured to death the way they did to Alex Mitchell.

Death was fine. After this ambush, he'd have nothing more to live for.

He opened the flask and gulped down the liquor. If he was drunk, his death might be painless. Drunk, but not so drunk that he'd cloud his mind. He did not intend to miss the show he'd come to see.

All was quiet on the grounds of the Jing Xin Temple. The temple's name meant quiet heart. When this was all over, would he find peace to quiet his heart?

The dawn light began to break. On the field below, a convoy of Japanese armored trucks drove toward the temple. Clark sat up and watched with quickened breath. The convoy stopped, and units of soldiers took their positions to swarm in. When they reached the front of the temple, a rage of gunfire broke out from behind the trees and the secondary halls surrounding the kill zone. The soldiers tried to turn back, but the Juntong fighters' bullets formed a deadly wall and none could cut through.

Behind the road, a second group of Juntong attackers lobbed a storm of grenades toward the convoy of military trucks. Explosions shook the air and gunshots rained. Clark rose on his knees and watched. His heartbeat drummed to the guns' pops and cracks.

Die! You group of beasts.

He gulped down the whiskey in his flask. What was happening below was glorious. Glorious!

All of you give me your deaths.

He gripped the flask and drank to the last drop. A stream of liquor dripped from his mouth down his chin. The burn of alcohol soaked his core, warming him all over with the heat of victory.

From behind him, a voice whispered, "Don't make a sound."

Clark's mind switched back from the scene of attack below. The man who spoke pushed the barrel of a gun against his back and grabbed Clark's pistol from his hand before he had a chance to react.

Clark closed his eyes, ready to let this be the end. But the man nudged him to get up. "Come with me."

Clark turned around. And so, the night would not end the way he planned after all. He won his last fight, but Fate had decided to give him a different final act.

He sucked in a deep breath and rose to his feet. Following the man's demand, he walked down the hill. Behind them, a field of bodies sprawled and the noises of the battle waned under the brightening morning light.

54

ESCAPE

IN A SHANTY by the Xin Liu River, the man who forced Clark to follow him apologized again. They had met once before, when he brought Peng Amah's grandson to Clark's home after the massacre in Nanking. The man, Fan Yong-Hao, was a member of the Heaven and Earth Society.

"Yuan Xiong," Fan addressed Clark with the honorific for a brother, "I hope I didn't frighten you. I didn't mean to. The situation was volatile at the time. It was the best way to bring you away without drawing any attention."

Wen-Ying, who was all too glad to see him, grabbed both of his hands. "It's so good you came back safely." She laughed in relief. "I was worried to death! Good thing Fan Yong-Hao found you."

Fan smiled. "You two take your time and talk." He left the shanty and closed the door.

"I couldn't let you die like that," Wen-Ying said.

"Wen-Ying, I—"

"Listen to me," Wen-Ying interrupted him. She let go of his hands. "If you don't want to fight on, I understand. I further understand you don't want to go into hiding and live a life devoid of any meaning. But I think, if you can leave China and go to America, you may find something there to live for."

Leave China? Go to America? How? "What are you telling me?"

"Greg Dawson offered to bring me to America. That silly man. He asked me to marry him." She raised her eyebrows and laughed.

"Marry him?"

"Yes. He sent me a message. He gave me a strong warning Shanghai is no longer safe now that it is entirely controlled by Japan. As if I don't already know. He said he's in love with me, and if I become his wife, he can legitimately bring me back to America. He arranged a secret route to transport me out of the occupied regions to Henan and onto Chungking. From there, he would meet me and fly me to Kunming."

"Will you go?"

Wen-Ying laughed. "Of course not! Who wants to go to a shabby place like Kunming!"

Clark couldn't help laughing too. "Right, I can't imagine you in that undeveloped part of the country."

She toned herself down. "Seriously, it's not that. If it's worthwhile, I would go anywhere. Besides, he said Kunming's changed. A lot of wealthy Chinese have fled there, and the city is now quite built up."

"Then why don't you accept his offer?"

"Really, Ge." She paced a few steps away. "What about the second half of my life? Be a housewife on a Kansas farm?"

Clark laughed again. "You can convince him to move."

"Never mind. It won't happen. I don't want to go to another country. Besides, I'm a member of Tian Di Hui. I still have unfinished business here."

"You really don't want to leave?" Clark asked. He felt full of worries again.

"No. But you should. Instead of me, why don't you go and let Greg's allies transport you to him?"

"If we do this, it doesn't feel right. Besides, what would I go to America to do?"

Wen-Ying peered at his face. "To see Eden Levine?"

To see Eden . . .

The foggy drunken stupor cleared from his mind.

"Isn't that what you want for yourself all these years? To be able to be with her?"

He gazed at his sister. So she knew all along. Nothing escaped from Wen-Ying's eyes. She just never brought this up with him.

"If I don't go, Greg will be disappointed for sure. But with his good heart, he won't be angry at you. He's friends with you too. He'll be happy you escaped." She came closer to him. "Ge. This is your one chance to get out of here. Don't let it get away."

Clark's mind turned. A new path had unfolded. Shanghai, China, Japan, the Communists, Dai Li, the KMT. He could leave all these behind now. He could go and find Eden.

"How will I get to America?" Clark asked. "Greg can't possibly marry me."

Wen-Ying shrugged. "Greg told me you have friends in America who want you there, isn't that right? Talk to him. He can put you in touch."

Friends in America. She was right. He had no value anymore to the KMT. But in the United States, he might still have something to offer to the Americans yet.

55

BROOKLYN

AT THE GRAND Central Oyster Bar in Manhattan, Clark waited anxiously for Eden to arrive. It'd been ten months since they last saw each other. That time, they thought they were saying their last goodbye. He thought they'd never see each other again.

The waitress brought him his drink and he opened the menu. He didn't want any food, but he needed something to distract himself so he wouldn't be so nervous. He didn't want to overwhelm her when she arrived.

The tables around him cleared. The lunch rush had ended. It being Grand Central Terminal though, the place was still more than half full with guests. If he'd picked their place to meet, he would've chosen somewhere quieter. Somewhere more upscale. Somewhere more romantic.

He propped the menu on the table and smiled. He was getting ahead of himself.

Although, why did she pick this place? It was such a big, impersonal place. Didn't she want to talk to him? They had so, so many things to say to each other.

He flipped his wrist and checked his watch. It was almost

three. She wasn't late. He'd come early. Way too early. Besides, she was coming all the way from Brooklyn.

And he'd come all the way from Washington, D.C.

After he left Kunshan, he followed the men in Greg Dawson's network to travel to Chungking. It wasn't easy sneaking his way out of occupied China, and it took him five months to arrive at his destination by a circuitous route. But eventually, he got there.

Once there, he didn't contact anyone at the KMT. Greg personally flew to Chungking and took him to Kunming. For a short while, Clark helped the AVG, the American Volunteer Group of U.S. fighter pilots led by General Claire Chennault and of which Greg was now a part. He translated and deciphered maps and other records and documents. The AVG, nicknamed the Flyer Tigers, was sanctioned by the American military. While working with them, he also made contact with Joseph Whitman. Whitman worked his network in Washington and got him a job in D.C. to work for the United States Office of Strategic Services.

As he expected, his bilingual skills and his Chinese background, coupled with his extensive knowledge of the inner workings of the KMT, made him a person of value to Washington. Now that America was officially at war with Japan, his insights became an asset too when it came to analyzing information.

But none of that mattered as much to him as coming here today. War, international conflicts, he'd given more than he ever wanted to all that in this lifetime. He'd do as much as he could for the United States government because it was now his job. Was there any idealism behind it? No. He couldn't honestly say there was. The world moved on each day. His own part in it had very little influence. China, especially, was a giant, ancient creature. Its centuries-old body carried too many abscesses and parasites, more than the naked eye could see, let alone heal. He doubted he would see the kind of world he once envisioned for his native country in his lifetime.

For him now, what was more important was coming here to see the woman he loved.

He picked up his Manhattan and drank. Maybe the alcohol could calm his nerves.

At the entrance, the silhouette of the woman of his dreams appeared. He recognized her instantly. Without thinking, he stood up, his heart palpitating as he gazed her way.

The host gestured for her to follow. She turned her head. Those eyes of hers. The eyes with a soul. They hadn't changed at all.

Immediately, she saw him. Her face filled with anticipation, she smiled back.

But wait. Something about her looked different. He couldn't grasp it at first, but as she came closer, he began to see. Her dress. Her waist.

Slowly, his hopes dashed. His smile disappeared. How could this be? He'd come so far. How could this be?

She came to his table. The host pulled out her chair. She stood by the table and thanked him. He showed her the menu and walked away.

"Hello, Clark," Eden said.

"Eden." He didn't know what to say. He fell speechless.

She put her hand on her stomach. "I wanted to tell you in person."

Clark looked at her from head to toe. This wasn't how he expected things to turn out at all. So, he was too late.

He was too late.

He took a deep breath and tried to gather his thoughts. What was he doing? He was letting a pregnant woman stand. "Excuse my manners. Please, sit down." He held his hand out to her seat.

"Thank you." She sat down across the table from him. The waitress came and Eden ordered a cup of tea.

After the waitress left, Eden smiled at him. "It's good to see you."

"Yes. It's good to see you too." He tried to think of what to say. He had so much he wanted to say to her. But now, he was completely lost for words. What was there to say?

She put her hands on the table. "I can't tell you how glad I am you made it out of China. When we left Shanghai, I felt so bad. You did everything to help us get out, and we had to leave you behind knowing how dangerous the city had become, and I didn't know what would happen to you."

"Yes." Clark forced a smile. "I never thought I'd make it out of there either. I never thought I'd be in America a year later. Had I known . . ." He couldn't finish. He choked up.

"Had I known too . . ." she said, her voice cracked. The waitress returned with her tea and they looked away from each other.

Eden started again, "I know you wanted my family and me to come to America to start a new life. But when I left Shanghai, I felt so empty. I felt so broken. I felt my heart broken twice over and more." She flicked away a tear dropping from her eye. "Part of me just wanted to turn around and run back to be with you. Inside me, I felt this empty void. I didn't know how I could go on by myself without you."

Clark dropped his shoulders. Didn't she know? He wanted to run after her too.

"When the ship sailed away, I didn't know what lay ahead, but I knew one thing. I could never fall in love with anyone else again. There might be love. Love of family, love of a friend. But not the kind of love I felt for you and everything else I left behind."

"You shouldn't think like that," he said. It felt like the right thing to say, but didn't he feel the same way too? The emptiness she was talking about. Wasn't that why he wanted to give up his own life for one final fight if he could win?

"Anyway," she said, "I tried to hold on, but inside, I was falling apart. It was so hard to go on, when all around me, I saw the deepest depth of human depravity. We risked ourselves to fight for what's right, and yet we couldn't defeat evil. And knowing what happened to Alex, and even Isaac, I couldn't get over those nightmares. Alex, it makes me want to throw up every time I think of what they did to him."

"I know," Clark said. He wanted to console Eden, but he knew nothing he could say could take those memories of hers away. He couldn't forget Isaac's bruises and wounds either after he was released from the Bridge House, and he could imagine the torture Alex suffered. Further, he could never forget holding his sister's wounded body in his arms before she died. These nightmares would follow them for the rest of their lives.

She wrapped her hand around her cup of tea. "We came to America. Somehow, I needed to find the strength to go on. You gave us a new chance at life, and I couldn't disappoint you and waste it. All this time, Isaac was there. He gave me his arms to hang on to. And I thought, who else besides him would ever know all that we've been through? I could never fall in love again, and I'll never meet anyone who would understand what I knew. Isaac, he didn't need me to tell him. He sees and feels my pain without me having to say a word."

"Yes." Clark nodded. "Yes."

"Soon after we arrived, we got married. It wasn't an elaborate ceremony. Neither of us wanted that anyhow. We decided to start a family. We thought, if we can't mend the wounds and damage in ourselves, we'd try our best to give our children the life we dreamt of for ourselves. And that would give us something to live for."

"Of course." Clark bit his lip. "I should say congratulations. I'm happy for you. I'm happy for you both." He forced out those words through the broken pieces of his heart.

"And I have grown to love him. Not the kind of love that I would feel as falling in love, but the love of a partner. Love of someone I care for, and someone I know I can depend on. He knows that. He's okay with it. He suffered too, and I'm the only one who can understand him."

Clark looked at her face. She was still beautiful. Still radiant. And there was more. Her face had rounded out a bit. When she moved, she carried the placid air of an expectant mother. Despite all she had said about her pain, when she smiled, her face glowed.

He should be happy for her. A new life was truly about to begin. What they could not have in this lifetime, maybe the next generation could find, if all the world's wars would be over and they could grow up in peace.

"What's Isaac doing now?" Clark asked.

"He joined the U.S. Army."

"What?"

"He felt he had to. Look around. All the American boys and men are being drafted. How could he stay here to save his own life while these men go to battle to fight for him?"

"Will he be okay? If he has to go back to Europe . . ." Clark stopped. He couldn't bring himself to say, if Isaac had to go back to Europe and fight, what if he met fatality at battle?

He frowned and sat up.

"I think he'll be fine," Eden said. "He's gone to training camp. It sounds like they want to put him in intelligence. He speaks fluent German, and he knows how the Germans think and behave. They'll have better uses for him behind the lines than at the front."

Clark breathed a sigh of relief. He relaxed his arms on the table.

"Having said all that, I want you to know I still love you." She reached out and held his hand. "I don't know if I'll ever stop loving you." She tried to hold back her tears. At this moment, she failed.

He turned his hand and laced his fingers between hers. Around them, guests began throwing glances their way. The sight of a tearful pregnant woman holding the hand of an Asian man invited much unwanted curiosity, but he didn't care anymore. He grasped her hand.

"Did you know," he said, "the Chinese believe a person can live multiple lifetimes? It's a belief that came out of the Buddhist teaching about the cycles of rebirths. The Chinese believe when a person dies, he'll be reincarnated. In our folklore, there are people in love who couldn't be together during their lifetimes. But they were meant to be together, and they meet again in their next life. In their next life, they're finally reunited. They're together, as they should be, and they're happy again." He caressed her hand gently with his thumb. "I haven't given you up yet. In our next life, I'll find you. I'll search for you to the edges of the earth. When I find you, I won't let anything stand in our way again."

As he spoke, a flood of tears fell down her face. She held on to his hand. For one more time, he let her hold on to his hand for as long as she could.

MEMORIES ON THE BUND

JUNE 1986.

On the plane, Clark opened his Agatha Christie novel to the page where he'd inserted the bookmark. The stewardesses had finished their last round of collecting the meal trays and were getting ready to show the in-flight movie on the cabin's screen. Soon, most of the lights would be turned off, and the passengers would either watch the film or fall asleep.

It was a long flight. From JFK to Hongqiao International Airport in Shanghai, with a layover in Seoul. Although, it was a flight he couldn't have made until recently. For thirty-four years since the Communist Party took control of China in 1949, he had no hope he'd ever return.

A rush of emotions washed over him. He put down his paperback and took a photo album out from his carry-on bag. The first photo was a black-and-white one of him and his family in front of their villa. They took this picture right before his parents sent him off to go to school in America. He was only sixteen then.

"Is that you, Professor Yuan?" Priscilla Chen, the girl next to him, looked over from her seat. She was one of his students who was coming on this trip.

Actually, he wasn't a professor. "Professor" was what all the students called the lecturer of their classes. With mainland China opening up to the West again for foreign investment under Deng Xiaoping's new economic reforms, the world was taking a renewed interest in China. The Dean of Princeton's Woodrow Wilson School, a good friend of his, invited him to teach a class on China as an emerging economic and world power. The invitation brought him out of retirement.

And that was a good thing. Gardening was fine, but doing too much of it hurt his back.

This trip was part of an educational exchange for students organized by the university to meet with business and local leaders overseas.

He pointed at the boy in the photo. "Yes," he told Priscilla. "That's me. The two girls are my sisters, and the two adults are my parents. This was our house."

"Your house?" Priscilla widened her eyes. "It's huge! Was this in Shanghai?"

"Yes."

"Are you going to go back to visit it when you get to Shanghai?"

"I don't know," he said. "It's not there anymore." Years ago, Wen-Ying had written and told him the villa was burned down during the war.

"That's a shame." She turned to the boy next to her. "Arata, look. It's Professor Yuan's . . ." The boy had already fallen asleep.

Priscilla made a face. Arata Ono was a student at Princeton too. He wasn't in Clark's class, but he was Priscilla's boyfriend and he had wanted to tag along.

Clark smiled and turned the page. These were photos of Mei Mei, his father and mother, and Wen-Ying and himself. They were taken during the Autumn Moon Festival, and the Dragon Boat

Festival, the year after he returned to Shanghai from studying abroad, before Japan launched a war and everything changed.

How lucky these photos were preserved. Thank goodness Wen-Ying thought of saving them before she left home that day he told her to run away and never to return to their house again. Of course, he would've kept them too, but he thought he'd be dead after he bombed his battery plant and tricked a Japanese troop to enter a death trap.

He turned another page. The picture of a young woman with beautiful bright eyes—eyes with a soul—stared back at him. Her smile still brought a tender warmth to his heart.

Wen-Ying even searched through his room and found this. When she saw him off back in 1942, she gave him these photos. They were the best parting gifts she could've ever given him.

"Who's this?" Priscilla asked. "She's gorgeous!"

"She is," Clark said. He brushed his fingers down the protective film over the photo as if caressing her face. "She was my girlfriend in Shanghai."

"Really? Wait! She was your girlfriend? How long ago was that?"

"I met her in 1936. She was Jewish. She grew up in Munich. In the 1930s, the Nazis passed a set of laws against the Jews. Things started to get very bad. Her family left Germany and went to China to escape Hitler." He thought of the first time he saw Eden. "For me, it was love at first sight."

Priscilla looked at him with the dreamy smile only a nineteen-year-old could summon. "What happened then?"

What happened? Clark sighed. "It's a long story."

Priscilla gazed out to the cabin's movie screen and to Arata sleeping in the seat beside her, then grinned at Clark and raised her brows. "It's a long flight."

Clark laughed. They did have fifteen more hours to go. He touched Eden's photo again. "I'd just returned to Shanghai after graduating from college . . ."

The pilot's voice came on the speaker as the plane began to descend. "We're now approaching the Gimpo International Airport. The time is now 7:30 a.m. We'll be landing in approximately thirty minutes. The weather . . ."

In her seat, Priscilla's whole face fell as she looked at Clark with her sad eyes and drooping mouth. "So that was it? You never saw her again after the Grand Central Oyster Bar?"

"No." Clark closed his photo album on the tray. "We sort of kept in touch. Every year, she would send me a Chinese New Year greeting card. She always included a letter to tell me what was happening with her and her family. I'd send her back a postcard." He put the photo album back in his carry-on and tucked it under the seat in front of him. The stewardess walked by and told him to put up the tray.

Priscilla threw off her blanket. "We're not done. I have to go to the bathroom. I want to hear the rest later." She turned to her other side. "Arata." She pushed her boyfriend's arm. "Arata. I have to get out."

Arata, who was listening to his Walkman, shook as he was jolted out of his music. He picked up his Walkman and got up from his seat to let Priscilla out.

The plane continued its descent and Clark raised the window shade. The sunlight of the Pacific shone in, as if bringing light again to a part of his life he'd closed and left behind. He'd just spent the entire night telling a young girl the story about his life he'd never told anyone else.

The flight arrived at Gimpo right on time. After hustling through the terminals to catch their connecting flight, Priscilla settled into her seat as the plane to Shanghai ascended into the air. "What happened after you separated from Eden? You said you never saw her again. Did you meet anyone else?"

Clark unhooked his safety belt and reclined the back of his

chair. "No. I never did meet anyone like her again. I had relationships. If I'd wanted to, I could've married one of the women I met later. But I didn't. I didn't feel it would be fair to them because I could never love them the same way. Not even close."

"Oh." Priscilla moaned, her expression filled with sympathy. "So you never married?"

"No." Clark looked at his bare ring finger. He wondered if Wen-Ying would give him a good chiding about that when they saw each other again. She always wanted him to have children and carry on their family name.

"What did you do then, after you came to America?"

"I worked for the Office of Strategic Services in D.C. until it was dissolved and the government restructured it into the CIA. Over the years, I worked as an analyst for the CIA and the State Department, and sometimes the White House as an adviser. With the Cold War and China closing itself to the West, it was very difficult for us to gather information on what Mao's government was doing and how it would affect global politics. I also worked for a think tank later on until I retired."

Priscilla nodded. She flashed a glance at Arata next to her. He barely noticed as he bounced to the beat of the music from his headphones. Priscilla rolled her eyes and turned back to Clark. "And Eden? You said you kept in touch. What happened to her?"

"She's fine." Clark smiled. "She and Isaac have two kids, a son and a daughter. Isaac did go back to Europe with the U.S. Army and served as an intelligence officer. He searched for his parents in France." Clark paused. "He found out they were sent to Auschwitz. They didn't make it out."

"Oh no!"

Clark lowered his head. "When the war was over, Isaac returned to the States and took a job as a salesman for medical equipment and supplies. He never did make it to medical school.

When he became a father, he had different priorities. But his son and daughter did. They're both doctors now."

"That's good." Priscilla cheered up.

"Eden started freelance writing for a local Jewish newspaper. When her children got older, she took on a full-time position and became the paper's editor."

"Do you think you'll see each other again? It's been so long. Why don't you all meet up?"

Clark thought about her question. Why hadn't he ever broached the subject with Eden about seeing each other again? So much time had passed. Couldn't they meet up like old friends? They did have good memories too. Couldn't they meet up and have a drink, and talk about the old times?

No. For him, it would be reopening old wounds. Some wounds never heal. They are only covered up. If you take off the bandages, you'd find it's still bleeding, and nothing in the world can ever treat it and compensate for all your losses. You can only cover it, grit your teeth, and summon all your inner strength to move on.

Priscilla sank back and pouted. "It's so sad. You were both so much in love."

Love. Clark blinked at the memories before his eyes. "In times of war, love was a luxury we couldn't afford."

At Hongqiao International Airport, Clark waited by the carousel and collected his suitcases and bags as they came down the conveyor belt. He almost had to laugh at himself. What a Chinese thing to do, to haul back such an excessive amount of goods and gifts. He didn't mind though. The two bags he had to pay extra for carried the things Wen-Ying and her husband and children never had the chance to enjoy while he lived a free life overseas. Even with the import taxes he was about to pay, they didn't nearly make up for all the things they had missed over the last four decades.

He dumped the first piece onto the cart. It took the wind out of him. He almost forgot he wasn't a young man anymore, and the suitcase was very heavy.

"Professor Yuan!" Arata Ono ran up to him with Priscilla by his side. "Here, let me. Is this everything?" He pointed at Clark's luggage, then loaded them onto the cart. Priscilla, too, offered a hand. When they finished, they insisted on rolling his cart for him too.

Clark followed them to the customs officials' stations. It felt so strange to hear Mandarin spoken all around him. The public signs, though, were hard on the eye. Everything was written in simplified Chinese. It took a while for him to get used to it.

When all the procedures were over, the Chinese official waved them through. The rough, impersonal way the government workers interacted with them made him feel slightly uneasy. This was something new. Something he wasn't accustomed to. These people were the products of a police state. The effect carried over to their manners and behaviors.

Arata and Priscilla led the way out to the arrival lobby. The other students and faculty members along on the trip exited with them. Their excitement bubbled over as they bounced questions from one another about their itinerary and places they'd come to see. For Clark though, his emotions were on a different plane.

He was back. He'd come home.

"Ge!" A clear voice he recognized cut through the crowd. He turned his gaze in the direction of the voice. Unable to control himself, his eyes welled.

"Ge!" An old woman, dressed in a loose cotton shirt and a pair of ill-fitting charcoal-gray pants, waved to him.

"Wen-Ying!" Clark rushed over to her. He'd seen photos she'd sent him, but he still couldn't believe his eyes. What struck him wasn't the wrinkles of old age, or the white hair revealing a life lived. Those features, he expected. But where was the hard-headed Wen-Ying he remembered? Where was the elegant, sharp-minded woman who'd made the Yuan family proud every time she stepped out? The woman in front of him looked small, like a beaten, submissive animal who didn't dare to raise her head, although her body had taken on a certain sturdiness. The kind of sturdiness of someone who had spent years performing physical tasks. Her lips, when closed, pressed into a hard, thin line, like she was bracing for the next hardship that would come her way. Her eyes had lost all their fire.

His heart broke, but he didn't dare to tell her what he thought.

"Ge." She grabbed his hand, as though she couldn't believe he was standing before her.

"Wen-Ying." He threw off all boundaries of cultural customs and gave her a hug. Yes, it was Western, but she'd just have to put up with it. He hadn't seen his sister for forty-two years. He wanted to give her a hug.

He thanked Arata and Priscilla for pushing his luggage. They waved to his family and went to join the rest of their group.

"Guo-Hui Ge," said the old man beside Wen-Ying. This must be her husband, Yang.

"How are you?" Clark shook his hand.

"Ge." Wen-Ying led him to the couple and the thirteen-year-old boy behind her. "My son, Ping-An. His wife and child, Jian."

The family greeted him. Clark took a good look at his nephew and his great-nephew. He'd seen their photos. In person, they finally became real to him.

But such basic names. Ping-An, safe and in peace. Jian, healthy. Not the kind of names usually chosen by more aspirational parents. They were more usual among the common class folks, although the meanings behind them were clear.

Clark left his thoughts aside and gave them a heartfelt smile. "Finally, I get to meet you. Oh, I brought you a lot of gifts." He pointed at his luggage filled with jeans, shirts, J. Crew and Polo sweaters, belts, Pepperidge Farm cookies, Godiva chocolates, Pond's face cream, hand lotions, Irish Spring soaps, Tylenol, and cigarettes, jewelry, and watches.

"Later, later," they said, but there was no hiding the joy on their faces. Inside his suitcases and bags, they would find not only gifts. Through the gifts, they would finally be able to see and touch the world outside of the only one they ever knew.

On the street once known as Avenue Edward, Clark and Wen-Ying strolled along as she recounted all that had happened to her after he left China in 1942. As he listened, Clark took note of all the changes that had taken place since he was last in this city. All the streets had been renamed. The Western ones were discarded in favor of Chinese. Many old buildings still remained, with their French, art deco, and neo-classical architecture all intact. The difference was, no Westerners lived in them anymore. Even the most magnificent mansions had been converted into government offices or subdivided into multiple homes.

Not a trace of the city's old glamour could be seen. All the glitzy nightclubs and restaurants were gone, of course. No more luxurious shops and fancy cars.

That wasn't all. It seemed to him, the people were still awakening. After the decades of oppression and hardship, they'd forgotten how to break out of the mental prison telling them they couldn't step out of bounds even when the chains had been unlocked.

At least they didn't all have to wear the Mao uniform anymore.

Wen-Ying led him around the corner. "When the world war ended, the KMT and the CCP resumed their fight. Tian Di Hui broke apart. Some factions wanted to support Mao, others wanted to support Chiang Kai-Shek. I myself didn't care about politics. What I cared about was justice for Mei Mei. She died because those red thieves tricked her. I would never stand on their side."

"You should've come to America like I suggested," Clark said. "In 1946, I could've gotten you out of here."

"I thought I had a duty to stay and support my Tian Di Hui brothers and sisters," she said. "It was hard, seeing them break apart and turning against each other. We sacrificed so many brothers and sisters' lives revolting against Japan. How did we come to this?" She sighed. "Around that time, I met Yang. I still had some of our family money left. At first, we went into business together. We started a trading company. Over time, we came together as we got comfortable with each other. Our businesses didn't do all that well. Inflation made profits impossible. And then, Mao's people were winning. They took over Shanghai. Yang and I thought about leaving then for Hong Kong, but his mother fell ill because of age, and I became pregnant." She paused. Her lips quivered.

Clark stopped. What happened to her then? He was afraid to ask. He didn't know anything first hand, and she never told him too much in her letters, but he knew the measures Mao took. "Wen-Ying . . ."

"I can't remember when the crackdown began." Wen-Ying resumed her steps. "When Mao took over, the Shanghai branch of Tian Di Hui disbanded too. We were pretty disorganized and broken at that point. Yang and I tried to mind our own business, but the CCP turned all private businesses into state-owned enterprises. They took our company and we were now working for the state. But that wasn't enough. The CCP arrested all my brothers and sisters who supported the KMT. They rounded up anyone they accused of being a bourgeois too. A lot of our old family friends were taken, even though by then we were all living in poverty. They arrested actors, actresses, news reporters, and all the people they said were advocates for the capitalist elites. There was an actress who became quite famous after the war with Japan ended. They shaved her head and paraded her down Nanking Road. They said her pretty hairstyles and fashion were marks of a capitalist. At the end of the parade, she had to go on stage and confess to her crimes. I heard she was sent to labor re-education camp a few years later."

"What about you?" Clark asked. "Were you arrested too?"

"I was." Wen-Ying tightened her lips and nodded. "I thought it would be the end of me for sure. You wouldn't believe it even if I told you. For once, I ran into my lucky star."

"How so?"

"Do you remember Liu Zi-Hong?"

"Liu Zi-Hong," Clark said. He hadn't thought of that name in years. Remember him? Did he ever! Even now, the mention of his name made his blood boil.

"He rose up the ranks very fast in the CCP. I didn't ask for his help, but he pulled his connections and got me released."

"He helped you?" Clark's mouth fell open.

"Yes." Wen-Ying nodded. "Mei Mei's little love affair . . . it ended up saving my life. After I was released, no one came to hassle me anymore. As long as I kept to myself and didn't cause any problems, I'd be all right and my family would be all right. As for me, I just wanted to let Ping-An grow up well."

Liu Zi-Hong. That little pipsqueak. He would have never guessed.

"He got far," Wen-Ying said. "He's still a CCP high official. He got married, and has a daughter. You know what he named her?"

"What?"

"Nian-Li. He named his daughter Liu Nian-Li."

Nian-Li. Remembering Li. Remembering Wen-Li.

"From beginning to end, he did truly love Mei Mei."

Clark's throat soured. Liu Zi-Hong, wasn't his love, too, a casualty of the time they all lived?

"Eh! Ge, we're here." Wen-Ying pointed to a building ahead of them.

Clark raised his gaze. He could vaguely recognize the street. When he was a child, he used to play on this street every day after school. As for the building Wen-Ying was pointing at? That should've been their home.

Their home was gone now.

They walked closer until they reached the building. It was an entirely unremarkable building. Just a residential flat, and no one who lived there now had any sense or recollection of the past glory of the home they replaced.

Wen-Ying stared at the spot. "I burned it down with my own hands."

She did. And he didn't blame her. He blew up and burned down their factory. All she did was finished what he started.

He put his hand on her shoulder. "At least, our enemies never got to defile what belonged to us."

———

The tour of the Bund began with the guide waving her yellow flag and pointing to the building with the iconic green pyramid roof. "That's the Peace Hotel," she said into her megaphone. "It was built in 1929. Back then was called the Cathay Hotel. When it was built, it was the number one hotel in the Far East . . ."

Clark followed along behind his American colleagues and their students as they made their way up the waterfront. To all the students, the view here and the buildings were an experience in discovery and a lesson in history. To him, well, that was another matter altogether.

He gazed out to the boats gliding up and down the river. It was a strange sight to see not a single luxury steamer or ocean liner occupying the water. The HMS *Peterel*, the USS *Wake*, and the IJN *Idzumo*, those were long gone too.

They passed by the spot where the statue of the Angel of Peace used to be. Here was the spot where he and Eden had first confessed their love.

The Angel of Peace was no more. The Japanese removed it in 1943. Its smashed remains were found in a scrapyard in 1947. That was what the Shanghai University administrator, who was their designated liaison, told him.

The tour guide pointed at what Clark saw as the HSBC Building. "That's the Shanghai Municipal Government Building. The building next to it is the Custom House . . ."

Clark knew all these buildings well. They might have different names today, but he knew this place as well as anyone.

Above each building, the red flag of Communist China flew.

"I dream of a day when all the nations' flags would fly in the unity of peace."

The voice of yesterday shook his core and he closed his eyes to steady himself.

Could there be hope? Fifty years had passed since he and the woman he loved stood here and shared this dream. The world war they fought was over, but the world that came after it continued to battle. The countries holding the most power continued to threaten to destroy each other.

There was hope. The same hope he and Eden held when they stood here when China and Japan stood on the brink of war. Gorbachev had recently announced the policy of *glasnost*, and Ronald Reagan expressed his interest in continuing to engage with the Soviets.

Maybe one day, the world would really learn to live in peace?

"Professor Yuan!" Priscilla Chen and her boyfriend Arata Ono came over. "Would you take a picture for us?" She held up her camera.

"Sure." Clark smiled and took the camera. The girl and her boyfriend struck a pose against the backdrop of the stretch of historical buildings behind them. "Say cheese."

"Cheese!" they answered. Clark snapped the picture and gave them back the camera.

"Thank you, Professor!" said Arata. He grabbed his girlfriend's hand and they walked on ahead.

"I dream of a world where no law or human divide would stop two people from falling in love."

His body trembled as the echo of yesterday's voice swept through his heart. He watched the two young people standing on the spot on the wharf where he himself once stood. Peace, perhaps, might not arrive yet today. But love.

That part of their dream had come true.

AFTERWORD

At last, we come to the end of this story. I knew writing *Shanghai Story* would be hard, but I didn't anticipate how hard it was until I was already at the point of no return. WWII in any European country is a complex subject. WWII in China is even more so, given that during the pre-war era, China had a very young, unstable government and a new, budding economy. It lagged far behind the rest of the world in technology, science, and education. It was also burdened by geopolitics unlike anywhere else in the world at that time. To bring all that history into one tale and make it easily comprehensible to readers—some of whom might know nothing about the subject—was truly daunting. Nonetheless, I wanted to bring to WWII fiction readers a saga that chronicles how WWII happened in China. I'm glad the story is now available to everyone, and I hope I did history justice.

With regards to Clark and Eden, I first conceived of the idea of their romance from a contemporary Chinese fiction novel I read years ago. The novel's title was *Round Dance* (my own translation). It was written by the very popular Hong Kong author, Yi Shu, who writes mostly love stories. I never did figure out what kind of dance she had in mind in that book. It was clearly a Western style of dancing, and it entails dancers changing partners throughout the dance. At the end, each dancer would end up with his or her original partner. But in her story, the two main characters did not end up together after missing each other many, many times, even though the heroine of the story was sure she and the man she loved would be together in the end, like the dance. I had the same vision for Clark and Eden, and I struggled with the ending of the story for a long time because I know from some of you who had written to me that you were looking forward to seeing them happy and together. Even as I was writing *Shanghai Dreams*, I had conversations with my editor whether I should write an ending that might make readers happy instead. Nonetheless, changing how I saw the story from the start never felt right. It felt forced and inauthentic.

In the end, I think this was the right ending, because their love story was a reflection of the story of China and WWII. Unlike the Allies in the West, the war did not end in victory for the Chinese, nor did they experience any closure. When WWII ended, China plunged right back into a civil war and its population didn't have a chance to recover. There was no heroes' welcome home for soldiers. The people only felt weary, and they wanted all the misery to be over. By 1949, Mao Ze Dong and the Communist Party had won control. We are all basically familiar with what happened since then. The country became a dictatorial state, the Great Leap Forward led to famine, and the Cultural Revolution killed and devastated millions.

The *Shanghai Story* trilogy ended with a time jump forward to 1986. At that time, Deng Xiaoping had reopened the Chinese economy to the world. There was a lot of hope, even some optimism, that China would eventually loosen its tight grip on its society, and the country would over time allow more freedom. For some years thereafter, the Chinese regime did go down that road, the Tiananmen Square incident notwithstanding. But in recent years, the government under Xi Jinping seems to be going backward. As I read about China during the pre-war era for my research, I kept looking back and wondered what might have been if China was given a chance to avert communism. I want to note here that Chiang Kai-Shek was a very imperfect leader, and he was no less brutal in the ways he crushed and massacred his opposition. But it remains for speculation whether China might be different today if the Japanese invasion never happened, and if it had a chance to continue the course of modernization under the influence of democracy instead of communism. Unfortunately, we will never know the answer.

As I wrote this final volume of *Shanghai Yesterday*, a mass protest was taking place in Hong Kong. The protest began on June 12, 2019 with a demonstration of more than one million people, and Hong Kong's total population is seven million. The protest started out as a demand for the kinds of basic freedom we in the free world often take for granted and are too willing to give up for the sake of fear or convenience. The conflict has been going on all summer, with massive demonstrations every weekend. Initially, the demonstrations were peaceful, but over time, they have become more and more violent as the government and police continue to clamp down on the protestors. As I write this Afterword, there are reports that those who are still protesting have become rioters and are now inflicting violence on civilians who disagree with them. The conflict is still not resolved and the violence is getting worse as this book goes into print for its official release. For me, it was a very surreal experience to be writing this book while watching the deterioration of the situation in Hong Kong every week. Sometimes, it even felt like I was witnessing with my own eyes the violent incidents I was writing about.

While on the subject of freedom, one theme that struck me as I was writing *Shanghai Yesterday* was the pursuit of the freedom of speech. We know the Nazi regime suppressed freedom of speech.

Hitler burned books and established the Ministry of Propaganda, through which Goebbels implemented censorship policies. During the war, suppression of speech also happened in the occupied areas of China, and it was equally horrifying to read about the brutalities inflicted upon those who spoke out against the oppressors. By oppressors, I'm referring to not only Japan and the Kenpeitai, but also the Chinese collaborators and those who were part of the puppet regime. I was in awe of the courage of those who put their own lives at risk to speak out. The character Alex Mitchell is a composite of all the brave reporters in Shanghai during the pre-war era. In particular, he was based on Carroll Alcott, who was in fact a star radio personality on the radio station XHMA. Prior to that, Alcott had worked as a reporter for the *Shanghai Evening Post and Mercury* and the *China Press*. Alcott luckily escaped death when he returned to America in September 1941 for an extended home leave. Ironically, he was Washington, D.C. trying to convince the U.S. government to give China total support in the months before the Pearl Harbor attack.

Others were not so lucky. In this book, I had already written about the murder of reporter Tsai Tiao-Tu of the Chinese newspaper *Shen Pao*. In 1943, American reporters Victor Keen of the *New York Herald Tribune* and J. B. Powell of the *China Weekly Review*, and H.G.W. Woodhead, a European editor of the *Oriental Affairs*, were all arrested and tortured at the Bridge House. (Woodhead also wrote a daily column for the *Shanghai Evening Post and Mercury* and broadcasted twice-weekly on two Shanghai radio stations.) Of course, there were more victims, and these were only the ones I had discovered in my research.

In this book, Alex Mitchell is a tribute to all of those reporters. In times of peace, it is easy to forget that freedom of speech is a right people had to die to attain. It also fascinates me that people would go to the extreme of killing others to stop the speech that upsets them or casts them in a bad light. After all, speech is only words. By itself, speech cannot cause any literal harm.

Today, technology has brought us to a new frontier where freedom of speech has become a major source of discontent. On social media, private individuals are brigading to de-platform, "cancel", and even harass those whose speech offends them. Corporations are removing employees and even customers who speak out against injustices if the speech of the employees or customers infringe on profits. Various groups around the globe pushing political or ideological agendas are using technological platforms to spread false information, create confusion, manipulate opinions, or even worse, incite hatred and violence. Companies that own internet platforms are suddenly given vast, and perhaps undeserved and unwanted, powers to decide what speech is or is not allowed. Their powerful algorithms determine what they think we want to see, and hide from us what they think we don't want to hear. Some governments, of course, are exercising their powers to censor speech on all media, as governments have always done. The Chinese government is one of the prime examples.

The world has yet to figure out or learn how to grasp what is happening and how to deal with these new developments. Meanwhile, social media and the internet have amplified all the voices that disagree with us, regardless of what beliefs we hold. They make us all feel under attack. Understandably, our immediate reaction is to wish for those voices to go away. It seems we've even accepted that censorship as a norm. A few years ago, I would still occasionally see people say online, "I disagree with what you say, but I will defend to the death your right to say it." Today, I don't see this quote anymore. Where censorship is not imposed by government or corporate authorities, we selectively censor speech we don't like by blocking all the voices we don't want to hear.

I want to clarify that I am in no way trying to tell anyone what they should read or listen to. It is not my place to tell anyone what choices they should make. What I do feel is important is that we should not take for granted our right to free speech and free press. As I read the stories of all the reporters in Shanghai who had given their lives to speak out, I'm reminded that freedom of speech is a hard-earned right. This right is also very fragile, and it is not a certainty that we would always have it. With *Shanghai Story*, I have written a story about China, but I honestly don't know if these books could see daylight in any Chinese press or media in mainland China if, theoretically, an opportunity comes up. After all, the parts where I had written about the Communists were not always positive.

Hopefully, going forward, we will find a way to manage the changes new technologies have brought to us. If we are wise, we will be learn to protect our freedom of speech and use our right to speak to engage with each other, and to find common ground to make our society better. Until then, I hope we won't forget what a valuable right it is to speak freely.

Lastly, I what to share my thoughts on the ending of the character Yuan Wen-Ying, Clark's sister. When I started writing this story, I only had a general idea of her personality and background. But right from her first scenes, she jumped out from the pages. It kind of reminded me of Jesse Garland in my *Rose of Anzio* series. Her character was quite riveting. When I was asked to join the *Darkest Hour* multiauthor anthology project, it was obvious to me that I had to write a story about her. That story ended up being the novella *The Moon Chaser*, and I was glad to have a chance to show her in war and in love. It seemed to me that in the end, she should take her emotional love story with Masao Takeda and ride off into glory.

But that wasn't how her story came to me in the end. The reality was, Mao Ze Dong's policies of suppression and economic destructions could wipe out anyone's soul and spirit. In Mao's China, people were just trying to survive. After forty years, I didn't see how Wen-Ying could've turned out any other way. She would've been very strong to simply survive.

I hope you've enjoyed this story. If you do, please consider giving it a review on Amazon. Your endorsement will help get the words out to readers who are interested in reading about WWII China, and those who have yet to discover there are stories in the Pacific front of WWII.

Alexa Kang
October, 2019
www.alexakang.com

Author's Notes

When I write my stories, I make a serious effort to stay true to historical facts. In my previous books, I had taken artistic licenses. When I did, I felt comfortable that the liberty I took did not change or misrepresent history in any substantive way. However, in Shanghai Yesterday, I had to fictionalize certain people and incidents in order to keep the plot coherent or enjoyable as a fiction reading experience. The fictionalization deviated enough from truth that I feel it is necessary to set the record straight.

The Heaven and Earth Society (Tian Di Hui): Tian Di Hui is a real organization. It was initially an association identity adopted by farmers, traders, and migrant workers who formed vigilante groups to protect themselves. The association's stated mission was to revolt and overthrow the Manchurian regime that ruled China during the Qing Dynasty and to restore the Ming regime. The groups operated separately, but under the same umbrella and followed the same rituals. At times, they also helped the poor, and took justice into their own hands when the poor and the weak were mistreated. However, there is no evidence that they were involved in any way in the resistance movement during WWII. That was pure fictionalization on my part.

The organization still exists today, with branches located worldwide. Some are local community organizations. Others are criminal syndicates or semi-criminal gangs.

Hayashi Yukichi: Hayashi was notorious for his attempted assassination of Tony Keswick in January 1941. He was the chairman of the Japanese ratepayers association in Shanghai, but he was not a member of the Shanghai Municipal Council. The actual Japanese members on the Council were Okamoto Izamu and Ikeda Kyoshi. I combined Hayashi and Ikeda into one character and made Hayashi an SMC member for plotting purposes, and also to avoid introducing more characters into my already extensive cast, which now rival the Game of Thrones.

SMC Election Dates: The Japanese's proposal to increase their representation on the SMC and the ballot stuffing scheme by the British and Americans did happen. However, the actual date of the election was not the same as written in my book. The real election took place in April 1940. I changed it to November to fit my plot.

Tan Shao-Yu: In Chapter 3, Clark assisted Pearl in a plot to assassinate Tan Shao-Yu, a former member of the Nationalist government who was recruited by Japan to lead the provisional puppet government. This character and his assassination were based on the real historical figure Tang Shaoyi. I fictionalized his character because I was unable to match the actual date of his assassination to my plot. Tang Shaoyi, the real person, was killed in September 1938. Tan Shao-Yu, my fictional character, was killed on July 7, 1938. I adapted Tang's personal background and the details of his assassination into my story.

Xi Shi-Tai: In Chapter 27, I wrote about the assassination of Xi Shi-Tai. Xi was a real person who was killed by Juntong. However, he was not the puppet police commissioner. His actual position was the principal secretary to the puppet Shanghai Police Commissioner Lu Ying. I made Xi the police commissioner for plotting purposes.

Miss Shanghai Pageant: In my book, this beauty contest was held in July 1940. The pageant was traditionally held every year in July, but in 1940, it was actually held on June 18. I changed the date to July to fit my story's timeline.

The *Shanghai Story* trilogy is over, but don't miss this spinoff story. Find out what how Clark's sister, Yuan Wen-Ying, continued her fight with the underground resistance in:

The Moon Chaser
A spinoff novella of the *Shanghai Story* trilogy

In one night, Yuan Wen-Ying can take down the Japanese commander who slaughtered masses in Nanking. Can she set the plan in motion if she has to destroy the unrequited love of the only one remaining by her side?

Get your copy now on Amazon.

Subscribe for a free story

On his last night in New York, a young grifter sets out to turn the table on those who shorted him before he leaves for the draft. Will he win or lose?

Sign up for my mailing list and receive a free copy of the WWII story **Christmas Eve in the City of Dreams**, plus news on book releases, free stories, and more.

http://alexakang.com/newsletter-2/

About the Author

———

Alexa is a WWII and 20th century historical fiction author. Her works include the novel series, *Rose of Anzio*, a love story saga that begins in 1940 Chicago and continues on to the historic Battle of Anzio in Italy. Her second series, *Shanghai Story,* chronicles the events in Shanghai leading up to WWII and the history of Jews and Jewish refugees in China. Her other works include the WWII/1980s time-travel love story *Eternal Flame* (a tribute to John Hughes), as well as short stories in the fiction anthologies *Pearl Harbor and More: Stories of December 1942, Christmas in Love,* and the USA Today Bestseller *The Darkest Hour*.

I would love to hear from you.
Contact me or follow me at:

www.alexakang.com
alexa@alexakang.com

You can also find me on Facebook and BookBub.

Also by Alexa Kang

The Rose of Anzio Series

A sweeping saga of love and war, **Rose of Anzio** *takes you from 1940s Chicago to the WWII Battle of Anzio in Italy and beyond.*

Book One ~ Moonlight

Book Two ~ Jalousie

Book Three ~ Desire

Book Four ~ Remembrance

New Release

Nisei War Series Book One

Last Night with Tokyo Rose

Official Release Date: January 22, 2021

Get your copy now on Amazon

Available also on Kindle Unlimited

Manufactured by Amazon.ca
Bolton, ON

31784962R00333